THE
FORGIVING
KIND

Center Point
Large Print

Also by Donna Everhart and available from
Center Point Large Print:

The Education of Dixie Dupree
The Road to Bittersweet

**This Large Print Book carries the
Seal of Approval of N.A.V.H.**

THE
FORGIVING
KIND

Donna Everhart

CENTER POINT LARGE PRINT
THORNDIKE, MAINE

This Center Point Large Print edition
is published in the year 2019 by arrangement with
Kensington Publishing Corp.

The text of this Large Print edition is unabridged.
In other aspects, this book may vary
from the original edition.
Printed in the United States of America
on permanent paper.
Set in 16-point Times New Roman type.

ISBN: 978-1-64358-115-6

Library of Congress Cataloging-in-Publication Data

Names: Everhart, Donna, author.
Title: The forgiving kind / Donna Everhart.
Description: Large Print edition. | Thorndike, Maine : Center Point
     Large Print, 2019.
Identifiers: LCCN 2018058066 | ISBN 9781643581156 (hardcover :
     alk. paper)
Subjects: LCSH: Domestic fiction.
Classification: LCC PS3605.V4454 F67 2019 | DDC 813/.6—dc23
LC record available at https://lccn.loc.gov/2018058066

Forgiveness is the fragrance
the violet sheds on the
heel that has crushed it.
—MARK TWAIN

Acknowledgments

I am fortunate once again to have the opportunity to express my immense gratitude to the following people for their unwavering commitment, encouragement, and support of this latest novel.

To my editor, John Scognamiglio, I am endlessly appreciative of your steadfast guidance, and genuine enthusiasm for these Southern stories I love to write—even if I sometimes write the sort of characters you'd like to punch!

To my agent, John Talbot, thank you all over again for believing in me and my work all those years ago. You took a chance on one singular story, and we haven't looked back since.

To Vida and Lulu, a virtual standing ovation for what you both individually do. Your passion and commitment as you strive to promote my work goes above and beyond.

To Kris, thank you for all you do on my covers, and to all of the others in my Kensington family who quietly labor behind the scenes, thank you so much for working so hard on my behalf.

A special shout-out to fellow Kensington authors Eldonna Edwards and Mandy Mikulencak, thank you for the gift of your friendships as we celebrate our individual successes.

A heartfelt thank-you to all of the independent bookstores who have helped me build my readership by supporting my work.

Thank you to Jamie Adkins, owner, The Broad Street Deli and Market, for providing the residents of our small town a place to purchase my books locally. (We're gonna need a bigger shelf.)

A special thank-you to my Trio tribe, Shari Smith, Jana Sasser, Bren McClain, Radney Foster, Cyndi Hoelzle, Eddie Heinzelman, Billy Coffey, Judith Richards, Deborah Mantella, Daren Wang, Beth Fennelly, Sheryl Parbhoo, and all the rest for your friendship. Attending "Southern literary church" with y'all influenced me to reach for new goals, and to keep growing. I love all of you.

Again, I would like to extend my thanks to book advocates and cheerleaders, Kristy B, Susan Peterson, Susan Roberts, Linda Levack Zagon, and too many others to name here. From the bottom of my heart I appreciate all of you promoting my stories across social media with such heartfelt enthusiasm.

Thank you to each member of my big, loving family, specifically my "moms" who always read my stories first—and of course love them!

And most of all, to my husband. Your quiet,

supportive presence is the foundation for my work. Thank you for always reminding me how proud you are, for making sure I eat, and for watching over me. I love you and I couldn't do this without you.

THE
FORGIVING
KIND

Chapter 1

Daddy never wanted to do nothing much other than grow cotton, and the way he'd gone at it, we figured that would be the thing to kill him, but it wasn't. We got three hundred acres in Jones County, North Carolina, first-rate land he calls it. For a girl like me, meaning a girl who'd rather spend time outside more than anywhere else, there was no better place on earth. Some might think we're stuck out in the middle of nowhere, that what we have ain't no different than any other farm along Highway 58. I see things different—I see what he does. The way freshly plowed soil looks like that rich chocolate powder Mama uses for baking. How the leaves on a cotton plant are heart shaped, and how on a sunny day, their vivid green color gets so intense, you have to squint your eyes. There's these little buds on the cotton plants, called squares, and when they bloom, they turn pale yellow, like fresh cream. Within days they go to a light pink, and then darker pink, self-pollinating, Daddy says. When our fields turn those different colors,

I can't imagine how nobody wouldn't think it wasn't the prettiest sight they'd ever laid eyes on.

In the spring when trees have started to bud out, and flowers reach for the sun, their sweet odor only beginning to drift on the air, we know it won't be long before cotton-growing season has come again. The Fort Hill creeping phlox, Virginia spiderwort, and jonquils dare to emerge, while Mama's Chestine Gowdy peonies begin to peek from the ground. Soon, the yard plumb bursts with colors too, always changing, always pretty. I like the hottest months, that time when a shimmery haze appears at the edge of the fields looking like water. In the fall, tiny, fluffy white clouds of cotton come, and we're in an entirely different world by then, with everything dying off and such. Even the coats of deer and squirrels change, turning mostly gray so they blend with the trees and bushes.

All of us, Daddy, Mama, Ross, Trent, and me, we're required to work real hard, hitching burlap bags over our shoulders, picking the cotton from dawn to dusk, fast as we can. School allows a break so anyone growing, which is most everybody, can get their fields picked. Afterward, the stalks get plowed under, and the land that was already flat looks even flatter. For instance, I can see a crow land in a tree a mile from our front yard. I can see someone driving down Turtle Pond Road toward our house minutes before they get here. That's why our little town's name suits this place. Flatland is where we live.

Our farmhouse is painted snowy white, like the cotton we pick, with a dark green tin roof. It's split right down the middle by what's called a dogtrot. The kitchen and living room set off to one side, and the bedrooms and a bathroom are on the other. The two sugar maples at each corner in the front, and a big oak tree in the backyard offer shade from a sweltering summer sun. Our land stops where Turtle Pond Road dead-ends in a thick row of longleaf pines, lined up like a natural fence. Beyond them are woods so dense and thick, during the warm months you can't see over to Frank Fowler's place, the only neighbor for miles and miles around. The only other thing visible sets off to the east, the small, silvery shape of the water tower that catches sunlight just so at certain times of the year.

Daddy said I appreciate the land like him, and while Ross is most like Daddy, Trent has got a wild streak long as the entire county. He absolutely hates farming. Daddy said the land's soaked into me the way blood soaks into wood, a permanent, everlasting mark. Three years ago, when I was nine, he placed an old willow branch in my hands, and showed me how to do what he's been doing since I can remember, something he calls "divining water." Turned out I could do this too. Since then, my attachment to the land beneath me has grown even more. I ain't never forgot how it felt, or how he'd looked either, like a cotton boll 'bout to burst open, all filled up with pride.

It was an early spring morning and as we walked toward a field to start work, we took our time, moseying along the path made by the tractor tires, him with one arm slung round my shoulder, the weight of it natural as my own breath. He pointed at all that surrounded us.

"That's a mighty fine view, ain't it, Sonny?"

"Sure is, Daddy."

The sun painted the edge of the sky like the inside of a peach, all orangey and red. We strolled along, taking in the morning before us. Ross was already at work, listing the dirt into neat, tidy rows. The hum of the tractor in the distance was as familiar and common as spring robins calling for a mate. At sixteen, he was allowed to drive pretty much anything he wanted. Not Trent. At fourteen, he's old enough, but last week when he was supposed to take one of the tractors to the barn, he got out on the road, and gassed it like he was driving a race car. He ended up in the ditch somehow and after Daddy found out he wasn't dead, he was ticked off but good. Trent was told he'd have to use money out of his allowance each week to pay off what it cost for repairs. Daddy said he could also forget climbing on anything with a motor until he straightened up and earned the right again. At twelve, I'm considered old enough to drive the tractors too, but I prefer the quiet of working with a hoe, which Trent said was dumb.

Daddy dropped his arm off my shoulder.

He looked to his left, toward Trent already at work without being told. "I see he's still thinking he can persuade me to change my mind."

He grinned down at me before he took off to check the fields we'd done the day before. I grabbed a hoe leaning against the fence, and went to work on the early nutsedge and morning glories. The work was something I could do while allowing my thoughts to drift as unpredictable as a dandelion pod caught by a breeze. I thought about Daniel Lassiter. Daniel has always been a head shorter than me until this past year when he'd abruptly shot up fast as a cornstalk. His family lives directly in Flatland, city folk we consider them, though our town's not much of a city. He likes to come here 'cause we got us a stage of sorts set up in one of the old barns. Daniel fancies himself a director, says he's going to make us movie stars one day. That, or he said he'd be a scientist.

Trent's voice interrupted my daydreaming. "Sonny, geez, hurry it up!"

Gosh, he was almost at the end of his row whereas I was only halfway. I didn't want to hear him gripe, so I chopped good and fast.

From where we worked, I had a perfect view of Daddy, moving along parallel to us, his hair shining like pale gold. We had the same hair color, his eye color too, a clear green Mama said looked like new shoots of grass.

Whenever we were at Wells' Grocery or Slater's Supplies, someone would inevitably say, "Sakes alive, if you Creech kids ain't the spitting image of Lloyd."

My arms were burning by the time I caught up to Trent and I took a minute to stretch my back muscles. We'd plant soon as it was warm enough, and this was the last field to get ready.

I was already in the process of starting again when Trent, his voice cracking like it had been doing lately, said, "Sonny, get a move on, Ross is almost done!"

I didn't even bother to look up. "I ain't in no race with you."

"Just hurry it up."

I mimicked him under my breath, glancing toward Daddy. He was so far away, he looked like a tiny baby doll. He bent down, but it was what happened next that caught my attention. He stumbled backward, the way you would when ou found a root, and pulled harder than necessary to get it loose. He lifted his arm over his head and brought it down quick, an odd movement, as if he'd tossed something away. I shaded my eyes. Daddy was looking right at me. I waited to see if he'd go back to work. Something about the way he stood so still wasn't right. He never wasted time just standing around. He was always on the go, in constant motion, sunup to sundown.

I leaned the hoe handle against my shoulder, cupped my hands around my mouth and yelled, "Daddy? Everything all right?"

The question in my voice got Trent's attention. Daddy didn't wave, or acknowledge me. He looked like a scarecrow standing there. I started across the field, still not sure there was anything wrong until he went down to his hands and knees, his overalls and T-shirt creating a blue and white lump in the middle of all that brown dirt. I kept thinking he'd stand up again 'cause he was strong, never sick a day in his life. I was confused, and when he didn't rise, a shivering kind a chill shot down my back and I started running, the soft, freshly turned soil making it hard to gain speed. I tripped, stumbling over the rows in an awkward manner, as if my leg muscles weren't getting the proper signals from my brain. I couldn't breathe, and the air was suddenly thick with heavily scented, overturned soil.

I yelled as I ran. "Daddy?"

Seconds later Trent passed me, his overalls stained dark with sweat, face already tanned almost the same color as the straw hat clamped on his head. Behind us the tractor shut off.

Ross's voice was faint as he yelled, "What's wrong?"

My hat slid off, fell to the ground, and my braid slapped against my back as I ran. It felt like it took forever to get to him when it only took seconds. Daddy lay balled up on his side, face contorted, his breath whistling in and out like a tire with a hole in it. Trent and I dropped to our knees in the warm, loamy soil. Daddy's hands clenched tight around the handle of his hoe, and he groaned. There was a trace of blood on his lip, like he'd bit it. One of his legs tremored, knocking against the ground, a spastic, foreign movement that was scary to see. Seconds later, Ross dropped down beside me and Trent.

I said, "Daddy? What is it?"

Ross swiped at Daddy's face with the tail of his T-shirt to wipe the sweat away. Daddy held his arm up. We looked. We saw, and understood. I put my hand over my mouth, covering the O shape of shock. Daddy's arm had two deep puncture wounds, and his forearm was already puffing up. Trent pointed at a long brown thing, not hardly fifteen feet away.

He said, "Rattler."

The snake squirmed, its body twisting and coiling, then uncoiling before slithering along a trench made by the tractor.

Trent jumped up like he would go after the

snake, and Ross said, "No! Leave it. We got to get Daddy to the house."

The sun burned too hot right then, as if it would sear our backs as we stared down at the man we'd only ever seen upright unless he was sleeping in the bed or sitting at the kitchen table eating. Ross and Trent got on either side of him and helped him stand.

Daddy gasped, "Don't know why I didn't see him. Bent . . ." He stopped to pant through the pain, then continued, "Down . . . to pick . . . up rock. There he was."

Ross turned to me. "Sonny, go tell Mama to call the doc. We'll get him to the house quick as we can."

Holding back tears, I took off for the house running hard as I could go, stumbling back the way I'd come, across the neatly laid rows, the tracks I left as erratic as the path of a small tornado. We'd left Mama tending to early English peas in the kitchen garden. She wore a pair of Daddy's work pants, cinched with a belt at the waist, and cut off at the bottom so they wouldn't be too long. Daddy had only joked this morning about how they looked like clown pants.

Within a minute I was bolting across our back yard screaming, "Mama! Mama!"

My eyes searched the garden, just past the clothesline where white T-shirts and underwear snapped in the wind, to where I'd last seen her picking peas. She wasn't there. I ran up the back steps, onto the porch, the boards creaking beneath my boots. I flew down the dogtrot, around to the side of the house where the outdoor cast-iron sink sat into a weather-worn wood table. This was where we brought tomatoes, okra, beans, cucumbers, and squash, and pumped the handle of the well to rinse them off. Granddaddy Creech had built all this about sixty years ago, and nothing had changed. There was a picture of Grandma Creech on the wall in our kitchen, and she was standing at the very sink Mama was bent over now.

Mama was motionless, eyes wide as she looked at me, auburn hair spilling out from under the pink kerchief she'd tied around her head, hands amongst the little green peas she'd shelled. Her face, usually flushed and pink, was milky white, as if my screams had already delivered bad news.

I gasped, half-sobbed, "Daddy. Snakebite. Rattler."

She jerked her hands from the water and rushed by me, and the uncomfortable squeezing sensation stuck in my middle grew as I hurried after her, my face crumpling while trying to keep myself from bawling out loud. We went through the kitchen where yellow curtains waved pleasantly in front of the open window over the sink. There was the smell of sausage still lingering from breakfast. I don't know why I noticed these small things. It was as if my senses had gone to a heightened state of alarm and took in everything, whether important or not. She picked up the receiver on the black rotary phone sitting on a small wooden table near the doorway to the living room. Beside it was a pad and pencil attached with a string, and a list of cotton-planting items Daddy had written for Slater's Feed and Supply, in his quick scrawl. The only sign of distress was her left hand, which she flapped up and down, an invisible signaling to someone on the other end to hurry.

She slammed the receiver down, then picked it up again, hitting the buttons in the cradle repeatedly. Having a phone was a new thing out here, and we shared a party line with four others in our small town. There were a couple of women who were always on the line gossiping.

Mama shouted into the mouthpiece, "Brenda Sue, clear the line, it's an emergency! No! You and Dottie got to hang up now!"

She put a hand over it and said, "Go see if the boys have got him here."

I turned to leave as the operator broke in on the call.

Mama said, "Eunice! Get me Doc Meade, quick!"

I ran back out into the yard. Ross and Trent were midway into the field closest to the house.

Each had one of Daddy's arms over their shoulders, his feet dragging, like his leg muscles had gone to rubber, although one foot caught the ground every now and then like he was trying to help himself along. His head hung down and I couldn't see his face.

I cupped my hands around my mouth, and yelled, "Hurry!"

Mama had come out and ran toward Ross and Trent as they half-dragged Daddy into the yard. She'd brought a sheet and laid it on the grass, motioning for them to put him there. In the short time since he'd been bit, I was stunned by his appearance. His arm was already twice its size and turning a funny color. His breathing was raspy, like he was fighting even harder now to suck in air. Mama dropped by Daddy's side and yanked the kerchief off her head, and her hair fell forward as she leaned over him, hiding her face from us. He gasped loudly and his eyes remained closed tight in a hard squint, his body twisted in pain. I wanted to do something for him and didn't know what, so I simply knelt by him too, my eyes going from him to Mama.

She said, "Doc Meade's in the middle of delivering a baby over to Chinquapin. The nurse said he's got some antivenin with him. We got to get him there quick as we can!"

Daddy panted, struggling to speak.

Mama lay her hand alongside his face.

"Lloyd. Oh dear God, Lloyd. What is it? What are you saying?"

Daddy gasped, "Water."

Her voice shaky, fearful, she said, "Get him water, Sonny, and get some aspirin too."

I jumped up, glad to do something, and ran back down the dogtrot and into the tiny bathroom where the scent of the gardenia bush right below the window drifted in. The medicine cabinet door creaked from rusted hinges caused by high humidity. I opened the bottle of aspirin, dropping the white tablets into my hand, but they were shaking so hard, a bunch of them fell out of the bottle. They hit the floor and the side of the sink, sounding like sleet on the windows in winter. I hurried back to the kitchen, yanking the freezer door open, and grabbed a metal ice tray. I yanked on the handle to loosen the cubes, accidentally dumping half on the floor while managing to get the other half into a mason jar. I threw the tray in the sink where it clattered like I'd dropped an entire drawer of utensils.

The water from the tap was like the slowest of trickles, and I mumbled, "Come on, come on!"

Finally, I ran back outside, and Mama took the jar and held it to his mouth so he could drink. He sputtered, and gagged, then gulped half of it down. She was trying not to cry, but the whites of her eyes were bloodshot, making the blue of her irises stand out even more. I wished I didn't have to see how he heaved and wrenched his body as he lay on the ground. Daniel had shown me journals he kept, ones where he'd drawn plants in and had written descriptions. One page said white snakeroot was good for rattlesnake bites, only we'd rid our land of it long ago when we'd had cows who might eat it and get milk sickness. What I wouldn't have given to know if we still had any. Even one tiny plant might be somewhere on all this land, but there was no time for that.

Daddy's feet thumped against the ground, jerking without control. Mama let him sip more ice water and said, "Here, Lloyd, take these."

Like a baby bird, he opened his mouth, and she dropped two aspirin in. She helped him drink only he was having trouble swallowing, water spurting from his mouth as he gagged and choked the pills down. Mama was on the verge of panicking, and so was I. It was too scary to watch, and I turned my head away, my eyes hurting as I held back tears. Trent hadn't said a word the entire time, his mouth downturned, trying not to cry too as he knelt by Daddy's head.

Mama said, "Get the station wagon. Hurry, Ross."

The wind picked up and Mama's hair fluttered about, like a bird caught in a cage as she bent over and tended to Daddy. They'd grown up together in Jones County, and had gone to the same schools all their lives. After Daddy got back from North Carolina State College, they got married and had lived with Grandpa and Grandma Creech, until my grandparents were killed in a crash when a car ran a stop sign and T-boned them. My only knowledge of them came from a photo Daddy kept on his dresser.

Ross pulled the Chevy around, left the back door open, and hurried over to help. He and Trent got the top corners of the sheet, while Mama and I got the corners down by Daddy's ankles. Though the spastic movement of his legs had slowed a bit, what was worse was he was no longer responding to us. We'd only known one other person who died from being snake bit. Mrs. Graham who went to our church had been down to her pond catching bream for her supper like she did a couple times a week. A cottonmouth was in the weeds and when it struck, its fangs sank deep in her calf. Everyone knew if the bite wasn't deep, you stood a better chance. I didn't want to think about how quick Daddy's arm swelled, already looking like it might pop. I had the notion the bite was deep, so I prayed hard Doc Meade's antivenin would work and tried not to think too far ahead.

I centered my thoughts on the fact nothing bad would happen. Nothing ever had. The worst thing to ever come visit us directly had been that wreck with my grandparents, but that was so long ago I had no memory of it. I guess you could say I considered myself pretty lucky, and this helped ease my mind as we rode to meet Doc Meade. I felt like that 'cause I have parents who loved one another, and hardly ever fought. They've always made even the simplest of things special, even grocery shopping together, 'cause Daddy would always buy us all ice cream sundaes when we were done. I loved how on Saturday nights, we sat together in the living room to watch a movie on TV, our hands dipping into big bowls of popcorn, while slurping on Pepsis, or hot chocolate, depending on the weather.

Shoot, I even got along with my brothers better than most siblings, least I thought so. We'd always done lots of things together, aside from work, and not 'cause we lived under one roof, and had to, but more to do with the fact we wanted to. In the humid summer months, Mama and Daddy didn't mind if we went swimming in the pond, sometimes staying out there until midnight, floating on our backs, staring up at the stars and talking about how big the world was, and how tiny we were in it. And Ross would always offer to help if I got stuck on something with my homework when Mama or Daddy were too busy. Sure, Trent was impatient with me sometimes, but mostly we got along, particularly if I did something with him he liked to do. We'd spent lots of afternoons shooting cans off the fence, and once he brought me a small turtle as a pet 'cause he knew how much I liked animals.

Daddy groaned, then breathed in a way that sounded like he was being squeezed tight. I swallowed hard, and thought again, *can't nothing bad happen.* How could it when everything had always been perfect.

Chapter 2

1952

The willow branch was shaped like a Y. I held the two ends the way Daddy showed me, each between my thumb and forefinger, my elbows against my ribs, the straight end pointing in front of me. I started walking, my eyes staring ahead. I wasn't looking at anything in particular, yet, I was keenly aware of everything. The way the sun's rays came through the trees, streaks of light spearing the ground. The rough ends of the branch resting in my palms, still warm from his hands. The heavy, sweet scent of honeysuckle. It was late summer, our cotton well established, and needing only a little tending now and then. For long as I can recall Daddy would go to other farms in the area, usually when someone wanted a new well dug, or to set up a way to irrigate their crops and he'd take this same stick, walk the land, and find water.

I went slow, placing one foot ahead of the other. My bare feet created no sound except a soft whispering noise through the grass. I had an expectation of what should happen, only I didn't know if it would. I was afraid, and excited. I didn't know how I was supposed to feel, or how *it* would feel. My mouth went dry as my anticipation grew.

Daddy said, "Don't think about anything, just keep going along toward the well. Relax."

"Okay."

I wanted for it to work, real bad, but I wasn't sure why, except that Ross tried, Trent too, and nothing happened for neither of them. Daddy had been real disappointed. Even Mama tried one day, half fooling around, and when the stick didn't cooperate, Daddy had chased her around the yard. He'd caught her, shrieking and laughing, and turned her over his knee, acting like he was going to spank her with it, only it turned into a kiss. I liked it when they got caught up with one another and forgot we were there. Even though Mama's attempt ended on a high note, I think Daddy was worried he'd be the only one left who had the ability until he decided to let me try. If it worked for me, Daddy said I'd be the same age he'd been when he'd started. Nine years old.

I kept going, taking measured steps, the sun hot on my head, the honeysuckle smell stronger as I passed by the old fence post covered in it. I could see him keeping pace with me out of the corner of my eye. I wanted to look at him to see if I was still doing it right, but as I turned my

31

head, a weird sensation started in my feet, crept up my legs, a sensation like something pulled at my skin. I sucked in my breath and stopped.

Daddy said, "Sonny?"

I couldn't speak as it traveled to my middle and then down my arms. For some reason, I wanted to cry. My lower lip trembled, and I couldn't look at him again. It was as if I *had* to move forward, like I was walking down a steep hill.

Daddy said, "You're okay. Keep going, slow now."

He hadn't told me what to expect, but I knew this was it, the same thing he must've felt. I was covered in an allover shiver and then it changed, what I could only describe as a *thereness,* like my body had somehow attached itself to the ground through my feet. Like I'd grown roots as I got closer to the well. And then, without warning, the stick moved. I hadn't done nothing, but down went the long end of it, slapping against my pants leg. It startled me, scared me. I let out a little scream, and dropped it. I stared at it like it was something I'd never seen. Wonder stretched my face muscles so my mouth was wide open and so were my eyes.

My breathing grew fast, and a warm feeling swirled in my middle. I smiled and looked back at Daddy. He stood with his hands on his hips, grinning.

He said, "Girl, you're the first Creech female

ever with the gift. That's what divining water is, what you did, right there. That's it!"

He came over to me, and hugged my shoulders, squeezing tight. "How about that, huh? Did you like it?"

I nodded. I did like it, now that it had happened. What I liked even more was that he was proud. I bent down and picked up the willow branch, and stared at it, like it was this magical object, not purely part of a tree.

Daddy said, "I've had that a long time."

"Is this your first one?"

"It is."

"But, how does it work? How does it know?"

"It doesn't. It's you. It's only a tool, a way for your body to interact with what's underneath you. Water underground is like water above ground, flowing in rivers and streams. It's in more places than we know, and you can find it if you're sensitive to it."

I didn't understand the connection between me and this piece of wood, but I didn't need to. I only knew I liked the way it became an extension of me, like if someone cut into it, it would bleed my own blood, dripping on the ground to soak into the water it found.

I looked at the Y-shaped end, at how it was darkened by his sweat, the wood worn and smooth, slick from years of handling. Without a word, I went back to where I'd started, situated the ends back into my palms, tucked my elbows tight once more, and I began walking again. I wanted to sense that tugging on my lower leg muscles again, that almost electric-like feeling as I got closer to the water source, in this case, our well. I did it over and over again, eventually in different places so I could learn how different spots felt. Daddy followed me, watching, wearing this little grin. I only stopped when it was too dark to see where I was going. I didn't hardly sleep a wink that night, and the next morning when I woke up, and before I got on the bus to go to school, I was back outside, making sure I hadn't dreamed it all.

Exactly like the night before, when I got close to our well, it came again, a stirring through my feet, tingling up past my hips and on down my arms. Ross and Trent watched, then Trent declared I was faking it.

He said, "You're moving it on your own."

"I ain't."

"You are too, I can see it."

Ross only said, "Do it again," like I was performing a magic trick.

I let go of one end, and the awareness I had with what was below my feet faded. I went back to the back porch steps, re-positioned the stick, and began my approach to the well. About ten feet from it, the branch wobbled and then another pace and down it went, very hard, very fast.

Trent made a dismissive gesture and said, "Shoot. She's doing it. It ain't real."

I said, "It is too! You're just jealous."

Trent started for me, probably to make me take it back, but right then Daddy came outside, cup of coffee in one hand, Lucky Strike in the other. He came over to me, my feet feeling fastened to the ground, and the branch still pointing down. I don't think I would've been able to pull it back straight if I tried.

He motioned at Trent. "Come here."

Trent wore this perpetual sour look most days. He straggled over to stand near Daddy.

He said, "Sir?"

Daddy said, "Sonny, don't move. Son, pull that end up so it's pointing at the well."

Trent repeated himself. "Sir?"

"Pull on it, pull it up."

Trent shrugged, reached over, grabbed the end closest to the ground, and lifted. Or tried to.

His face turned red.

Daddy said, "Try again."

He did, and I could tell he was really trying. Same thing. I could feel him trying, but it stayed pointing at the ground. I only had to hold it. Trent looked stumped, even I couldn't understand this.

"She's doing that! She's holding it so it won't move!"

"You saying your nine-year-old sister's stronger than you?"

35

Trent stumbled over his words. "N-no! She ain't, but . . ."

"Are you saying what I do ain't real neither?"

Trent's shoulders drooped, and he mumbled, "No, sir."

Daddy glanced toward the road. "School bus is coming. Go on."

I let go of one end and felt the release, like having my muscles all tensed and then letting them relax. Smiling at Daddy, I handed it to him.

He took it and said, "I'll put it in your room and cut me a new one. This one's yours now."

It was like he'd given me a million dollars.

Later on that week I went with him to discuss dowsing Frank Fowler's land for an irrigation system. I'd never met our neighbor before, but the other kids at school said he had money to burn and the most land of anyone we knew. There was also mystery about him, particularly about his own daddy. How they'd found him shot when Mr. Fowler was about fifteen. How they'd never been able to determine what happened, if it had been suicide or foul play. It had been in the paper, according to Daddy, and consumed the town for a long time, while Mr. Fowler and his mama went on like usual. That was what had caught everyone's attention. Their apparent lack of emotion over his death.

Soon as we arrived, Mr. Fowler opened the Farmer's Almanac, and read from it, emphasizing how the summer of '52 was expected to be hot and dry. He wasn't taking no chances. Mr. Fowler was average height, his skin scorched by hours in the sun, and one ear stuck out from his head a little farther than the other, and despite that, you could say he looked a little like Clark Gable. His black hair was slicked back with hair tonic, making it look like coal. The longer hair at the front flopped onto his forehead, and he'd shove it back. That's when I noticed how ridiculously large his hands looked compared to his arms.

He motioned at me standing by Daddy's side, and asked, "This your daughter?"

Daddy had draped his arm across my shoulder. "Yes, this here's Sonny. She's a dowser too."

"That so?"

"Good as me."

"Hm."

The way he said it was like he didn't much believe him.

He said, "How old is she?"

His eyebrows drew together, making a solid line across his forehead. I cleared my throat and tried a little smile.

"Nine, sir."

"Manners. Nice. I like that."

He immediately walked away, the move assuming we'd follow. Daddy looked at me, gave me one of his funny looks to put me at ease. Mr. Fowler led us through the house, each room bigger than two of ours put together. The walls were covered with thick wallpaper, and were of terrible hunting scenes with dogs, their teeth bared going after a bloody deer, and on another wall, a fox. Both deer and fox had terror in their eyes. I hated that wallpaper. The windows were framed with heavy drapes, and all around sat finely crafted wood tables, leather chairs, and plump couches with fancy tapestry pillows. We went into a wood-paneled room filled with a couple of deer heads mounted on wood plaques, stuffed pheasants, and quail, along with more pictures, all hunting scenes. He pointed to a leather chair for Daddy to sit in.

Daddy said, "No, I'm a might dirty. I'll stand."

I'd stopped just outside the room to look at a painting in the hallway.

Mr. Fowler, in a voice that sounded prideful, called out to me and said, "Don't touch it. That's a reproduction of Monet."

My hands were behind my back, so I had no intentions of touching it, but I remained quiet. I'd learned about Monet, and that's why I was staring at it to begin with. My third grade teacher believed in elevating our knowledge of The Arts, as she called it, and she'd shown us pictures of paintings like this, rolling through them one by one, showing us slides of places we'd never go. She said they were French Impressionistic.

Before I could tell him what I knew, he said,

"Maybe folks like you wouldn't know about artists like that."

His comment made me look at Daddy, at his calloused, rough-knuckled hands, coveralls stained with machine oil, and his T-shirt a little grimy since he'd been lying under the tractor earlier. Me, I'd come in my own work attire consisting of an almost too small threadbare blouse, dungarees with patches on the knees, scuffed penny loafers instead of my usual boots. I cataloged the comment in my mind, and began to form an opinion of him. Thing was, Daddy was well read, well educated in fact, in spite of what Mr. Fowler thought. His and Mama's room held books he called classics, like *The Great Gatsby*, *Pride and Prejudice*, *Moby-Dick*, and *Of Mice and Men*. He had a degree in agriculture from North Carolina State College. Our farm had been one of the early test farms through Daddy's contacts at the college for chlordane, a pesticide used to eliminate the boll weevil everybody was having problems with.

Daddy, ever amiable and laid-back, ignored the insult.

All he said was, "Well, sure. That's right. Can't imagine many of us from the sticks smart enough to 'preciate a fine picture like that."

He winked at me, then smiled slightly at Mr. Fowler. Moments later they shook hands over an arrangement.

We dowsed his land that spring and Daddy charged him twice what he'd have charged anyone else.

Daddy never had a bad word for anybody, but I'd overheard him tell Mama, "He's a real piece of work."

Mr. Fowler never saw me dowse 'cause I worked the back side of his property, marking where a pump should be set with a stick planted upright. When the job was done, Daddy used the money to fix the tractor. He built a new chicken coop for our laying hens, and put a down payment on a new cotton stripper. He bought Mama a new dress, got Ross a new pair of cleats for playing football like he'd been wanting to do. Trent got some new work boots and I got new school shoes, the usual black Mary Janes I loved. There was no drought that year. We had plenty of rain, and Mr. Fowler didn't need the irrigation at all. Maybe he'd get his money's worth out of it next year. We didn't see him again though, not until three years later after everything changed.

Chapter 3

We'd buried Daddy on the land he'd tended with such steadfast devotion, on a small rise beneath a cluster of pines. I got to where I'd visit him most every day. I wanted to talk to him, yet finding words to say eluded me. There was no stone yet, so I stood next to the mound of dirt and stared at it, the divining branch loose in my hands. I suppose it looked like I was waiting for something, and in a way, I was. I kept hoping what Preacher Moore said was true, something about the ones who leave stay with us in some capacity. I waited for Daddy to show up the way we found water, an awareness that would come like the pulling on my arms and legs. I wanted the assurance of it.

I considered maybe I could find him in the places we'd walked, so I started wandering the fields, holding on to hope. Just before sunrise one morning, days after we laid him to rest, I walked into a field, trying not to set my expectations too high. I began where I left off the day before, going up and down, row by row, over and over, the Y

41

end set inside my palms. The spot I kept coming back to was where it happened, where he'd fallen. I passed over it again and again, waiting for the slightest hint of a vibration. What I felt was disappointment, and eventually stupid while my feeling of loss grew. This powerful association I'd had with the willow branch was fading, becoming no different than picking a twig up off the ground. I considered putting it away and never using it again. Making my way back to the house, the early morning sun colored a low cloud bank with bright pink but the beauty of it angered me 'cause my world was ugly without him in it.

Back in my room I turned on my record player, picked up the needle and placed it at the beginning of my one and only favorite record, the one I had to have after I'd learned of Elvis. *That's Alright Mama* played, and with the volume low, I went to my dresser. I picked up the small article from the local paper and unfolded it. I could have recited it word for word, Daddy's entire life captured in a paragraph on page three. I'd read it many times, especially the part about the water. I lowered myself to the edge of my bed to read it again.

Jones County, North Carolina
Local Man Dies from Rattlesnake Bite

Lloyd Simpson Creech, age 41, was working his cotton field on April

42

19th when he encountered an Eastern Diamondback Rattlesnake and was bitten. Doctor William Meade, in the process of delivering a baby, directed the family to quickly bring Mr. Creech to him at the Newmans' residence approximately twenty miles away. There Mr. Creech was administered antivenin, but passed hours later, at home. Doctor Meade stated there were never any guarantees, and circumstances are all different. That, along with the ingestion of water by Mr. Creech prior to treatment, he concludes, led to Mr. Creech's unfortunate death. Mr. Creech, an upstanding individual with a talent for many things, from farming to crop management, to his unique insight locating water, was a lifelong native of Jones County. He leaves behind a wife of eighteen years, Mrs. Olivia Walters Creech, two sons, Ross Lloyd, 16, Trent Walters, 14, and a daughter, Martha Simpson (Sonny), age 12. Funeral services will be held April 23rd at Calvary Baptist Church, Highway 58 at 11:00 a.m.

Mama went to rip it in half when she saw it, but I'd said, "No!" and grabbed it from her.

There was a black-and-white photo of him below the words. He was standing in the middle of the cotton field, eerily close to the same spot where the snake had been. He wore a straw hat pushed back on his head and a big silly grin on his face. It captured a time before us kids were born, and was like looking into the past. The corners of the article were already smudged from me handling it so much. I folded it up and put it back on my dresser.

Aside from that, and the willow branch, there were other things of his we'd kept around. His work boots sat inside the back door like always, his coat for winter was still on the hook too. I took it down the other day, sniffed at it good and hard, catching a faint whiff of his hair tonic and cigarette smoke. Trent found me with my face buried in it.

In that tone he gets sometimes when he's spoiling for a fight, he'd said, "Quit being weird."

"I ain't. I'm only holding it for a second."

"Put it back."

He stood close, like he'd pinch me if I didn't do what he wanted, so I'd put it back like he said. He'd gone out, slamming the screen door so hard the spring that connected it to the frame made a funny *wawawa* sound. His shotgun rode his hunched shoulders, and he kept his head down, like he wished he didn't have to look at this world without our daddy in it. I started to yell at him I'd tell Mama if he got to shooting at the squirrels again. I hadn't 'cause I didn't want him coming back, not in the mood he was in. Trent not only had a wild streak, he had a bit of a mean streak too, rarely seen when Daddy had been around. Daddy used to say he was a might hot headed, and that hot headedness had been showing itself a lot lately.

I got up off the bed, smoothed my bedspread, and stopped my record player. I opened my door and heard the phone from the other part of the house, ringing the special ring, two long, and one short, which meant a call for us. Even though the sun was barely up, people wanting to pay their respects were already starting to call and I went to get it. I spent the rest of the day opening the door to accept offerings of fried chicken, soups, casseroles, pies, and cakes. It was a fact no one would ever go hungry if somebody died in these parts. Friends came to console us, to share their memories of what they remembered about Daddy, and it did help. I figured some also came out of curiosity, as if they could relive the horror of the moment by looking out across our land to the spot where he fell. Everyone tried to maintain a polite inquisitiveness that wouldn't offend, but sooner or later they'd get around to asking the details.

As the day wore on, Mama took to her bed and shut the door in such a way, I believed she might not ever open it again. Me, Ross, and Trent kept greeting visitors when they came knocking.

Soon as they heard she was resting, most would hand over what they'd brought, offer condolences, and leave, while some came in, like the Hudsons and the Pritchetts, and sat down in the living room, piling food onto plates from what was put out on the kitchen table and counters, laughing and talking like it was a supper party. Some of the women came from the church and stood at our kitchen sink to wash and dry dishes like they were in their own kitchens. We weren't offended. It was the way of things, how it had always been done, except it had always happened to other people. Not us.

Aunt Ruth called right before suppertime, and Mama left her room long enough to talk to her. Her manner of speaking was clipped since she was still so distraught, but she assured Aunt Ruth she didn't need her to drop what she was doing to come all the way from Rocky Mount.

"No. I'm fine. I'm fine. There's no need, really. You've got your teaching job. Maybe this summer. That would be nice."

She hung up the phone without looking at us and shuffled back down the hall and into their bedroom. Click went the door.

The one visit I assumed I would be glad for was when Daniel came with his mama, who he called Brenda, not Mama, and his sister, Sarah. They pulled up in their ancient Pontiac, and it was backfiring loud enough to scare the birds from the trees. The front bumper hung at an angle, about to fall off. Daniel had always said Brenda couldn't drive worth a lick, and judging by the looks of their vehicle, he was right. They came in and he barely glanced at me. For the first time ever in our years of friendship, the naturalness had disappeared. I figured it was due to his mama being there. His brown hair fell almost into his eyes in front, and over his ears on the sides. It was even longer in back. Daniel was always searching for a way to differentiate himself, like letting his hair grow when all the boys at school had crew cuts. This difference was him to a tee. He said useless words, and I said some back, all of it nonsense like we'd only just met. That's the way it felt, like we didn't know each other.

Him: "Hey."

Me: "Hey."

"How're you?"

"Okay, I guess."

"Well. That's good."

Normal would've gone more like this.

Him: "Your daddy should a killed that sumbitch 'fore it got him."

Me: "Ain't that the doggone truth!"

Him: "I'm gonna hunt that sumbitch down and kill it myself!"

"Not if I get to that sumbitch first!"

"Well, come on then, let's go!"

We would've then gone on a snake hunt or at

least acted out one, seeking some sort of vengeance on Daddy's behalf. The normal Daniel would've made this terrible situation a little better. He would've showed up dressed to play some part after searching every closet in his house to come up with a perfect costume. But he didn't say anything like that, not with his mama talking ninety miles an hour, controlling the conversation and his sister making it known she was more interested in trying to get Ross's attention than conveying sorrow for the death in our family. It was the first time in my memory I was glad when he left. Having that feeling didn't seem natural, not when we'd been best friends clear back to first grade, and I think we would have been even before then except Daniel had skipped kindergarten altogether. Everyone rumored he'd missed it 'cause his mama didn't register him, and the county had no idea he was supposed to even be in school. It made no difference since Daniel was smarter than most, and that was easily recognized his first day.

Our first grade teacher, Miss Rutherford, said, "Children, a few of you at a time are going to come to the reading circle at the back of the room, and we're going to start in our *Dick and Jane* primers and learn to read, won't that be fun?"

Daniel, who had avoided looking directly at anyone since he walked in the door, sat two rows over from me, and when I glanced over at him, our eyes locked on one another. Neither one of us smiled, but in that split second, there was a recognition, like seeing someone we know, even though we'd never met. Miss Rutherford took one student from each row, and Daniel ended up in my reading circle, sitting beside me. Boy, was she in for a big surprise. She went through explaining how we'd sound out words using our knowledge of the alphabet that we'd learned in kindergarten. She called on Daniel to try first. He stared at her, down at the page, and then closed the book.

She said, "Daniel? Won't you read?"

He said, "It's too easy."

Miss Rutherford said, "What, what do you mean too easy? Do you already know how to read?"

He nodded.

Surprised, Miss Rutherford handed him a book off her desk, one she was reading herself. "Can you read this?"

She opened it to a page and handed it to him. He began, and she simply let him read a whole paragraph. I think she was so stunned, she didn't think to stop him.

Finally, she said, "My word. Very good, Daniel."

She took the book from him, then said, "What else do you know?"

He froze up, and even then, I was already able to see he was uncomfortable, didn't like the close scrutiny.

She said, "Come up here."

Daniel followed her slowly to the front of the room. The other kids who were supposed to be busy copying the work from the blackboard while we were in the reading circle stopped what they were doing to watch.

Miss Rutherford picked up a piece of chalk and put, $1 + 2 = \ldots$

She handed the chalk to Daniel and he wrote, 3.

She wrote, $5 - 1 = \ldots$

Without hesitation, he wrote, 4.

I could see she was confounded. What was she supposed to do with Daniel? How had he learned all this? On his own?

She asked him, "How did you learn all this?"

He said, "I don't know."

Junior Odom let out a loud fart, his obnoxious reputation having already been established the year before.

Miss Rutherford, now distracted by the class, which had exploded in laughter at Junior's disruption, allowed Daniel to inch his way back to the reading circle.

He sat back down beside me, and I said, "You're real smart."

"No, I ain't."

"You are too. Will you teach me?"

"Teach you what?"

"To read, like you do?"

He stared at his shoes, the toes of them scuffed pale brown.

He said, "Okay."

I opened my book, and he pointed at the first word, and specifically, the first letter.

He said, "What's that letter?"

"G."

"What's this letter?"

"O."

"How does the 'g' sound?"

I made a hard g sound. He nodded.

"And this one?"

I said, "O."

"Add it together."

The meaning clicked, and I said, "Oh!"

He shook his head and looked so disappointed. "Not oh."

I grabbed his arm and said, "No, I mean *go!*"

Daniel smiled at me like I'd just figured out something huge. I grinned back at him.

From that point on we were near about inseparable. Luckily, we always ended up in the same classrooms too. As we grew older, I became Daniel's protector when his smarts made him a target. For me, he was the most interesting person I knew, his mind always percolating with new ideas to keep us amused, usually by acting out his movies, or sometimes his scientific interests were the highlight. Like the time he asked if we had any ammonia and bleach. He made the both us pure tee sick when he "experimented," and mixed the ingredients together in a small container we found. Bent over it, we inhaled the noxious fumes, got dizzy and then lolled about on the porch swing, both of us feeling queasy. Mama asked why we didn't eat our bologna sandwiches at lunch, and we claimed we'd eaten too much breakfast.

I was forever begging her, "let's go get Daniel" on weekends when I couldn't see him in school. His own mama always seemed glad to get him out of the house, like he was something of a burden to her 'cause he interrupted her "fun." I recollected a time when Daniel was in a grumpy mood on one of those days we'd picked him up. There was nothing he wanted to do. Mama had got him as we drove to the grocery store, and he didn't say a word when he got in, on the way to the store, or back to the house.

Mama finally asked, "Daniel, are you okay?"

Nothing.

I tried to get him to talk too. "Hey, Daniel, maybe when we get to my house, we can fix that light a little better near our stage, and maybe we can find some wood and add a platform to stand on, and maybe . . ."

Daniel finally spoke and cut me off. "I ain't feeling like none of that."

"Oh."

There was only silence then. I noticed his arm had a red mark, like a scratch. Mama glanced at me, and shook her head ever so slightly, a signal to let him be. That visit was terrible, with Daniel all out of sorts, and me trailing after him as he wandered about our farm like a lost puppy. We figured something must have happened, but what we didn't know. Something he didn't want to talk about. I was torn when it was time for him to go home. It had been no fun at all, yet I was troubled too. His presence that day was so heavy and unnatural, I worried about what he faced back at his house. I had to hand it to Daniel though. His ability to bounce back from those times was extraordinary. Next time I saw him, it was as if that dark day was erased and never happened. I never did find out what made him act that way, but when I think about how his mama is, and how his sister can be, he was due to have those off moments now and again. They probably set him on edge, made him uncomfortable not knowing what might come out of one of their mouths. For us, Daniel fit in like he should've been a part of our family instead.

That was why that feeling of being glad he and his family were gone didn't fit with how it usually went with me and him. After they'd left, here came Vernon Slater, from Slater's Feed and Supply. Trent said a cussword, and Ross smacked his head. They were hungry and worn down from the constant flow, and I was bone tired too. But, Mr. Slater, he'd known Daddy near about long as anyone. He came shuffling slowly up the drive, hanging tight to the wrought iron railing at the front steps. He was about seventy-five and walked in a manner that said he hurt somewhere, maybe everywhere. Before he even knocked, I swung the door open, catching him with his hand in the air suspended. It was as if he had to lower it in order to raise his head so he could look at me. He gave me a weak smile and stepped inside. I took his hat, and hung it next to Daddy's, and in doing that, it was as if it was any other day. I had an unusual, out of touch moment where I could imagine him still here.

Mr. Slater turned to Ross and said, "Couldn't hardly believe it when I heard it."

Ross said, "We couldn't hardly believe it when we saw it."

Mr. Slater sucked on something in his teeth and nodded. "Well. Y'all know your daddy was a fine man. Been knowing him since he was knee high to a grasshopper. He never did think a farming like work. Reckon if he was called home to the Lord, might as well been working in the place he loved best."

I motioned toward the couch, and extended him the sort of welcome Mama would've offered. "Mr. Slater, won't you sit a spell?"

He made a delicate turn, and shambled over

to it, then did another slow turn, looking behind himself twice as if to make sure the couch hadn't moved before he eased himself down. We took a seat with him as was warranted, Ross in Daddy's chair, me in Mama's rocker. Only Trent stood by the kitchen door, looking put out. Mr. Slater's watery blue eyes circled around to each of us, and then stayed on me.

"You know when your daddy was 'bout ten years old, he fell into Mr. Montague's new well after him and your granddaddy dowsed the property."

Ross and Trent looked at each other. We hadn't heard this story, and I leaned forward a bit.

Mr. Slater said, "There he was, bent over, looking into the hole and there he went, head first. Your granddaddy tried to grab him, got only his shoe, and it slipped out of his hand. Everybody heard the splash when he went in. They put a board crosswise, tied a rope around it and your granddaddy went down to get him, said he was knocked out cold, floating in the water. What was funny about it was, after they finally got him back out, someone found a piece of quartz rock somewheres on his person. Not in a pocket, but inside a his britches, or his shirt, something like that. Purty one too, clear as glass."

I interrupted him. "He's still got it, it's on his dresser."

Mr. Slater said, "Don't surprise me none. He

55

was like that about what held sentimental value to him. Things some wouldn't call important was to him."

Like the divining branch he'd given me. Daddy said he could've used any branch, but it was the one his daddy give him. Mr. Slater was right. Daddy put a value to things some would think worthless.

Mr. Slater cleared his throat and said, "Well, either way, y'all would serve him well to grow up and be like him."

Ross said, "Yes, sir," while Trent only narrowed his eyes and looked elsewhere. I nodded at Mr. Slater, who kept an endless supply of Mary Janes and Tootsie Rolls for the kids who came into his store.

He said, "Your daddy was real proud a y'all. Don't never forget that."

"No, sir."

He turned to Ross and asked, "What's your plans now, son?"

Ross said, "I reckon we're gonna get back to planting the crop soon as we can."

Mr. Slater pursed his mouth, like he was thinking hard on something.

Ross went on. "I mean, we were preparing the fields and all when . . . it happened. Daddy had a list ready for what he'd intended to plant. I can get it for you, then come by the store to get it once it's all gathered."

Mr. Slater pressed his hands on his knees, and stood. "Hang on to it for now. I got to speak to your mama first, the sooner the better, if possible."

Ross looked confused. "Okay."

I got his hat for him and he slapped it on his head.

When he got to the front door, he leaned toward me, and half-whispered, "You were extra-special to your daddy. He was real proud of you and what you could do."

It pleased me, what he said, and after he went out, I shut the door, and hoped no one else would show up, now the sun had gone down. And no one did. Matter of fact, once Mr. Slater came and went, the visiting slowed to a point that soon enough, there were no cars venturing down the road, no one bringing food, and the phone went silent except for the ring tones signaling calls to others. The people Daddy had known had paid their respects and now it was time to get on with their lives. It was all we could do too, but how do you do that when such a huge part is missing? Mama sure didn't appear up to it. She'd not been out of her room except to attend to the necessities of life.

A couple of days later, I came through the dogtrot, heading toward the kitchen after another early morning walk around the fields, and no luck. I usually gave up when a reddish sliver broke the horizon, as if daylight revealed the reality and futility of what I was trying to do. I could hear the low rumble of Ross's voice, talking to someone.

"We got to think about the planting."

I expected it to be Trent, but no, it was Mama. She sat at the kitchen table, a steaming cup of coffee in front of her.

Her voice was hoarse as she responded to him. "I guess. Got to get on, get by it. Somehow."

Her face was white, thinner. There were dark circles under her eyes. Her hair needed a washing, and hung limp against her cheekbones. She noticed me looking through the screen door, and her expression softened. I came into the kitchen and went around to the back of her chair, leaned over and wrapped my arms around her shoulders. She put her hands on my arms and leaned her head against me. She smelled of cigarettes, Jergens hand lotion, and sorrow, and I noted how her shoulder blades, all jutted out and sharp, poked into my chest. I squeezed her tight and then moved to the other side of the table to sit.

Mama stared at me. "Sonny, you look like something the cat drug up."

I'd been dressing in the same clothes for a week, a pair of droopy dungarees, a torn shirt that had a streak of brown on it that might have been gravy, and my scuffed, muddy work boots.

I hadn't unbraided my hair the entire time either and stray frazzled ends stuck out from my head, wild and unkempt. I'm not sure if I'd been brushing my teeth much. I hadn't really cared about how I looked.

I stared down at myself. "I reckon so."

I scratched at my head, and Trent came inside at that moment, his face going from glum to hopeful when he saw her.

He hugged her too, then stepped back to look at her carefully. "Mama, you all right?"

She rested her head down on her arms, and stayed like that for a few seconds. She eventually lifted it, reached across the table, and slid a cigarette out of the pack Daddy had left near the salt and pepper shakers. She put it in her mouth and lit it.

After she exhaled, she said, "I'll be all right. We're gonna be all right. We'll get through this."

There was conviction in her voice, on her face too. She looked and sounded determined enough to me. Mama came from tough stock, having grown up on a chicken farm with only Aunt Ruth, and Granny Walters, a life of hardships after Granddaddy Walters died of a stroke, dropping dead right on the kitchen floor. She'd wrung a lot of necks, more than most mamas who only threatened to, if they got aggravated enough at their young'uns. She swore long as she lived, she'd never raise that many chickens again. She'd talked about the strong ammonia odor along with a wet, fusty, feathery smell she felt she couldn't ever get out of her hair or clothes. After Granny Walters passed from emphysema, she and Aunt Ruth sold their childhood home, and split the money. By then Mama and Daddy were married, and used it to buy what they needed for the farm. Mama once said Aunt Ruth likely squirreled hers away, burying it in jars around the small house she'd bought up in Rocky Mount. One could say Aunt Ruth was a tad eccentric.

Mama was wearing a pair of Daddy's old pants, and they hung off her thin frame. She had a kerchief tied around her head, like she always did when she intended to work. Looking like she was ready to do something made me get up and get the apron off the hook by the stove. I cracked eggs into a bowl, and moved the skillet to a burner to heat it up. Soon the familiar sounds of cooking and the smell of food filled the kitchen again. I split some biscuits brought by someone who'd come by earlier in the week and put them in the oven to heat up. Mama needed to eat, and I didn't bother to ask if she wanted anything. I fixed the food, and put a plate in front of her and said nothing. I filled plates for Ross, Trent, and myself. Mama stared at the food and then, to my relief, she picked up her fork.

It grew quiet as we ate scrambled eggs and

biscuits, and drank up the entire pot of coffee. We sat together as a family for the first time in what felt like months. Mama's gaze suddenly fastened to the empty area at the end of the table. Daddy's chair wasn't there since someone had moved it into the hall by the phone.

She brushed a crumb from the corner of her mouth. "You know, all you do and say would matter to your daddy. Before you speak, make a decision, or go to do something, you think about him, how he'd go about it."

The three of us replied, "Yes, ma'am."

Mama said to no one in particular, "Bring his chair back over here where it belongs."

Ross got up and slid it back into its rightful place. That small correction made a big impact 'cause even without him sitting in it, there was something right about it being there than not.

Ross returned to his earlier topic. "Mama, Mr. Slater wanted you to come by the store. You up to it today?"

"What's he want, you reckon."

"I don't know. He said he needed to talk to you."

Mama said, "Today's good as any other," and Ross's face relaxed from looking so worried.

He was like Daddy in that way, full of get-up-and-go. Mama got up from the table, and left the kitchen. When she came back, she'd put on a touch of lipstick. She didn't wear it around the house, and though she wasn't vain, she never went out "in public" without it.

She said, "Let's go."

We piled our dirty dishes in the sink, went out, and got in the truck. Trent climbed into the truck bed, and I followed, which is how we always rode when it was nice. I leaned against the back of the cab, thinking the drive to Slater's could have been like any other if I closed my eyes and let myself believe Daddy was driving. I'd already found out thoughts like that were useless, and only made me feel worse. I stared through the back window at Mama holding onto the list, her thumb going over and over the pencil marks Daddy had made. It was early May at this point, and there were acres filled with cotton plants as well as tobacco, corn, soybeans, and sweet potatoes.

Ross's head swiveled left and right. I could imagine what he was saying. "Gosh, look a there, that cotton's almost six inches high already," and "Doggone, that corn's shot up a foot since I last seen it."

Trent leaned against the opposite side of the cab, pretty much ignoring me. He messed with his pocketknife, opening and closing the blade, and pressing it against his arm as if to test the sharpness. The gravel lot at Slater's was filled with a half-dozen trucks and one tractor. Slater's Feed and Supplies was a flat-roofed cinderblock structure, with a wooden front porch that went end to end. Ads were painted on all sides of the building. A giant-sized Pepsi Cola bottle cap was on the front left, while the Purina Dog Chow checkered symbol was on the right. A message for a brand of defoliant stretched down the full length of it, and showed withered leaves from a cotton plant on the ground, indicating a successful leaf drop. I already knew on the other side was an ad for fertilizer.

We parked under a tree, and I hopped down out of the back. I followed Mama and Ross inside, while Trent took off to where Mr. Slater kept shotgun shells. Cool air from massive ceiling fans whirling overhead caused anything loose to flutter, spin, or flap. Customers had lined up in orderly fashion to get what they needed at the back, with the colored farmers waiting for the whites to pay up first. They stayed huddled together in a corner, out of the way, talking softly amongst themselves. I'd asked Daddy why that was one day, why the colored people had to wait and let the white people go first.

We were sitting inside the truck after coming out of the store, and he'd said, "It's complicated, Sonny, although it doesn't need to be. There's people who think different, those who believe the coloreds ain't as good as us. Can't change their minds, the way they think. They're just ignorant, is all."

"Does Mr. Slater think that?"

"I doubt it, but I'm sure he does it this way only to keep some of his customers happy."

Today, only white people were in the store, and I felt a sense of relief 'cause it had always made me uncomfortable, like I was somehow personally to blame for colored people having to wait. I'd been taught to respect my elders, so it didn't ever set right to be allowed to go before they did, especially if we'd just walked in.

Junior Odom was stocking shelves, and when I walked by he stared rudely, his face holding the same ugly smirk he wore in school. He was filling bins with nails and didn't act like he cared half fell on the floor. Mr. Slater was talking to Mr. Cornell about lime, and after he finished, he turned to Mama. She went to hand him Daddy's list, but he didn't take it.

Instead he leaned over the counter, said something, and pointed to a door that said, "Office."

Usually, all we had to do was hand someone the list. Whatever we wanted was put on Daddy's account to be paid after the crops sold. This was highly irregular and Mama looked uncomfortable. She and Ross followed Mr. Slater into the office while those standing in line stared after them. I felt self-conscious, like everybody knew something we didn't. They were only in there a couple minutes, but boy, when they came out, Mama looked fit to be tied. Ross's face was blood-red, making his blond hair stand out even more. She motioned sharply for me to follow and given her expression, I wasted no time.

"What's wrong? Ain't we getting anything?"

Her jaw was squared, and she didn't answer. Ross was behind her, puffing like a locomotive.

Near the front door Mama spotted Trent and said, "Trent!" in a voice we rarely heard.

I couldn't see him, but I heard, "Hey, I want . . ."

Mama said, "Now!"

Her tone matched her look, hard and angry.

Ross spoke. "I can't believe it."

Mama shushed him. "Ross, not now."

Ross was too disturbed though, his voice emphatic. "It ain't right! We're paid up, and we've always paid on time, every year!"

"I said, keep your voice down."

Junior snuck into the aisle closest to us, eavesdropping. I wanted to go over there and tell him to mind his own business, except Ross's voice was loud enough for everyone to hear anyway, even Mr. Slater, who looked our way, his eyes drooping with sadness.

"It ain't fair!"

Mama put her hand on his back and moved him toward the door. "Fair ain't how you stay in business."

Junior hovered even closer, and when I scowled

at him, he put both hands up to his cheeks, and pulled his skin down in a fake expression of distress. I could've knocked him into next week, if I'd have thought Mama wasn't looking.

Ross scrubbed at his head. "Now what're we gonna do?"

I waited for her answer, but she didn't have one.

Chapter 4

Mama kept the list Daddy made which included a new cottonseed called pima, a special variety he'd wanted to try, and which Mr. Slater had ordered. Not only was it more expensive, it was a kind of cotton that required a special picker, or even hand picking, and no one was going to buy something particular and new for one kind of cottonseed, or hire a bunch of people either.

Mr. Slater had offered up his advice about Daddy's decision. "Could a been a good thing, risky, but good. Sells at a higher price, but considering all, it was mostly risky. I was going to talk to him about the new policy. Never got the chance."

Mama tried to get Mr. Slater to do what he'd always done, on credit, but on account of some not paying, he was no longer allowing that. Daddy had gotten loans from the bank before, but for the past few years, he'd settled up with Mr. Slater at the end of the season.

Ross said, "I wished Daddy hadn't sold off all the seed from the crops last year. We'd at least have that to plant."

Mama said, "Can't nobody see into the future now, can they?"

None of us said much on the ride home.

We were at loose ends without the usual field work to consume every minute of the day. Ross and Trent went to work mending areas of the fencing even though we had no cows to keep where there were pastures. After that, they patched up some holes in the chicken coop and then it seemed all they had to do was bicker about stupid things.

"When you put that screen on that hole, it ain't gonna hold up 'cause you ain't done it right."

"Shut up."

"You shut up."

There was a scuffle and a thump. "If I say shut up, then . . ."

Why did they always have to fight like two cats with their tails tied together? Mama yelled out the back door, like a referee directing two boxers.

"Ross! Ain't you got something else needs fixing? And Trent, get your tail end over there and help Sonny weed that garden!"

Trent mumbled something and stomped his way to the toolshed, yanked the door open and got out a hoe. Mama took a minute to cool off, her body a silhouette caught between the two sides of the house as the breeze blew through the dogtrot and fluttered the skirt about her knees. She'd quit wearing Daddy's work pants, since sometimes she needed to drive into Flatland to return something she'd mended, or it might have been that wearing them made her sad. She'd been calling around, talking to folks about maybe taking in some ironing and sewing.

She had a nice Singer sewing machine Daddy got her one Christmas and she'd turned out some pretty dresses to wear to church. After the funeral service, Mama said we were taking a break from going to services on Sunday.

"I can't face them people, God bless'em. I just can't. Besides, I need to spend what time I can on sewing, making ends meet. Somebody's got to be needing them a new skirt or blouse."

"Yes, Mama."

She felt God understood, and then she said she knew He did when someone accepted her offer to sew them a new dress. Her voice, as they worked out pattern style and material went from hesitant to excited, like the moment you get any sort of good news. She had a couple of other jobs crop up too. Mrs. Aiken asked if she could make her some curtains, and repair a couple skirts since she couldn't see none too good anymore. Mama had also found out Mrs. Poole's daughter, Bobbie Lynn, was getting married, and so she was set to iron a stack of tablecloths for the wedding later in the week. All of it together might bring in twenty dollars.

I hacked at the weeds even harder, my own

frustration getting the better of me. Mama's grief was poured into her pursuit of money. She'd directed me to gather eggs once a day, put them into a crate with some straw, and have Ross to drive me into town where I was to sell them.

She said, "Every little bit helps, right?"

"Yes, Mama."

One of the first times we went, I urged him, "Geez, don't take me to nobody I don't know."

"Huh? Why?"

"It'll be easier if I know the person."

"Aw, Sonny, you're only selling eggs, it ain't like you're asking them to buy a car. You can't be choosy, and 'sides, we ain't got gas to burn going all over the place."

Mama had no idea how much I hated doing it, just as much as when I had to get up in front of my class to give a book report—which I despised the way I did taking a spoonful a castor oil if my stomach was off. She said I'd get used to it after I'd done it for a while, but my legs shook just as hard as I walked up to the door at every place we stopped.

Sometimes I got this reaction. "Hey now, sugar, ain't you Sonny Creech? I'm sure sorry about your daddy; that was so unexpected! Here you go, I'll take a dozen."

Some said, "Oh my, how nice, but no thank you, I get mine down to the A&P in Trenton."

And some said, "Have mercy, this what you

Creeches are doing now your daddy passed on?"

They weren't any more shocked than we were.

Beyond the egg selling, lots of little things bothered me more than ever. Like how Trent was hacking at the weeds at the moment, coming so close, I was sure he intended to chop my foot off.

"Trent, can't you see my foot's right there."

He only whacked harder, staying just as close. He made me so mad I could spit. I took my hoe and walked out of the garden.

He yelled, "Get back here!"

"No!"

Trent yelled, "I'm not doing this alone!"

"Sonny! Trent! What in God's name is wrong with you kids?"

Mama stood on the back steps, her face flushed, eyes red rimmed. Her mouth was set in a thin line of frustration. I wanted to tell her, only that was being a tattletale, plus she looked like she'd had a bait of it, between all of us.

She lifted a hand and let it drop, a sign of exasperation as she turned to go back inside. "Cut out the damn fighting."

Ashamed, I headed for the cotton field near the house where the center of several rows remained mutilated and damaged through the middle, like a drunk had somehow stumbled around before finding his way out. This was where I'd run, and my brothers had half-dragged Daddy to the house. I stared at the crooked, broken path what resembled my own insides, just as twisted and torn up. Trent continued slashing at the weeds like a madman and I entered the field, stooped over, and began to fix the soil, my motions tender and soft, as if repairing the earthly wounds.

The sun quickly heated up my back as it penetrated through my thin blouse. I didn't look up much. It was too hard not seeing Daddy in a distant field on a tractor, or driving the truck up and unloading something we needed, or walking to the shade of one of the trees in the yard, where we would eat our noon dinner together. He'd always been with us, his steady hand and words creating the stability we needed, showing us what hard work could do if we kept at it. He'd always answered Ross's questions, resolved the irrational actions of Trent, considered all I said as if it was the most important thing he'd heard all day. My parents had leaned on one another the way Preacher Moore leaned on the arm of God and his congregation. They had encircled us with their love and held a deep regard for all our petty little gripes. There was a section missing in our familial loop, our way of living, thinking, and doing spilled out of the brokenness, creating a weakness whereas we'd always been so strong.

I finished smoothing the rows, rebuilding the hills, but it didn't really make me feel any different, any better. I went to put my hoe up only I noticed Trent wasn't nowhere in sight, and weeds still grew thick around the corn. With a sigh, I went back to the garden, and before long, I found myself hacking at them the way he'd been, working out all that was in me until my mind slowed down and my back hurt. I finally finished, and put the hoe away. I figured something had to give sooner or later.

That something showed up a few days later.

Down Turtle Pond Road came a truck going faster than most would go. Ross and I were just back from selling eggs and he'd gone around to the back side of the house while I lifted crates out of the truck bed. I shaded my eyes, trying to figure out who was driving like the devil was on their tail. This beat-up truck pulled into our drive, parked, and when the door opened, Mr. Fowler got out. Though it had been at least three years since I'd seen him, he looked the same as I remembered, only the truck was as mismatched to him as a hammer with a screw. The paint was two-toned, blue and white, the darker blue starchy looking, dulled from sitting out in the sun. There were a couple of rust spots on the lower half, the metal so corroded, I could actually see through it. I'd have figured him to have something spit shined and polished.

He left the door open and I got a glimpse of the inside. There was no trash on the floorboard like ours where Ross's accelerator foot was always colliding with a Pepsi bottle rolling around, or peanut and candy wrappers. Mr. Fowler acknowledged my presence with a glance, then looked toward the house. He turned to stare at the barn, the chicken coop, and finally, he stared at the fields.

"I wonder why there ain't no cotton?"

He wondered that, while I wondered why he talked like I wasn't there. Didn't he read the papers? Did he not go into Flatland and maybe hear some mention of Daddy? He remained by the truck, hands hanging loose by his side as if unsure of what to do. He wore work clothes, a pair of dark blue pants, and pale-blue work shirt, only his were clean, pressed, and without stains. Daddy's clothes, even though they might have been clean, always had some sort of stain Mama could never get out. I recollected when we'd dowsed Mr. Fowler's fields, several men, mostly colored along with one or two whites, worked in and around the outbuildings. And while they'd always worked in a spot we weren't, somehow I doubted Mr. Fowler ever lifted a finger around his place. Instead, he'd point, *do this, do that,* and his spotless clothes proved it.

I could smell him even though he stood a few feet away as he looked around. He smelled like he'd only just got out of a bath, the sweet odor of soap and maybe aftershave. His gaze returned to me, and he angled his head toward the house.

He said, "Is Mrs. Creech in?"

He didn't ask, *is your mama home?*

"Yes, sir."

He pushed his hair back off his forehead, also in that way I remembered, using the palm of his hand. His mouth was curled up at each corner, like he was smiling a little, only he wasn't, since his eyes didn't crinkle up. He went to the back end of his truck, propped himself there against the dropped-down tailgate, arms crossed, and stared at the prepared fields as if waiting. I turned and ran inside, the screen door slamming behind me, earning a look of aggravation from Mama. She was on the phone with someone else, and in the process of saying goodbye to whoever she'd called. She exhaled a cloud of smoke, and stabbed the cigarette out as she eased her way out of what sounded like an awkward exchange.

"Well, I figured with you having them two babies you might need some help with the washing and ironing, or some new baby clothes. They grow so fast! Oh, no, it's fine, Betty. We're fine. No, we don't need a thing, but thank you again. Bye, bye."

Mama set the receiver in the cradle, and gave me a look that said she hated what she was having to do as much as I hated selling eggs.

I stuck my thumb over my shoulder while leaning in, like Mr. Fowler might hear me. "You ain't gonna believe who's here."

She got up off her chair and went to look out

the door where he remained propped against his tailgate. "I hope it ain't nothing wrong."

"He asked if you were home."

Mama narrowed her eyes at him, then stared down at herself. She untied the apron she had on and went out the door like she meant business, head held high, and with a confident step. I followed, right on her heels. As soon as he saw her, he unfolded his arms, and stood straight.

Mama was direct. "May I help you, Mr. Fowler?"

The change in him was remarkable. His mouth stretched big and wide, and that standoffish manner he'd held with me flew the coop as he extended a hand to her. She hesitated before she took it. After that, she crossed her arms over her chest. For the first time since Daddy died, she allowed a tiny polite smile to soften her face as she tilted her head to look at him, like she was curious why he was here. I found I didn't really like her smiling at him, and I wasn't sure why, although maybe I was jealous on Daddy's behalf, as if no other male ought to have her smiles, only him. I wondered whether or not Mr. Fowler had ever been married. He looked to be about the same age as Daddy, maybe a little younger.

Mr. Fowler said, "Noticed them empty fields. Used to seeing cotton growed up a good bit by now. Decided I'd see for myself what was going on."

Mama was no longer smiling. "Have you not heard about my husband, Mr. Fowler?"

"It's Frank."

Mama shifted away from him a little, and looked toward the fields. She'd shut down, digesting the way he'd responded to her question.

He pushed his hair back. "Heard about it. Condolences to you, and your family."

Mama said, "Is there something else?"

"Don't mean to get into your business, but, ain't you planting this year?"

Mama started to reply, but he kept on, sounding like he was quite disturbed about the empty acreage as they stood side by side, facing the empty fields.

He gestured at the land, and then, like he was continuing this private conversation with himself, he said, "Sure, sure. Time's needed for the grieving and such. Look here at these empty fields. Got to make do somehow though."

Mama didn't say nothing, likely thinking he was a nut ball. Maybe thinking it wasn't none of his business.

When she said nothing, he went on talking again to himself. "Always been something in the ground by now. Reckon they could be in a bind."

He waited then, and said no more. Mama, strong woman that she is, put a hand up to her cheek, and embarrassment is what I read in her expression.

She lifted her shoulders, and let them drop and said, "That's about the extent of it."

He reached into his shirt pocket for a cigarette. He smoked no-filter Camels, cigarettes Daddy had said would singe the insides of your lungs if you weren't used to them. He shook one out and offered it to Mama. She hesitated like she was deliberating on how it might appear, his offering her a cigarette, and then shook her head.

She said, "No, thank you kindly."

He stuck it in his mouth.

After he lit it, had a puff or two, he glanced at me, and the tone to his voice altered a degree, coming out a little less soft. "Where's them two boys?"

His eyes narrowed, and I had the thought he would snap his fingers under my nose for me to answer—quick—if Mama hadn't been there.

She answered before I could. "Ross is around back somewhere, and I'm not sure where Trent is at the moment."

He turned back to her. "They work the cotton?"

"They do."

"They know what to do and all?"

Mama said, "Course, they growed up doing it."

Mr. Fowler smoked some more, then said, "What about her?"

He dipped his head toward me.

Mama said, "Sonny works it too. Matter of fact, she's like her daddy. Loves it."

"That so?"

She nodded, turned to me, her lips curved upward and it made me feel a bit better 'cause when she could smile, it told me she wasn't none too worried about the conversation.

"Thinking on something, but it's up to you entirely. No skin off my back if you say yes or no."

Mama raised her chin a bit and said, "Oh? And what's that?"

"A few years back, kind a had a little interest in the land here, only your husband, he won't into selling. Offered him a nice, tidy sum seeing as it backs right up to the end of my property."

I hadn't heard about this before.

I had a split second of anxiousness that's what he was after again before Mama cut him off. "I remember, and I'm not inclined to sell, Mr. Fowler, particularly not now."

"Didn't imagine you would be. Got a different proposition, more like financing the crop this year. Buy the seed, and you all tend to it, and come time to harvest, maybe get some help here, and when it goes to market, we agree on a cut. Should give you enough and some to set aside for next year."

Mama angled her head, as if studying on his suggestion. I couldn't say I really knew his ways, other than to think he might have a little higher regard for himself than was warranted, but, although his idea didn't sound so bad, why would he care when he ain't never come over here in all these years?

I was relieved she didn't jump right on the idea. "Well, I've taken in some ironing and such, and if Ross can get a part-time job . . ."

He stopped her. "Won't make enough to pay bills and keep this place up to boot."

Mama's shoulders drew up, and I recollected Daddy always talking about the cost of the upkeep with so much acreage. We had to keep fields mowed we didn't plant in, which meant we needed fuel, plus there'd be repairs to equipment meaning the cost of parts, and that didn't count the regular bills, or the fact that I liked to eat and so did Ross and Trent.

Mama paused a moment, and then she asked, "What's it to you, exactly? What's the catch?"

His eyebrows raised up, and he rubbed his hands together. "Why see? Knew you'd want to hear an offer 'fore you turned it down."

Mama said, "Why wouldn't I?"

She sounded annoyed. She didn't much tolerate foolishness from anyone.

"Figured a fifty/fifty split would be about right."

Mama said, "I don't know about that. We'd be doing most of the work from the start and into the end of growing season. If I were to even consider it, I'd say more like seventy/thirty."

He actually chuckled, and it made him less severe, almost easygoing like Daddy. Maybe he took warming up to, and once he'd got to know folks, he allowed his true self to show.

He said, "Sixty/forty and that's more than fair. It's a risk, and that's the final offer."

There was that word again—risk. Mama didn't answer right away, and neither one of them were really smiling. No, they looked more like they were trying to gauge who might win the negotiation. If this worked out, Ross sure was gonna be happy 'cause he'd been at his wit's end, drifting around like he didn't have a thing to do. Trent came around the corner of the house and when he saw Mr. Fowler, he came over and stood beside me, staring while Mr. Fowler kept talking.

Trent said, "What's going on?"

I mumbled, "We might get to start planting, courtesy of him."

Trent frowned. "What? Why?"

"Said he'd buy what we needed, and . . ."

Mr. Fowler turned to look at us, so I quit talking.

Mama said, "Let me talk about it with the kids tonight."

Mr. Fowler looked toward me and Trent, and I allowed a bit of a smile, like I'd done all those years ago. He offered nothing. Not even a blink. But boy when he looked back at Mama, he did that thing again I couldn't quite call a smile, it was more of an expression that implied he was real easygoing about anything she said or did.

He said, "Whatever makes you comfortable, but your decision ought to come pretty quick, as it's already getting into May."

Mama said, "You'll have it by tomorrow."

He spun on his heels and headed for his truck, while Mama went over to the clothesline and started taking clothes down, already moving on to the other things she had to do as if his visit were of no concern to her. What struck me was his expression when he'd turned away from her. The way his entire face flattened out, and everything from his eyebrows to his mouth went into a straight line, so different from how he'd looked when he'd faced her, appearing pleasing and friendly. I can't say I'd ever seen someone look so different from one minute to the next, and I concluded he was pretty good at hiding what he was thinking.

Chapter 5

At the supper table Mama talked about Mr. Fowler financing our operation (that was how she put it), and Ross looked ready to hop on the tractor that minute. Trent did what Trent does, which was to raise a shoulder up in an "I don't care" manner, while he kicked Ross under the table. Trent sure did hate to work the cotton.

Mama turned to me. "Sonny, what do you think?"

Trent spoke up. "Who cares what she thinks, she's a girl."

Mama smacked her hand on the table, and the sound was sharp, like she'd actually hit his face. By the look on hers, she was tempted.

"Trent Walters Creech. Don't never let me hear you say such a hateful thing, ever. You understand?"

Trent slumped in his chair, wearing that sullen look he'd had lately.

Mama tapped his arm, like she wanted him to really understand she meant business. "I want to *hear* you understand me."

Trent mumbled, "Yes, ma'am."

She said, "Sonny?"

I didn't know exactly how to respond 'cause I could see the reason in it, while my doubts about Mr. Fowler stuck. Yet, I wanted to see cotton growing no matter how it got there. Empty fields didn't seem right, and made me think about Daddy.

I said, "Do I got to sell eggs if we plant?"

Mama said, "You'll keep helping in any way you can, as usual."

She stared around the table at us, her look saying she'd made up her mind and I went to bed that night knowing somehow, after tomorrow, everything was going to be different. In my room I listened for maybe the millionth time, the smooth velvety voice of Elvis and his declaration, "that's all right, Mama," hoping that was true.

The next morning when Mama picked up the receiver and punched the buttons a few times to get Eunice, I watched with mixed feelings.

"Eunice? Patch me over to Frank Fowler." There was a pause, and she snapped, "Frank Fowler, yes, that's exactly who I said."

She rolled her eyes. There was sure to be gossip over to Wells' Grocery at the very idea of her calling him.

After a few seconds she said, "This is Olivia Creech. I've thought about it, and I'll accept your offer."

There was quiet on her end for a few seconds. "No. Sixty/forty." More quiet. "Yes. Fine. Of course, we'll do our best."

She hung up the phone, came back to the table, and sat down. "Guess we're gonna find out how that might go."

For a while it was only the sound of forks scraping on plates as we finished up breakfast.

When I was done, I wiped my mouth, sat back, and said, "What you reckon Daddy would think?"

"He'd want us to do what we needed to do to get by."

It put me in a mood, something between relieved and troubled. I couldn't explain my worry any more than I could describe how the dowsing stick worked. Some things just weren't meant to make sense right away. My concern was as mystifying as the need I felt to march across the acres while waiting for some signal from Daddy in his heavenly home.

At school, I was all keyed up. It didn't help when "Lil" Roy Carter and Junior Odom started shooting spitballs out of their mouths at everyone's heads until Mrs. Baker finally separated them. It was just my luck Billy Watson's desk beside mine was empty 'cause he was out sick, and that's where Mrs. Baker put Junior. I didn't look at him even though he kept trying to get my attention by mumbling my name every few seconds.

"Sonny. Sonny. Hey, Sonny. Pssst."

I stared at the clock over Mrs. Baker's graying head, wishing the bell would ring. I wanted to finish my earlier conversation with Daniel. Junior got to making some wild moves the more I ignored him, first shifting one way and then the other. Daniel finally looked my way and mouthed, *coming over today*. Happy, I relaxed and sat back to listen to Mrs. Baker talk about nurses coming to our school to give out them newfangled polio vaccines the following week. She droned on and on while I stared down at my reddened cuticles, and jagged nails where I'd taken to chewing on them even more. Mama hadn't noticed yet. I recalled her dipping my thumb into the pepper sauce when I was about two so I'd quit sucking on it, and thought she'd do the same thing again if she could see my fingertips.

Finally the bell went off and there was the usual hectic scramble to the door with Mrs. Baker yelling at us to not forget to do our homework. I felt sorry for her sometimes. Daddy used to say she was old as Methuselah since she'd taught him too. Junior pushed his way in front of me, then stopped so I almost ran into his backside.

"Move it, Junior, geez!"

Daniel waited beside the door, and walked with me to the bus, while Junior tried to get under our skin.

"Aw, look at the two lovey-dovey birds. Go on, Lassiter! Why don't you kiss her? Sonny and Daniel sitting in a tree! K-i-s-s-i-n-g!"

My face burned. I'd never considered Daniel in that way, although recently he'd grown lanky, and he was getting what Mama called peach fuzz on his upper lip. I didn't want anything to change. I wanted things to stay like they'd always been, our ease together as comfortable as my oldest, worn-out dungarees. Daniel refused to look at Junior, who started squeaking like a mouse, although something flickered in his eyes when Junior bumped into me again.

I said, "Quit, Junior Odom! You almost tripped me."

Junior's look shifted to something hateful, but he moved away so at least I didn't have to smell the liverwurst and cheese sandwich he'd wolfed down at lunch. Daniel did that thing I liked where he slung his arm over my shoulder like Daddy used to do, while Junior stayed on our heels. Some days I wished Daniel would stand up to him, give him one good solid whop. I bet he'd think twice about messing with us. Sarah sat in the parking lot waiting on him, the back end of their car smoking hard as she was. Daniel rode with her to and from school instead of the county bus like us.

I said to him, "You might not be able to stay at our place long. Mr. Fowler's supposed to be there, and we got to get on with the planting pretty quick since we're so far behind."

"What's he like?"

"He's all right, I guess. He doesn't talk much to us, but he's real nice to Mama."

"Dang. I bet he's making moves."

"Making moves?"

"You know, on your mama. She's all alone now, except for you and your brothers. Remember what went on with Mr. Earl and Mrs. Grissom."

That rumor had held the town captive for months until it became a fact. Mr. Grissom wasn't dead six months hardly when next thing we know, Mrs. Grissom was becoming Mrs. Earl. I gave Daniel a doubtful look. He gave me a smug one, and then the thought of it sort of made me mad.

I huffed at him. "Have you lost your marbles? Mama loved Daddy, and still does. She'll always love him, and no one else. If he was up to something like that, she wouldn't stand for it. She'd tell him to go to hell."

"Okay, calm down, I'm just saying."

I made my way toward the bus. "He's more interested in our land, I think, which I don't much like that either."

Daniel followed me, and he said, "Well, maybe that's all it is."

Alarmed, I said, "All it is? Shoot, that's everything!"

I stewed over Mr. Fowler's possible motives. The idea he might be interested in Mama was as bad as him wanting our land. Any consideration of either would be like turning our backs on Daddy, and his memory.

I climbed the first step on the bus and Daniel said, "So, you want me to come over or not? I got a new scene we can practice."

We'd been doing bits and pieces from *A Streetcar Named Desire* for a year now, the same ones over and over, and I was getting sort a tired of it. Daniel got obsessed with stuff like that. He watched shows at his neighbor's house, an elderly lady who gave him cookies and milk, and talked his ears off, while he sat in front of her set. He always took pencil and paper and scribbled details about different movies for us to reenact although we'd sometimes carry on off-the-cuff, saying what came to mind instead of what was really supposed to be said. Daniel said that was improvising.

I stopped and faced him, which put us eye level, and said, "I guess."

He took my answer as a sign of disregard and said, "Ain't got to if you don't want me to."

"No. I do."

I stared at Daniel a second longer, his eyes like maple syrup, warm and golden, and my heart gave a strange, new little quiver. I hurried onto the bus without looking back at him again.

I took a seat where I could watch him walking toward Sarah who kept an eye out on the other kids coming from the school. She didn't wear what most girls her age wore, the poodle or circle skirts with matching sweater sets, bobby socks, and oxfords. She liked them tight-fitting pencil skirts, and flats. I couldn't help but think she might have a "reputation." Boys Ross's age talked about girls like her, the ones who snuck behind the bleachers in the gymnasium or out on the baseball field and "made out" with them.

The sort they called fast, a girl who goes all the way, or "puts out."

Mama had that discussion with me this past birthday. She needn't have bothered. I'd had no inkling in that direction whatsoever. Sarah scanned the parking lot, and spotted Ross coming from his school across the street, his letter jacket and books slung over his shoulder, heading for the bus. She immediately tossed her cigarette aside and waved at him enthusiastically. He had to have seen her she was so animated, but he didn't wave back. He looked past her, shouting and waving to Addie Simmons instead. Ross used to like to go to the Pavilion down to the beach now and then to dance, until Hurricane Hazel tore it all to pieces last year. He was good at Carolina shag, and had won a contest or two. Sometimes at night, I could make out the *shuffle shuffle, swish swish* noise of him practicing steps in his bedroom, his transistor radio tuned in to a station out of Carolina Beach.

Sarah's hand fell, and that happy look of hers dropped into a pout. I almost felt sorry for her, until she slapped Daniel as he went by, as if he was to blame for Ross not giving her a single glance. That ended any sympathy I might have had. Daniel only gave her an annoyed look and got in the car. He never stood up for himself, and between his mama and Sarah, I was certain he got shoved into the background a lot, as if their words and opinions were always more important than his.

The bus lurched out of the parking lot, and I settled in beside my friend Becky Hill, a smart girl who liked to draw pictures of horses and had earned every single badge there was as a Girl Scout. I liked her quiet ways, and she could tell when I didn't want to talk. I stared out the window at the countryside we passed, acres and acres filled with cotton, tobacco, and corn, fields filled with money, and all the good things that could be bought when a crop was successful. Ours was the third stop, and when the bus came to Turtle Pond Road, the land lay brown and empty, not one tiny little plant in sight. But that wasn't what drew the attention of the bus-load of kids. No, after Ross, Trent, and I bailed out, the inevitable murmur began from those who still found it interesting to talk about how

Daddy died when they thought we couldn't hear.

"Said he couldn't breathe . . ."

"Swolled up like a balloon . . ."

"Mama said what them Creeches were doing was evil. Whoever heard tell of finding water with a damn stick."

"My daddy said it was a bunch of horseshit."

"Hey, water witch! Sonny Creech is a water witch!"

They made me mad and didn't even know it. I wanted to shout "shut up!" at the top of my lungs as the bus pulled away leaving us in the stench of its smoky exhaust. I held my books tight against my chest. Ross walked with me, knowing I'd heard the comments as they flowed out the open windows, words tossed like trash on the ground. My school shoes smacked against the dirt road, and my dress swung around my legs since I was walking fast like my feet were on fire. Trent lollygagged behind, stopping to investigate the stink of something dead in the ditch.

"Don't pay them no mind."

"I ain't."

He reminded me more of Daddy every day, not only the way he walked, loose-jointed and relaxed, but even his expressions. Ross understood me, almost as good as Daddy had. We hurried along, anxious to get home. Mr. Fowler's truck was visible soon as the house came into sight.

Ross said, "Well, he wasn't fooling."

Hearing Ross's comment, Trent, who'd caught up to us, said, "I never thought he was. I knew he'd stick to his word."

Ross snorted, and I shook my head. Since when did Trent know anything about Mr. Fowler anyway? We went around to the back of the house. When we walked into the kitchen, Mr. Fowler was parked at the table, cup of coffee in front of him and a half-filled ashtray. The room smelled of cigarette smoke and his hair tonic.

Mama said, "Mind your manners."

Ross stepped forward and shook his hand as did Trent. After Trent, I stuck my hand out, and Mr. Fowler grabbed it, and then stared at my fingertips.

I pulled my hand back as he said, "Young ladies don't bite their nails."

Mama frowned and reached for my hand, staring down at my chewed nails.

She let my hand go and said, "We're coping with what's happened best as we can."

Mr. Fowler's demeanor changed right away, and he said, "Oh, sure, sure. Didn't meant nothing by it. Just commenting, and probably shouldn't."

He sort of laughed, and then stopped abruptly, like it was something he wasn't used to doing.

Mama motioned to us. "Go on and get out of your school clothes."

We filed out of the kitchen, and headed down the dogtrot to our rooms. Ross mumbled, "Danged if he ain't kind a strange."

Trent said, "I didn't see nothing strange."

I said, "Wonder why he ain't never been married."

Trent said, "Maybe he has, we don't know."

I said, "I wonder if he's going to be coming around here all the time."

We went quiet as we took a moment to think about the implications of Frank Fowler in our lives.

Then, Ross echoed my own thoughts. "I sure hope not."

Trent drew up his shoulders like it wouldn't bother him none. In my room I quickly changed into a pair of clean dungarees, a T-shirt, and my work boots. My fingers worked to capture my hair in a braid as I stared at the soft pink walls Daddy had painted and the white curtains with ruffles Mama had made. My bed was what Mama called a spindle, with swirly posts of dark wood. Some had scratches 'cause it was old, and had been passed down from Mama. At the foot was a quilt made by Granny Walters and Mama when she was about my age. It was soft, and colorful, patches of worn materials from various dresses, and other pieces of clothing. Farther up, in the center, sat Dolly, a porcelain doll I'd been given once Mama decided I was old enough not to bust her head. She too had been Mama's when she was little, brought back by Grand-daddy Walters from Paris after WWI. She had real hair, blond like mine, and she wore a red dress and a velvet black collar. She was mighty fine to look at, even though one blue eye didn't open all the way, giving her what Daddy had said was a "drunken look."

Mama had said, "How would you know?"

Daddy winked at her and said, "That's the exact look I had after I saw you."

I finished my hair, feeling nervous. I hoped by evening, I'd know enough about Mr. Fowler to ease my mind. He tended to come off in a prickly manner, like he was irritated, or found some--thing not to his liking most of the time, but maybe once we got to know him, he'd be fine. I slapped my straw hat on my head and went back toward the kitchen.

"Hey, Sonny!" came from across the yard.

Daniel had decided to come after all and I ran up to him as he leaned his bike against the side of the house.

"Hey there!"

He wore dungarees like me, a striped T-shirt, and high-top Keds. I was glad he'd not shown up in a "costume" like he was prone to do, least not with Mr. Fowler here. Last time he'd come in one of his sister's dresses, and he said a couple men tried to run him off the road, and had yelled

95

something at him. I'd laughed till my sides hurt when I saw him. Paired with his high-top tennis shoes, he'd looked like some crazy old lady and claimed Blanche Dubois would be offended at my laughing.

He pointed at Mr. Fowler's truck and said, "What's going on?"

I said, "We're about to start planting. We ain't never done it this late before."

We walked over to the truck and looked at bags upon bags of seeds in the back along with a tray of seedlings about a week old.

Mr. Fowler came outside and said, "Git away from there."

We backed up and he tilted his head like he was trying to figure out where Daniel had come from. Trent and Ross walked outside from the kitchen. They'd grabbed a leftover biscuit from our morning breakfast and my own stomach growled.

Remembering my manners, I said, "Mr. Fowler, this here's my friend Daniel. He comes over sometimes, just to visit and such."

Mr. Fowler didn't hardly give Daniel a second look.

He said to no one in particular, "Ain't no time for visiting when there's work to do. He's got to go."

My mouth fell open. I looked at Daniel, who'd gone the shade of a strawberry. Without a word, he walked to his bike, hopped on it, and started down our drive.

I yelled, "Daniel, wait!"

Mama came out, took one look at my face, and then stared after Daniel, who was now out on Turtle Pond Road, his shirt flapping behind him like a flag in a stiff wind.

She said, "What's going on?"

My eyes burned, and my entire body was hot.

I managed to say, "Mr. Fowler told him to leave."

Mama turned to Mr. Fowler who had started unloading the truck, a question on her face. Mr. Fowler set the bag of seeds down carefully.

He gestured toward the back end. "Got more of this coming. Got to be planted and quick. Ain't got no time for playing around. This is an investment here and everybody's got to be on it and on it hard if it's gonna work out. I asked him to leave, so we could get some work done. Can't see as how that's so bad."

He didn't tell it right. He hadn't asked at all.

She said, "I suppose you're right. I'm sure Sonny didn't think about that."

He made a dismissive motion with his hand. Quietly, we began to unload the truck while Mr. Fowler got to whistling like he was already over it.

Chapter 6

The whistling stopped soon as Mama went into the house to start on supper. As the minutes went on, silence filled the space between us and him, and I was sure he was peeved by my own attitude. After we unloaded everything, Mr. Fowler got to asking Ross and Trent about fertilizing and tillage, and what all did they know about soil compaction, sounding conversational at first—until they hesitated. He repeated the questions again. It was like a pop quiz at school, him firing questions at us, and then sort of glaring, waiting on an answer. Then he asked a real oddball question.

He asked Ross, "Son, you know what cotton is?"

Ross gave him a funny look, and I wasn't sure if it was 'cause he'd called him "son" like Daddy used to or if it was the question itself.

Ross hesitated, and then he said, "It's . . . a plant."

Mr. Fowler's mouth bent in what I supposed was a smile, but was as friendly appearing as a snarling dog. "No, what *is* it?"

Trent quickly piped up with a know-it-all look. "Fiber."

"No," Mr. Fowler snapped.

Ross and Trent glanced at one another. I wanted to sink into the background, and hoped he wouldn't ask me. His demeanor said he wasn't sure we were worthy of his time and investment. He walked stiff legged, reminding me of a peacock strutting about.

He said, "Nitrogen, oxygen, and carbon. That's what makes up all plants and that's why we don't need fertilizer, and why we won't be using it. Cotton plants don't take it from the soil, they don't need it."

He squatted down and wiggled his finger underneath a little seedling in the crate.

Ross said, "We've always fertilized. That's what Daddy did and our crops did all right."

Mr. Fowler didn't move for several seconds, then he raised his eyes and stared at Ross so long it became as uncomfortable as when Daddy decided one of us needed a whipping. He used to send us to wait for him in our room, and that was worse than the actual punishment. Mr. Fowler's silence changed the air, like when a cold front comes through. Ross gestured with one hand, as if he wanted to plead his knowledge about what he'd just said.

Mr. Fowler made a huffing sound of aggravation and when he spoke, his words were slow and measured. "Son, don't never correct me."

The color left Ross's face as he realized he'd offended Mr. Fowler in some way.

"No, sir."

"Been learning about this a lot longer than you. Know what I'm talking about."

"Yes, sir."

"Your daddy, he done all right. Could a done a lot better, if'n you ask me."

We looked at each other, dumbfounded. What gave him the right to judge how Daddy ran things? Mr. Fowler went to the front of his truck and reached inside. He lit one of his Camels before he went back to remove the seedling. He held it aloft, turning it this way and that.

He pointed at it. "See them two little leaves? Them are called cotyledons."

We were quiet, not really knowing what else to do other than listen while he gave us a lesson in what we already knew.

He said, "Say it. Co-ta-lee-dons."

We repeated the word as prompted, our voices low with uncertainty. We didn't dare explain Daddy had already taught us all this, or that he'd been asked to teach down to the Agri-Extension once, but turned it down to farm. The back screen door banged shut and I sighed with relief. Mama was coming, and she wasn't smiling. When she got close, I caught a whiff of whatever she was cooking, and my stomach rumbled.

She crossed her arms and looked from us to the truck to Mr. Fowler. "Y'all about to start?"

Mr. Fowler's voice was soft. "Oh, sure, sure. Just thought I'd tell them a bit about cotton. Thought it might be a good idea so they know what they're working in, what they're planting."

Mama said, "Lloyd's taught them all they could ever know and then some."

She gave a rather pointed look at the sun, holding her hand to her forehead.

Mr. Fowler offered Mama a nice, friendly smile and said, "Right, how about that. Okay, well, come on, then. Let's get to it!"

Mama said, "Supper will be in a couple hours. Mr. Fowler, you're welcome to eat with us."

He said, "Might do that."

She walked away, and it was only when the back screen door slammed again, he turned to us and said, "We'll start in them fields near my property." He pointed to Trent. "Go get the tractor and bring it over here."

I noticed a sharp movement from Ross and admired his ability to keep his mouth shut. Trent didn't waste a second. He ran to the shelter at the side of the barn and it didn't take him no time to bring it around to where we waited. He idled it down, and Ross lifted the tops to the planters on the back and dumped seeds in.

Mr. Fowler gave Trent a thumbs-up. "Boy snapped to it. Good job, son."

Trent grinned while I bit my tongue, wanting to remind him he was disrespecting Daddy. After Ross filled the planter, Mr. Fowler motioned at Trent to get going, and he took off down the tractor path.

Mr. Fowler turned to Ross and said, "You ride the tailgate, make sure none of that stuff dumps out. Set them seedlings over there. We'll plant 'em later." Then he motioned toward me and said, "You ride up front."

I'd have rather rode with Ross, but I said not a word and got in on the passenger side. I hung my arm out the open window, remembering how Daddy would slap the side of his door when he wanted the boys to hurry it up.

Mr. Fowler slid into the seat and looked over at me, but I stared at my lap, hiding my chewed up nails by curling my fingers against my pant leg.

After he started the truck and began to pull around so he could go down the path alongside the field, he said, "You miss your daddy?"

I swallowed hard, and both my eyes and nose unexpectedly wanted to run. I looked out the window so he wouldn't see. I thought about something, anything I might say, to change the subject. I cleared my throat, and began to recite every single thing I could think of about cotton, mostly to let him know we weren't ignorant like he seemed to think.

"Daddy said a single cotton plant has about a hundred bolls. The small buds that grow first, those are called squares. The fringe on them? Those are called bracts. And, a boll is considered a fruit 'cause it has seeds. One acre of land can produce a bale of cotton, and a bale of cotton weighs about four hundred and eighty pounds. We usually get about two and a half bales per acre."

I could have said more, but I clamped my mouth shut. Mr. Fowler had his wrist hung over the rim of the steering wheel and his other hand rubbed his chin. He kept his eyes straight ahead.

After a minute or so, he said, "Manners, and real smart. How about that."

I was getting used to Mr. Fowler's habit of making comments as if I wasn't sitting right there. If he was surprised by what I knew, he didn't let on, but he sure didn't try to tell me anything more about cotton. We rode the rest of the way without talking.

Planting time was something I usually enjoyed, but Mr. Fowler had given me a reason to dread it in this case. I was tensed up, like something was about to happen, like he would find fault just in the way I was sitting in his truck, and maybe point out the clumps of dried dirt in the floorboard that had come off my boots.

His truck rolled and bumped over the ruts along the tractor path, and he stopped at one point where the path came to a T and hollered out the window, "Which way?"

Ross shouted back, "Go right!"

We finally made it to the field that was set off to the far east of our land, what Daddy had called the "top corner." I was out of the truck before Mr. Fowler got it in park. Ross and I didn't do like usual, moving off to do our own thing, and when Trent came up alongside the truck, Mr. Fowler motioned at him to kill the tractor's engine. He looked at how the field had been listed and prepared for planting, what seemed like a really long time ago when we'd done it.

He said, "This here's what we're gonna do," and he went to the back of the truck, dropped a bag of seeds by the tire, and walked over to the tractor.

"Gonna show you how we're gonna plant, so it gets done right."

He motioned at Trent to get off, and he climbed on, started it up, then he angled it so the planter fit directly over the rows, all the while shouting out to us that the seeds would be dropped about every foot or so.

Ross mumbled, "Geez. We already know this."

I said, "Yeah."

Trent said, "He's the one spent the money, reckon he just wants to be sure."

Mr. Fowler stopped after he'd gone about halfway down the field.

He left the tractor idling and came back toward us.

He said, "Like that. Ross, you and your sister ride with me over to them other fields."

Ross stomped over to the truck, his straw hat setting low on his head but it didn't cover his downturned mouth. He wasn't none too happy. Trent shot us both a smug look as he took off on the tractor. Mr. Fowler drove us to several more spots, and Ross would jump off and drop a bag of seeds for refilling the planter. We ended up in the bottom left field when Mr. Fowler finally cut the engine on the truck.

He said, "Get them hoes out and work on them weeds there."

It was like Mr. Fowler was just giving us something to do. He pulled out a Camel, and got to smoking, sitting inside the cab of the truck. Daddy would've been right alongside us doing what we did 'cause it was necessary to have as many hands as possible. Like I said before, what I'd seen of Mr. Fowler was he liked to point and direct. The only sound was the distant hum of the tractor as it went along. There was none of the usual good-natured bantering like when we'd worked with Daddy.

Mr. Fowler would shout every so often. "Got to keep at it. Can't be dillydallying. Still got a long ways to go."

I used a tremendous amount of strength,

pounding at the earth with the hoe. Mr. Fowler was concentrating on me and how I was working.

He called out, "Why you doing it like that?"

I stopped and stood motionless, uncertain what he meant.

He strode over to me and said, "I reckon I got to show you."

He snapped his fingers, and I handed the hoe to him. He stepped into a thicket of weeds, chopped and slung them off to the side, making the area look like a hog had run around in circles, disturbing the uniform look I'd been giving it.

"Like that."

"That's not how we were taught."

Mr. Fowler's voice went low. "That so?"

He bent down and stared right straight into my eyes.

"How about you just do it the way you been shown."

I whispered, "I was."

"That right? Well, what I was taught was do as I was told."

"Yes, sir. That's what I was doing."

He said, "Maybe you ought to remember who bought this seed. Ain't doing this for fun, like you got you a pretty little garden to play in. You're here on account of me. I spent my money so y'all could have something this year. You got that?"

"Yes, sir."

I allowed a sideways look at Ross as I went back to work.

He whispered, "Jackass," and winked.

I couldn't even wink back. Knowing Mr. Fowler was watching, I promptly lost my natural rhythm. I was clumsy and less efficient, like a truck with a flat tire, bumping along, turning this way and that. When it grew dark, Mr. Fowler gave a high-pitched whistle just as the sun dipped out of sight, waving down Trent, who'd worked his way to the end of a row. I envied Trent not having to be part of these up close interactions.

Mr. Fowler stood with his arms on his hips like he was mad, and as we made our way toward him, Ross mumbled, "I ain't never seen nobody so contrary."

Mr. Fowler's whistle cut in again and he waved at us emphatically, as if he had somewhere to go.

He said, "Y'all lollygagging like it's a Sunday afternoon."

Ignoring him, I hopped onto the tailgate.

He gave me a look, and I felt I ought to explain. "I'm hot. I can cool off better back here."

"Young ladies ought to ride in the cab," he said.

The things he said. This young lady could work a field, but ought to ride inside a truck? He climbed in the cab, and maybe it was me, but

when he got going back down the path, I was
sure he drove a little faster, turned the steering
wheel a little harder, and did nothing to avoid
the ruts along the way.

Ross said, "Sumbitch didn't drive like this
coming out here."

Trent laughed like he thought it was hilarious,
and hollered, "Faster!"

I held on tight thinking we shouldn't never
want to make Mr. Fowler mad.

Chapter 7

Mama sat on the back porch waiting for us, and even in the twilight it was obvious how much she'd changed since Daddy died; we all had, really, in our own little ways. There was a milky whiteness to her face, and her eyes were sunken and had dark rings around them. Her cheekbones rose higher and sharper, and she'd become all edges and angles, layered in sad quietness. She wore one of her old day dresses saved for kitchen work, and it hung loose on her frame as she got up from the chair to come down the steps, walking slower than usual, as if she was no longer sure of where she was going, or had no real purpose. She met us in the yard by the clothesline, arms folded across her middle.

She said, "I thought I was going to have to come get y'all."

Ross's agitation showed as he rubbed at his scalp, over and over, stroking across the brushy flatness of his crew cut.

He was about to speak when Mr. Fowler said, "Let them do what they could, long as they could." Then he said, "Girls ought to be in the house, learning how to cook, wash clothes, and sew. Ain't no call for her to be in the field like some nigga gal."

Mama frowned. "Mr. Fowler! We do *not* talk that way around here! Besides, Sonny's always worked around the farm. She doesn't much care for inside work. Her daddy didn't see nothing wrong in her learning what them boys know."

Mr. Fowler hesitated, then with an emphatic tone, he said, "Telling like I see it, is all."

My brothers and I were sweaty, tired, and hungry, and our clothes were dirty like we'd been rolling on the ground instead of standing above it. What Mr. Fowler said shocked and aggravated me, but Ross nudged me with his elbow, warning me to keep quiet, while Mr. Fowler, to my relief, appeared put out, and started for his truck.

Mama, apparently having a split second of doubt, called out, "Won't you stay for supper?"

He hesitated, and I prayed he'd go on, but instead, he said, "Might as well."

My insides tightened.

Mama said, "Well, y'all come on into the house, then, and get washed up."

She pointed Mr. Fowler to the bathroom down the hall and said, "You kids clean up in the kitchen."

Of course as soon as we were alone with her, she asked, "Tell me, how did it go?" and all of us started at once.

She said, "Sh! One at a time."

I said, "All he did was stand around smoking and calling out orders."

Mama's eyes tightened but she didn't speak. After the usual shoving, Ross and Trent moved away from the kitchen sink, and I was able to wash my hands and face, then we settled into our usual places, and waited. And waited. The food was on the table and I kept eyeing the bowl of steaming mashed potatoes. Mama had fried pork chops, made gravy, and there was a big bowl of stewed okra we'd put up from last year, and the inevitable bowl of English peas, dazzling green and shiny with butter. I wanted bad to get me a big ole biscuit, but I satisfied myself temporarily by leaning in to catch the smell coming off the bowls, pungent and rich.

Mr. Fowler finally came into the kitchen, and Mama pointed him to a chair beside Ross. Maybe he hadn't seen her gesturing at him 'cause he took Daddy's chair at the head of the table.

She cleared her throat and said, "Mr. Fowler? I'm sorry, but could you sit here please?"

Mr. Fowler jumped up. "Sure, sure, sorry about that, there was a little more room there is all."

Mama waited while he moved to sit beside Ross. You ask me, him sitting in Daddy's chair would've been like cheating on his memory. We started passing around bowls, and soon as our plates were filled, we put our hands in our laps.

Not Mr. Fowler. He picked up his fork and got to eating. I glanced at Mama. Everybody knows you say the blessing before you dig in.

In a gentle voice, like she didn't want to embarrass him, she said, "Mr. Fowler, we give thanks to the Lord first, if that's all right?"

He lowered his fork, appearing flustered as he looked at her from across the table, almost like he'd been caught peeing on the vegetable garden.

He said, "Oh, sorry, it smelled so good."

Mama nodded, and then bowed her head. We all followed suit. About halfway through I had the urge to peek at him. I kept my head down as I did so. Why, he didn't have his head bowed at all, instead, he sat reared back in his chair, arms crossed and he was openly staring at Mama, his mouth sort of slack. I dropped my eyes quick, and tried to interpret his odd look.

Mama said, "Amen," and when we lifted our heads, I looked his way again, and he was still looking at her.

She handed him the butter, and he almost dropped it. I was certain his face went a deeper shade than the sunburn he had, though she didn't act like she noticed. Once we began eating, it was too quiet for my own sense of ease. Supper time had always been about catching up, our usual chitchat back and forth as easy breezy as a Sunday afternoon. There would have been laughter. Joking around. Mr. Fowler didn't even offer up polite talk like most guests, but then again, neither did Mama.

The moments went by, with only the sound of the kitchen clock over the stove ticking along, the noises of a meal being consumed, and an occasional, "Pass the salt, please," or "Would you like some potatoes?"

We were on our best behavior, like when Preacher Moore came by to eat Sunday afternoon dinner. After seeing the way Mr. Fowler looked at Mama, I got to thinking his offer of help might have more to do with her. It grew hot and stuffy in the kitchen, and though I'd been hungry at first, my appetite dwindled. I ate a bite here and there, waiting for the meal to end. Mr. Fowler ate like somebody might snatch his plate away. He finished first, and right when Mama looked like she was about to ask him if he wanted seconds, he reached over and speared another pork chop—with his own fork—even though the serving one sat beside the serving plate. Mama sank against the back of her chair, and put her hands back in her lap, twisting her napkin into a long swirly looking tube.

Finally, Mr. Fowler pushed back his chair, and stretched and rubbed his stomach like he was the only person in the room. I waited for him to belch considering he appeared so unconcerned about where he was. I looked at the counter where Mama had set out the small cut-crystal goblets specially reserved for serving ambrosia, a quick dessert she could put together for such an occasion as this—the unexpected supper visitor. I waited to see if she'd offer him some, and if she did, it meant I had to serve it. I tried to imagine him holding one of those delicate glass dishes, and realized our circumstances were just as fragile and vulnerable as one a them in his hands.

Mama said, "Thank you for joining us for supper, and thank you for what you're doing. We sure do 'preciate it."

Mr. Fowler threw up a hand and said, "It's what any good neighbor would do."

Mama hesitated and said, "How about some dessert?"

Mr. Fowler appeared to think about it, and then he said, "No, thanks. Got to get on home. Great meal though. Very good, thank you."

Mama said, "You're quite welcome."

She followed him to the door, and he said, "Be back tomorrow, same time."

Mama nodded. "Fine."

He said, "Won't be a problem whatsoever, us all working together, right?"

His eyes landed on each of us for a brief second.

"No, sir," said my brothers and I, our answers sporadic, fractured, and broken sounding as the odd warble of starlings.

It was only when I could no longer hear his

truck did my muscles go lax and my breathing become regular like.

I said, "He's got to come every single day?"

Ross said, "Yeah, if we're doing all the work, why does he even need to show up?"

Trent said, "Ha, I get to drive the tractor again."

Mama sighed and said, "Come on, let's go have that dessert."

Ross said, "I was hoping I could take Addie for a milkshake."

Trent whistled and did a low hoot and Ross shoved his shoulder. Trent shoved back.

Mama said, "Enough," and then, "Be back by ten."

"Yes, ma'am!"

Trent and I sat back down at the table where I could still detect the lingering odor of Mr. Fowler's hair tonic, or his soap. Ain't nobody ever worked in the fields before ever smelled that good at the end of a day. As I took a bite, I suddenly got hungry again. I looked at my almost untouched plate, and grabbed the pork chop. Mama watched me eat, her eyes gone soft and indulgent, the way they'd looked before Daddy died. She brushed a hand over my hair, and rubbed my back as I chewed and swallowed.

"I couldn't imagine why you weren't eating. I knew you had to be hungry."

I said, "I can't eat around him, he makes me nervous."

Trent rolled his eyes and said, "He's all right. I like him," while Mama actually chuckled.

I marked it as exactly thirty-three days since we'd got to hear that light, airy laugh. I took another bite of pork chop, and then a bite of potatoes with gravy too.

"Oh, Sonny. He's just a man," is what she said.

Chapter 8

Whatever it was that brought Frank Fowler to our supper table every night since the first night wasn't exactly clear, though I had my ideas. The second, third, and fourth time he sat to eat with us went much like the first, only now he knew to wait for the blessing, and that there would be dessert. Last night we'd had fried fish. Mama made coleslaw and cornbread to go along with it, and I could've sworn Mr. Fowler's eyes rolled back in his head when he took a bite of creamy coleslaw. The butter he'd slathered over the cornbread melted and hit his plate like soft yellow tears. His enjoyment irritated me for reasons I couldn't put a finger on. The next morning before we had to catch the school bus, I hinted at my disapproval to Mama.

"Is he gonna be here *again,* tonight?"

"Who? Frank?"

It was Frank. Already. That started on the fourth or maybe it was the fifth night, and likely contributed to my inner turmoil and dismay.

"Yes, him."

The *him* came out in a low distasteful tone, like

I'd taken a dose of castor oil. Mama sighed, and reached into her apron pocket for her cigarettes and shook one out of the pack. She lit it, blew smoke toward the open kitchen window before she answered.

She said, "Sonny, ain't no harm in that man eating supper with us. He's not taking food out of your mouth, is he?"

To hear Mama put it that way made me feel a little bit guilty.

"No, but why can't he eat at home?"

"Some don't like eating alone."

"Geez, what's he been doing before now?"

"All I know is it's the least we can do, considering what he's doing for us, right?"

Mama trivialized my concerns so easy, especially when I couldn't explain my reasons for thinking of him like he was trespassing on our property and stomping all over Daddy's memory.

"Yes, ma'am."

I looked out the kitchen window at Ross driving our tractor out to the field Daddy had been in that day, and it gave me a twisty feeling in my stomach. He worked carefully around Mr. Fowler's precious little seedlings. The day they got planted Mr. Fowler was even more uptight than when we'd started on the seeds. He'd also had one of his workers bring one of his tractors over and told Trent to use that one. A brown cloud followed Ross, shadowing him like a ghost, and I imagined it like Daddy's presence, caught up into a soft formation of our land.

Mama broke my thoughts by commenting, "Them boys are fast at planting."

If Mr. Fowler was pleased about the progress, you couldn't tell. You couldn't tell one thing about him unless Mama was around and he engaged her in conversation, acting natural, not twitchy and irritated. I'd noted her sorrow was deeply layered as the ground beneath our feet, like the soil chart Mrs. Baker recently showed us. Humus, topsoil, eluviation, subsoil, regolith, bedrock. Mama had sunk under the bedrock, I was sure of it. When Mrs. Baker discussed the chart, I remembered what Daddy had said about water underground, and raised my hand.

"Yes, Sonny?"

"What about the water?"

Mrs. Baker said, "Good question! We're going to talk about that tomorrow."

A hateful, whispered, "water witch!" came, which I ignored.

Mama rubbed at her eyes, then looked at me close. "How's Daniel been lately?"

"All right, I guess."

"Why don't you invite him for supper this evening?"

"What about Mr. Fowler?"

"What about him?"

"Won't he mind?"

"Why should he?"

"I don't know."

"This is still our house. Tell Daniel I'm fixing his favorite, country style steak."

Mama smiled, encouraging me.

I perked up at her suggestion and said, "Okay."

The bus was coming, and I hurried to kiss her cheek, then ran out the back door. Even though I got to see Daniel in school, him turning up out of nowhere at our house several times a week is what I missed most. Daddy used to laugh at his way of describing his mama and sister. How Sarah would sneak into their mama's room, and pilfer her "gotta find me a good man" clothes, sometimes accidentally burning a hole in a blouse, or she'd spill ketchup or a milk shake on a dress, then return them to the closet damaged or dirty for his mama to find. Daniel said they got into some knock-down, drag-down fights over stuff like that.

At recess, by swing sets, I got him off to the side.

Before I could say a word, he said, "I saw a movie called *All About Eve*."

He was pretty excited about it and I listened to him quietly until I spotted Junior and Lil Roy sneaking around the swing sets, clearly up to no good. Junior abruptly hit Lil Roy, signaling him to run, and they came toward Daniel fast. Daniel had his back to them and didn't know something was about to happen.

I shoved him away from me, and yelled, "Watch out!"

Junior had thrown a rotten apple at his head last time, and it had splattered, covering his hair with a sour, mushy pulp so he'd smelled vinegary the rest of the day. Junior needed a comeuppance, is what he needed, only Daniel wasn't bold enough. He wasn't fast enough either. He hesitated, and now Junior was only inches away.

"Ha!" Junior yelled as he whacked his hand against Daniel's back, and kept running. Lil Roy did the same.

They whooped and hollered, cackling with glee. They stopped several yards away, and Junior bent down to scrub his hand on the ground. He actually gagged, and with a sense of dread, Daniel pulled at his shirt from behind, trying to see what was on it.

I said, "Turn around."

He did and smeared down his plaid red and blue shirt were two dark marks. That unique Daniel smell I'd come to recognize as a salty, outdoor, boyish odor I really liked was overtaken by another distinct, sharp smell.

I yelled over my shoulder, "Junior! You're a disgusting creep!"

Junior's retort floated back. "That's what happens when you think your shit don't stink!"

Daniel, his voice shaking, said, "Is it . . . ?"

Damn Junior Odom.

I said, "Hurry, go try to clean it off."

The bell rang.

"I can't! Recess is over!"

"Mrs. Baker ain't gonna allow you in class like that, Daniel."

"I'm gonna stink up the room."

"You will if you don't go get it off. Go!"

He took off while Junior and Lil Roy laughed, falling on each other while pointing at him. Mrs. Baker stopped him and he pointed at his back. Junior and Lil Roy stood hunched together, whispering, waiting to see if Daniel would tattle. They'd know if she looked their way and then they'd really have it in for him. Mrs. Baker only gave an exasperated shaking of her head like it was somehow his fault. I went hot at the way she grabbed his arm, marching him toward the double doors. She let him inside, then waved at the rest of us to hurry it up. I still hadn't had a chance to tell him about supper.

I ignored Lil Roy's hooting at my back as I hurried inside. At my desk I tore a piece of notebook paper, and scribbled a note. Daniel came from the restroom and Mrs. Baker even wrinkled her nose as he passed her. His face was pale, looking like he might get sick. He sat two rows over from me, and as the afternoon wore on, an off odor wafted around the classroom while Junior and Lil Roy made sure they complained loudly until Mrs. Baker opened the windows.

I nudged Laurie Ward to get her attention and showed her my little folded square of paper that said, "Daniel."

She kept her eyes forward, dropped her hand down, and took it. She held it for a minute before she swapped hands, and sent it on to Becky Hill, who sat right behind Daniel. My note said, *Mama invited you to supper. She's fixing your favorite.* Poor Becky. Sitting right behind Daniel, there was no getting away from the stench coming off him. She flipped the note over his shoulder while leaning back far as possible, her nose tucked under her shirt.

I side-eyed Daniel as he opened it, read it, and hesitated. I could almost read his mind. *What about Mr. Fowler?* He glanced at me, then Mrs. Baker, who'd moved to the blackboard. I gave him my best tormented look. He nodded once, barely a flick of his head, then went back to staring at his desktop, letting his hair fall forward to hide his face, his discomfort obvious. You could hear those near him whispering.

Somebody said, "Fee-yew!"

Mrs. Baker interrupted my scrutiny of Daniel and his torment.

"Sonny?"

"Ma'am?"

"Would you care to show us how to conjugate our next set of verbs?"

"Yes, ma'am."

I stood to go to the blackboard, feeling their eyes shift from Daniel to me. Once there, I began until Mrs. Baker threw me a curveball.

"In present continuous, please."

"Yes, ma'am."

It was going to be a long afternoon.

At home I changed from my school clothes to work clothes. The deep rumble of Mr. Fowler's voice talking to Mama in the kitchen wasn't hard to miss, and with a good three hours of daylight remaining, it left me questioning why he was already sitting inside. I got my dowsing stick and went to the kitchen. Mr. Fowler sat at the kitchen table looking quite comfortable. I set the dowsing branch by the door, not wanting him to comment on it, and went to the cookie jar. Mama was already busy with supper preparations.

She said, "Daniel coming?"

"Yes, ma'am."

"Good."

I bit into an oatmeal cookie.

Mr. Fowler said, "That boy that was here the other day?"

She said, "Yes."

"What's his last name?"

"Lassiter."

Mr. Fowler repeated it. "Lassiter."

"He lives in town with his mama and sister."

Mr. Fowler chewed on a toothpick. He pushed against the table edge with his hands and set the chair on its back two legs. Mama drew up, wanting to say something. How many times had she asked us not to do that very thing?

Instead, she said, "Is there something wrong?"

"No, no. Just trying to figure out what a boy like that does."

Mama's voice was carefully inquisitive. "What do you mean?"

"Boys need work to keep their minds occupied. So they stay out of trouble."

She visibly relaxed. "That's the very thing Lloyd used to say."

I swallowed, and then spoke up, full of pride, "Daniel's going to be a director."

Mr. Fowler leaned forward, setting the chair on all four legs.

His eyes were intent as he said, "A director? Of what?"

Strangely, Mr. Fowler's cold, unblinking stare was like that of a snake, and I shivered inwardly. Telling Mr. Fowler what Daniel dreamed of doing suddenly seemed disloyal. I was convinced if I said "direct movies or plays," he'd dismiss the special thing that set Daniel apart from everyone else. Daniel's dreams were sky high, as far as the stars, and the moon. Lofty goals, Daddy had said. I hesitated, thinking hard. It meant he'd leave Jones County, maybe go to California or New York, and that meant Daniel would eventually leave me. I'd never thought of it this way before, and this new realization completely stole the words I held on the tip of my tongue. My lack of response caused Mr. Fowler to appraise me in a knowing way, like he'd concluded Daniel held no real purpose worthy of his time.

Mama, her hands coated in flour, turned slightly toward Mr. Fowler and said, "They got themselves a little stage set up in the barn. You know how kids pretend things."

"Nope. My folks saw to it I stayed on the straight and narrow. Didn't play no games. Had chores to do." He rubbed his hands against his thighs and concluded, "Boys got to stay occupied doing a man's work or else they come to no good."

Mama said, "Daniel's a good boy. He and Sonny been friends a long time."

Mr. Fowler said, "Boy needs a man to show him the way. My own father, he was strict as they come. I only made a mistake once, never again."

Mama said, "Daniel's father left when he was just a baby. His mama's doing the best she can, raising him and his sister on her own. It can't be easy."

Mr. Fowler said, "You get what you ask for."

The cookie turned to sawdust in my mouth. Mr. Fowler didn't like Daniel, the way he looked, or maybe even the fact he was coming to eat.

I said to Mama, "I'm going outside to wait."

When I picked up my dowsing branch, Mr. Fowler said, "You gonna take that magic wand of yours, wave it about, and get your work done?"

I pretended not to hear him while Mama explained that too. "Her father gave that to her, so it's right special to her."

Mr. Fowler's answer was vague, and then he started asking questions about Daniel's family. What did his mama do, and did Mama think he was a good influence on me. I went down the steps, and walked past the clothesline. I didn't want to hear anything more from him. I went to the garden, and drifted up and down the rows of sweet corn, tomatoes, and okra. There weren't many weeds, but I pulled a few here and there, and noted we'd need to stake the tomato plants soon. Next I went to the chicken coop, scattered feed for the hens and filled their water pans, their clucking soft and soothing as I dropped corn around my feet, making my own little noises at them.

Ross waved his hat at me as he went by, the tractor's sound smooth and steady. I waved back and then went behind the barn, where I wouldn't be interrupted. I clenched the stick against my palms, and tried to relax. There was a warm breeze, and the afternoon sun was pleasant, not too hot yet. That familiar drawing on my legs began as I went along, a reassuring sensation. I couldn't explain why I thought today would be the day I'd sense Daddy's presence. As I walked, instead of getting stronger, the sensation faded. A contrasting shiver rode up and down my backbone, and then the pulling was gone altogether. I stopped and went back to where I'd started and did it again with the same result, a faint tug, and that was all. I worried that maybe it had only been Daddy's own gift all along. Maybe it had never really been mine. I hurried to the spot he fell with a sense of urgency, a clear question in my mind.

Are you here?

"Hey."

My eyes went wide and I spun around. Daniel stood a few feet away, holding a brown paper bag clutched in his hands.

"Gosh, Daniel! You 'bout scared me to death!"

He smiled and pointed at the branch.

"Any luck?"

I was too embarrassed to tell him what I was really doing, certain he'd think I'd gone clear off my rocker.

I didn't answer and instead I said, "Come on."

We walked back to the house, and he followed me to my room where he threw himself across my bed, and yawned. I put my dowsing stick in the corner by the window, and thought about the day he'd had at school, but he didn't act bothered by that anymore.

I said, "You tired?"

"Yeah. I didn't get much sleep last night. Mama was up till dawn."

"Doing what?"

"What do you think? She had a *friend* over."

"Oh. Ew. Hey, what did you bring?"

"I'll show you, come on!"

We went back outside, running by the chicken coop, making the birds flutter and squawk. He reached the barn first, and I followed him into the stall nearest the door. This particular one was best 'cause the back ones were too gloomy, even in broad daylight. Plus this one didn't have used, greasy tractor parts, stacks of cotton sacks, or flattened tires. Here is where we'd fashioned a crude stage using wood crates to create a platform. We had a curtain we'd hung by fastening a piece of rusty wire from one end to the other, and draping an old piece of cloth Mama let us have. We could even pull it open or closed. We had an old floodlight Daddy let us use for what Daniel called special effects. It would flicker erratically, but was still useful when it was nighttime. Daniel pulled items from the paper bag.

Two dresses.

"Your mama's gonna have a fit."

"Nah. These ones are old. She won't miss'em."

Daniel tossed me one, and we tugged them on over our clothes. I was always amused at what Daniel came up with. Mine was a chestnut-brown color, with small beige flowers and hung off of me while Daniel's was pale blue. He began taking big long strides around the stall, going into his "director mode," explaining what we were going to do, confident and sure of himself. Director Daniel was different than School Daniel. He was bold and assured.

"You"—he leaned in close, our noses almost touching while breathing in a dramatic fashion—"will be Eve Harrington. I'm Margo Channing."

He spun on his heels, enthusiastic and eager, the curls of his hair and the dress swinging as he paced, explaining the scene. I was fascinated by his excitement; it was contagious, and my own enthusiasm grew as he went on until Mr. Fowler appeared in the opening of the barn, and the smile I'd had vanished. Mr. Fowler placed his hands on his hips, and stood in the shadows, a self-righteous look on his face, like what he saw confirmed a thought, a perception he'd held in his mind.

Daniel hadn't noticed him, didn't see how his eyes narrowed until they became small and glittery, like solid black marbles. Mr. Fowler spit on the ground as if wanting me to know what he thought, as if what we were doing was wrong. His reaction made me uncomfortable. He definitely did *not* like Daniel. With an eerie grin, he walked away, and I was sure what he'd seen would cause a problem, and sooner rather than later.

Chapter 9

I looked at the now vacant opening as the sound of Mr. Fowler's truck filled the barn. He revved the engine hard several times, the pitch of it matching the look I'd seen on his face. Daniel went still and looked apprehensive. Mr. Fowler stopped mashing on the gas, and let the truck idle for several minutes. Finally came the sound of him leaving, and a few seconds later, the barn was quiet again. I hoped he wouldn't be back for supper.

Daniel walked over to the barn door, and looked out. "Did he come in here?"

"He sort of looked in the door."

"Oh."

Daniel yanked the dress over his head. He grew quiet, withdrawing the way he did at school, his energy and liveliness tucked away until it was safe to come out again. I pulled the dress I had on off too.

Even though Mr. Fowler was gone, I remained a little on edge. "Let's go down to the fishpond."

I could see him stewing, his good mood fading. Wanting to reassure him, I said, "Don't let him bother you. It doesn't matter whatever he thinks any old way. He ain't got a thing to say about it, and if he does, well, we'll kick that sumbitch's ass."

That brought a little smile to his face, and hopeful he would perk up, I said, "Come on, I'll race you!"

We took off, and several minutes later we stood by the pond, breathing hard. It was relatively hidden at the end of our property, situated close to the woods separating our land from Mr. Fowler's. The grass hadn't been mowed around the edges the way Daddy liked to keep it safe, so I began searching for a couple of fallen limbs under the trees. I chose two that looked like they could withstand the heavy whacking to scare off water moccasins. I gave one to Daniel, and we got to beating on the weeds up to the edge of the small wooden dock. Daddy had built it, and it wasn't nothing fancy, just four posts, and a wood surface big enough for us to lie on.

Daniel went alongside me whispering, "Be gone, agkistrodon piscivorus!"

No task went without a tiny trace of showmanship from Daniel. We went onto the dock and sat on the graying, weathered wood. I drew my knees up, wrapped my arms around them so I could rest my chin on my kneecaps. I waited for him to talk. Daniel was holding onto that moment back at the barn, sitting quiet, the breeze

133

ruffling his hair. I inched toward the edge, rolled up my pant legs, pulled my penny loafers off, and stuck my feet in the water. I was hot, and the water was cool, not tepid like it would eventually become by the end of summer.

"We could go swimming," I suggested, while I gazed up at the sky, and the thickening clouds to the west.

"Nah."

"It's warm enough. Feel."

I grabbed his hand and pulled.

He leaned over and stuck his fingers in the water. "Uh-huh."

He sat back up and wiped them against his pant leg.

It was quiet again for a few seconds, until I said, "Daniel?"

"Hm?"

"Remember that time I finally beat you?"

He made a noise and looked at me, smiling a little. "Yeah. First and *only* time."

We'd been nine years old, and it was a day he'd beaten me time and again, with me growing madder by the minute. I'd swam naked before, until Mama insisted I wear a swimsuit when I'd turned seven. When I stripped my suit off and jumped back in, Daniel had sat with his mouth open in disbelief. I'd wanted to beat him bad— just once—but the bathing suit Mama made me wear hindered me with straps that kept falling down. I'd laughed and splashed water at him, not feeling the least bit uncomfortable.

He'd grabbed my suit, flung it at me, and yelled, "Put it back on!" turning away, the back of his neck to his toes red like he'd got an instant sunburn.

I threw it back and said, "Not 'til you race me. I can beat you. I know I can."

"I ain't racing no nekkid girl."

"You're just scared 'cause you know I'll beat you."

"Ain't."

"Are."

"Dang it, Sonny. I ain't racing you less you put the suit on."

"You'll lose."

Daniel waved his hand at me without turning around. "No I wouldn't."

"Would."

"Wouldn't!"

"Then, race me."

"Promise you'll stay on your own side. Don't come near me."

"Geez, Daniel. It ain't like I got cooties, ya know."

I started to climb out of the water, and Daniel actually screamed.

I stopped. "What is it? I got to get out to dive in."

"No you don't!"

"Yes I do!"

I put my hands back on the sun-warmed wood, and went to pull myself out of the water again and he'd faced away from me, yelling, "Don't!"

He jumped in so fast it looked like he fell. I'd never seen him so worked up, so panicked by my presence.

I couldn't resist looking all around myself as I swam a little closer, saying, "Eeeew! Look! What *are* these?"

Alarmed, he came a little closer and said, "What, what is it?" real concern in his voice.

I lunged and tried to grab his arm, screaming, "It's a cootie!"

Daniel said, "Dammit! Quit playing around! You ready?"

My competitive side took over, and snickering to myself, I swam back to the dock, gripped the edge with my fingers, and focused on the other side of the pond.

My jaw set, I said, "Yeah."

"On your mark. Get set. Go!"

I plunged forward and began kicking for all I was worth, my arms going over and over, my body feeling as if I was skimming over the surface. I ended up beating him by a few seconds. He couldn't believe it.

I climbed out to do a victory dance, and he yelled, "Get back in!"

I cannonballed him, and cavorted about with

glee. He was stunned, but mostly mad. He climbed onto the wood and made me look away, taking off his own swimsuit, wanting to prove he could beat me back, and he did. Who knew if the suits really had a thing to do with being faster, but every time we went swimming after that, eventually, they came off. By then we'd discovered we liked the freedom and we grew comfortable around one another, sometimes even lying on the wood side by side to dry off. It was a carefree, natural feeling, and though I'd been a little curious about Daniel, after I discovered he looked like my brothers, who I'd seen plenty of times when we were little, we quickly went back to being our nine-year-old selves.

Ross had caught us once too. He'd appeared out of nowhere, coming for a swim, and there we were, like white chicken meat floating in a bowl of gravy.

Ross yelled, "You better get them bare asses outta that water, now!"

I'd yelled, "Go away, Ross! Quit spying on us!"

Daniel said, "We ain't doing nothing!"

Ross said, "Like hell you ain't! You're swimming nekkid with my baby sister! I'm gonna turn my back, and you're both gonna put them suits back on, or I'm gonna go and get Daddy!"

Furious, yet scared, I said, "You do and we'll have plenty of time to get them on. Our word against yours, Ross Creech!"

"And who you reckon he's gonna believe? Me or you? Why would I make up something like that? Huh?"

He had a point.

Grumbling, I said, "All right. All right. Come on, Daniel."

We scrambled out of the water, wiggling quick as we could into our suits while Ross stared at the sky. Once we were decent again, I stormed off with Daniel following close behind me, both of us worried he'd tell Daddy anyway.

He hollered after us, "Daniel Lassiter, I'll whup your ass and tell my daddy, you ever do that again!"

We'd done it a few more times, always keeping track of where Ross or Trent might be, but as we got older, and Mama had talked to me 'bout boy and girl things, that took the fun out of it.

I sneaked a peek at Daniel, sitting like me, arms around his knees.

"What do you want to do, then?"

"Just sit here for a while."

"Okay."

I lay on my back, and twirled a piece of grass. I reached over and got another and sandwiched it between my thumbs. I put them vertical to my mouth and blew. It didn't work right the first time, but the second time it did, and I produced a fuzzy sounding whistle, much like the noise of a gnat. Daniel looked at me, annoyed.

Innocent, I said, "What?"

He shook his head.

I sighed. "Let's go back to the house. Mama's bound to have supper almost ready."

We walked with me bumping into Daniel to knock him off the path, and him doing the same to me. By the time we got there, both John Deeres were parked under the oak tree. The hopper lids were up, and Ross and Trent were in the process of cleaning the equipment, checking the various parts. This was something Daddy had taught them as well. I could hear him clear as if he was here. *You can't just jump on'em and go. You got to keep'em up, that's just as big a part of the job as usin'em to tend to the crops.*

Trent said in an irritated voice, "No fair you go off playing. That field I was in could have used some hoe work."

"I'll do it tomorrow."

Trent acted like he hadn't heard me or didn't want to hear. I caught a whiff of supper drifting from the open windows of the kitchen and motioned to Daniel, who didn't see since he was watching Trent climb back on the tractor. I had a sudden thought. Maybe he wanted to learn how to drive one. He'd never worked on a farm, and maybe he was wishing he could learn to do some of the things my brothers did.

I said, "Hey, Daniel, you want to see if you can drive the tractor? Trent can teach you."

Daniel looked at me, his expression hopeful while Trent looked downright ornery at my suggestion.

He said, "I ain't got time to be giving no lessons! I got another field to plant."

Daniel shook his head quick. "That's okay. He ain't got to . . ."

Trent cranked the tractor up as Daniel was speaking, popped the clutch, and almost did a wheelie. He took off, driving like he'd done the day he'd ended up in the ditch. Ross shook his head, grumbling about it.

I said, "Come on, let's go in."

Daniel looked over his shoulder at Trent as he flew down the road. I was pretty darn sure he wanted to learn how to drive that tractor.

Mr. Fowler was nowhere in sight at supper and nobody asked about him. It was almost like old times with all of us gathered round the table, except for Daddy's empty chair. Mama put so much food on Daniel's plate, even he looked alarmed. She said he was getting too thin. After we were done, Daniel swore he was about to pop, couldn't eat another bite. When he saw the banana pudding, the meringue all toasty brown, he somehow found room. After supper, Ross got the truck, and Daniel put his bike into the back. Ross and I gave him a ride home, talking about nothing really. At one point, the truck's headlights caught the two glowing eyes of a possum as it crossed the road.

Ross said, "Guarantee that's the only possum in Jones County ever made it to the other side."

A few minutes later we rolled down Daniel's street to see every single light was on in his house. Shadowy shapes of people passed by in the windows, and there was music. Loud music. Too loud even for a Saturday night hootenanny, as Daddy used to call somebody else's itch to get drunk, play records, and sing along. Daniel climbed out reluctantly. He shut the door, leaned against it, and twitched at some loud noise from within that was followed by loud laughter.

He said, "Well. Guess I better go see what's going on. Sounds like furniture being moved around."

I said, "Reckon your mama's having a party, huh."

"Yeah. No sleep for me tonight."

I said, "Want us to wait? You can come stay at our house you know."

Daniel looked me, then Ross. "You sure?"

Ross nodded. "Go on and get your stuff."

Daniel looked relieved. "Okay."

We watched him walk up to the house, slump shouldered, and thirty seconds later he hurried out.

He got in, slammed the door, and said, "Thanks. Mama said it was a 'supper party,' but it looked like a drinking party, you ask me."

The front door flew open and Mrs. Lassiter

appeared, leaning against the frame, bottle in one hand, a cigarette in the other, and wearing a dress so tight you could practically count the bones of her rib cage. Her hair was all mussed up and a man appeared over her shoulder, smooching on her neck. I looked down at my hands, fighting the urge to bite my nails.

Ross said, "Is she . . . drunk?"

Daniel said, "Yep."

Without another word, he put the truck in reverse and we backed out of the driveway.

Mrs. Lassiter waved the bottle, and called out, "Mr. Langley wants you to staaaaay, Daaaaniel!"

Daniel said, "Hurry."

Ross gave it some gas and we took off. I looked over my shoulder at Mrs. Lassiter stumbling out into the yard. I turned to face forward, sorry Daniel had to live like that.

Mama was sitting on the porch swing smoking a cigarette, the tip end showing in the darkness when we pulled up. She stood, but didn't ask what was going on, intuitively knowing there must've been a problem.

She stubbed out her cigarette and said, "How about some more of that banana pudding?"

Daniel nodded. Mama fed you when things were going wrong, and if she'd been up to it after Daddy died, she'd of emptied the deep freeze, and cooked everything we had. She'd have fried chicken, fixed a meatloaf or three, and baked enough pies and cakes to feed the neighborhood. Mama put a second heaping bowl of banana pudding in front of Daniel again while I sat beside him, chin resting in the palm of my hand. I thought of Sarah, and speculated on whether she'd been in the house, in the middle of it all, sashaying around in front of everyone, mimicking her Mama, batting her eyes at whoever looked her way. I imagined the "things" that went on and probably shouldn't.

After Daniel finished, Mama went to the linen closet and brought down a flat sheet. She fixed the living room couch, added a pillow, a light blanket, and as she smoothed the sheet out over the cushions, Daniel yawned. We said good night to one another and for me, there was something nice about knowing he was only a little ways down the hall. After I got in bed, I imagined myself walking down the hallway, and into the living room, sitting on the edge of the couch, and running my fingers through his long hair. That idea gave me that new, curious feeling I'd had lately around him. I went to sleep worried what he would think if he knew something had shifted inside me where he was concerned.

The next morning before the sun came up, Mr. Fowler's truck was in the yard. Alarmed, I hurried to get dressed, wondering why he was already here. I made my way to the kitchen and found him at the table eating fried eggs with strips of brown, crispy fatback, biscuits piled high, and a steaming cup of coffee by his plate. Mama stood at the stove, still cooking, and that's when Daniel came out of the living room looking eager for breakfast until he saw Mr. Fowler. He looked like he was about to retreat. Mr. Fowler barely glanced at him as he picked up a piece of fatback.

He said, "Look a there. Sissy boy finally decided it was time to get up."

Mama motioned Daniel to the table while I sat beside him, frowning at that name Mr. Fowler called him.

Mama said, "Good morning, you two."

"Morning, Mrs. Creech."

"Morning, Mama."

"Y'all want some eggs?"

Mr. Fowler slurped some coffee and said, "Sure he does. Even a little flit's got to eat."

Mama put a plate in front of Daniel, then handed me one too, only I didn't start eating 'cause I'd seen her cut an evil eye at Mr. Fowler. I waited. She poured herself a cup of coffee, and sat down. She lit a cigarette and blew the smoke over our heads. I moved the egg around on my plate. She knocked her cigarette ash into the ashtray, then put her full attention on Mr. Fowler. She had that look she'd get if we sassed her, or did something she thought wasn't called for.

She quietly asked, "Why're you calling him that, Frank?"

I breathed out, and took a bite of egg. Mama would set him straight.

Mr. Fowler looked up, surprised. "Who? Him?" He pointed his fork at Daniel. "Hell, boy wears a dress, what else would he be?"

Mama actually laughed, but Daniel put his fork down.

Mama said, "Oh, Frank. Sonny tried to tell you Daniel wants to be a director. You know. Make movies? He and Sonny are always acting out little scenes. It's just pretend. Ain't no harm in it."

Mr. Fowler wiped his mouth with a napkin, and leaned back. "Seems to me like he don't need to put on a dress to do all that."

Mama said, "I don't see why it should matter to you what he does or doesn't do."

Trent and Ross came in and Mama got up to get their breakfast, while shaking her head. I peeked at Daniel, ready to let him know I didn't care not a whit for Mr. Fowler's name-calling. Daniel seemed to have got over his discomfort as he listened to Trent tell Ross about shooting his BB gun at some target, claiming he'd hit it fifty times in a row. Typical Trent talk. Daniel looked impressed, eyes alert as he watched Trent's every move.

Mr. Fowler dipped his head toward Trent and

made a general pronouncement, "That's what a boy ought to be doing when he ain't working. Shooting. Fishing. Hunting. Such as that."

All Mama said was, "More coffee, Frank?"

Mr. Fowler held out his cup, and offered a soft, "Thank you," as she filled it.

Thankfully he went on to a different topic. "Y'all ever think about irrigating this farm here?"

His question caught me by surprise.

Mama said, "Yes."

"Seems to me y'all would a done it by now, considering. 'Sides, Farmer's Almanac says there's a drought coming this year."

I could've reminded him he'd been wrong all those years ago.

Mama said, "Lloyd wanted to, but every year we had enough rain and the crops were fine. He always said, ain't no sense wasting time or money on what ain't necessary."

Mr. Fowler scrutinized Daniel again, who was now eating his breakfast with enthusiasm, matching Ross and Trent, bite for bite.

He said, "Ain't it the truth."

Chapter 10

School was over and we poured into the hallways, then out into the stifling air. We took it as a sign it would only get worse as the summer months went on. I hated to admit that Mr. Fowler and his Almanac might be right 'cause rain sure had been scarce. We walked down Turtle Pond Road, and it felt like I was breathing through a wet burlap bag. Ross and Trent were just a little ways ahead and I'd dropped back since they were arguing about something stupid. Who cared who could pee off the back porch and aim accurate enough to hit the dandelion weed growing to the left of the steps? At least I knew where they were peeing so I wouldn't walk there barefoot.

Trent said, "Hell, mine shoots piss like it's coming right from out of a cannon."

Ross said, "That's a lie. You got to have a magnifying glass to see that little pecker of yours. Hell, you can't get a stream past the tips of your toes."

Trent shoved Ross and said, "Now, that's a lie, and you know it."

Ross pushed him back, "Damned if it is . . . mine can . . ."

I cut them both off. "Lord a mighty, I can hear you, you know. I wished y'all would quit peeing in the yard where people got to walk too."

Ross said, "It don't matter none. Rain's gonna wash it away."

I said, "It's disgusting, and besides, it ain't rained in a while and draws flies. I'm gonna tell Mama to take y'all back to the church quick as she can if you want to keep acting like a bunch a heathens."

That settled them down, although the closer we got to home, talking tended to stop anyway. Sometimes he was in the yard, standing around smoking his Camels, as if waiting for us, but then he wouldn't speak. Sometimes he was in the house, and I always deliberated on how long he'd been in there, especially if Mama looked a little harried, rushing around, which gave me the impression he'd been there a while. He'd stayed for supper most every night except that one night when Daniel came, and out of nowhere he'd decided, or Mama had, why not come eat breakfast too. He'd been to our house every morning just before seven o'clock.

I stopped to get the mail. There was the light bill, a copy of *Farmer's Digest*, a magazine Daddy had subscribed to, the sight of it causing that familiar little pang, and last, a letter from

Aunt Ruth. Maybe Aunt Ruth was wanting to see when she could come visit. She'd talk about what we called big city news, how Roanoke Rapids was growing, who was doing what, and what she thought about it. She'd make it interesting even though we didn't know the people she spoke of. I took note of Mr. Fowler's truck parked in its usual spot under one of the sugar maples like he now owned that area and slammed the mailbox closed. He was nowhere in sight. On my way to the house, the dazzling white of Daddy's grave marker stood out like a beacon. It had been brought by a couple men on a flatbed truck after Mama decided since we now had a cotton crop, she could spare the money for it. I was glad it was there, for two reasons. It stood as a reminder to Mr. Fowler whose land he stood on, and on those moonlit nights I couldn't sleep, it was like a watchful eye as I traversed the fields.

I hurried to my room to pull on a pair of dungarees, T-shirt, and slid my feet into my work boots. The ground was pretty dry, and our new little cotton plants, now about six inches high, were starting to droop, even them seedlings Mr. Fowler bought. Weeds don't never let up no matter how little rain comes. They'd suck every drop of moisture from those tender little plants if we let them get out of hand, which meant I had to get to chopping. I got my dowsing stick too. I would start by the new grave marker, thinking, for some reason, it might could happen today. Mr. Fowler's voice carried down the hall and just the sound of it put me on edge, especially when it was followed by that harsh laugh of his that sounded cruel, not amused.

As I made my way along the dogtrot, I saw Trent already in the backyard standing with Mr. Fowler, staring up into the oak tree. They each held a shotgun, scanning the branches. I could see what they were up to, and I wanted very much to stop it, and if it had only been Trent, I would have tried. I'd have had a hissy fit at him taking potshots at the birds, or squirrels, but today, I kept quiet. My usual pluck, as Daddy called it, vanished when Mr. Fowler was around. Without any warning, Trent snapped to the right and fired.

I slapped my hands over my ears, an instant reflex to the noise, along with an alarmed, "Oh!" as the birds, only seconds before quietly chirping and calling out to one another, scattered like fireworks on the Fourth of July. The collective sound of their wings made a loud fluttering noise, similar to the sound of a moth beating against a window, only amplified. Trent immediately pumped the slide on his gun back, then forward, loading another shell into it. Seconds later, Ross came from around the back of the barn, his hands greasy with oil, face sweaty and looking pissed off. He gave Trent an irritated look, and then carefully spoke to Mr. Fowler.

"Sir, we ain't allowed to shoot them birds. Trent knows that. It's against the law."

Ross's expression as he spoke to Mr. Fowler was arranged to look as careful as his words. Mr. Fowler cocked his head one way, and then the other way. It was such a peculiar reaction, it gave me the chills.

Then he said, "Who the hell's gonna come out here and arrest us?"

He reached over to nudge Trent with his fist, laughing again, and Trent went right along with him and the word *traitor* come to mind.

Mr. Fowler said, "Hell, we're just having us a little fun, ain't that right, son? Ain't no harm done."

Trent grinned and said, "That's right." Ignoring Ross, he said, "Hey, look a there. I bet that's the damn squirrel been chewing on wood above my bedroom window, waking me up. I'm gonna get that sumbitch."

He put the gun to his shoulder and sighted on it.

I yelled, "Trent! Don't!"

A large crow, part of the flock scattered from the tree earlier, sat at the top of a distant pine and called out a brisk, "Uh uh! Uh uh!" as if it too, was telling him no.

The squirrel somehow sensed it was trapped. It sat motionless, flattened out along the branch, trying its best to hide. It was startled from the earlier shot, and eyeballed the humans who'd caused it. Daniel said squirrels were smart, part of the prairie dog family. We'd been working on one, trying to get it to eat peanuts out of our hands. What if it was this *very* one? I slapped my hand over my mouth as Trent's finger tightened.

BOOM!

It landed on the ground, the small gray body twitching once, scratching at the ground, and then it went still. I was so stunned, I couldn't talk. Trent walked up to it and pushed it with the toe of his boot, while Mr. Fowler propped his gun against the tree and casually lit up a Camel.

I uncovered my mouth. "Trent! You're just plain rotten!"

Mama came running from the kitchen, wiping her hands on a dish towel, her eyes frantic. She probably thought somebody had been shot.

She noticed the squirrel lying on the ground by Trent's boot, and she said, "Trent Walters Creech! You know the rules about shooting guns near to the house and about hunting!"

She put her hands on her waist, her forehead developing a row of lines as she gave *that* look to Mr. Fowler. He lifted his shoulders in a manner that suggested he didn't have a thing to do with anything that had happened in the past five minutes, quietly puffing on his cigarette, purely a bystander at this point.

She repeated what she'd said to Trent. "No shooting this close to the house."

Mr. Fowler said, "Aw, well he wasn't aiming toward the house exactly."

Mama made a strangled noise, and ignoring him, she said, "Trent. Get that squirrel."

Trent huffed, but bent down and grabbed it by its tail. The sight of it hanging limp from his hand, dripping blood made me queasy, but that didn't count for how I felt over what he'd done. Anger overrode a sudden rush of nausea, but it was a useless anger. *What's done is done,* is what Daddy would've said. He swung the squirrel back and forth, like it hadn't been a living, breathing thing only seconds ago. Like it was trash. Daddy would have had a conniption fit at the way he looked at Mama, like he'd forgot about respect. He would've tanned his hide, and I wouldn't be sorry about it one bit.

He said, "Should I put it in the burn pile?"

Incredulous, Mama said, "What? You know better than that! By God, no. You're gonna clean it, and eat it for supper tonight. Hurry up 'less you want to eat it raw. I ain't cooking it."

Ross, Trent, and Daddy had taken in their share of squirrel eating, while Mama and I didn't care for them a whit. We looked at them more like common backdrops to nature, intended for decorating tree branches—like birds.

Trent didn't look none too happy, and stood defiant, swinging the squirrel by the tail. "What're you cooking?"

Mama said, "Fried chicken, rice, and gravy, and if you do as I say, you'll be lucky to get some. Now, quit waving it around."

"I'd rather eat chicken."

"Too bad. You chose your supper tonight."

Mr. Fowler said, "That's a good lesson to teach them boys. Makes 'em think twice."

Mama ignored that too, and went back to the house.

Mr. Fowler winked at Trent behind her back, whispering, "Unless they don't get caught."

Boy, I wished Mama had heard him say that. Her aggravation was evident by the sound of the pots and pans banging which we could hear clear out to here. Ross disappeared around to the back of the barn again, leaving me with Mr. Fowler and Trent.

Trent grumbled, "I ain't in the mood for eating no damn squirrel," as he stomped off to the sink on the back porch to clean it.

Mr. Fowler took one last puff on his cigarette, dropped it on the ground, and scraped some dirt over it. I looked toward Daddy's grave, still holding tight to my dowsing stick with sweaty hands. There was an uncomfortable moment as I hesitated, wishing I could just walk away. I couldn't think of a single thing to say to him. He looked like he couldn't think of nothing to say to me either.

He finally said, "Them fields could use some chopping."

The dowsing branch was colored dark at the ends where Daddy's hands had held it for years. I placed mine in the same spot, the slick wood a comfort, before I raised my eyes to meet his.

Mr. Fowler pointed at the cotton, his tone conversational, almost friendly. "Got to have some rain soon, or they're gonna start dying. They're calling for a drought."

I held the willow branch up. "I could try and locate where the water is running. Maybe we could irrigate."

"Shit. I ain't 'bout to rely on no twelve-year-old girl for something important as that."

He delivered the stinging dismissal as easy as a compliment and then walked away, leaving me feeling I mattered as much as that squirrel had to Trent. Trent came around the corner holding the pink, skinned body. It looked like one does when it's first born. Innocent, defenseless. Mama appeared like magic at the back screen door, and Trent kicked at the ground at her motioning for him to come inside.

It was clear he thought she'd give in, letting him get by with what he'd done. "Aw, Mama!"

She said, "Get in here. Frank?"

"Yes, Vi?"

Vi?

"He ain't to shoot near this house."

Frank in that pleasant tone he used only with Mama, put his fingers up to his head, like he was tipping a hat, "Yes, ma'am, you got it," and Mama actually smiled as she held the door open for Trent.

Frank went to mumbling, doing that talking to himself thing. "Got to see about pesticides for the boll weevils on the field closest to here."

My eyes widened at the mention of boll weevils. We sure couldn't afford that on top of everything else.

"Daddy used to call down to some place in Tallulah, Louisiana, about boll weevils. He tested an insecticide for them. It worked real good."

"Your daddy knew it all, huh."

I lifted my chin. "He knew about everything."

His voice went low and soft. "Knew about everything, and then died from a snake bite. How 'bout that."

He whistled as he went back to his truck, while I fumed. He was plain mean is what he was, except around Mama and sometimes Trent. As bad as I hated to admit it, I thought he'd taken a liking to her, while Trent was maybe a little like him. One kind recognizes another. Trent held a mean streak inside of him. He used to yank my hair so hard it brought tears to my eyes, or punch me hard enough to leave a bruise. He'd get this conniving look, and I'd be on pins and needles all day, nervous about what he might do to me. Sometimes it was hard to imagine the nice moments we'd shared. Like, last Christmas when he'd given me a leather headband he'd braided and a plaque inscribed with a poem he'd written himself, etching words into the wood with his wood burning kit.

Step carefully
oh divining daughter,
How deeply runs,
that hidden water
T.W.C. 12-25-54

It wasn't the prettiest thing I'd ever received, but it meant more to me than a store-bought gift. He was different since Daddy's passing, as if the absence of his firm hand and watchful eye had turned him more spiteful, and mean, like he was souring from the inside out, turning into a stranger.

Long as I can remember I'd trailed behind my brothers, wanting to be part of whatever they were up to, if they'd let me. I worshipped both of them, but Trent had only thought of me as this worrisome little pest who wouldn't leave him alone. There was a day, when I was around eight, he'd shoved me down for staying on his heels, asking him questions. I skinned my knees and banged my chin. Mama tended to the cuts and scrapes, painting my skin orange with Mercurochrome while Trent stood in the doorway, defiant.

She waved him away. "Go to your room and wait for your father."

When she said, "father," and not "daddy," we knew the thing we despised most was going to happen. I begged her not to have Daddy whip him.

I pleaded over and over, "He didn't mean to. He didn't mean to."

All Mama said was, "It'll teach him to be more careful. He's got to learn his lesson."

I was so worried, I thought I might get sick. Daddy came in from the field and Mama pointed to my bandaged chin and knees, while I sobbed they didn't hurt, they didn't hurt at all. Daddy wasted no time taking his belt from his pants, and went down the hall toward my brother's bedroom. I followed him, and stood by the door as he went in.

I cried even harder when I heard Trent saying, "I'm sorry, I'm sorry, I'm sorry."

Daddy said, "Don't apologize to me. When I'm done, it's your sister you'll apologize to. Son, this is gonna hurt me worse than you."

He always said that. Then he told Trent to drop his pants, and when the sound came, I jumped. The noise of it hitting his bare skin was sharp and quick as were Trent's howls of, "Ow! Ow! Ow!"

It was never more than three licks, but it seemed like a lot more to me.

Daddy always ended our punishments with "Now, you sit there a while and think about what you did, and when you're done, you apologize."

"Yes, s-s-sir."

Daddy came out, the belt coiled around his hand.

He gripped my shoulder and pulled me along with him, saying, "Let him be, Sonny. Let him cool off."

Later, the apology Trent offered was quick, done out of duty than any real remorse. His face still splotchy, he was mad as a hornet held in a jar. He let me hug him, he didn't dare push me away after he'd just been punished, yet the way he held his body, unyielding, told me it was all he could do to stand my embrace.

I overheard Mama telling Daddy, "Where does he get these moods?"

"You."

Mama gave a soft laugh. "To a degree."

Trent got back at me later on, but I kept my tongue. He pushed me down, at least twice, each and every day, an act of opportunity, on the sly, and away from everyone else's eyes. It went on until one day, I stayed down, my knees bloody once again, my clothes grass stained and dusty, my head bowed. Satisfied, Trent walked away. I never followed after him again.

I glanced down at the willow branch in my hands. It meant nothing to Mr. Fowler. He'd never believe I could find water, just like I'd never understand Trent. I took it back to my room, and after getting a hoe out of the shed, I followed the tractor path down to the field where Ross plowed. I got to chopping with a vengeance, a way of ridding myself of what I was thinking and feeling in that moment. Ross turned around at the end of the field and was on his way back when I motioned at him. He idled the tractor down, and I climbed up, and told him what Mr. Fowler said about Daddy getting snake bit.

He wiped the sweat off his face, and pushed his hat back a little before he spoke. "I don't care nothing for him, but keep quiet about it, understand? We'll see this through to the end, get our money and be done with him."

"I ain't gonna say nothing."

Ross nodded and said, "It'll all work out, wait and see."

When we sat down to eat later on, the atmosphere around the table was stagnant with unspoken words. Ross and I were in a snit about Mr. Fowler's comment while Trent fumed at the idea of us enjoying Mama's crispy fried chicken, tasty gravy, and fluffy biscuits. He stared down at the scrawny, somewhat charred squirrel, and leaned against the back of his chair, his demeanor saying he might put up a fight. He looked around the table at everyone's plate, then back down at his.

Mama said, "You can have what we're having after you finish that, but by God, you're gonna eat it."

Trent glared at the squirrel like it was the squirrel's fault for being there on his plate.

Mr. Fowler helped himself to gravy, and out of the blue, he said, "Do as your mama said."

Ross and I shared a disbelieving look while Trent leaned forward and grabbed hold of a leg. If Mama thought anything about Mr. Fowler inserting himself, it was hidden as she rose from the table to pour him some sweet tea.

Chapter 11

June went into July with no rain in sight. In the mornings, the sky was a steely blue, and by afternoon, large billowy clouds appeared like ghosts on the horizon. The most they offered was a quick splattering of a few large drops lasting seconds, and then the sky cleared again, and soon there was serious talk about drought. Ross and I went to pick up a couple things Mama needed and I saw something that scared me, even though I had nothing to worry about. It was as if the weather set off a fever in some folks, gave them a case of heatstroke so they would act out, do things they ought not be doing.

Ross said, "Damnation. Look there."

He didn't need to tell me to look 'cause how could anybody miss it. Smoldering in a front yard of a family I knew to be colored was the remnants of a burned cross.

Shocked, I couldn't stop staring, and I had to twist around in the seat to keep it in sight until we rounded a curve.

I faced forward and said, "When you reckon that happened?"

He pressed on the gas pedal, putting distance between us and what we'd seen.

His voice was low, and he said, "Looks to have been just last night."

We'd heard of such before, but had never caught sight of such doings. Daddy had once brought up another similar incident after reading about it in the newspaper. Hearing and seeing sure was different though.

Without thinking, I said, "I'm glad I'm not colored."

Ross made a noise and said, "It shouldn't matter."

"But it does, doesn't it. I mean, if we were colored, we might have somebody burning a cross in our front yard."

"It ain't *supposed* to matter, is what Daddy used to say."

"I know, but it does, doesn't it?"

"To some around here, it seems to."

"You mean them people who dress up in white. They look scary to me."

"Them, and even some ain't part of that."

"Well, if I was colored, I'd be scared."

"You'd have a right to be."

We both grew quiet. I don't know what Ross was thinking, but I was thinking how the front door of that house stood wide open, and how the screen door swung back and forth in the breeze, like whoever'd lived there was long gone. I couldn't blame them, except they'd had to give up their own home, like they had no right to it, or no right to live their life like everyone else all 'cause they had darker skin. It stuck with me the rest of the ride into Flatland, and nagged at me as we entered the store, my sense of it causing me to seek out if there were any coloreds inside. There weren't, but I realized from that point on, I'd probably pay more attention to what went on with them.

After we got what Mama needed at the A&P, we stopped to get a drink at Slater's Supply.

Ross gave me a warning before we went in. "Don't say nothing about that cross back there."

"Why not? Don't you reckon everyone's seen it?"

"Oh yeah, sure enough, but they'll act like they don't know nothing about it."

We went in and Ross headed for the drink machine off to the side. He slipped a dime into the coin slot and pulled the narrow glass door open. He handed me a sweaty Pepsi, got himself one and all the while, there was a running commentary by men standing near the register at the back. Nobody cared about that cross. They were all focused on what appeared to be a more important matter. The lack of rain.

"We're long overdue, I 'spect."

"Ain't seen it like this in a while."

"It hit the mid-nineties yesterday. That's ten days going."

"Corn already done dried slam up over to McNeely's place."

Ross grabbed some Nabs off the shelf and made his way to Mr. Slater, who looked happy to see us.

He snapped open a small brown bag, dumped the crackers in, took Ross's quarter, and asked, "How's that newfangled cotton crop turning out?"

Ross said, "Like everyone else's, I reckon. Needs rain."

Mr. Slater said, "Sure could use it. Everything's drying up."

There was a murmuring of agreement, boots scuffling against the floorboards, creating a soft rustling, like dried corn stalks rubbing together. I looked at the sun-burned faces, creases around eyes as deep set as a furrowed field, hands as roughened as the sides of a weather worn tobacco barn. They'd been farming long enough to know what they talked about. I recognized a couple of the men standing around, the ones who'd had Daddy dowse their land. They didn't seem quite as worried. Daddy had said our pond was spring fed, and it would take a real mean drought for it to ever get low, but long as we didn't have a pump and generator to get water to the fields, it wasn't doing us much good. Mr. Fowler already made it clear he'd find it difficult to accept my word on finding water anyway. I couldn't quite figure out why he wouldn't want to help things along, considering the money already spent. It was like he was wanting us to fail somehow.

Mr. Slater said, "Frank Fowler's been in here a few times, said he's working over to your place right much."

Ross's answer was shorter this time. "Yeah."

Mr. Slater looked like he wanted to keep asking more questions and the others gathered grew quiet which told me everyone was curious about what was happening at the Creech farm. Daniel's words came back to me about Mr. Earl and Mrs. Grissom getting married so quick after Mr. Grissom's passing. Is that what everyone here was thinking?

Ross grabbed the little bag and said, "We got to go."

Silence followed us and I was relieved to get outside. There was an odor in the air, one of things drying up, an arid, parched scent like cut hay in the fall, and it was blended with the underlying aroma of the large chicken houses, powerful and strong. They could be miles away but on a day like this, you could smell them like you were standing right next to one. The door handle sizzled when I touched it and I had to use my shirttail to pull it open. I slid into the cab, and the vinyl seat burned through the backside of my dungarees and T-shirt. I pushed my hair off my forehead and fanned myself with my hand, then took another swig of Pepsi.

I glanced at Ross and said, "Everyone thinks it's weird about Mr. Fowler."

Ross said, "That's 'cause it is."

He pulled out of the parking lot and I dug into the bag for a pack of Nabs. I looked at the fields of cotton growing, along with tobacco, the soybeans, and corn. The corn was lost. Some of the cotton crops looked about like ours, the leaves going limp, instead of bearing up under the relentless sun. Then there were those who had irrigation lines set up, the portable pumps and diesel generators stationed, flinging water over the plants and that cotton looked great. It was a fascinating thing to see, like defying Mother Nature. We rode with the windows down, munching on the crackers, chasing them with cold swigs from our bottles, and I remembered all the times before when we'd done this very thing, back when Daddy was still alive. In the course of a few months, Ross was not only walking and acting like him, he'd even started to look more like him, more mature, with his upper lip and jaws showing he'd started to shave, evident by a tiny nick here and there. He'd also been spending time with Addie Simmons, and I figured they were getting along good 'cause he usually came back looking pretty happy. He slowed down as we neared Turtle Pond Road.

He cleared his throat and said, "Reckon you could find water?"

Ross believed in me, and with his encouragement, I wanted to try.

"I think so. But he doesn't think I can."

I didn't have to clarify who.

Ross said, "What? Why?"

" 'Cause I'm twelve."

"He don't know a damn thing."

I pictured Ross and Trent digging where I showed them, then bringing up bucket after bucket of underground water. With proof, Mr. Fowler ought to have no problem buying whatever was necessary. Soon there would be water running down the neatly chopped rows, and the cotton plants would draw it in, and stand tall and green once again, as if Daddy's hands had guided my own, as if he'd finally answered me.

I said, "I want to try."

Ross rubbed his head, thinking, and as we rounded a curve, an out of place red spot appeared ahead of us in the road. With hope, I leaned forward, and sure enough, as we got closer I could see who it was pedaling so furiously.

"Hey, there's Daniel!"

Ross said, "Now there's a crazy fool in this heat."

He honked the horn and Daniel glanced over his shoulder, then came to a stop and waited until we pulled up beside him. His red shirt was damp, and his hair too. He put a hand over his eyes, shielding them from the glaring sun and I noticed the shine of sweat on his arm. His face was flushed, but Daniel looked so handsome to me in that moment, I was almost as starstruck at the sight of him as I would have been at Elvis Presley.

He was breathing hard and said, "Hey . . . y'all."

A slight breeze caught hold of his hair and waved it about his head. He shook it out of the way, and my heart did that new little fluttering thing again, while any words I would have normally spoken lay puddled inside my mouth.

Ross said, "How about a ride?"

Daniel nodded with relief. I watched in my side mirror as he lifted his bike into the back, noting how the muscles in his arms twitched. I forced my eyes forward, staring out the windshield instead. I slid over so he could climb in on my side bringing a whiff of sweat, pine trees, and the sun. I inhaled deep as I could, and let my breath out slow. Ross put the truck back in gear and we continued on. I offered Daniel some of my Pepsi. He took the bottle and drank, wiped his mouth and handed it back. We'd shared many a cold drink just this way, but I'd never considered my mouth being where his had been, and liking the idea of it. I thought about that as I drank a swallow or two. I offered him more, and he took the bottle again, and between us we finished it off quick.

I asked an obvious question, just to hear his answer. "Were you coming to see me?"

Daniel rolled his eyes and said, "I sure ain't coming to see ole what's his name. Oh, Ross, Sarah said hi."

Ross merely grunted.

It only took us a couple more minutes to get back to the house. On the back steps, as predicted, sat Mr. Fowler smoking a Camel. A tiny groan came out of me when he stood like he'd been waiting on us. We got out of the truck and he stared at the empty drink bottles we held.

He threw his cigarette on the ground and said, "Where y'all been?"

Ross started for the house with Mama's things, tossing an explanation over his shoulder, while holding up the box of detergent. "Mama asked me to get her some stuff in town."

Mr. Fowler said, "Wait just a minute," and he pointed at the drink bottle I'd held. "I'm thinking them drinks ain't part of what your mama asked for."

Ross paused, and then with careful deliberation, he said, "And I don't recall you being put in charge of everything we do around here."

I wished I'd been the one brave enough to say it.

Mr. Fowler's eyebrows went together, a solid

dark line of agitation. "Oh, I get it now. I bet you thought *you* were supposed to be the one in charge after your old man died, is that it? Is that it?"

Ross looked uncomfortable like Mr. Fowler hit a nerve.

Mr. Fowler said, "Shit, you're still wet behind the ears, boy. You got a long ways to go before you know what you're talking about, much less what you're doing. You listen now. You better think twice before you say something like that to me again. You better learn to appreciate what's being done for you."

Ross said, "We've been busting our tails ever since you got here, doing everything you tell us."

Mr. Fowler's voice got louder. "We got a long ways to go, and that means we ain't got no goddamn time for y'all to be riding about the countryside, drinking cold drinks, and picking up the likes a him on the side of the road."

Ross said, "Thirty minutes hardly accounts for much riding around when we work till dark as it is."

"Every single minute counts, boy."

"I ain't got to listen to this, and his name is Daniel."

Mr. Fowler looked like he might not be well. He grew shaky and pale at every comeback Ross had. I peeked over my shoulder again, looking for Mama, but she was nowhere in sight.

I considered running to get her when it looked like they might actually start fighting. Mr. Fowler stepped closer as Ross backed away.

Mr. Fowler said, "We got a shitload of work to do around here. Them fields need cultivating, and all the while, here y'all are wasting time."

Ross made a dismissive gesture and trudged toward the barn, and Mr. Fowler said, "Get back here!"

His breath came heavy and his voice had gone hoarse. Daniel and I didn't dare walk away like Ross. Mr. Fowler grabbed his pack of Camels out of his shirt pocket, tapped another one out, and lit it. His hand shook, and he wiped his forehead.

"Ungrateful little bastard," he said as he pulled hard on the cigarette.

I don't know why I spoke up right then.

I said, "What if I try and find water?"

Mr. Fowler rolled his eyes and said, "That's supposed to be the answer. Like your daddy, Mr. Know-It-All?"

"It worked for you."

"How do you know? What if I said them pumps done ran dry? What if I said I paid all that money and barely a drop come out of 'em this year?"

Quiet as can be, Mama said, "Good heavens, Frank, what are you going on about?"

Grateful, I looked over my shoulder. She was holding a bowl filled with tomatoes, their red color matching the high color of her face. Mr.

Fowler put his hands up, spread flat and wide, showing her his palms like he was surrendering.

His voice, his whole demeanor changed, going soft and persuasive. "I guess I'm a little riled up. It's different nowadays, ain't it? I mean, hell, taken half a day off for joyriding like these kids did here, it ain't something I'm used to."

Mama frowned. "Joyriding?"

It was amusing to watch Frank rethink his words. His mouth opened and closed, like bream in the water.

He rubbed his arm, picking at something there, then he said, "I only want to do right, you know? I want it to be a good crop so you don't have to worry, and I've been working real hard to make it so. Don't you see?"

The rigidness in Mama's posture relaxed some.

She said, "Of course. We all want that, Frank. These kids were taught responsibility." She sort of laughed and said, "Shoot. Their daddy preached it every morning at breakfast during cotton-growing season."

Frank said, "I'm worried is all. This weather don't break soon, we're gonna be in a real fix."

Mama set the bowl on the railing and shielded her eyes. She looked across the backyard toward the fields, and even from where we stood, it was easy to see the wilting cotton plants struggling under the harsh sun.

She said, "I know."

I spoke up again. "I could try to find water. That's what I was telling Mr. Fowler."

She turned to me and gave me a little smile. "That would be wonderful, wouldn't it, Sonny?"

I nodded. "Yes, ma'am."

There was a mumbled "Jesus," from Mr. Fowler, but Mama didn't appear to notice.

She said, "What do you think, Frank? Lloyd always said she was good as him. I've seen her do it. It's amazing, really. Irrigating might be the answer. Lloyd always wanted to do it . . ."

Mama had herself a weak moment then and she wiped her eyes. Seeing her upset made my own eyes hurt as I held back tears, and wished with all my might Daddy was still here. Mr. Fowler rubbed the back of his neck hard, like she'd made him uncomfortable.

He said, "It's gonna take some doing."

Mama cleared her throat, and went on like she was thinking out loud. "Course, I guess we could just go right on along like we have been. Wait and see what the weather does. Seems silly not to try and do what we can though."

Just like that, she flipped the tables on Mr. Fowler.

He stopped and said, "Fine, fine. Let her try. Jesus. I just don't like the idea of spending a bunch of money on the whims of a twelve-year-old."

"Lloyd said Sonny was accurate most every time."

At the mention of Daddy's name for the third time, Mr. Fowler quit talking while Mama kept on about how good we'd been at finding water. Meanwhile he'd puffed so hard on the cigarette, it was already smoked down to a nub. He tossed that one on the ground as well, and Mama shot him a look while he sent smoldering looks at Daniel, as if he was somehow to blame. Then he turned his attention to the floundering cotton plants, their pitiful droopy leaves looking like they were begging us to get on with it.

Finally, he gave her a response, more like a bark. "Fine."

Mama said, "You seem upset, Frank. If you're worried about money, then say so."

His tone sharp, he said, "It ain't that."

Mama spoke quietly. "It's not such an outlandish idea. You did it."

Mr. Fowler softened his tone, and said, "I'll do whatever you want."

Mama smiled like she'd won a prize. It was the first time I noticed their interactions resembled hers and Daddy's whenever they hadn't agreed with one another. I knew right then I *had* to find water. I had to so that cotton would grow as high as the sky, and we'd get at least five bales per acre. We'd make enough money to pay him off, and be done with him interfering in our lives. Daniel had gone from being red-faced and hot to looking a little pale. He never had liked arguing of any sort. Mama reached out and smoothed down a few stray hairs hanging loose from my ponytail. She placed a cool hand along my hot cheek before adjusting the straw hat on my head. Mr. Fowler lit another cigarette and moved to stand under the oak tree. He wore an aggravated look.

She said, "What you reckon, hey, Sonny? Go on, get that willow branch of yours," as she turned to Daniel and said, "Honey, how you doing?"

I hurried into the house, hope and fear making my heart thump such that I could hear it in my head. In my room the window was open and a whisper of a breeze came in. I stood there a moment to calm down before I picked up my willow branch and ran my fingers along the wood, while sending a little prayer up. Maybe what I'd experienced last time, my sense this ability was growing weaker had been only a temporary. I went back outside where Mama and Daniel waited and Mr. Fowler scowled at the sky and headed for the closest field. As I passed under the sugar maple, a low whistle came from overhead. I glanced up and there was Trent, resting among the branches, appearing to have enjoyed the showdown from a perch on the lowest limb. He dropped down to the ground and fell into step beside me.

Mama and Daniel, caught up in conversation,

walked slower, so no one heard Trent. "It ain't gonna work. I bet it ain't never worked, you just acted like it did so you could think you were special."

I ignored him, while repeating *Daddy, help me,* over and over in my head. Ross was hooking up the cultivator at the back of the barn. When he spotted what I held, he stopped and fell into step beside me, opposite of Trent.

Trent started to repeat what he'd said, and Ross said, "Shut up for once, Trent."

I tried to only think about a strong flow of clear, cold liquid slipping by beneath our feet, rushing over that porous rock, and me sensing it. I pictured the moment it would happen, how it would feel. I bent down and collected a few small sticks in anticipation of placing them where the branch pointed. The soft whispery sounds made as we walked through dead grass and weeds along the tractor path sounded like someone shushing us, but no one was talking anyway.

Chapter 12

I couldn't make up my mind where I should start. Daddy would walk around, stand for a moment, and then he'd begin. I normally did the same thing 'cause there was some instinctual awareness, but with everyone counting on something to happen, except maybe Trent and Mr. Fowler, I hesitated, trying to figure out how I should go about it. I stared across at all that wilting green. I pictured the roots running here and there, desperately searching for the slightest amount of dampness. I imagined how they were shriveling up, drawing into themselves, unable to find the moisture they needed to channel to the stems and leaves, no different than the necessity of the life-giving blood flowing within my own body.

The cotton plants waved and flickered with the slight breeze, as if they were restless, like they were waiting on me, wanting me to hurry up and save them. I glanced at Mama standing quietly and smoking a cigarette. She looked calm, unworried.

She met my gaze and said, "It'll be fine, sugar. Even if you don't find water."

Had Mama lost faith in me too? Ross stepped into the field and walked along the rows, bending to lightly touch the tops of the plants, shaking his head now and then at their pitiful appearance. They weren't as tall as they should've been by now. Daniel was closest to me, with his arms crossed over his chest, and I felt better since he was here. I didn't dare look at Trent, knowing he'd give me some spiteful look.

Mr. Fowler was impatient. "What're we doing? Having a prayer meeting? Let's get it going."

Mama said, "Oh, Frank, you're so impatient. Give her time."

I moved past Mama into the field, the gentle brush of her fingers touching my shoulder as I went by. I had a moment of calm that quickly left when Mr. Fowler mumbled something. With my back to them, the Y setting in my palms, wrists up, I quickly glanced up at the sky where a relentless sun bore down, burning the skin of my arms and the top of my head. It was as if it had grown hotter, just in the past few minutes. *Daddy. Help me.*

The thought stayed as I began, focusing on the ground in front of me. After I went about thirty feet or so in one direction, I changed to the right, moving deeper into the field. I went along for a few seconds. Nothing. I looked back over my shoulder and Mr. Fowler leaned toward Mama, gesturing. She kept her eyes on me. My heart went nuts again, and my palms grew slick. Sweat gathered along my forehead and temple, trailed down my jawbone and off my chin while a hard knot formed in my throat. It ached like I'd swallowed a cantaloupe. I felt vulnerable, like I was standing naked in front of everyone, and that strange prickliness, like what happens when you know everyone's watching every move you make, crawled up and down my spine.

It didn't take long to know where I was at was no good. I came out of the field. I looked toward the pond, still hidden from sight and heard Daddy's voice in my head. *It's fed by an underground stream.* With the Y held tight, the long end in the general direction of the pond, I set off again. I hoped for a miracle, but the closer I got, the more I paid attention to the fact I still didn't feel a thing. I was close now, and without even a hint of a vibration. I knew then, "it" was gone, like Daddy. If anything was going to happen, it would have by now. I let go of one end of the branch. There was no need to continue, with everyone anticipating a signal from me, one that was never coming. I stood with the willow branch hanging by my side, tapping lightly against my calf. I held onto my tears, saving them for when I was alone and no one would see. There was a rustling noise behind me, but I stayed facing the pond, my composure as fragile as the wispy strands of a spider's web.

Sounding disappointed, Ross said, "It ain't gonna work this time, is it?"

I shook my head while my dream of healthy cotton dissipated as fast as a drop of rain hitting the bone-dry ground.

I looked over to Mama and said, "I'm sorry, I'm sorry."

She came to my side and gave me a hug. "Oh, honey, it ain't the end of the world. Least you tried."

That wasn't good enough, not when everything counted on it. I stared at the divining branch with a sense of betrayal. I had a sudden surge of anger, bad enough I wanted to snap it in two. I actually heard a tiny crack as I pressed the Y ends as if to join them. If it hadn't been for Daniel coming over and giving me a quick hug like Mama, I think I would have broken it. Embarrassed, he stepped back, and when I looked at him, he returned my gaze with open sincerity, like he still believed in me. He gave me hope 'cause the warmth in his eyes was gentle, kind. As if I couldn't ever make a mistake. As if it was something else wrong, something not of my own doing. I took a deep breath and let it out.

Mama said, "Come on, let's go have us some dinner."

She started back to the house and everyone was strangely silent, even Mr. Fowler.

Ross and Trent followed Mama, but Trent

paused long enough to lean down and hiss in my ear, "Told you so," before he hurried to catch up to Ross.

I waited for Mr. Fowler to say something, only Mama looked over her shoulder, and without a word, he hurried to walk with her. I lagged behind, my disappointment enormous over the loss of something special. It troubled me like nothing had before.

Daniel said, "Wait till you're alone. You can't do nothing like that with everyone breathing down your neck. It's just like performing. You got to have the right atmosphere."

"I guess, but everything's changed. Something ain't right. Last few times . . . nothing happened."

Daniel said, "What do you mean?"

I said, "When it works, it's . . . different. It's hard to explain, but sometimes even before I start walking, I can tell I'm going to find water. It's a feeling of fullness."

Once we got to the backyard, Mama went into the house along with Ross and Trent. Mr. Fowler stayed outside by the oak tree, watching me and Daniel approach. He had his hands on his hips like he was just waiting on me to explain myself enough so he could give me an earful.

I went by him, and he yelled out, "Hey! Wait just minute."

I stopped and oddly, in that moment, I realized he'd never said my name. He'd never addressed any of us, me, Ross, or Trent by name, only Mama, and by the special one he'd given her.

Daniel said, "Sumbitch," under his breath.

Mr. Fowler came close and said, "You ain't so smart now are you? Bet you ain't feeling so full of yourself."

It wasn't that I was full of myself at all. I only wanted to help Mama, figure out a way for us to help ourselves, and when it came time, to be able to give him what we owed him. Mr. Fowler spit on the ground.

"Answer me what you think that was?"

We stood before him wide-eyed, and I was starting to feel a bit afraid.

"I was . . . trying to find water. That's all."

"Showing off is more like it. Wasting everybody's time. As if I'm gonna spend more money for you to point here, there, or wherever. Hell no, it don't work like that, not with me."

He stomped off toward the house mumbling under his breath.

Once he was out of earshot, I said, "I honestly can't stand him."

Daniel shook his head and said, "Me neither."

"He acts like he owns the place."

"He sure does."

"He's pure tee evil is what he is."

"Yeah. Worse than the devil hisself."

Mama came to the door as Mr. Fowler went up the steps.

She held it wide for him, and when Daniel and I stayed where we were, she said, "Well, ain't y'all gonna come on in? The food's getting cold."

I called out, "Yes, ma'am," and then I mumbled to Daniel, "You watch. He'll be sweet around her, won't be no fussing and nitpicking about this or that."

Daniel said, "I'm telling you. He's got plans for your mama."

"Gah, don't say that!" I pinched his arm, and he said, "Ow!"

The smell of chicken pastry, and Mama's cornbread met us at the screen door, and my stomach flopped. Mr. Fowler was already seated, no sign he was mad, or upset about a thing. He talked to Mama good-naturedly about getting a pump to irrigate by using the pond water. It couldn't reach all the cotton, but it would reach some, he said. We went in and sat down. I set my willow branch on the floor beside my chair, and debated on whether or not I'd be able to eat even a bite.

Mama was saying, "Maybe rain will come."

He said, "Maybe. Maybe not."

"Your crops doing good?"

"Oh, sure, sure. Everything's looking just fine."

I nudged Daniel. That right there proved he'd told us a flat-out lie. Mama gestured at Daniel to serve himself. Much as I loved her chicken pastry, the sight of slick, gloppy looking dough, and chicken meat floating in thick gravy was enough to roll my stomach again. We said a quick blessing and then everyone started eating like there was no tomorrow while I tried not to watch. The sight of food entering their mouths, and the smell made me stand up quick, my chair scraping along the floor.

Mama said, "Sonny, you all right? You look plumb washed out."

I said, "I'll be right back."

Mr. Fowler waved his fork around and repeated himself, "I keep saying girls ain't supposed to be traipsing around a farm doing a man's work. They got delicate constitutions. They should be in and around the house tending to the garden, cooking, and such."

Like he cared. He'd have me chopping cotton an hour from now. My belly tightened until it felt like I couldn't breathe. I hurried to the bathroom, certain I might throw up. I closed the door and leaned against it, and stared at the mirror. Mama was right. I was looking just about the color of them pastry strips, all pasty white. My green eyes stood out in vivid contrast, and my upper lip and forehead shined with sweat. I went to the sink, bent over, and splashed my face with cold water. I kept my forehead against the cool porcelain.

Daddy, why didn't you show me where?

The curtains flapped in the hot breeze, and the sound of cicadas revving up in the sugar maples and oak tree only made it seem all that much hotter. My stomach settled, and I rinsed my face again. I felt better, but now I was only killing time so I wouldn't have to eat, but I didn't want Daniel to think I wasn't coming back and leave before we'd had a chance to even visit. When I went into the kitchen, they were finishing up, drinking their last swallows of sweet tea while Mama looked at me, worried. She got up from her chair, wiped a hand down her apron, and put it on my forehead.

She said, "You ain't hot. You want me to set you a plate aside for later?"

"No, ma'am."

Mr. Fowler said, "Well, that was real good as always. I think we've wasted enough of the day on that other mess, time to get back to the real work."

His comment was as abrasive as the scraping of his chair as he slid it back.

Mama said, "My word, Frank, the things you say. You're gonna hurt Sonny's feelings."

Frank said, "Aw, Vi, I don't mean a thing by it, I'm just teasing."

His tone suggested a familiarity I didn't like. He even winked at her, and she actually offered him a smile. I didn't much like that either. Daddy used to tell her he loved that smile of hers, and here she was giving them away to somebody who didn't deserve them, not a one. Mr. Fowler could easily get the wrong idea. My thoughts were interrupted when he focused in on Daniel, like sighting in on a target.

He said, "Come on, sissy boy, we ain't got time for your kind of fun and games. You got to work to earn that food you just ate."

I said, "But, he came to visit me."

Mr. Fowler sucked at something in his teeth, and with Mama there, his response was mild.

"The way I see it, men spend time with men. Women spend time with women. Come to think of that, maybe he *should* stay behind here with y'all."

He slapped his knee as he laughed. Trent joined in until Mama gave him one of her evil-eyed looks and his snickering petered out.

Her voice held a warning. "Frank."

"Aw! I'm just messing! Lordy, y'all got to lighten up! Come on now!"

Ross said, "Hey, Daniel, you wanted to learn to drive that tractor didn't you?"

Mama said, "There you go, that's good, Ross. You and Daniel go on and do that while Sonny helps me clean up in here."

Mr. Fowler didn't look none too happy, but he conceded to Mama's decision with a loud belch, and no apology, before he went down the hall to the bathroom. My brothers went out, and Daniel followed. Even though Ross had said not to discuss anything with Mama about Mr.

187

Fowler, I wasn't going to keep my mouth shut any longer. He was acting like he was all of a sudden in charge of everyone, like he was man of the house. We scraped leftover food from the plates into the scrap bucket we kept for the burn can, and I ruminated on how I would say what I wanted. Mama hummed as we cleared the table and filled the sink with hot soapy water. She was still too thin, fragile looking, yet she appeared to be so peaceful, I almost didn't want to bother her.

"Mama."

"Hm?"

"Can I ask you a question?"

"Of course."

I tried to get my thoughts straight, and finally blurted out, "What would you think if I said I didn't like Mr. Fowler?"

"I sort of guessed it already. You get a look when he's around. You remind me of your daddy. He had a similar look as that, like he was hurting somewhere."

And here I thought I'd been doing pretty good hiding it.

She said, "What is it you don't like about him?"

"Everything."

Mama actually laughed when I said that, and I could see why. My voice was so glum, so grim.

She said, "I know it ain't like working with your daddy. Frank's not as patient, but in all fairness, Sonny, he bought that seed when he didn't have to, he's been here every day when he's got his own crops to tend. I think things would be really different if we'd have had rain."

"Or, if I could've found water."

"Oh, honey. Don't you go and carry that burden now. Ain't nobody blaming you for that."

"Mr. Fowler is."

"What do you mean?"

"He said I wasted everyone's time. That I was showing off."

"When did he say that?"

"A little while ago. And, he's mean to Daniel. I don't like him calling him that name."

"I don't like it either, but Frank's got a different sense of humor. That's all. I'll speak to him about it."

I didn't think that was a good idea. "Don't Mama. It's okay."

"No, I'll speak to him. Everything will be fine. Here, take this out."

She handed me the scrap bucket to carry outside and dump. Outside I noticed Ross and Daniel moving around the tractor with Ross showing him what was what. Trent was already on Mr. Fowler's tractor, straw hat clamped low on his head as he headed down the tractor path. There was a breeze coming out of the east, making the pines sway. I glanced at Daniel again, wanting to catch his attention. I held my arm up, waving it a little, only he wasn't looking my way, and he wasn't paying attention to what Ross was trying to show him either. Instead, he was staring at Trent with the same expression he'd get when he talked about going to California or New York one day. What I thought of as a thirsty look, longing for something out of reach, lasting until Trent was out of sight.

He turned back to Ross who was coming from around the other side of the tractor and said, "Ain't you listening to me?"

Even from where I was, I could see he looked embarrassed.

Mama came to the screen door and said, "Sonny?"

"I'm coming."

I went up the steps slowly, looking back over my shoulder. Daniel climbed up on the tractor and Ross hopped up behind him, standing on a small metal piece, and reached over Daniel's shoulder to start it. The engine chugged to life beneath him and Ross said something in his ear, then pointed at his foot. Daniel pushed on the gas, and the tractor backfired. He pressed on the gas again, and got to revving the engine like Ross or Trent would do, grinning the whole time.

Mr. Fowler came out of the house, brushed by me, and hollered, "Hey! Y'all quit the fooling around now!"

That was when I figured it out. Maybe Daniel wanted to be friends with Trent too, but I couldn't imagine why, especially when Trent acted the way he did.

Chapter 13

Mama was at the sink, and while she washed, I dried and kept a lookout from the window. On occasion I'd see a brown swirl of dust float by as Ross drove the tractor up and down the rows with Daniel on the back. Minutes later he was back inside, wearing a coat of dust, and looking like he'd had enough.

I finished wiping the last glass and said, "Come on, Daniel, I got to go to the field."

He probably wanted to practice some scenes, but with Mr. Fowler around, I had to chop cotton.

Mama said, "Take some iced water with you."

She filled mason jars with ice first, then water from the tap. She wrapped each in a hand towel. She also put some brownies in wax paper and put them in a bag.

"Daniel, will you be staying for supper?"

He hesitated, and I could tell he wanted to.

Mama leaned her hip against the counter, wiped her hair off her forehead, and said, "I'm fixing stew beef over rice, in case you were wondering."

Another one of Daniel's favorites. She gave him a smile to go with her invitation.

"Thank you, but I have to go home in a little while."

She said, "If you change your mind, I'll have plenty."

Outside, I went to the toolshed and got a couple hoes. Luckily, Mr. Fowler was nowhere in sight. Daniel held the jars and the brownies as we made our way to a field, and I glanced at him a few times, realizing he was *not* prepared for this sort of work. I wore a long-sleeve shirt, my hat, and long pants. It seemed crazy to dress like that, but it was actually cooler 'cause it kept the sun's rays from making my skin feel like it was under a broiler. But Daniel, he had on shorts, *and* a short-sleeve shirt, and Converse sneakers.

Hesitant, I said, "Daniel?"

"What?"

"Maybe you should sit in the shade while I do this?"

He turned to me with a look so ugly, so unlike himself I took a step back in surprise.

I gasped, "What? What is it?"

He spit the words out. "What do you think it is?"

"I don't know. I just said . . ."

"You think I'm what he says. Sissy boy."

"No I don't! But, you're gonna get slap burnt up!"

"Oh, sure. Yeah. That's it."

"What's the matter with you?"

The look he gave me was as searing as the sun over our heads, his expression like he wanted to say something else.

I grabbed up my hoe and said, "Do what you want. Least I don't pout like a baby when I'm upset. You didn't see me having a hissy fit or being hateful to anyone earlier, right?"

Daniel grabbed his hoe and launched it like a spear. It landed about three rows away, right on top of the cotton, crushing the plants.

"Daniel!"

He ignored me and stomped across the field to get it. And where he ended up was where he stayed. I began to feel sorry for myself while I worked. I was the one who ought to be upset, considering. I whacked everywhere I could see pokeweed, horseweed, killing the things growing that shouldn't be. I could hear Daniel doing the same, violently stabbing the dirt, making little grunting noises as he did so. The afternoon wore on. I stopped for a drink of water, and Trent rolled by heading for another section of field. He looked over at Daniel, still hunched over the plants, the hoe rising up and falling. He shook his head and went on. I looked at Daniel who refused to pay me or even Trent any mind. His arms were turning the color of his shirt. I stared at the sky and estimated it was going on three o'clock, a long ways to go yet. After a little while, Daniel broke his silence. He was still three rows over, but close enough I could hear him.

"Sonny?"

I didn't stop working. I didn't feel chitchatty after an entire afternoon of silence.

"Hey, Sonny."

"What," said I, emphasis on the *t*.

My response was flat as the hoe blade. I sighed and quit murdering the weeds. I stared across the tops of the cotton plants and fought not to bust out laughing.

I cleared my throat and said, "Let's get a drink."

Daniel hurried ahead of me over to the shade of the pine tree. He almost glowed, and I was certain he regretted his impulsive decision. A few clouds had formed and tried to offer us respite from the direct rays. The breeze had kicked up too, and I picked at the end of my shirt, pulling it from my skin, letting air get in. We stood side by side, sipping the still-cool water, and eating brownies.

Daniel swallowed the last of his and said, "You know, sometimes I feel like I just don't belong nowhere."

He wasn't telling me anything I didn't already know. The difference was, he'd never mentioned it before.

I licked my fingers and said, "Well, you are a little weird, ya know."

He shoved my shoulder in a playful manner, coming back around to being Daniel.

Then, with a cautious tone, he said, "Do you think I am?"

"Think you're what?"

"Weird?"

"No, silly. I was only kidding."

"Maybe you are, but the rest of them ain't. Ain't nobody at school ever asked me to play baseball, or football, or you know, be on a team. Or to even eat lunch with them."

"Do you *want* to play ball?"

"No, but that ain't it. You're my only real friend. Heck, even my own family acts like they don't want me around half the time. At home? Brenda and Sarah pretty much ignore me unless they want me to do something for them."

Daniel started to pace and droplets of sweat fell from the ends of his hair, which was stuck to his neck. He put a hand underneath the strands, and lifted them so the breeze could get to his skin. It was something I'd do with my own hair, and the gesture suddenly stood out. I couldn't picture Ross or Trent doing such a thing. That was it. It was his hair.

Excited to have figured it out, I said, "Daniel, it's your hair!"

"Huh? My hair? What's that go to do with anything?"

"Just now, the way you did that thing to get it off your neck."

"It's hot, what else am I supposed to do?"

"Cut it?"

He was quiet, like he was thinking about what I said. Like maybe I'd brought something to his attention he'd never thought of before.

He shook his head. "It's more than that. I don't want to talk about it anymore."

He clamped his mouth shut, and the idea he had a secret he was keeping from me hurt my feelings.

Wanting to ease his mind, and hoping he'd share it, I said, "Well, you fit in here, with us."

"I used to. Not anymore, not with *him* around."

We were quiet for a minute, then I said, "I told Mama I didn't like him. I told her how he is, things he says when she ain't around."

"What did she say?"

"She was gonna say something to him, but I didn't want her to. I thought it might make him mad."

"Yeah."

"Yeah."

Just before six we'd worked our way closer to the house, and as we came out of the field, I took a good look at Daniel and said, "Oh my God."

"What?"

"Your skin."

Daniel mashed a finger on his arm and a white spot showed and quickly disappeared.

"Ouch," he said.

Mr. Fowler happened by, and gave him an assessing look. "Looks like the little flit got scorched. You gonna run home to Mommy and cry?"

He put his fists up to his eyes, twisted them against the lids, and made a *wah, wah, wah,* baby crying noise. Daniel and I ignored him. I followed him to get his bike while Mr. Fowler's low singsong, "Aw, boohoohoo," followed us. Daniel got his bike out from the back of our truck.

I said, "Mama's gonna be disappointed you ain't staying."

He tipped his head toward Mr. Fowler. "Not a chance. Not with him."

I couldn't blame him. I had all sorts of bad thoughts about Mr. Fowler as I stared at my friend pedaling down Turtle Pond Road like he was being chased by something I couldn't see.

I never prayed so hard for rain as I did that night, and I also prayed for the cotton season to be over, and repeated my wish for more bales per acre than ever before. I pictured it in my mind and swore up and down, sideways and straight, for the plants to ignore what they weren't getting. I prayed Mr. Fowler would never come around here again. I was praying for miracles, and as I held Dolly tight, stroking her blond hair, I somehow knew none of it was possible.

There would be no miracle 'cause if miracles were going to happen, it should have been for Daddy to live through that rattlesnake bite. It would have been the only one needed.

Chapter 14

After a few days of frantic searching, I finally broke down and asked Mama had she seen my willow branch. Trent and Ross were cramming bologna sandwiches and chips in their mouths, chased by Pepsi 'cause Mama had been too busy to cook like usual. She'd been making black--berry jam all morning long, and was twisting the top of the last jar.

Looking a little flustered, she said, "No, honey, I ain't seen hide nor hair of it."

"Darn."

She plopped a crate I'd used to sell eggs up on the table, and started putting the jars into it. "Did you look in the barn? Maybe you left it there."

"I've looked everywhere."

There was a hitch in my voice as the words bumped over the knot forming in my throat. She didn't know how long I'd been looking. The kitchen was overly warm from the boiling pots she'd used for the preserves while the humidity level rose outside too. We'd put a fan in one of the windows of the kitchen, facing outward so it would pull out the sticky air. It worked until about noon, and after that, nothing would help except to wait for the sun to go down.

Mama wiped her forehead and said, "Well, keep looking, honey, and I'll help you after I get back. I got to go take this blackberry jam I made to Mrs. Aiken."

I nodded and she went to the car, crate resting on her hip as she opened the door. She'd only just made a decision to get back to making a little extra money and I was sure it had to do with the cotton. This made me feel even more guilty. Trent and Ross kept eating, not looking at me. Maybe they were thinking the same thing. It was my fault. The phone rang with our special tone. I'd tried to call Daniel earlier and didn't get an answer, and I hoped it was him.

I ran over to the hall table and answered, "Hello?"

"Hey, Sonny."

"Well, hey there, Daniel."

"What's buzzin', cuzzin?"

"Huh?"

Daniel sighed. "What's new?"

"Daniel, you got to come quick."

I held my breath, unsure if he would.

He said, "Why?"

"I can't find my willow branch!"

"Is *he* there?"

He wasn't—yet. He'd be coming sooner or later, and I found myself wanting to lie about it if it meant Daniel would stay home. I wanted to say he hadn't been around for days, but Daniel would know by my voice. He just knew, somehow.

"Not yet."

"I'll come, but you better not laugh when you see me. And, if *he* starts anything, I'm leaving."

"Why, what's . . . ?" and I got dial tone.

I drifted back into the kitchen and made myself a bologna sandwich, making sure I spread the slices heavy with mustard.

Trent offered a suggestion. "Did you look in a tree? That's where most branches are found."

He laughed at his own joke, while Ross said, "Shut up, Trent."

"You shut up."

"No, you . . ."

I picked up my sandwich, and went outside to sit on the porch swing to eat. I moved it back and forth, pushing gently with one foot, while watching the road. Trent and Ross came out a few minutes later. Trent headed off toward the barn, while Ross dropped down to sit beside me.

He said, "Want me to help you look?"

I shook my head and said, "No, that's okay, thanks anyway."

He yanked on my ponytail, and went off to work in the barn, wiping his hands down the front of his dungarees. Thirty minutes later I knew why Daniel said what he said. He rode into the yard on his bike, got off, and came up the steps and flopped down beside me. I couldn't say a word. His skin looked like a molting snake. It was peeling and flaking all over, making his face and arms look like a speckled egg. The end of his nose was shiny and red.

He said, "I told you, don't laugh. Geez, I'm itching like crazy."

He rubbed on his arms hard and pieces of skin floated down to settle around his feet.

I said, "Geez, Daniel. You'll be like a whole new person when it's all over with."

"Maybe that would be a good thing."

"Hmph."

He joked, "I bet if anyone was behind me, they thought it was snowing."

"Yuck."

"When was the last time you remember having it?"

"The day I tried last. You know."

"Yeah."

"It's got to be around here, somewhere."

We left the porch, and began searching the tool-shed, even pulling the shovels, rakes, and hoes from the hooks on the wall, just to be sure. We went into the barn, looked around our stage, in all the empty stalls, on the floor, and even up in the loft, although I'd not been up there this year.

We came out, and there stood Mr. Fowler.

"What are you two up to?" He did a double take, and said, "Mother of God, look at you. You just got yourself a new name. Flake any better?"

Without a word, Daniel spun on his heels and started for his bike, intending to make good on his promise. He climbed on.

I said, "Wait! Daniel, don't go yet!"

Mr. Fowler said, "What's he doing here anyway? There's work to be done."

Something boiled up in me, and I pictured it like an underground geyser, like the pictures of Old Faithful erupting I'd seen in the World Britannica Encyclopedia set my brothers and I got for Christmas a couple years ago.

In a voice I'd never, ever considered using with an adult, I yelled, "He's helping me, that's what! I invited him! This is our house, not yours! This is our yard, and he's my friend!"

Mr. Fowler shoved his hat back on his head and his eyes went icy, and fixed on me like a crow's would, black and beady and without depth. Daniel heard me and paused, and Mr. Fowler glanced at him, his expression something close to hatred. His mouth stretched thin, he turned back to me, almost poking his finger in my chest.

He said, "I ain't taking no sass from you, you hear me?"

I looked at Daniel, my eyes begging him, *don't leave.* What happened next was as odd as seeing that five-legged frog I'd found close to the pond one afternoon. Mr. Fowler appeared to reconsider. I was sure he was thinking about

Mama's words, and whatever she'd said to him on my behalf was working.

He said, "You two got thirty minutes to waste time, and then you need to get on with your chores and he either needs to help, or go on home."

That wasn't to my liking at all, but I gritted my teeth and said, "Daniel, please? Just for a bit."

He rolled his bike back over to the oak tree, and leaned it against the trunk, but he made no move to come closer.

To my surprise, Mr. Fowler asked, "What were you two looking for?"

I wasn't sure if he was going to make fun, or if he was planning to say something mean. He still had no expression, the features of his face as lifeless as my doll. He did that funny thing with his head, tilted it one way, then the other, and again.

It really was such a creepy habit, I averted my eyes and mumbled, "I can't find my willow branch."

He said, "That old thing? Hell, it was probably about half-rotten anyway. It sure as hell wasn't any good to you the other day, now was it?"

"It was my daddy's, he gave it to me."

He said, "Yeah? So?" He picked at something in his teeth, then said, "Hey, I know what to do. Stay right there."

He sauntered over to one of the sugar maples

and snapped off a smaller branch near the bottom. I had no idea what he was up to, but then, he closed his eyes and began to act like he was in a swoon. Trent came out of the barn in time to see him fluttering his eyes, and staggering about the yard, mimicking me. He weaved one way, and then the other.

Suddenly, he snapped his eyes open, opened his mouth wide while pointing the stick at the ground. "Ah ha! Here. And here. And here. And there! Waaaattter! It's everywhere!"

Daniel narrowed his eyes. Trent thought it was hilarious and slapped his leg and hooted. He and Mr. Fowler were still carrying on when a curious noise came from Daniel.

He suddenly charged Mr. Fowler, his arms stretched out in front of him, shouting, "Leave her alone!"

Mr. Fowler simply waited until he was close enough, then he made a backhanded motion, hitting him hard as he could with the stick. It hit Daniel's chin, and went down and across his chest.

I yelled, "You can't hit him!"

Daniel folded over. Mr. Fowler grabbed him by the front of his shirt, and all Daniel could do was grip Mr. Fowler's wrists as he was picked up so his feet barely skimmed the ground.

Mr. Fowler shook him and screamed in his face, "You fucking little flit! Who the hell do you think you are? I'll beat your little ass you mess with me!"

Ross came running out of the barn, wild-eyed, unable to grasp what was going on. Mr. Fowler tossed Daniel aside like he was a sack of potatoes.

I shouted, and pointed. "Help him, help Daniel!"

Trent was stuck in place like I was and it was Ross who charged at Mr. Fowler, lowering his shoulder the way he would when he played football. He took Mr. Fowler's feet right out from under him, and Mr. Fowler landed with a solid thud on his back. This was the scene Mama came up the drive and saw.

The car jerked to a stop and she jumped out, yelling in that way she would when she was confounded by what she saw. "What in God's name is going on?"

Daniel and Mr. Fowler were both still on the ground, and Ross looked guilty while Trent stood stone-faced. Mr. Fowler's elbow was scraped and he looked a bit dazed. Daniel got up, and his chin had an ugly stripe across it. Mama didn't know who to go to first, Daniel or Mr. Fowler.

Her breath came rapidly, her eyes darting around to each of us. "What has happened here?"

I was so upset, I couldn't get any words out except, "He . . . he . . . he . . ."

Ross said, "He hit Daniel!"

Mama looked at Mr. Fowler and said, "You hit him?"

He rolled over onto his knees, pushed himself up. He brushed dirt off of his pants carefully, taking his time. When he straightened up, his mouth was bloody, like he'd bit his tongue or something. He worked his mouth a little, then spit. He pointed a finger at me, Daniel, and then Ross, like he was targeting us and I began to think about everything that happened. In hindsight, I could see how my side might sound from Mama's perspective, especially when Mr. Fowler got to telling his version.

"This whole thing"—and he jerked his thumb at me—"happened when I says to them two, her and that boy there, there's work to be done, and she goes off half-cocked, yelling how this ain't my house or yard. Even then, I was still nice about it, and I allowed they could take some time to look for that stick a hers she done lost. Couldn't a been so important you go and lose the thing, you ask me. I said they needed to get on with the work, and that he could work too, or go home. I was only fooling around, having a little fun, and there wasn't any call for her to behave like she did. Him neither. That's when he came at me, trying to hit *me*."

I shuffled my feet. "That ain't exactly the way it happened."

Mama spoke my full name, indicating how upset she was. "Martha Simpson Creech."

"Mama . . ."

"Martha. Did you raise your voice to Mr. Fowler?"

Her calling him Mr. Fowler told me whose side she was on. I hesitated. There wasn't much I could do but answer truthfully.

"Yes, ma'am."

Mr. Fowler coughed. "Downright disrespectful is what it was."

Mama gave me a disappointed look, a tightening of her mouth and eyes, and then she looked at Daniel.

"Daniel, were you going to hit him?"

Daniel had nothing to lose, I suppose.

He said, "Yes, ma'am. I sure was. It ain't right for him to poke fun at her like he was doing. It ain't right he keeps on calling me them names."

Mama stared at Daniel like she was considering what he'd said.

She turned to Ross. "Is that what happened?"

He scrubbed his hand over his hair, and said, "I didn't see all of it. I came out at all the yelling, and when I did, he . . ." He gave Mr. Fowler a distrustful look, his eyes narrowed. "He had Daniel jacked up by his shirt collar. Sonny was screaming at me, and I didn't really think . . . I just tackled him."

Mama shook her head, and last she faced Trent. "Trent?"

He lifted his hands, and said, "I didn't do nothing."

Mama gave him a hard look, and Mr. Fowler said, "He's the only one who didn't."

Mama put her hand up to her forehead. "Jesus," she whispered as she shot a furious look at Ross and me. "Haven't all of you been taught better than this? Didn't your daddy teach you better?"

Mr. Fowler, sounding a bit smug, said, "Look. If an apology from me helps, then I'm real sorry. I sure didn't know they would get so doggone upset over a little bit of funning. Damnation, I believe I got a loose tooth."

Mama said, "All of you, apologize immediately. Martha, you first."

"Mama . . ."

"Martha! Now."

I was sure to choke on those two bitter words, yet I managed a strangled, "I'm sorry."

She looked expectantly at Ross, and like me, he could barely get the words clear of his mouth.

"I'm sorry."

She turned to Daniel last. He returned Mama's look and the red streak striped down his chin was bleeding, and it traveled across his neck. There was a tear in his shirt, and it was apparent Mr. Fowler had not held back at all.

Daniel said, "I ain't apologizing."

Mama said, "Daniel, what you did is wrong, don't you think?"

Daniel said nothing.

I was proud of him for standing his ground until Mama said, "If you won't apologize, you can't come visit until I say so."

"Mama! It's not fair!"

I shouldn't have ever said anything to the sumbitch. I shouldn't have let my anger get in the way. Mama ignored me.

She turned her back on Daniel and said to Mr. Fowler, "Let's get some ice on that."

He followed Mama into the house, holding his lower back.

Sick, I went to Daniel and said, "What're we gonna do?"

He delivered a sad look in my direction before he went and got on his bike. I noticed another whelp on his arm. I wanted to take those hurts away, only they went deeper than whelps, and it showed in his eyes when he'd looked at me seconds ago. He pedaled down our drive, and I half-heartedly trotted after him.

I called out to him, "Call me, okay?"

If he heard me, he didn't react. He turned onto Turtle Pond Road, and his shirt began to flap the faster he went. He stood up on the pedals, and not once did he look back at me. It was as if the sun had gone behind a dark cloud, and would never come out again. Unsettled by what happened, resentful toward Mama taking Mr. Fowler's side, I moped about in the kitchen garden, picking at the weeds sporadically. Ross and Trent had crept away silently, disappearing somewhere. It was quiet after all the commotion, and the afternoon took on a strangeness where familiar things weren't any comfort, only a reminder I was out of sorts with all that was around me.

I went to the chicken coop, and the hens came and stood expectantly by the wire fence staring at me like little convicts. It was too early to feed them, but I scooped corn out of the sack into a pan, and opened the gate. I stepped in and scattered it around, taking my time. They followed after me, heads bobbing, and turning so they could watch as I dropped the corn, some of them bickering over a kernel. There was a jockeying for position, a hierarchy amongst them that was quickly decided with a determined peck or two.

If only it could be so simple with people.

I put the pan away and left the coop. The screen door banged, and Mr. Fowler came out of the house. I ducked behind the toolshed, not wanting to see him. I felt too raw, too stung by what had transpired. The last thing I wanted was to have to face him so soon after what had taken place. Mama followed right after him, and I could see them talking rather intently. She nodded, eyes on the ground, but I was too far away to hear. Mr. Fowler ticked off on his fingers, a this, this, and this gesture. I could imagine what he might be saying, most likely reminding her of all he'd done. Mama stared after him as he got in his truck and left. It was only about five o'clock in the afternoon, and his early exit gave me hope he wouldn't be back.

I came out from behind the shed, and took a chance. "What was he talking about just now?"

Mama waved a hand and said, "About the generator, a pump, the hoses needed."

More ways for us to remain indebted to him.

"He ain't got to spend it. He . . ."

"Martha."

She was still mad 'cause she was using my formal name. She went inside and I went and sat on the porch swing. I stared at the sky, willing the few clouds there to come together and bring us rain. The more I thought about what happened, the angrier I felt. Not knowing what else to do, I walked out to Daddy's grave. I sat on the ground, the mound now covered by grass. I leaned against the stone, and sent my confused thoughts out to him.

As usual, there was no response.

Chapter 15

It was out of character for us to behave the way we had earlier, so everyone was subdued at supper. Soon as we'd finished, Ross and Trent went to their room, leaving me with Mama.

Bothered by her demand we apologize, I said, "It all started when he got to making fun of my dowsing. Daniel stuck up for me. Mr. Fowler's different when you're not around. He doesn't like us, but he especially doesn't like Daniel."

Mama kept rinsing a plate, and minutes went by until I gave up on her talking any more about it.

Finally, she said, "He's never had young'uns. He's treating you like adults is all, or trying to."

Shoot. If he was treating us like adults, why wasn't he acting like one?

Mama said, "Even when you believe someone else might be in the wrong, sometimes the best way is to simply forgive them. Don't you think?"

I wasn't sure about this, not when it came to him, but I said, "I reckon."

She could tell I wasn't satisfied. "What's the matter?"

"It ain't fair about Daniel."

Mama shook her head, and sighed heavy.

I persisted and repeated my earlier statement. "He was only sticking up for me."

"He let his temper get in the way of his better judgment."

"But Daniel doesn't *have* a temper, Mama. You know how he is, you can't hardly get him riled up over nothing."

"It seems to me whenever he's been around lately, is when trouble starts."

"It ain't true! Daniel's been coming here a long time, and ain't never been no trouble until now. He ain't causing it. It's *him!*"

I could tell Mama was tired of it when she swiped at her forehead in an agitated manner.

"We ain't got time for this, not when everyone is worrying about that crop out there. That's all I'm going to say about it."

A couple of days went by without any sign of him, though he called Mama to talk. Her voice would get lower, and I hated knowing it was him, and couldn't figure what they had to talk about outside of the farm. His absence reminded me of how it used to be, how it could be, and I relished when cold weather would come, the cotton would be picked and there would be no reason for him to be around. My sense of peace ended on the third morning when I spotted his truck back in its usual spot. The sun crept over the horizon and with it came the promise of another hot day. Sniffing the morning air as I walked along the dogtrot, I caught a different scent that overrode everything else, a sharp, spicy odor that wasn't unpleasant but wasn't Mama's gardenias or hyacinth. I entered the kitchen and found the source. His dark hair was slick and wet looking, every hair in place. The smell was his aftershave and it overrode the heavy odor of the fatback Mama fried.

And Mama? *She had on lipstick.*

She set a cup in front of him and filled it with coffee. She slid the creamer and sugar bowl over to him too. He watched her every move, and this too was another routine too much like how it had been with Daddy.

Agitated, but determined not to show it, I said, "Morning," to no one in general, and got a greeting from Mama.

"Morning, you hungry?"

"Not really."

They were smoking and drinking coffee, and I had the distinct impression I'd interrupted something. After a minute or so, he cleared his throat, and tapped the long papery looking ash into the ashtray.

He said, "We could irrigate that section over near to the pond. I'll do whatever you want me to do."

I stopped buttering my bread for a second and looked at Mama. She looked nice with her hair curled under like Bettie Page. She blew a puff of smoke toward the ceiling. I was torn. I wanted the cotton to have a chance, even if only a small portion of it, and at the same time, I realized we'd be indebted to him even more. I slid the bread into the oven and set the broiler on high.

She said, "How much would it cost?"

"Thinking about five grand for fifty acres. On the other hand, this drought's liable to break any day now."

Mama said nothing. She smoked the rest of her cigarette. He kept glancing at her, and fiddling with the handle on his cup.

He repeated what he'd said before. "Whatever you think is best."

She got up, refilled his cup, and then she said, "It's a lot of money, but irrigation equipment can come in handy no matter what. I reckon we ought to just go on and get it. Lloyd was planning on doing it at some point anyway. Just add to what I owe you."

Mr. Fowler shifted in his chair at the mention of Daddy's name, but he only said, "All right."

I smelled my toast and yanked the oven door open, grabbed the pan, and set it on the stovetop. It was burnt. I got a knife and scraped it to remove the burnt part and the noise brought his eyes my way.

"You ever find that stick of yours?"

I didn't answer.

Mama prompted my manners. "Sonny."

"No, sir."

Mr. Fowler leaned back in his chair, balancing on two legs, and Mama drew up. He rocked away on them two legs, all that weight of his causing them to creak and groan. Mama got up and went to the sink like she couldn't bear to watch.

He said, "Just as well. I ordered you a dowsing kit. Found it in a catalog down to Slater's. What you think about that?"

That sure caught me off guard. I had no idea you could buy such and or that he'd bother to even buy something for me. He'd made it pretty clear what he'd thought about my strange ability. Mama smiled, then prompted me about my manners again since I was still trying to grasp what it meant. There had to be a reason behind it.

She said, "Why, that's real nice, ain't that real nice, Sonny?"

My response was half-hearted. "I guess."

Mama's voice went deep with disappointment. "Sonny."

"I'm sorry, Mama, but I'm still looking for the one Daddy gave me."

"That doesn't mean you forget your manners. Didn't you tell me they were copper, Frank?"

"That's right."

Copper?

I couldn't picture how that was supposed to work, much less how it would ever feel like the willow branch, which held the warmth of my hands, as well as the natural smell of sun-soaked wood. I could almost feel the Y in my hands right then, the memory creating a tingling sensation in my palms for want of it. It was a longing much like the one I had when I thought about never laying eyes on Daddy again, never hearing his voice, or his laugh.

Mama said, "See. They ought to last you a good long time."

I nodded, already knowing I couldn't hardly stand the idea of accepting them. Besides, what good was copper? A branch from a willow tree was intended to find water since it did best growing near rivers, streams, or lakes, according to Daddy. This idea of Mr. Fowler's seemed outlandish, strange. How appropriate coming from him. I picked up my toast and went toward the door.

Mama said, "You want an egg?"

"No, ma'am."

"I'm going to need you to get them tomatoes and okra out of the garden today."

"Yes, ma'am."

She said, "Oh, and Aunt Ruth's coming next week."

"She is?"

"Yes, but she can only stay a few days.

She got a summer job tutoring some students."

Mr. Fowler set his chair back on all four legs and said, "I didn't know you had a sister."

Mama said, "You never asked."

I went outside and flopped down onto the porch swing, setting it in motion with my foot. I stared out at the fields, my spirits lifted over Aunt Ruth's visit, considering what *she* might make of it all. I finished eating and headed down the porch steps toward the barn to tell Ross about the irrigation and Aunt Ruth. When I passed the burn can, a shape caught my eye. I went closer, and then snatched at what poked up over the edge, staring in disbelief. It was my willow branch, the distinctive Y-shaped end scorched, one side almost half gone. *How would it have gotten in there?* The screen door slammed. Mr. Fowler was heading for his truck. I pressed my mouth together and marched back across the yard, up the steps. Mama was picking up the phone as I burst into the kitchen, waving it in the air.

"Look! It's my dowsing stick, all burned up! I'll never be able to use it again! He threw it there!"

Mama hung the phone up, giving me an exasperated look. "Who did?"

"Mr. Fowler!"

"Oh, Sonny. Why would he do that?"

Outraged I said, "That's why he spent money to buy me that other one! He's feeling guilty!"

I could see uncertainty in her eyes, but she only said, "Calm down. It ain't right to lay blame when you don't know for sure."

"Who else would've done it? *I know* it was him!"

Mama glanced over my shoulder. Mr. Fowler was standing just inside the doorway. I'd been so busy yelling, I hadn't heard him come back in.

Calm as could be, he said, "I ain't touched it. Hell, it don't even look like the same one to me."

Giving Mama a pleading look, I willed her to believe me, only she said, "Sonny, you're not being fair."

My chest heaved up and down like I'd run all the way to the house from one of the back fields. She stared at me with such sadness, I realized she would take his side on this too. Maybe it was where he stood in the shadow of the doorway, or maybe it was that my vision had gone blurry, whatever it was, I was certain he'd smirked as she said that. I rushed back outside and took off across the yard.

Mama called, "Sonny!" but I only ran faster, heading straight for Daddy's grave. When I got there, I dropped to my knees and leaned my forehead against the stone. I cried out of anger over Mama not believing what I'd said, and then I cried about her taking his side over mine. And, I missed Daddy, his closeness. Mr. Fowler tested loyalties and I felt betrayed. All of it came pouring out, but instead of feeling better when I finally quit, I felt worse. I stared down at my poor, soot-covered willow branch. I was going to keep it anyway. I wasn't ever going to throw it away.

I spoke out loud. "Things sure are different now you ain't here."

I stared toward the cotton fields, and my chest hitched again. It felt like I'd cried enough tears to drench an acre. If only that were possible, I'd have cried an ocean in order to save us all.

Chapter 16

Aunt Ruth pulled into our drive in the blue Buick she'd had for years, arm hanging out of the window and waving with enthusiasm. She was the distraction we needed, and as she climbed out and stretched, I was again reminded how much she resembled Mama, only a little taller. Mr. Fowler upon finding out Aunt Ruth was arriving today had decided he'd spend the time buying what was needed for the irrigation. He would be gone most of the day. I wished her visit would keep him away for as long as she was here, but that was a pipe dream.

She and Mama did that thing, grabbed hands and started jumping up and down while going in a circle and laughing. They had to stop to catch their breath after a few seconds. Aunt Ruth stood with her hands on her hips to study me and my brothers before hugging each of us in turn.

She said, "My word, you all have grown like weeds."

Her manner of speaking was more precise, as if her teaching mode was never turned off. She grabbed Ross's arm and playfully pulled him around to the back of the car to help her get what she'd brought. He lifted out the expected and welcome crate filled with jars of spiced peaches. She gave Mama a soft brown paper package, tied with string, likely a pretty material for something she could make. She gave Trent her suitcase, and to me, she handed a box filled with magazines and books. Mama's favorite, *Good Housekeeping*, was on top.

We headed inside, and once we got into the kitchen and set things down, Aunt Ruth grew teary eyed.

She said, "Oh, Olivia, I'm so sorry about Lloyd. You know how much I cared about him."

Mama couldn't speak since it was still too hard to talk about Daddy as a memory. She drew a handkerchief from her apron and dabbed at her eyes. Ross and Trent shuffled their feet, while my eyes welled up and spilled over. Aunt Ruth hugged Mama hard, and after a few seconds she let her go.

Mama blew her nose and said, "God, it was awful. He was in so much pain."

Aunt Ruth shook her head. "I can't hardly bear to hear it. Lloyd was such a good man. You know, I got to thinking about the time I was about seven and you were five."

Mama nodded. "Jimmy Flynn."

Aunt Ruth said, "Yes. He barely got nipped by some kind of snake, I'm not sure if they ever knew, but my word. How his arm swelled up and turned color."

"I remember."

Whoever this Jimmy Flynn was, he must've died.

Curious, I said, "What happened to him?"

Aunt Ruth said, "They amputated his arm. All the way up to the shoulder."

I said, "He didn't die?"

Aunt Ruth shook her head. I wished what happened to Jimmy Flynn had happened to Daddy. He might not have had an arm, but he'd still be here.

Aunt Ruth sighed, and pointed out the window. "I see the fields got planted. The neighbor you mentioned?"

Mama nodded. "Yes." She cleared her throat and said, "Frank's been a godsend."

I shifted, and Ross coughed into his hand.

Trent said, "He sure has got a lot of money."

Aunt Ruth quickly picked up on Mama's use of his first name. "Frank, huh?"

Mama flipped her hand, dismissing any meaning behind it. She got her cigarettes, lit one up, and Aunt Ruth stuck out a hand, wiggling her fingers.

Mama frowned and said, "Since when did you start smoking?"

Aunt Ruth said, "Since I started back teaching sixth grade instead of fourth."

She smiled at me knowing I was going into the sixth grade, while Mama handed over a cigarette and the matches.

Ross grumbled his opinion of Mr. Fowler. "He's real good at telling us what to do, that's for sure."

Mama gave him a warning look while Aunt Ruth's expression was curious. "I remember you saying you had a neighbor, but didn't really know him."

"Yes, before Lloyd's accident, we didn't see him much."

Aunt Ruth regarded Mama like a cardinal looking for food, tilting her head, examining her closely. I wanted to tell her how hateful he was, but Mama kept talking like she needed to get ahead of herself with some sort of explanation.

She said, "We spotted him a time or two in town, or in one of his fields when we'd drive by the place. He was just always busy, I suppose."

Trent said, "He's got a lot of land. A lot more than us. About a thousand acres."

Ross said, "Ain't nobody cares about that but you."

Trent shoved Ross, and before they could get into one of their tussles, Mama said, "Boys," and then continued, "he noticed the fields weren't planted. That was on account of Slater's Supplies had quit allowing credit on purchases. If it hadn't been for him, we wouldn't have a crop this year."

Aunt Ruth was looking a little bewildered. "You never said a word about that when we talked, Olivia."

Mama said, "There was no need for you to worry. I handled it."

"But . . . why didn't you tell me?"

"What could you have done?"

"I could've helped!"

Mama said, "Lord have mercy, I know you ain't forgot how much it takes to run a farm, have you? It takes a lot of money, even one this size."

"But, to take from a stranger?"

Mama breathed out heavy and said, "I didn't see as it's much different than credit at Slater's. Oh, sure, I suppose we could have gone without the crop. I'd already taken in sewing, done some ironing again, working my fingers till they were numb and it wasn't enough. Sonny could've sold some of the vegetables out of the garden along with the eggs. Ross could've got him a part-time job. It wouldn't have been enough."

"What about the bank?"

"We're already carrying a large note. We borrowed against the house a few years ago when we'd had a bad year. Lloyd only just said we didn't need to get in any deeper with it."

"But . . ."

"I did the best I could."

Aunt Ruth said, "I'm just a little surprised is all."

Mama waved an arm toward the windows. "Weather sure hasn't helped."

Aunt Ruth shook her head. "No. I can see that."

Mama said, "Frank's decided we ought to irrigate a few acres."

Aunt Ruth said, "Hm."

She finished her cigarette, stubbed it out, and said, "When do I get to meet this helpful neighbor?"

I spoke up. "He's here for breakfast, dinner, and supper, and most times in between."

Her expression almost made me laugh as she raised her eyebrows at me, then even more markedly at Mama.

Mama brushed it off and said, "Ain't nothing wrong with him eating here considering. The least I can do is cook him a meal."

I said, "Meals."

Mama ignored me and said, "You'll meet him soon enough, I reckon. I asked him to come for supper tonight."

Aunt Ruth said, "I can't wait."

I couldn't wait to see what she thought of him. Aunt Ruth was blunt and said what most people thought but were afraid to say. I'd seen her and Mama butt heads a time or two in the past when she came to visit, though it didn't happen often.

She looked at me and smiled. "Are you and I bunking together?"

I liked her being in my room with me. "Yes!"

Mama said, "Boys, get the cot out of the attic."

I grabbed the suitcase from Trent and took it to my room. I loved remembering some of the great conversations we'd had after everybody went to bed. Let's see what she thought about things after I filled her in tonight. I went back out into the hall and watched as Ross pulled on the cord that brought down the attic door. He unfolded the ladder, and climbed up. He handed the cot down to Trent, who carried it to my room and set it by the window. I got extra sheets out of the wardrobe in the hallway, and made it up. Just seeing it in there, and that suitcase by my bed meant it was officially summertime.

I went back into the kitchen where Mama and Aunt Ruth sat at the kitchen table catching up. Sometimes I wished I'd had a sister when Ross or Trent got to acting foolish, and I found myself smiling a little bit even though I had no idea what they were really giggling about. Mama eventually got up and filled the metal ice trays, then washed out a set of small glasses she kept in the top cabinet. Aunt Ruth set them on a silver tray she'd just polished.

She held it up to eye level, checking out the shine she'd given it while commenting, "This was Mama's favorite piece."

Mama nodded and said, "It sure was."

Aunt Ruth took it to the living room and Mama took the tablecloth she'd soaked in starch out of the freezer. I used a Pepsi bottle with a rubber sprinkler top and shook water in droplets onto the frozen material when needed. There was something satisfying about pressing the hot iron to the cold cloth. I especially liked hearing the little spitting noise the iron made as I worked to remove the wrinkles. Steam rose up, and the scent of starch was as fresh as cut grass.

Mama came by occasionally as I moved sections of it around the ironing board, telling me, "Don't forget that corner" and "There's a spot there."

She helped me carry it and place it just so on the table. The final touch was when I went outside to cut some of her white peonies. I arranged them in a pretty crystal vase, and set it in the middle of the table. I stood back a little and stared at the setting, and considered its overall appearance. Fancy. Like when Preacher Moore would sometimes come to eat Sunday dinner. Mama was going to put out a big meal just like for those occasions. She'd already fried the chicken and had bowls filled with rice, gravy, and the purple hull peas I'd shelled on the porch earlier. There was a plate of cucumber strips and tomato slices, so pretty and colorful. She'd made two pitchers of sweet tea and they sat chilling in the refrigerator. She'd made a chocolate pie with meringue and it was on the counter.

Trent and Ross hovered about like unwanted

flies at a picnic, their hair still wet from cleaning up.

Mama said, "Can't you two find something to do? If you're not helping, out of the kitchen."

They drifted off with minor grumbling to go listen to the radio on the back porch. Aunt Ruth had gone to take a bath, and when she came out, Mama took one. They both had dresses, freshly starched too. Mama's was pink, and Aunt Ruth's was blue. I wore a dress that was one of Daddy's favorites. It had a white collar, and was pale yellow. Mama said it went real nice with my hair, which I'd braided into two pigtails and tied white bows on the ends. I loved getting dressed up. I pulled on a pair of anklet socks with lace, and finally, my spit shined black Mary Janes. They made a clopping sound like a horse's hooves as I went down the hallway. I stepped into Mama's room where she was in her bra and slip, sprinkling talcum powder in the crease of her bosoms.

I said, "Mama, can I use some of your perfume?"

She spritzed it in the air and said, "Walk through it," which I did.

It smelled of peaches, a bit of cinnamon, and other things I couldn't quite pinpoint.

"Which one is it?"

Mama said, "It's Youth Dew by Estée Lauder."

Daddy had given it to her for her birthday a

couple years back. I noticed she was almost out, and regretted asking her to share it.

Mr. Fowler showed up at six o'clock, hair tonic holding every strand of hair in place for a change and wearing a dress shirt like he was attending a church service. Each time he moved, the aroma of his aftershave, or whatever it was he wore, drifted my way, and after a while, I started to get a little headache between Mama's perfume and that. Daddy never wore that sort of stuff. He smelled like rain and hay. Wind and dirt. He smelled of the outdoors, the scent I love best.

Ross and Trent had followed Mr. Fowler inside, so now everyone was crowded into the kitchen, which was a bit steamy still from all the cooking earlier on. In a matter of seconds, Mr. Fowler's forehead beaded up with sweat. Nervousness or awkwardness was not what I expected out of him, but that had to be the reason he kept tugging at the collar cinched around his neck, and clearing his throat. Mama made quick introductions. He offered Aunt Ruth a brief handshake before he stuffed his hands back into his pockets.

After the introductions, Mama said, "Frank, would you like a cocktail?"

Relief melted his features into something almost pleasant. "Sure, sure, that would be real nice."

Aunt Ruth wagged a finger and said, "Follow

me," and Mr. Fowler went along with her like a puppy being led away on a leash, docile and meek.

Mama pointed at my brothers and me, and said, "Go on. Get yourselves in there and be polite."

We filed into the living room behind them where Mr. Fowler acted like a different person, his voice low-key, soft and he barely made eye contact with Aunt Ruth. She mixed him a drink and gave it to him with a little linen napkin. She mixed two more and told me to take one to Mama in the kitchen. I did, and Mama grabbed at it, took a big swallow and then scrunched her face like she'd just sucked on the lemon Aunt Ruth just used.

She lowered the glass and said, "Whew," licked her lips and then took another, bigger sip. It must've been better the second time since she didn't make a face. I went back to the living room to find Aunt Ruth studying Mr. Fowler from over the rim of her glass. I kept waiting for witty conversation to begin like she'd have done with Daddy, but she didn't have much to say. Mama breezed in, pink cheeked, and looking so pretty if Daddy could've seen her, he'd have jumped up and danced her around. The living room slowly filled with a blue haze of cigarette smoke, while a beam of sunlight filtered through the parted curtains, and reminded me of when the sun breaks through a hole in the clouds.

My headache grew. Mama got to talking up a storm about the drought, about the cotton, about Daddy, about anything she could think of, clearly nervous too. A few minutes passed and the adults sipped on their cold drinks some more. Soon things loosened up and the conversation flowed more naturally.

Mr. Fowler reached over and jokingly punched Ross on the shoulder in a playful manner, earning him a confused look before he aimed his thumb in my direction and said to Aunt Ruth, "This gal here's got herself a unique talent. I went and bought her the real deal. Copper rods. What I'll call no fail rods."

He chuckled in a way I'd never heard.

Aunt Ruth said, "That's real nice, but, Sonny, what happened to that willow branch of your daddy's?"

I said, "It got ruined."

Mr. Fowler said, "She'll have that brand-new one I bought her. Won't be no different."

Like he hadn't spoken, I said to Aunt Ruth, "I found it in the burn barrel."

Aunt Ruth said, "How on earth did it end up there?"

Mama said, "By mistake, I'm sure."

I said nothing.

Aunt Ruth said, "Well, that's too bad, sugar. I'm sorry. I know how special it was to you."

"Yes, ma'am."

I'd tell her all about it later, I was sure. Mr. Fowler changed the subject and I was actually glad.

He said, "We planted a new type of cotton. Think it would have done real good if we'd had enough rain. We'll put in some irrigation though. That ought to help us out."

There was that *we* and *us* thing again.

Mama shifted in her chair and said, "I sure owe you a debt of gratitude for stepping in to help out."

Mr. Fowler said, "Well, it'll all come out in the wash."

That sounded like something Daddy would say to Mama when they were discussing a problem to ease her mind.

Mama stood, the tone of her voice pitched a little high as she said, "Anybody hungry? I'm sure the biscuits are ready by now."

Mr. Fowler put on a fine display of manners as he stood too, and then made a sweeping gesture with his hands and said, "Ladies."

Aunt Ruth went first, then Mama, then me, followed by Mr. Fowler, with Ross and Trent bringing up the rear.

After everyone found a seat, Mr. Fowler said, "Shall we say the blessing?"

I frowned. He really was putting himself all out there for Aunt Ruth. As we bowed our heads, there was the soft crinkle of paper being unfolded. I didn't dare try and see what it was, but when he smoothly delivered a decent enough blessing, I was sure he'd been reading something.

When it was over, everyone said, "Amen."

After we raised our heads, he kept his hands underneath the table. Mama began passing the bowls left to right and Mr. Fowler leaned off to the side and surreptitiously slipped the paper back into his pocket. The drinks made him a little more easygoing and he got to telling stories about being in the war, waving his butter knife around, to emphasize certain points. I don't think any of us knew he'd fought in WWII, or had any idea he'd been to all those foreign places.

"Yep, I ended up in France, and then in Italy. Fought over there for a while."

Trent was awestruck and even Ross looked a little bit impressed.

Trent said, "What did you do?"

"Drove a tank. Shot up some people."

Mama said, "More crowder peas, Frank?"

He took the bowl and put some on his plate, and handed it back to her.

Ross said, "How did you end up in the Army?"

"Drafted."

Trent said, "Mama, why didn't Daddy get drafted?"

"He had a deferment due to the farm."

Ross looked at Mr. Fowler and said, "But, you had your farm too, didn't you?"

"No. Mother had it. Had a bunch a workers running it. She didn't need me, so I went off and killed me some Nazis."

Mama shifted in her chair while Mr. Fowler took a huge bite of chicken, and tore it off the bone, part of the skin hung out of his mouth. He poked it in and kept chewing.

Trent's eyes lit up, and he sounded a little too eager. "How many did you get?"

Mama said, "Eat, Trent."

Mr. Fowler spoke around the food in his mouth and said, "We won, didn't we?"

Aunt Ruth said, "It's admirable to serve one's country," and then she looked at me. "That's why a lot of women started factory jobs, and some did the family farming too. There was an advertisement for women to come and do the jobs men used to do. They used an icon for the manufacturing jobs known as Rosie the Riveter." She looked at Mama. "We could have been Rosies."

Mama grinned and said, "We sure could have."

Mr. Fowler waved his fork in the air.

He said, "Them women shouldn't have been allowed to do that sort of work. Housework. That's their job."

Aunt Ruth sat back in her chair so hard, it creaked.

She said, "Who was going to do it when most of the men were off fighting?"

Mr. Fowler swallowed and said, "A woman's place ain't in some factory. Too hard for 'em."

"Is that right? Funny, somehow they did it, hard or not. Tell me. What do you mean by hard? Intellectually, or physically, Mr. Fowler?"

Mr. Fowler appeared to ignore the question, even though he was looking right at her. He ran his tongue around the front of his teeth, and made a sucking noise, like he was loosening a piece of meat that got caught. The whole time, he gazed at her with that same look he had for Daniel, his head cocked off to one side. It was plain to see he'd decided something about Aunt Ruth. He didn't much like her or her questions.

Chapter 17

Mr. Fowler stood under the oak tree, his foot propped on the bumper of his truck, drawing hard on the cigarette, enough so his cheeks sucked inwards, and he had to squint his eyes against the smoke he released.

Aunt Ruth leaned against the counter and said, "Well, well, well."

Mama was quick. "Well, what?"

Aunt Ruth said, "He's quite the know-it-all."

Mama had no reaction.

Aunt Ruth went on. "Impatient."

Mama said, "He doesn't seem like that to me."

Aunt Ruth said, "He gets his dander up quick."

"Oh, he's fine, Ruth. He's like most men."

"Lloyd wasn't that way."

Mama sounded sad when she said, "No. He wasn't."

Aunt Ruth looked thoughtful. "Why isn't he married?"

Mama ran water into the sink, added soap, and put the dishes in.

She looked toward the screen door, then back to Aunt Ruth, and lowering her voice, she said,

"How would I know? Sounds like he was in the war and then he came here to work the farm after his mother died. Sh! Here he comes."

He opened the screen door and Mama motioned for him to have a seat. She immediately began serving pie and coffee, hovering at his shoulder, pouring him a cup when she saw it was almost empty. Like she'd have done for Daddy. Aunt Ruth sat quietly sipping from her cup, watching it all. When it came to eating pie, she barely nibbled at her slice. Her earlier comments and questions made me feel better, knowing I wasn't the only one who thought the way I did. He was starting to give me a feeling something was happening I couldn't stop.

Then Mama asked him what happened to his daddy. "My father? Oh. We ain't sure what happened. Mother found him in the barn. Shot."

Mr. Fowler left at nine o'clock, and when the door shut behind him, it didn't take long before Mama and Aunt Ruth found themselves in a little war of their own. Aunt Ruth was only trying to open Mama's eyes a little, wanting her to realize maybe she was a little blinded by how he was, and couldn't see beyond his perfect manners. How funny it was to think so differently about the same person right before our very eyes. Ross and Trent were sprawled on the floor in the living room in front of the TV and the sound of Indians whooping meant they were watching a

Western. They had the volume up, but as time went on, it got pretty loud in the kitchen too. Mama and Aunt Ruth didn't seem to care I was standing right there, drying dishes and stacking them back into the cabinets, and their interaction became like the gunfire on TV, one shooting words, and the other shooting back.

Aunt Ruth started in with, "I'm telling you, there's something to be said for him appearing all of the sudden. He's got something up his sleeve."

"It's only a business deal, Ruth. We agreed he'd get part of the profits and that's why he's sticking around, to see it through."

"That's not all he wants."

"Oh, Ruth! Really!"

"Yes, really!"

Mama said, "You're always jumping to conclusions. Why can't someone simply be helpful?"

Aunt Ruth said, "I see what I see."

"Your eyes need checking."

"Rather convenient for him, you here all alone."

"I'm not alone. The kids, remember?"

"You know what I mean."

"No, not really."

"Oh, Olivia. Why didn't he ever come over here before Lloyd was gone?"

"I never thought about it, to tell you the truth.

I was too busy worrying about where this farm was headed."

Aunt Ruth gave her an exasperated look. Daniel's voice echoed in my head again, hinting at the same thing as Aunt Ruth. I couldn't imagine this. I hoped it wasn't true, but I knew how he acted around her, and how she was around him, wearing lipstick and all.

Aunt Ruth continued, "People have reasons for doing what they do."

Mama said, "Maybe."

Aunt Ruth made a noise. "I'm telling you, you best be careful."

Mama said, "You've always been so suspicious. Can't nobody change your mind once it's made up."

"That's a good trait."

"Not if you're wrong. You ain't been here but half a day, and you've already judged the situation."

"Not true."

"True."

Mama sighed. "Always got to have the last word."

"I'm only trying to get you to see what's going on here. Lloyd's gone. This neighbor who's never bothered to drop in before miraculously shows up. Offers to spend thousands of dollars? What's he doing here all the time? Sonny said he's here for every meal, and more. Doesn't he have his own farm to tend to?"

Mama looked at me like I was some kind of ratfink. She didn't answer. Exasperated, Aunt Ruth grabbed Mama's cigarettes and lit one up. She released the smoke in a manner that reminded me of a bull snorting.

Mama finally said, "He's got workers over there I guess."

"Don't you know? It seems you don't know a lot about him in general. You didn't know he'd fought in the war, even."

"I don't need to know his history. All I need to know about is this farm, and how to make ends meet."

"That's being naïve."

Mama stopped washing the dishes, and faced her sister. "You're always so self-righteous. You see things your way, and that's it. You've never married either. What's the big deal about that? All I know is it would have been a lot worse if not for him. Despite that, we're not going to do well, Ruth. That crop's not going to bring in near enough money the way it's looking."

"Which is why, if it had been me, I wouldn't have gotten myself tangled up with him to begin with. Now you've got not only your bills to pay, but him too. You've dug your hole even deeper and you can't see it?"

"What would you have done?"

"Not this."

And then Mama dropped an even bigger bombshell. "Let me tell you something. This is exactly why Lloyd married me instead of you."

All movement ceased. Mama put her hand to her mouth. Aunt Ruth dropped her eyes and stared at the floor. I don't know exactly what I'd expected to come out of this evening, but I sure hadn't anticipated that. I didn't know who to look at. Mama bit her lip, looking like she regretted what she'd said, while Aunt Ruth looked hurt.

Mama said, "I'm sorry, I shouldn't have said that," and then she said to me, "and, Sonny, you shouldn't have heard it."

Aunt Ruth brushed it off, and acted indifferent, although there was a sheen to her eyes that said otherwise. "What difference does it make? That was all a long time ago."

Mama's voice was filled with regret as she said, "Yes. Yes it was."

Aunt Ruth's voice had gone soft in a tired, beaten down sort of way. "I think I'll turn in. It's been a long day."

Even though they hugged good night, I could tell that might have been exactly why Aunt Ruth ended up in Rocky Mount. The fact she'd never married herself said a lot too. Had she loved Daddy so much no one else after was good enough? Mama wasn't the only one who'd lost weight. Aunt Ruth had too, and maybe it was for the same reasons. Mourning his death.

I said, "I'm gonna go to bed too."

I hugged Mama, and followed Aunt Ruth down the hallway. I was feeling a bit uncomfortable knowing this about her.

I couldn't look at her when I said, "You use the bathroom first. I'll wait."

She grabbed her cosmetic case and left the bedroom.

I picked up Dolly and whispered in her ear, "Boy oh boy. What a mess. Wait till I tell Daniel."

When she came back in, she had on her night-gown and housecoat. She had smeared cold cream on her face, and had pinned her hair up. Usually she'd joke with me about how she looked, or grab me and try to rub her face on mine, but tonight, she sat on the edge of the bed, looking serious.

Her words precise, she said, "I would like to read some, if you don't mind me keeping the light on?"

I shook my head and said, "No, Aunt Ruth, that's fine."

I went off to brush my teeth and when I came back, she wasn't reading. She held the book in place but her eyes weren't on the page. She didn't say anything though, so I climbed underneath the cool sheets on the cot and closed my eyes. I was tired, but I wanted to tell her I agreed with what she was saying and what she was thinking. I also wanted to tell her about what Mr. Fowler had done, and what I *thought* he'd done. And, then there was the whole thing with Daniel. I was bursting with what I had to share, and I wanted her to give me permission to talk to her, but she didn't. I rolled over on my side and thought about her and Daddy. Had it been the two of them first? Or had Aunt Ruth loved him, but he'd chosen Mama over her instead?

It wasn't long before she turned off the light and said, "Good night, Sonny."

Disappointed, I said, "Good night."

The next morning I woke up and realized I was lying crooked, with one leg hanging off the cot while a warm hand brushed my hair off my forehead. It was early, the sun not quite up yet. I turned over and looked at Aunt Ruth who sat in a chair by me, staring out the window.

Her hand came to rest on my arm, and I leaned up on my elbows. "Aunt Ruth?"

"Hey, sweetie, I hated to wake you, but wanted to let you know I was leaving a bit early."

"But, you just got here!"

"I know."

We stared at one another for a few seconds, and I said, "It was what Mama said."

She lifted a hand, and let it drop. "That all happened a long time ago."

"I know, but . . ."

I was afraid to ask about it. It wasn't none of my business 'cause it was an adult subject, as Mama would have said.

Aunt Ruth looked at me with patience. "But what?"

"Did you and Daddy date?"

Aunt Ruth looked away and said, "Well, it was more than that. We were engaged once."

I actually squeaked when I said, "You were?"

"Um-hmm. We were in the same grade. A thing through most of high school, you could say."

"What happened?"

"Oh, I don't know exactly. Your mama's right. I am opinionated. We broke up, and he started dating your mama a few months later. She's always been so easygoing, less of a tyrant than me." She gave a little laugh. "I guess she just suited him better. And besides, if not for them marrying, well, then I wouldn't have you, or Ross, or Trent. I am not unhappy at all about that!"

"But you've always been unhappy about what happened with you and Daddy?"

"Well. I did think he was real special."

"Aunt Ruth?"

She sort of laughed and said, "Sonny?"

That was our funny little thing.

"You're right about him."

"Who?"

I rolled my eyes. "Mr. Fowler, who do you think?"

She said, "Ah. Want to tell me?"

Once I got to talking I began listing everything fast as I could.

"He treats Mama real nice, but he calls Daniel names, like flit, whatever that is. Everybody got into a big scrap the other day when he made fun of me and my dowsing after I couldn't find water. Daniel stuck up for me, and Mr. Fowler hit him, and then Ross knocked him down, and Mama got real mad at us, but not him! And he's the one who started it! I also think he's the one who stuck my willow branch in the burn pile out of pure meanness. I don't like him at all."

Hearing myself ramble on and on made everything sound overly dramatic and I was afraid I sounded like a spoiled brat who was complaining when I ought to be appreciative of all he'd done.

Aunt Ruth brushed a strand of hair back off of my forehead, and she said, "Sonny, you'll always compare everyone to your daddy, you know that, right? No one will ever measure up to him in your eyes. And it's true, there are adults who have no idea how to act around children and I would agree with you, he's one of them. I don't think he knows how to act right around adults either, for that matter."

I took a breath, and let it out. "You ought to see

his house. It looks like a museum on the inside. I didn't like it when Daddy and I went over there. He had wallpaper that showed animals being killed."

She hugged me and said, "Keep in mind, your mama's smart. She's always thinking about you kids. You need to trust her."

With that, she picked up her suitcase, and turned to leave the room.

"Oh, and Sonny, one last thing."

"Ma'am?"

"You know I teach about science and all, right?"

I nodded.

"You probably couldn't find water with this drought. The water tables are really low. Remember?"

My eyes filled. I didn't want her to go for one thing and now she'd given me hope. Memories of her past visits started flashing through my mind, how it had been making homemade ice cream under the oak tree. How Daddy, Ross, and Trent would take turns cranking the handle until it wouldn't move, and how Mama would lift out the wooden paddle and we would gather around using our fingers to scoop ice cream off and then eat as much as we could hold, bowlful after bowlful. I could almost smell the hamburgers and hot dogs on the grill, and feel the warm night air as we sat on the back porch to watch fireflies flickering, pinpoints of yellow light like tiny candles underneath the trees. Aunt Ruth made the sweetest, best lemonade. She had a loud, infectious laugh. I liked how she walked with a long stride, and swung her hands in a carefree manner. Aunt Ruth's visits were part of our summer, and now she was leaving after just getting here. There was a finality to the precisely tucked bedspread, as if she'd never slept there, and her decisiveness about leaving was as if she believed she was unwelcome, all 'cause of Mr. Fowler. If I had to say there was something Mr. Fowler was good at, it was driving everyone away.

I lay on the cot, miserable knowing she'd been extra quiet, not wanting to wake me until the last minute so I couldn't argue about it.

I said, "Wait."

I got up and threw on the work clothes I'd had on before changing into my dress. I didn't care about the dirt stains on the knees, or the dribble of chocolate milk down the front of my shirt. I didn't bother to brush my teeth or my hair either as I hurried down the hallway with her, leaning my head on her shoulder for as long as I could. Mama was in the kitchen pouring cups of coffee, and without a word, she handed Aunt Ruth one of the cups. The thing that had been said, long past, yet still hurtful, had grown into something even bigger now when Mama's eyes landed on Aunt Ruth's suitcase. She looked offended, but so did Aunt Ruth. She drank the cup of coffee without a word, gave Mama a quick hug good-bye, me one last smile, and then she walked out.

I stood on the back porch, watching her car roll down our driveway just as a sliver of orange broke the horizon, signaling another sweltering day. She put her arm out and waved at me. I lifted my hand and waved back, and sat with a dejected flop on the porch swing. Mr. Fowler's presence was always causing some sort of commotion, either directly or indirectly. It made no sense why Mama couldn't see this.

Chapter 18

Aunt Ruth had been gone only a couple of days when the mail carrier gave a quick honk in the late afternoon, which signaled there was a package. Mama went out to the mailbox and came back in carrying a box and wearing a smile.

"Look what I have!" she said in a cheerful voice she'd been using, doing what Ross called "putting lipstick on a pig," and trying to make it appear everything was just fine.

I'd tried to call Daniel to talk to him about what I'd found out, but he was never at home, and I could picture him sitting over at his elderly neighbor's, stuffing himself on cookies and watching movies with her. I resented the fact he'd not bothered to try and call me at all. Mama handed the box to me with the name of some company I'd never heard of stamped in the upper left-hand corner.

She said in a singsong voice, "I bet I know what this is."

I did too. I dreaded opening it up, and sort of sat there staring at it.

Ross said, "Want me to cut the tape?"

I nodded. He took out his pocketknife and cut through it, and then stood back. It appeared everyone was waiting on me. I lifted the top and pulled back the paper. Inside were two copper L-shaped rods. They looked nothing, nothing like the willow branch.

Mama said, "Well, they're certainly official like."

I picked them up and looked them over, holding each one a little awkwardly.

Trent said, "Boy, you sure are gonna look even more weird walking around outside with them shiny things."

For once, he was right. I *was* going to look weird. Underneath the shipping paper was a small booklet that showed how you were supposed to hold them. Like pistols, with the short ends in your hands, the long ends pointing out straight. I read further, and according to the instructions, the ends would cross one over the other, making an X if you located water, oil, or whatever it was you thought you should try and find. I found this odd. We'd only used the willow branch to find water, while the booklet suggested for you to "have fun!" and hinted at it being like a magic trick. I quickly dropped them back into the box.

Mama said, "That's real nice, don't you think, Sonny? Frank's trying to get along, and make things right in his own way. Make sure you thank him when you see him."

I said, "Yes, ma'am."

Ross said, "Don't you want to try them? See if they'll work?"

"Not right now."

Mama said, "She will, maybe later, right, Sonny? Now, don't forget to thank him."

I sighed and stared at the copper rods, uncertain if I'd find water with them no matter what Aunt Ruth said. It was as if Mr. Fowler was telling me in his typical underhanded way what I did was only a game, a hoax, or, like the instructions hinted at, a magic trick. In other words, not real.

I picked up the box and said, "I'm gonna go put them in my room so I don't lose them."

Mama tapped a cigarette out of her pack and said, "Good idea."

On my way, I considered detouring out to the backyard and dropping them down the well. I didn't want a stinking thing from Frank Fowler, but doing something like that was too chancy. He was liable to ask me to get them, and then what would I say? I went into my room where Dolly eyed me from her spot on the bed.

I spoke out loud to her, holding up the box. "What you reckon I'm supposed to do with these?"

She gave me a blank stare, and I said, "Exactly."

I opened the closet door, and shoved them way into the back. I didn't care what anybody said. I wouldn't never use them.

Soon as I saw Mr. Fowler, I quickly thanked him as Mama had asked. I wanted it over and done with so I could go on and forget about them.

"Did you try them?"

"Not yet."

"They cost me a pretty penny."

I didn't know what to say to that, so I repeated my thank-you again.

Mama said, "Maybe you could try this evening, after your chores are done?"

I played with my ponytail. I wanted to make Mama happy, but it wasn't like I could snap my fingers and it happened.

I was cautious when I replied, "I might."

I hoped something would come up or they'd forget. His idea to buy them was his own doing, and I didn't feel obligated to entertain him. I was sure he'd only wanted the opportunity to do what he was best at, point out how he'd been right all along about my not really having any ability to find water. I could hear him now.

"See? Even with them special rods I bought her, she ain't able to do it."

Oddly enough it was Trent who saved me. By nightfall, he wasn't feeling well, and Mama's attention turned to nursing him. When she announced he had a high fever, Mr. Fowler, worried he'd catch whatever it was, hightailed it back to his place. He called the next morning to see if "the coast was clear," and Mama said, "Not yet. Give it another day."

I could only imagine what Operator Eunice must've thought at their choice of words, about how Mrs. Creech and Mr. Fowler had "something going on."

I didn't want Trent to be sick, but I will admit, I wasn't wishing for his fever to go away either, no matter what anybody thought of the phone calls. I tried Daniel again and finally, he answered. I told him about my burned-up willow branch, and how I was certain it had been Mr. Fowler.

"He did it, Daniel, I know he did."

"Yeah."

"Can you believe it?"

"Yeah, I can."

I also told him about the new dowsing rods and about Aunt Ruth. "There's a lot you been missing!"

Daniel said, "That's something about your aunt and your daddy."

"Yeah."

"You reckon them rods are gonna work?"

"I don't know. I don't really care. I ain't using them."

His voice grew cautious. "Why not?"

"I just ain't."

"Ain't you curious? What if they worked?"

I'd never considered that possibility.

"Why don't we meet near the pond? We'd have to be careful. Mr. Fowler's been out there checking on the irrigation."

"Nah. I can't."

"Why not?"

Silence.

"Oh, come on. Just cut down that path on Turtle Pond Road that leads to the back field, and I'll meet you by that huge pine tree. Say around four o'clock?"

I was being pushy, which Daniel hated.

"He could show up all of the sudden, like you said. He might as well be living over there as it is anyway. It's like he owns the place."

"Geez, don't say that!"

"It's true, ain't it?"

"I don't want to think about it."

Daniel was quiet, and I was quiet. I was sort of aggravated now, and about to tell him to forget it, that I had to go, when he said, "Maybe I'll come tomorrow."

My heart skipped a beat—or three. "You will?"

"I ain't promising. I'll try."

That was enough for me. After we hung up, I ran into my room and grabbed Dolly off the bed. I danced around with her, excited, even if it meant taking a chance.

I thumbed through the Sears catalog while sitting by the phone, and after Mama went by a time or two, she finally said, "Sonny, what are you doing?"

"Nothing."

"How about you go check on them hens. Get them eggs up."

"Yes, ma'am."

Like she did sometimes, she guessed exactly what I was doing. "If Daniel calls, I'll let you know. Don't you two be up to nothing. He ain't allowed to come back over here yet."

"No, ma'am."

How Mama figured this stuff out was anybody's guess. No sooner was I in the chicken coop bent over and reaching under a stubborn hen when she hollered out the back door, "Phone!"

I ran back across the yard, and slowed down to a walk when I got up on the porch so I wouldn't look too eager. When I went by Mama, she raised an eyebrow in warning. I kept my answers to Daniel cryptic.

He said, "I reckon I'll come, if you still want."

"Okay."

"At the pond?"

"Yes."

"I'll be there in about an hour."

"Okay."

I went back outside, adopting a certain non-chalance as I passed by Mama who was now sweeping the back side of the porch. I quickly gathered the eggs, took them into the kitchen, and set the basket on the counter, then went to my room for the copper rods which would make my trip to the pond legitimate.

As I passed Mama, I held them up. "I'm gonna go down to the pond to look at the new irrigation, and to try out the rods."

She looked as if she approved.

She smiled and said, "Frank will be glad you've tried them."

"Yes, ma'am."

I walked down the tractor path slow but when I got out of sight of the house, I took off running fast as I could, my feet smacking against the dried dirt, and stirring up the dust. Once there, the usual peacefulness was replaced by the rackety generator and pump working nearby, squirting water out of the pipes laid along the rows. We'd have to move it all again tomorrow. Mr. Fowler bought enough pipework to wet about five acres at a time, which meant by the time we'd done all fifty over the course of a few days, it would be time to move everything all over again.

In the long run, I supposed I'd rather have it than not, even if it had been expensive. We'd worked too hard to see it all go to waste. I pulled off my penny loafers, set the copper rods down beside me, and sat with my feet hanging off the edge of the dock, my toes skimming the coolness. Before too long Daniel came into view, his bike bumping along the uneven path causing the fender to rattle. I was unexpectedly shy. I gave him a little wave, and he returned it. He coasted over, getting close to me, while his eyes darted about like he thought Mr. Fowler might be hiding somewhere. In the distance I could hear the generators working the irrigation over at his place too, and it seemed no matter where I went on the farm, there were reminders of his presence everywhere.

I spoke first. "Hey."

"Hey."

He straddled his bike, holding onto the handlebars like he was thinking about leaving.

I looked over my shoulder at him again and said, "Ain't you gonna come and sit down?"

It was like we'd forgot once again how to act around one another. He sighed, and got off, knocking the kickstand into place. He dropped down beside me with a thud, and we were quiet for a few minutes, watching where fish and turtles kissed the surface, creating small circular ripples, some close enough to reach my toes. The tree frogs were going crazy, their noise competing with the cicadas and the nearby equipment. The smell of pond water mixed with the sweet odor of wild grapes growing thick and heavy, their vines creeping along the tree trunks, allowing the fruit to hang thick from the branches. Birds, deer, and anything else that could get to them ate them up almost as quick as they could ripen.

I wished I'd thought to grab a handful to eat while I waited 'cause they'd be gone before too long.

After a while, I said, "What's been going on over at your place?"

Daniel rolled his eyes. "The usual. Except one thing happened I ain't told nobody about yet."

"What's that?"

"Sarah's gone."

"What?"

"Yeah. Brenda said she's done run off with some man."

"Gosh, Daniel!"

I didn't know how to react since it was the most unlikely thing for him to have said.

He shrugged and said, "Ain't like it's no surprise it happened, considering how boy crazy she is. She falls in love with anyone who looks at her twice."

I remembered her crush on Ross.

"Have y'all heard from her?"

"Once. She called and said she was in Georgia."

"Did your mama call the police?"

Daniel looked at me like I was crazy.

"Brenda said she's on her own, said she's sixteen, and far as she's concerned she's made her bed, now she can lie in it."

"Oh."

"Yeah. Sarah's just as hardheaded. She ain't called since."

261

I didn't know what to make of Daniel's news. We sat quiet until he changed the subject.

He pointed at the copper dowsers. "You tried them newfangled rods yet?"

"No. I only brought'em so Mama wouldn't think I was up to something."

We were sitting close enough so that our shoulders touched if one of us moved a certain way. Eventually I leaned into him like I was trying to push him off, and he returned the pressure. We kept it up until we both got to giggling. It relieved the stiff awkwardness and took away the unease we'd initially had with each other.

I said, "Wanna go swimming?"

Daniel gave me an assessing sort of look, then broke the gaze and said, "Nah. I don't feel like it."

"Oh, come on. It's hot."

"You can. I'm not."

"Well, it ain't no fun to swim alone."

Daniel looked uncomfortable. Feeling a bit put out, I stood up and removed my T-shirt and shorts.

Daniel said, "Geez, Sonny!"

"It ain't like I'm naked. I got on an undershirt and my underwear."

"Well. It ain't right."

"What ain't right?"

"Being out here with no clothes on."

"We've done it before without anything on at all. Come on, dare you!"

Daniel hated when I threw out the dare 'cause then he had to step up or put up with me the rest of the day. He shivered, and then made a face like he would when he was confronted by something he didn't like. Where was the Daniel I knew? The boy who did whatever I wanted, who challenged me, who made me laugh at his carefree, funny antics? His change of behavior made me self-conscious. I crossed my arms and sat balled up.

I said, "Gosh. Not even a dare will do it? Since when did you get to be so prissy?"

He glared at me. "Don't say that."

Seizing on his reaction, I slapped my hands against the wood, and yelled with glee, "Prissy! Through and through!"

He grabbed for me, but I jumped to my feet and into the water, feeling sure he'd follow. I popped up to find him still standing on the dock giving me that same hard look. I couldn't let well enough alone.

"Ooooh, I'm scared of Mister Prissy Pants!"

I swiped water in his direction, and even though it hit him, he didn't move. He stayed in the same spot with his fists clenched.

He went red at my name-calling, and yelled, "Shut up!"

I shouted the name again, and when he yanked off his shirt and jumped in, I hollered victoriously. He lunged for my arm. I shrieked.

I yelled out, "Prissy pants!"

He dove underwater, and I screamed again, excited and afraid at the same time. I kicked hard to get away, but I wasn't quick enough. He grabbed at my legs and pulled me under. He held me underwater, and I sort of thrashed about like I'd done in the past when we were horsing around, and after a few seconds of struggling, I relaxed. That was my signal for surrendering, my way of saying "Uncle!"

Only Daniel didn't let go.

His hands squeezed hard as he gripped the top of my shoulders, his fingers digging into my collarbone. He pushed me down where the water felt cooler, and the clear green turned dark. My hands were on his, trying to pry them loose. I looked up at him through the murkiness, and found he was staring right at me. He didn't look like Daniel at all. The water made his features blurry, and his eyes looked like empty holes.

He used his weight to keep me down, and when I started to struggle again, he rose only enough to allow his head to break the surface. I realized I really, really needed to breathe too. I went to the right, and broke free, got one gulp in, when he grabbed my arm, his fingernails scraping my skin. I quit fighting, and tapped his arm in an urgent way but instead of letting me go, he'd worked himself overhead again and pushed me down once more. I began to fight in earnest. Whatever Daniel thought he was doing, I no longer found it funny. Each time I tried to get out of his grip, he grabbed me somewhere else. I twisted, and turned, went one way or the other and he somehow found another part of me to hold on to.

I'd thought we were only having fun. I'd thought it was just another play fight, and he'd let go, and we'd laugh about it. It was nothing like that, it had turned ugly, and frightening. I grew more violent, my need very real now. I'd run out of air, and through the water, I could still make out Daniel's eyes, dark and wide, looking at me like he hated me. It made me go motionless and we stared at each other through the greenish haze. He let me go. I rose to the surface and gulped in air. I began crying, half-afraid, half-mad, and very confused as I thrashed my way across the pond.

Daniel popped up beside me, and when he reached for me, I screamed, "Get away from me!"

I swam fast as my burning lungs would let me, my arms and legs straining like I was swimming through mud.

He yelled, "Sonny!"

I didn't stop. I was already winded, but I flailed toward the dock, arms churning and feet kicking until I could pull myself up and onto it. I lay on my side, at first choking, then panting while trying to grasp what just happened. Daniel didn't climb up right away. He stayed in the water, peering over the edge as I lay on the wood gasping the way a fish would.

He said, "Sonny?"

I sat up, then I got to my feet. I refused to look at him. I hurried to put my shorts and T-shirt back on. He repeated my name, his voice more desperate, and there was the slosh of water as he pulled himself up. I didn't care until he made a sound that made me stop. I knew that sound. I'd heard it only once before, when we were in second grade and Junior Odom had tripped him. Daniel had hit the floor hard, and split his chin. Blood came but he hadn't cried until our teacher poured peroxide on it right before applying a butterfly bandage.

His back was to me now. I sat down, staring at his wet head, hair down to his shoulders, the curls pulled straight. There was an unnatural movement of his shoulders. The bumps of bone along his spine looked like a long line of delicate pearls as he bent forward, bracing his hands on the edge of the wood. I tentatively reached out, wanting to touch him. I didn't. I withdrew my hand. We didn't talk for a long time. I stared across the pond toward the trees, while we sorted through our thoughts. I couldn't believe Daniel actually tried to hurt me. It was a stifling quiet that stretched on, and part of me began to feel sad, while the other part of me had the image of being held underwater, fighting for air. I was still mad about that. I didn't understand. Daniel finally spoke and when he did, his words hurt worse than what he'd done.

His voice was hoarse as he said, "You ain't no better than Mr. Fowler."

"What? How can you say that?"

"What you called me."

I frowned until I realized what he meant. Stupid me. I understood now why Daniel had reacted like he had. *Sissy boy. Prissy pants.* They weren't so different.

"Daniel, I didn't mean nothing by it."

"You think the same as him. You don't know nothing, nothing at all."

"I don't either think like him! Wait, what don't I know?"

His comment was confusing, while my denial and question sounded phony. I couldn't explain why I'd said it, it was too embarrassing to admit it came down to me wanting him to snap out of the way he'd been acting, like he didn't care whether we were friends or not, like I didn't matter so much to him anymore. I wanted him to stop looking like he had a secret he was keeping from me. I wanted it to go back to like it was. All I'd wanted was a reaction.

"I wasn't thinking. I said the first thing that came into my head, to make you mad."

He exhaled and said, "See? That's what I mean."

I went to put my hand on his shoulder, and he jerked away and I got mad all over again.

"Well, you tried to drown me!"

"You're nuts. I only held you under for a bit."

"A bit? I wished I could do you the same way, and see how you like it."

This time our silence stretched out even longer. I was pretty sure if I could see his face, see his eyes, I wouldn't like what they told me. They'd have that distant look I'd seen him get before when he got to dreaming big. They wouldn't be that unguarded golden-brown color as open and free as the sky above our heads. Instead, they'd be closed off, secretive once again. This new, uneasy stillness emphasized how much had changed since Mr. Fowler showed up, from Aunt Ruth leaving to this ever-growing rift with Daniel and me. Despite this unfamiliar and underlying distrust and anger that separated us, I was certain Daniel would come around eventually. I just had to bide my time.

I sighed, and looked across the pond, and my eyes fell on a spot among the pines to a color that didn't belong. I drew in my breath slow. A sliver of blue stood out against the trunk of a tree, part of a face peering around the edge, a hand going up slow and then back down. A wisp of smoke dissipated in a matter of seconds. I didn't say nothing to Daniel. He was staring down into the water. Mr. Fowler had to see me looking at him, but if he did, he didn't let on. He turned and disappeared through the woods, and the only thing that remained of him having been there was his image in my mind.

Chapter 19

I was sure Mr. Fowler would tell Mama he'd seen me and Daniel at the pond, if only to prove his point we were disobedient. He didn't though, and one afternoon I finally understood why.

It was getting on toward quitting time, and he said, "That boy ain't right. Glad you finally saw the light of day."

"Sir?"

"Down to the pond that day. The little flit and you. What was it you called him? Prissy pants? That suits him too. Best you figured it out now the boy's a little lavender lad if I ever saw one."

There was nothing I could say in my own defense, or in Daniel's. I didn't know what he was getting at, calling him those names. I knocked my boot against a step, and looked away. He kept calling him that and it sounded real ugly. Mr. Fowler went off whistling under his breath while I stewed over the idea he thought I was somehow on his side.

August was slow to come, then it dragged and although Daniel and I talked on the phone, it wasn't the same. Something had changed for him about me, and I wanted to fix it, only he gave me one excuse after the other about not coming over. I wanted Ross to take me into town, drop me off and then come back to get me, but he wouldn't.

"We ain't got gas money to burn up on gallivanting around."

He was harsh when he said it 'cause Mama had said something to that effect about him picking up Addie.

Rain fell one afternoon while we were sitting in the kitchen eating tomato and mayonnaise sandwiches loaded down with salt and pepper. Mama, Ross, and I put ours down and ran outside, looking up toward the sky. It had come too late, but maybe it would help a little. I ran out into the yard and stood in it, and was surprised when Mama followed me. We grabbed hands and spun around, laughing. Mr. Fowler stood on the porch staring while Mama twirled about in her bare feet, a happy look on her face. His gaze was so intent it made me shiver, and I let go of Mama's hands. She put them on her hips and turned her face up to the drops falling, unaware of the way he looked at her. The shower ended as abruptly as it began, and he came down the steps.

He spoke to Mama. "Got to run into town, you need anything?"

Mama, her hair plastered to her head, said, "More rain?"

Mr. Fowler gazed at her with this strange look and said, "If I could get it for you, I would."

Mama stared at him too, while I simmered over this little flirtation. The sun came out almost immediately after, and steam rose from off the road, swirling about like a low-lying fog. For a few minutes, everything carried a wet, damp smell. We looked toward the west where weather tended to come from, at the clouds already breaking apart to show the blue sky. Ross and I drifted back inside while Mama stayed out on the porch looking up at the sky. Trent hadn't budged from the table. He'd eaten his first sandwich and was working on putting together his second. He was scooping mayo out of the jar as we came in. He slapped a big white gob into the middle of a piece of loaf bread and smeared it around.

He said in a matter-of-fact voice, "I knew it was gonna stop. No sense going crazy for nothing. I don't get why everybody's so worked up. We've had bad crops before."

Ross reached over and flipped Trent's hat off his head. "Where have you been? I've seen that little booklet he keeps in his truck, and for every-thing he does, he writes it down. He licks the end of that stupid pencil and then ticks off one more thing to charge to us. There's all the gas he's bought. Parts to fix the tractors, them expensive seeds. The irrigation equipment. It's adding up. We'll be lucky to pay him back one red cent."

Trent said, "Shoot. It ain't like he's gonna kick us out of our house."

Ross and I both stared at him. Mama came in and sat down at the table. She slid her half-eaten tomato sandwich away, and lit a cigarette instead.

Ross pointed a thumb over his shoulder and said, "Do you know exactly how much we owe him?"

Mama said, "Of course I know! How about you let me worry about that?"

Trent said, "I wonder how much cotton we'll get outta them fields. Might be more than we think."

I stayed silent, waiting for an enlightening moment. A plan. A way she'd already thought of, like Daddy used to do when he believed we might have a bit of a squeeze financially. Aunt Ruth had said *trust her,* and I was trying but it wasn't easy when she brought Mr. Fowler into the conversation at every turn, as if all the answers rested with him and his way of doing things.

She cleared her throat and said something that gave me hope. "It has been a tough season. Reckon when we know what we got, we'll figure it out. I can always take in some ironing and sewing most likely, make more jam."

Ross said, "I could maybe get a little of the money we bring in, and plant winter wheat. We could sell that."

Mama said, "Have to see what all we owe first."

Ross nodded and went quiet again.

A few seconds passed, and then from nowhere, she said, "Frank *is* a generous, kind man," as if she were thinking she ought to say it. When the fields were laid bare and there was no crop to tend, would he still eat here, out of habit, or for other reasons? This possibility weighed on me with a heaviness not unlike what I'd experienced when Daddy died. Later on when I was still anxious, I called Daniel like I always did if I was troubled, but then I almost hung up on him after he repeated what he'd said before.

"I'm telling you. He's got it for your mama. You better get used to Frank being around."

I made an angry noise. "Why do you keep saying that? Ain't nobody around here thinking like that except you."

"I guess I don't think about things the same way you do."

"I don't know what that means, Daniel."

"I reckon I don't either."

I sighed. I didn't expect he'd want to sneak over so I didn't ask.

He surprised me by offering. "Want me to come over?"

I almost couldn't answer him. "Yes."

It was late evening as I waited for him on the opposite side of Turtle Pond Road, just out of sight of the driveway. He rolled his bike into a field of cotton, and laid it down so it was hidden well. We counted the rows from the drive to where he'd left it. Ten. We then skirted around the perimeter, stopping to pick our way around briars and to eat some of the blackberries that grew near the ditch. Alongside them he pointed out the big tall clusters of other berries, their magenta vines standing out against the sharp green of their leaves. I was familiar with them 'cause he'd shown them to me before, in that little journal of his, the one with the crudely drawn pictures, and what I'd remembered was the word *POISONOUS*.

Daniel nodded at the clusters of dark purple berries and said, "Phytolacca."

I shook my head.

He said, "Pokeweed."

I said, "Now that I recognize."

He turned to me and said, "Well? What're we gonna do?"

I had a crazy spur-of-the-moment idea to go to Frank Fowler's. "Let's go see how Mr. Fowler's cotton's doing."

Daniel hesitated. "Geez, what for?"

"Just to look at them fields closest to us. Sumbitch is probably got his cotton growing high as the sky."

Daniel nodded, and within a few minutes we were hunched down, peeking from the edge of the woods at Frank Fowler's fields. It made me all kinds of mad to see how good his cotton looked, tall and healthy, but I held a bit of pride too. It wouldn't look like that had it not been for me and Daddy. The sprinkler system worked on a pivot setup Daddy had recommended, and I found the whole process fascinating and infuriating at the same time.

I sighed heavy and said to Daniel, "That sumbitch is sure gonna make himself a lot of money."

Daniel was hunkered down alongside me and he nodded in agreement. "A bunch. Sumbitch."

We looked at each other and for a split second, it was the old way again. Daniel's mouth carried a purplish stain from eating blackberries, and there it came again, a little sparkle of a feeling, that flush of a reaction that happened on occasion without warning, like a sneeze about to come on. I don't know what made me do it. Later on I would excuse it as being out in the sun on a hot day with the scent of late summer in the air, or just plain curiosity.

He was close, only inches away. I was over-the-top happy he'd come without me begging him. My expression must've changed 'cause he leaned toward me, the way you would when you hold up a magnifying glass to study something. He stared like he would when he thought I was about to say something he ought to pay attention to. Without thinking of the consequences, I quickly mashed my mouth against his, trying to mimic what I'd seen in the movie theater when we'd gone and spent a whole Saturday afternoon at the movies watching *Gone With The Wind*. Daniel's reaction was to shove me so hard I fell on my rear end.

He swiped the back of his hand across his mouth and said, "Don't do that. Don't ever do that again."

I was beyond embarrassed.

All I could do was choke out a weak, "Geez. Okay."

My breath came rapid as I fought back tears of humiliation. I hung my head, unable to look at him. I'd set us back to that awkward, strange place we'd found ourselves more often than not. I'd been stupid again. I had an instant thought too; Daniel didn't like me the way I liked him.

I whispered, "Don't you like me, even a little bit, Daniel?"

"Not like that."

"Why not?"

"You're a doggone girl."

His answer sounded like something Trent would say. Maybe he liked somebody else. That created a new feeling, like how I used to feel when Daddy would take the boys off in the truck and leave me behind.

"Do you like somebody else? What's her name?"

Daniel sighed. "You're asking too many questions."

I didn't have time to think more on it. Mr. Fowler was unexpectedly close, too close. I started to raise my head to see where exactly, when Daniel poked a finger on my thigh, warning me with a shake of his head. Mr. Fowler was one row from where we were crouched, and I wished I hadn't worn such a light-colored shirt.

He said, "Godamighty, can't get no goddamn good help."

There was a rustling noise, and someone else spoke. "Doing all we can."

Mr. Fowler and an elderly man with a limp drifted by only a few feet of us. It was Charlie Cummings. I lowered my head as their footsteps came even closer, tensing up, sure we were about to be caught, but instead, they moved farther away, until it was quiet again. I poked my head up a bit to see where they'd gone. Not far enough. We waited some more. Finally, when I was sure I'd have a heat stroke, sprinkles fell on my arm like it was raining, only the sun shone down on us hard, and hot. Irrigation water hit us, and I turned and grinned at Daniel. He appeared to have recovered from my mouth touching his 'cause he smiled back, big and wide. We poked our heads up like gophers to see an empty field.

"Come on!" he said.

We ran up and down the rows, getting soaked, and the effort to stay quiet made it all that much harder not to laugh. Despite what had happened between us, for now we were only best friends once again, and I wished my time with Daniel would last forever.

Chapter 20

We understood what the drought did long before
the cotton was picked. It was obvious by the
small bolls. By Ross's estimation, he thought if
we got half a bale per acre for the dry land, we'd
be lucky, whereas the irrigated fifty acres fared a
little better, but not by much.

Mama said, "I'm afraid there ain't enough
money to buy no new school shoes, least not right
now. You'll have to polish the ones you wore
from last year real good till we see how things
are after we sell some cotton."

She looked almost guilty over this, and her eyes
turned a little misty.

Like Elvis's song, I said, "That's all right,
Mama," but of course I was disappointed.

First day of school I found myself looking at
everyone's feet. I was pretty sure we were the
only ones without the squeak and shine of new
leather. My toes felt pinched, but I'd said nothing
to Mama. The two sixth grade rooms were
located at the other end of the school, in a new
section built off the old. In some ways I was glad
to be back in a classroom, and that was simply

'cause the room was new, plus there was the excitement of being in a higher grade. It would wear off after the first week like it usually did. Our new teacher's name was Miss Young, and that really said it all about her since she didn't look old enough to be teaching. Lucky for her, Junior Odom and Lil Roy were in the other room. They would have done her in on the first day. Happy with them elsewhere, I was upset about the fact Daniel was too.

Everybody knew classes were set up by how we did at the end of each year. As in what grades we'd made. Daniel and I had compared our report cards and we'd both made mostly As, aside from the B I'd made in math, and the one he'd made in English. Junior Odom and Lil Roy had laughed and laughed about how they made mostly Ds and Cs, and maybe even an F.

I didn't understand why he was put in that class with them, and not in mine. I thought about grumpy old Mrs. Baker from last year, and recollected moments where she'd ignored his raised hand. Where she'd given him less than an A even when he'd had all the answers right 'cause she'd point out something silly like his penmanship, or not putting the date at the top of his paper and take off points. Little things like that. We finally saw one another at lunchtime. He walked past the line to get food, and sat in a chair. Becky Hill and Laurie Ward joined us at our usual table, but placed themselves on my side. They spoke to me, but not him.

I leaned into the table and said, "What did you do the rest of the summer?"

He looked at me, and shrugged.

"Did you watch any movies?"

"No."

I sat back. I kept having the same thought maybe what had happened between us had something to do with the change in him, but I couldn't be sure, 'cause every now and then there would be a tiny glimmer of the old Daniel. I was still mad at myself. I shouldn't have ever called him that name, and I really, really shouldn't have tried to kiss him, if that's what it could even be called. I'd made him aware of me in a different way, a way he didn't like.

By mid-September, after we'd been in school about two weeks, out of nowhere, the weather changed. We went from hot and dry, to overcast, and then came an unexpected drop in temperatures and rain to boot. Everyone who had cotton in the fields, irrigated or not, couldn't have been happy when the drought finally broke. The first day it showered, right after school, Ross immediately went out to see about the cotton bolls that had already opened. The rain had picked up at that point and came down in sheets. The wind was blowing it sideways, and when he came back in, he stood by the kitchen door, dripping and wetter than a fish.

He told Mama, "There's a lot of string out. It's pretty bad."

She looked out toward the closest field and shook her head. "Swear to God, if it ain't one thing it's another."

Rain and cotton don't mix. For the bolls that were already opened, the rain on the exposed fiber turned it into a stringy thread hanging off the plant, instead of sitting tight and puffy on the burr. Discoloration was common, and some of it would surely end up on the ground. When seeds within got wet, they could start growing so you'd have little roots inside. All this affected quality, and buyers wouldn't offer the going price. Plus, putting heavy equipment into a wet field, like that fancy picker Mr. Fowler kept talking about, could end up stuck.

Ross said, "Maybe it'll stop soon."

It rained the rest of that day, and the next, and the next. We gathered around the windows and anxiously stared at the fields. Mr. Fowler made a casual comment to Mama but the implications behind it were enormous from my viewpoint.

"Maybe we'll have a better season next year."

It about made me sick to my stomach as I tried to rationalize what he meant. That night I picked at my food and Mama threatened the castor oil.

I blamed it on missing Daniel. "When you gonna let Daniel come over again?"

Mama said, "There's too much going on until we get this cotton up. When we're done, then we'll see."

It wasn't the answer I wanted, but it was better than nothing. I picked up my fork and tried to force myself to eat a few bites.

Mr. Fowler said, "I ain't missed his smart mouth."

I put my fork back down and Mr. Fowler pointed at my plate.

He said, "Better not waste this good meal your mama's fixed."

Like he was my daddy or something. Mama looked at me with such a pitiful expression, I sighed and ate another bite. She smiled with approval, and I figured I'd rather make her happy than spite him.

He leaned toward me, pointed at a window where the rain spattered and sounded like hundreds of fingers tapping. "Hey, reckon you can find water now?"

His explosion of laughter was so startling even Mama jumped.

Trent joined in until Mama said, "Stop it, the both of you."

Mr. Fowler's laugh petered out, and he said, "Damnation, can't nobody take a joke around here?"

Mama looked irritated, and then he leaned closer to her and whispered, "Vi?"

She stared at him, genuinely curious. "What?"

He winked, then tried to grab her hand, only she yanked it away. He grabbed for it again, and she sort of slapped at him, then she laughed. I shot a look at Ross. He watched their playfulness, and he didn't like it any more than I did. Smiling, Mr. Fowler went back to eating, and when he put a bite in his mouth, he looked over at Trent and winked, and Trent grinned like they were in cahoots together.

The weather was so markedly different it was hard to believe we'd been running about barefoot, and in shorts and T-shirts only a few weeks before. At the end of class one day, I gave Miss Young the usual note excusing me the six weeks during the seasonal harvest as I'd done with every teacher ever since I started school.

She gave me some homework and said, "We'll miss you. Come back soon as you can."

"Yes, ma'am."

I went down the long hall, the waxed tiles shined to a gloss by the janitor, Mr. Green, and out the front doors to where Ross and Trent waited in the truck. We drove home, and once we were on Turtle Pond Road, I stared at fields nowhere near as filled with fluffy white cotton as we were used to seeing. The drought first, and then the rain had done a real good job. Even though the harvest would be lacking, it would still take about three to four weeks to be sure we'd got it all. I was anxious to get going. I wanted to know the end result. I wasn't feeling very optimistic as my eyes scanned the beaten-down plants and the pitiful strung out clumps desperately clinging to burrs. Ross stopped along Turtle Pond Road several times to get out and check the fields.

When we got to the house, Mama was at the stove, and he told her what he'd seen. "For them parts we couldn't irrigate, the plants are in pretty bad shape. Some's big, but not as big as they could be. I'm telling you, you ask me, we should a fertilized, and they would a took hold better. They'd have handled the stress from the drought better."

"Says who?"

Like a ghost conjured up out of nowhere, Mr. Fowler appeared on the porch, peering through the screen door.

Ross said, "My daddy, that's who."

Mama was stirring a pot of homemade soup and she gave him a warning look. "Ross."

He persisted and said, "Daddy always said fertilizing was a good thing. I reckon he ought to have known. He studied it. Had a degree in it." Ross pointed at Mr. Fowler and said, "I told him we should."

Mr. Fowler had stepped inside, and was kicking his boots off.

He said, "Nobody never said not to fertilize."

Ross's entire body drew up, and his voice rose in disbelief. "You said that very thing when we hauled them seeds out to the field that day. You said cotton didn't need it 'cause it was made of nitrogen and all, and didn't take it from the soil."

"Son, you calling me a liar?"

"Don't call me son."

"Ross! Please." Mama was near about wringing her hands, and I'd never seen her do that before.

Ross relaxed, and he said, "Sorry, Mama, but what he just said's a lie."

Mr. Fowler said, "That's right disrespectful."

I spoke up. "He did say that. I heard him."

Mr. Fowler went real still. Mama stared at us and then at Mr. Fowler. She was caught between us and him, and I could see it. Like Ross, I relaxed. She would side with us, it was two against one. I was sure of it.

Mr. Fowler said, "You misconstrued my meaning all those months ago."

Mama said, "Maybe you just misunderstood him."

Ross said, "I don't see how. He went through a long explanation about it."

Mr. Fowler insisted. "Y'all are taking what I said out of turn."

Trent came in at that moment and said, "What's to eat?"

Mr. Fowler sat down heavy in a chair and Ross looked anything but happy. Mama turned back to the stove, and once her back was turned, Mr. Fowler got to staring at Ross, and he didn't look away. Ross returned the look. It was like one of those staring contests Daniel and I would do, waiting for the other to blink. Mama busily ladled up bowls of homemade vegetable soup, ignorant of the confrontation behind her. They kept it up until she set the soup down in front of us. She put a platter of biscuits on the table and poured glasses of sweet tea. Finally, she sat, but instead of eating, she lit a cigarette and looked thoughtful.

She blew smoke toward the ceiling and surprised us all when she circled back around with a question to Mr. Fowler. "Did you say not to fertilize?"

Mr. Fowler stopped spreading butter on a biscuit dwarfed by his hand.

He gave her an incredulous look that changed to aggravated. "I thought this was settled." He pointed at Ross with his butter knife and said, "Somebody's trying to stir it up, you ask me."

Ross said, "It's a yes or no question."

Mr. Fowler set the butter knife down carefully. He rose from the table, went over to the peg by the door, got his hat, and slapped it on his head. He jammed his feet into his boots.

Mama said, "Frank. Come on, sit down. Eat."

He opened the door and said, "I ain't getting a sense of appreciation for what I've done around here. These kids don't seem grateful at all."

Mama stood up. "Yes, they are. I know they are." She looked at us sitting in silence around the table and said, "Aren't you? Children?"

What was there to do but say yes?

Trent who'd been slurping on his soup and watching it unfold like it was a TV show, said, "Yes, ma'am."

I said, "Yes, ma'am," too.

Ross didn't. Mama stared at him intently.

"Ross?"

"I appreciate it. But I don't appreciate him changing the story on what he said."

Mr. Fowler threw a hand up.

He said, "Like I said. No appreciation, no respect for that matter, not for nothing done around here."

He slammed out the door, and a few seconds later we heard the truck start and the engine rev a time or two. The smell of exhaust drifted in through the back door as he drove down the drive.

Mama turned on Ross. "You shouldn't have argued with him, Ross."

"But, he's lying! We all heard him."

I nodded in agreement while Trent went wide-eyed and innocent looking.

He said, "Honest, I don't remember."

Ross said, "Yes you do. Don't be sticking up for him."

Just as angry, Trent said, "I ain't. But I ain't stupid enough to bite the hand of the person who's feeding you. That's what Daddy always said."

Trent was right. Daddy had said that.

Mama said, "I declare, ain't there enough to worry about without all this bickering?"

We finished eating in silence. When we were done, Mama went and picked up the phone and asked Eunice to connect her to Mr. Fowler's number. She waited, then hung up. We washed the dishes, and then she tried again. She didn't have to say who she was trying to call. He must've answered finally 'cause she stayed in the hallway with the door shut. Still, I could hear her apology, like she'd done something wrong. After a minute or so, she came back into the kitchen and gestured at Ross, holding the phone out. He got up and went toward her like his feet were lead weights.

He took the phone, scrubbing his hand over his head as he said, "Hello?" and then listened. He tipped his head back to stare at the ceiling.

After another few seconds, he said, "Yes, sir,"

and handed the phone back to Mama. "He wants to talk to you."

Mama took the phone and said, "Yes?"

Her face went beet red. "Oh! Why, that's real nice. Okay, see you tomorrow, then."

I leaned over to Ross. "What did he say to you?"

He muttered, "A lot of what he'd already said here. That I was ungrateful and disrespectful. I wanted to tell him he was a liar and an ass, but . . ."

Mama sat down at the table and lit another cigarette. While she smoked, lost in her own thoughts, I finished cleaning up. Ross went back outside, and disappeared into the barn, while Trent went to watch TV.

She looked tired, and after the scene with Mr. Fowler, I didn't want to bring up something else, only I was curious, and I wanted to get her mind off of him.

"Mama?"

"Hm?"

"Aunt Ruth said her and Daddy were engaged first."

"That's true."

"Didn't it make you feel funny to marry him afterward?"

"No, not really."

"Why not?"

" 'Cause your daddy could take the most awkward of situations, and make it right."

That wasn't at all like Mr. Fowler. He did just the opposite. Couldn't she see that?

She said, "He told her we wanted to date before we actually started."

"Was she mad about y'all getting married?"

"Oh, no. She was my one and only bridesmaid."

Without thinking, I brought it right back to the topic I was trying to avoid. "Daniel thinks Mr. Fowler's got intentions."

Mama gazed at me through the bluish cigarette smoke, and if she thought my comment was surprising, her expression and response remained bland.

She stubbed out her cigarette. "One thing's for sure, I'll always love your daddy."

Like what she'd said about Mr. Fowler being generous, it was the sort of declaration that made me uneasy.

Chapter 21

Mama was quiet the next day and it also didn't go unnoticed Mr. Fowler didn't show up first thing either. I tried to figure out the reasons, but couldn't come up with anything. She cooked supper earlier than usual, and set covered dishes on the back of the stove to stay warm. Then she told us in a *don't ask me any questions* way, he was taking her out for supper, and it all made sense from the night before while she'd been on the phone with him, plus the heightened color to her face after she'd hung up.

When she went to take a bath, I was finally able to hiss at Ross, "I can't hardly believe it!"

He paced the kitchen floor, mumbling the same thing I'd thought. "It ain't been but five months."

Trent said, "Geez, it's only supper."

She stepped out of her room a little later wearing a dress that, although old, had been Daddy's favorite. It had pink flowers on a white background, and was made with material he'd bought her one Christmas. She held a sweater over her arm for the chilly night. Her refusal to meet our eyes confirmed her guilt. I wanted her to feel that way. She patted her hair, which I noticed she wore pulled up in a twist, then checked her lipstick in the mirror of her compact. She smelled of that Youth Dew. Maybe she'd worn his favorite dress and that perfume to remind herself she was still Mrs. Lloyd Creech. She snapped the compact shut when his headlights hit the kitchen window.

Mr. Fowler appeared at the back door, dressed like he'd been when Aunt Ruth was here. He looked as if he was all hepped up over this thing that looked and smelled a lot like a date. I was furious. My arms crossed, I glared at him as he held the back screen door open for her, and I continued to send several less than friendly looks his way as he greeted Mama.

"Vi, you look mighty nice."

"Thank you," said Mama.

He pretty much ignored us while I noted every single thing he did. His hand on her elbow. How he opened the door on the passenger side, and waited for her to sit, then pull her legs in. It was a car I'd never seen, and as shiny as a new quarter. They took off without a wave or a toot of the horn. The three of us watched from the kitchen window until the car disappeared around the curve on Turtle Pond Road.

Ross said, "I will be damned."

I could barely eat supper. Afterward, I washed the dishes and while Ross and Trent watched

TV, I watched the time. Seven o'clock, then eight o'clock came. I placed a collect call to Aunt Ruth.

She sounded half-asleep when she said, "Hey, honey, what's wrong?"

"Hey, Aunt Ruth."

Her voice became more awake. "Sonny, everything okay?"

I hadn't thought about the fact my sudden phone call might send her into a panic. "Everyone's fine, nobody's hurt. I just wanted to tell you something."

"My word, you gave me a start."

"I'm sorry."

"What's the matter?"

"Mama. And Mr. Fowler."

There was nothing on the other end. Maybe the line had been disconnected.

"Aunt Ruth?"

"I'm here. What's going on?"

"They went out to eat supper tonight. They left at six and they're still gone."

I could hear her sigh.

"Sonny, remember what I said? About trust?"

"Yes, ma'am."

"She knows what she's doing."

"I don't like him."

Aunt Ruth said, "I didn't care that much for him myself. That, we can agree on."

"What do you think will happen?"

"All I know is your mama's got a lot to think about, a lot of responsibility."

"I know."

"Honey, whatever happens, your mama loves you, you know that, right?"

I said, "Yeah."

Aunt Ruth sighed and said, "It'll be fine. Don't worry. Night, sweets. Sleep tight."

"Night, Aunt Ruth."

I hung up, and didn't feel any better. I looked at the clock. Almost nine. Ross was sprawled out on the couch and Trent was on the floor, both of them asleep. At ten, headlights looking like two huge pale yellow eyes crept up the drive real slow. The light was off in the kitchen so it was easy to spy on them as the car moved to the spot under the oak tree where he usually parked. I leaned forward so I could see through the screen better. The window was still open, and the night air held that first of the season coolness, while tree frogs still chirped, as did the crickets. The longer they sat, the more agitated I got. I could see two tiny orange circles go up, then down. They were having a smoke.

I went rigid with anxiety, my eyes locked on the car's dark windows, barely able to make out the shape of them. I urged Mama to get herself out of the darn car. Finally, the interior light came on and he exited. Would he walk her to the door, and try to kiss her? I squeezed my eyelids to slits, distorting my view while I held my breath. I almost wanted to shut them completely so as to block out what I was petrified to see. He held his hand out, and she took it, and that didn't set well either. Soon as she was standing beside the car, she pulled her hand from his. I let my breath out. They came toward the house, and while she was talking, Mr. Fowler listened with his head bent in her direction. I noticed Mama kept her hands occupied with her wrap, and her pocketbook. He came up the porch steps and I had the impression he wanted to come in.

Mama said, "Good night," and he went back down and out to his car. I scooted away from the window as she opened the door.

She flipped on the light, and jumped when she saw me. "Jesus, Sonny! What are you doing here in the dark?"

"Nothing."

Mama made a sound as if she found my answer lacking. "Hm."

To try and prove I wasn't snooping, I said, "I was just getting some milk," and then I cleared my throat and asked, "Where'd y'all go?"

Mama put her pocketbook on the counter, and crossed her arms. "To a steak house."

"Oh."

Gosh. He took her for a steak. Course there wasn't any sort of place like that around here to eat, only the local diner. I tried to imagine the two of them together. All that came to mind was what I was most familiar with, the sight of her and Daddy instead. How they used to sometimes tease each other during supper. How he used to hug her from behind while she stood at the sink washing dishes. How they'd sat at the kitchen table, ashtray overflowing, coffee cups at their elbows, the bills they'd spread out, working out finances and plans for the future. How we'd gathered in the living room and watched TV together, sitting crammed together on the couch with our hands blindly dipping into a big bowl of popcorn and peanuts while watching a Western movie. I couldn't imagine her and Mr. Fowler in that same way any more than I could Daddy being bit by a snake and dying from it.

She picked up her pocketbook, and yawned.

Subdued, and tired sounding, she said, "Where's Ross and Trent?"

"Asleep in the living room."

She poked her head in to look at them, stared for a few seconds before turning back to me. I tried not to look as bothered by her night out as I felt. As she studied my face, she reached out, and touched my arm.

She said, "Don't you worry none, Sonny."

Mama's attempts to ease my mind were useless 'cause for her to say "don't worry" only troubled me more.

I followed her outside and down the dogtrot,

and she whispered, "Good night," and disappeared into her room, leaving me standing in the cool hallway, worrying and worrying some more.

Mr. Fowler was back the next morning like nothing had happened the night before and nothing was any different. Business as usual. He got Mr. Johnson started in one of the fields at daybreak. He'd brought around a wood-sided truck with a scale, and normally it took about one acre to fill a wagon with at least twelve hundred pounds of cotton, which was the minimum weight needed to go to the gin. In our case it was looking like it would take two acres, maybe even three. Ross, Trent, and I set out with our picking bags and began. They had nine-foot bags and I had a six-foot. A handful of other pickers Mr. Fowler hired were already bent over like bizarre humped animals moving down the rows.

The familiar weight of the bag on my shoulder dragging the ground made me sad as I remembered picking cotton with Daddy. At first my fingers were cold, stiff, and clumsy as I carefully worked to pry cotton away from the opened boll. I kept at it, waiting for the smoothness of the routine to settle in. I sucked on the ends of my fingers, as they were pricked, and as I moved from plant to plant I noticed I was only spending about half the time on them as was usual. In many instances, the cotton was so strung out and discolored I hesitated to get it. A lot of the bolls hadn't opened at all.

The most I'd ever picked was forty pounds, while Trent and Ross could usually get up to seventy or so. We weighed in around mid-morning. It had warmed up some by then, and I'd shed the lightweight coat I'd been wearing, tossing it into the back of our truck. I went to the wagon with the scale, and handed Mr. Johnson my bag. He doubled them up so they didn't touch the ground, then he'd add either a one-pound or four-pound weight, called "peas," to the other end of the hook to level things out. Mr. Fowler stood nearby and he gave me a "look" that conveyed what I'd done wasn't hardly worth it, while Mr. Johnson was nice.

"Every little bit helps," is what he said when he tossed me my empty bag. Thirty pounds, even though I'd covered a lot more rows than normal.

Noon we had another weigh-in and the wagons were only halfway. We stopped long enough to eat our dinner, and while Ross and I used the tailgate of Daddy's truck to sit on and devoured leftover biscuits stuffed with fried eggs, Mr. Fowler sat on his with Trent. We ate fast, while Trent ate slow as he could, then laid back and put his hat over his face like he might take a nap. I drank some water from the jug being passed around and then I was ready to get back to work. Ross went by and slapped Trent's boot.

He said, "Come on, Trent. We ain't done yet, not by a long shot."

Trent made no move. Ross looked at Mr. Fowler as he talked to Mr. Johnson about what the wagons were weighing in at. He slapped Trent's boot again, and Trent sort a kicked at him. Ross grabbed hold of his feet and yanked him so hard he pulled him off the tailgate, and Trent landed on the ground with a hard thump. Trent jumped up and next thing I know, they're fighting. Everyone stopped working and when Mr. Fowler came running over, I was certain he'd pull them apart.

But, no.

He yelled, "Git'em!"

I yelled, "Stop it, you two!"

Mr. Fowler said, "Hit him in the gut!"

I didn't know who he was encouraging. It was like he just wanted them to fight. A circle of workers gathered around as they rolled in the dirt, getting bits of cotton on their sweaty skin, their faces flushed as they tried to best one another. Mr. Fowler actually made boxing-like motions and called out advice as they went at it again. And here came Mama, carrying more jugs of water and a big paper bag that probably held cookies or some other sort of snack.

She walked at a fast clip while yelling, "Ross Lloyd Creech! Trent Walters Creech! For shame! Look at you!"

Mama's voice penetrated their stupidity. They quit tussling and separated, breathing heavy, clothes covered in soil, cotton, and defoliated leaves. She dropped the jugs of water on the tailgate along with the bag.

Hands on her hips, she said, "What have you to say for yourselves?"

Panting, neither one spoke.

She pointed a finger at them and said, "What would your daddy say?"

There was shuffling of feet, and downcast eyes.

Mama said, "He'd be ashamed of you, that's what!"

Everyone, even Mr. Fowler, was as quiet as when somebody got up to testify at church. She glared at those who'd come to watch and they drifted away and got back to picking.

She gave a look to Mr. Fowler, and he said, "It's just boys being boys."

"My boys don't do this."

"Boys gotta know how to fight, how to stand up for themselves."

"Not brother against brother."

Mr. Fowler leaned his head back, his eyes almost sleepy looking and said something more surprising to me than the fistfight between my brothers.

"Dang it, darlin', of course you're right."

Darlin'?

And worse, Mama softened up like butter left out of the fridge.

She said, "We ain't got time for this sort of tomfoolery."

Mr. Fowler continued to smooth things out. "We sure ain't. All right, boys, you heard your mama."

We went back to work. I went to the other side of the field to pick so I wouldn't have to see Mama and Mr. Fowler sitting on the tailgate of his truck. All that happened made for a long afternoon.

As the sun went down, we had the last weigh-in, and Mr. Johnson announced, "Got about thirteen hunnert pounds."

Mr. Fowler motioned for the tractors pulling the wagons to head for the gin located down Highway 58, about a mile or so past Slater's. It was owned by Morris Strickland, a man I remember Daddy saying ate like he had a tapeworm. His coveralls fit him no better than a scarecrow's would. The gin was in a brick building, longer than it was wide, with a sign on the side that said, Quality Cotton, Inc. Mr. Strickland and seven other men worked inside. One in the engine room, one in the office, three at the gin stands, and three who worked the press boxes to compact the cotton into the appropriate size, a government-regulated rule in order to transport by train. More workers were in the yard managing the suction, and taking finished bales off to the warehouse. Ross drove the tractor while Trent and I rode in the full wagon like we used to do when Daddy was alive. It didn't escape me that Mama and Mr. Fowler rode together in his truck. When we got to the gin, Trent and I bailed out of the wagon, picking bits of cotton off our clothes. I hurried up to Mama, chattering about this and that, about nothing really. I kept talking so they couldn't. I didn't care to hear any more "darlins" coming from out of his mouth.

Fifteen minutes later, Ross pulled the wagon forward, last of the four with our cotton. Mr. Strickland went by, arms waving and directing, while chewing on what looked like beef jerky. He motioned for Ross to get into the back of the wagon since his other guys were busy. Ross grabbed hold of the big giant suction hose and sucked out all the cotton, and that was it. Twelve acres had been cleared today, and I quickly calculated in my head and figured it would be three weeks to get it all in, maybe less. We'd do it all over again until all three hundred acres were done. After the first pass, we'd go to what was called scrapping, meaning we would go back for any "scraps" left behind. That was all that would be left anyway.

We went through the entire crop in two weeks, only making one additional pass. It was mid-

October, and the only thing left was considered waste, tiny shreds of dirty white fiber, not worth going after. Ross looked discouraged and Trent, who'd been in his usual cotton-picking sour mood, looked relieved when he realized it was almost over with for another year. He kicked at a dirty clump lying at the edge of the field.

He said, "Ain't worth making another pass."

Ross said, "I guess not."

I stood between them, my burlap bag at the ready. There had to be more. This wasn't enough! I started back out to the field again, but Ross put a hand on my shoulder.

"It's a waste of time."

I looked down at my fingertips, reddened and sore. I contemplated what Ross had figured we'd harvested. About a hundred and fifty bales total when we usually got something like seven hundred and fifty. If I'd found water, we wouldn't be in this predicament. I said as much, and Trent made some grumpy noise.

Ross said, "It ain't your fault."

"But, we'd have a lot more cotton."

No one said anything and we started back to the house. Mama was on the phone with someone from Jones County already asking about taxes, when they had to be paid, and if there was a way to delay. The buzzing sound of a voice on the other side went on and on.

Mama repeated the information, her voice

low-key. "That much interest? Okay. Well. Thank you for your time."

She hung up and looked at the table covered with various bills, organized into piles of must pay, and what could wait. The pile of must pay was a lot bigger than the other. She chewed on the pencil the way I chewed my nails.

She picked up a sheet of paper and said, "I found some things still owed I had no idea about."

She held out a couple pieces of paper, and Ross took them.

He said, "Oh yeah. This is the bill from when Daddy bought that new disc."

She put her head in her hands and said, "Well, this is when the rubber meets the road."

I said, "Mama, you want I should fix supper?"

She barely glanced at me, continuing to read the numbers, and said, "I don't care."

I looked in the refrigerator. There was some hamburger meat wrapped in white butcher paper. I got it out, and made hamburger patties, cooked some rice, made gravy, and opened up a jar of crowder peas we'd put up last year. When I put food on a plate and stuck it in front of her, she ate, but never stopped adding, and erasing, and adding again. We'd got our cotton samples, each a foot long and wrapped with a strip of brown paper, like the yarn Mama would buy from the store. It came in the mail with a card telling us the grade. It had been classified as "strict low middling," or SML, the lowest. The highest grade, M or "middling," was going for thirty-two cents a pound. We wouldn't get that.

By the time we finished eating, Mama put the pencil down, rubbed her reddened eyes, and said to Ross, "Them cotton samples, I knew when I saw them it wasn't good. With only twenty cent to the pound, it's as bad a crop as we've ever had."

He looked glum while Mama drummed her fingers on the table, then reached for her cigarettes.

She said, "I could pay the taxes, and give half what I owe Frank, and some on the disc. That would give us a few months toward the light bill, groceries, but nothing else until harvest next year except what we could scrape together here and there. We could maybe plant some winter vegetables to sell."

Ross leaned forward, dangling his hands between his knees as he thought. I stared down at my plate, pushing a pea around on it. I couldn't recollect having money problems like this before. We'd had a small Christmas a time or two, but Daddy had always found ways to get around the tough times. I'd never worried when he was here.

Mama said, "I'll pay the taxes so we don't lose

this farm. Then I'll have to see about how to manage the rest."

That simple statement soon turned into the unexpected.

Chapter 22

Mr. Fowler got somewhat scarce after the cotton was done, but then he started calling. Mama would always disappear around the corner to talk. I suspected she was arguing about money 'cause the sound of her voice would rise, and then drop. After she hung up, her face was always flushed, and her eyes glittered with some emotion I couldn't pin down. I'd peeked at her scribblings on the notepad, saw the total of what was in the bank, what we owed, what we needed month to month, and thought about telling her we ought to get ourselves on back to church and pray hard. She'd not mentioned a word about returning since Daddy passed. She might have been struggling with the idea God allowed such hardships.

Preacher Moore's wife had always said, "Lord only gives you what you can handle."

Ross got a part-time job as a bag boy down to Wells' Grocery. I was in the kitchen with Trent and Mama when he came in from work and told her when he'd get paid.

"First paycheck comes next week."

She said, "How much you reckon it'll be?"

"He's paying me seventy-five cents an hour. I've worked about twenty."

"At least we can buy some groceries, maybe some gas. That's real good, Ross."

She'd gone back to calling around for anything she could get her hands on to sew, iron, or mend. There was always plenty of that sort of thing with the holidays coming. She agreed to press and starch pants, shirts, tablecloths, fix broken zippers, reattach buttons, and hem things. She tried not to let us know she was upset, but sometimes her red nose and eyes gave it away.

She looked at the three of us and said, "You all hungry?"

We nodded. She got up and did what Mama loved to do when she needed to think. She dipped a cup of flour into a bowl and worked in some lard and water for a pan of biscuits. She got souse out of the fridge, sliced it, and set the pieces in the frying pan. My brothers and I sat at the kitchen table like we'd done since we were little, quiet, watching her every move. On occasion as she turned the meat, and checked on the biscuits, she'd turn to look at us, like she wanted to know we were there. She got to talking about Daddy, and that made me feel better. She set the food in front of us, then sat and watched as we ate, her eyes gone dreamy and satisfied, as if feeding us soothed her frayed nerves, and proved she could care for us.

We went back to school, and for the first time in a month as I went down the lunch line, I saw Daniel. He was searching for a place to sit. He carried an enormous brown bag, the size people use in the grocery store. In the old days I would have poked fun, asked him why he was carrying a suitcase for one little sandwich. In the old days he would've laughed, and thought of something funny to say back. These days it was better not to do that. I balanced my tray and cautiously tapped his shoulder. He spun around and the relief in his eyes told me how things had been going since I'd seen him last.

I said, "I got stuff to tell you," and pointed at the nearest table.

He dropped into a chair and I sat on the other side, and looked at my lunch tray. Mama had only said this morning we'd have to start taking our lunches 'cause she wasn't going to be able to give us money to eat. That was going to be fine by me 'cause today was meatloaf and the portion one of the lunch ladies plopped into my plate looked like a plastic gray square with a splat of red ketchup to top it off. I decided maybe the mashed potatoes might be okay if I mixed in the peas.

Trent came in while I was busy trying to make

my lunch appetizing, and Daniel was unwrapping the wax paper around his cheese sandwich. As Trent weaved his way through the lunchroom with a couple of his buddies, Billy Perdue and Norris Delaney, Daniel's attention strayed. It was routine for Trent to ignore me and he drifted by, his friends punching each other in the arm, and laughing a little too loud. Daniel watched with interest. I waited, wanting the right moment to tell him Mama had said he could start coming over again except he kept his eyes on Trent, and had that same wistful look from months ago when I was sure he'd wanted to learn how to drive the tractor.

Unexpectedly, and in a louder than normal voice, he said, "Hey, Trent!"

Trent froze. Billy Perdue leaned toward Trent and made the same stupid kissing noises like Junior Odom had done with me and Daniel. I frowned, confused, and glanced at Daniel, who stared at his sandwich like it was a foreign object. He held a stillness, like a startled rabbit. Trent pushed Billy, and Billy pushed him back. Norris cast a nervous look over his shoulder, looking for the lunchroom monitor, Mrs. Brown.

He said, "Hey, you two, cut it out or she'll be over here and we'll have to sit with her to eat."

That was Mrs. Brown's way of dealing with the students who didn't obey rules. She had a table

312

set aside, and would make those who ticked her off sit with her, a less than pleasant experience.

Billy started to push Trent again, only Trent said, "Cut the shit, Billy. I'm warning you."

I said, "You ain't supposed to be cussing."

He whirled around and said, "You shut up. And tell your weirdo friend here not to talk to me."

Shocked, I said, "What's Daniel done? Gosh, Trent, all he said was hey."

Trent stooped down and came so close to my face, I leaned back, unsure of what he was about to do.

He said, "I reckon you're too stupid to see it."

I reckon I was 'cause I didn't know what he was talking about and said so. "What're you talking about?"

He gestured at me with his thumb, and laughed as if my question proved his point. Norris and Billy laughed with him, and I got irritated about the little secret they thought so funny.

"Just tell your weirdo friend not to talk to me," Trent said.

I turned to Daniel, mystified. His eyes were now focused on the big brown bag which sat crumpled and folded, much like he was, like he was ashamed, shrinking into himself. Trent impatiently motioned to Billy and Norris, signaling he was done wasting his time.

He leaned down to Daniel and said, "Don't talk to me, creep," while Daniel was so mortified by

313

it all, he looked physically sick. I got madder than I'd ever been right then. I jumped up, knowing exactly what I would say. Billy and Norris quit snickering as I pointed my finger at Trent, making like I might stab it into his chest.

I said, "Daddy can see and hear every single ugly thing you do, and if he was here, he'd whip your ass up one side of this room and down the other."

I was so mad, I was almost wheezing. The tables beside us grew quiet and those who could hear nudged one another and nodded in our direction. Trent tried to play it off. He lifted his hand and dropped it, the gesture signaling indifference, but I could tell I'd got to him by the dirty look he gave me before he drifted off, his friends following. I stared after them and then I turned back to Daniel. He hadn't moved, and he kept swallowing, over and over.

"Daniel?"

He shook his head, unable to speak.

"Wanna go outside?"

He stood so fast he caused his chair to fall over. The noise silenced the rest of the lunchroom.

He yanked it up, and when I started to grab his sandwich, he shook his head and said, "No! Throw it out. Let's just go!"

"Okay, okay."

I hurried to turn my tray in, and tossed his sandwich in the trash, earning a dirty look from

Mrs. Brown, who hissed at me, "It's a sin to throw away perfectly good food!"

"Yes, ma'am. My friend, he ain't feeling good."

"*Not. Not feeling good.* And maybe if he'd eat, he wouldn't be so sickly."

"Yes, ma'am."

We hurried onto the playground, to our favorite spot at the chain-link fence. We leaned on it and faced the sun. It was brisk, with a slight breeze. We didn't talk. I was beginning to understand something about Daniel; not just in the way he'd grown in the past year, but more about the ways he'd acted. It had to do with what just happened with Trent. I stared at him and thought about how he'd become less showy, less loud, withdrawing more and more, the way the evening primrose only blooms at night, like he thought he ought not be seen. Like he needed to be in the shadows, less conspicuous, as if he'd become aware of how people reacted to him whereas he'd not cared before, or it hadn't mattered. It mattered now, for whatever reasons, though I couldn't figure out why. He leaned against the fence, huddled tight to it like it would anchor him in place.

He said, "You know what he means, don't you."

His voice was light, almost like a whisper, but not, and what he'd said was like a question, but not.

"I don't know. Maybe a little."

He exhaled. "It don't matter."

"It does to me, if you're sad, Daniel. And you seem sad, lately. A lot."

He bounced one time against the fence. "I'm fine. I miss Sarah, even if she was a pain."

He didn't look at me when he talked.

I said, "You ain't heard from her?"

"Nope." He cleared his throat and said, "So, y'all got the cotton done?"

I wanted to talk about him, but that would only make him not talk at all, so I answered his question, my tone gloomy. "Yeah. Sort of."

"What's sort of mean?"

"It was a bad crop. It got a low grade. We didn't get nowhere near the money we would've, so Mama's been trying to figure out how we're gonna get by."

"But . . . you got some money, right?"

"It was like working for nothing by the time we finished. There's something else, too. Two things actually. One is Mr. Fowler took Mama out to eat steak."

Certain he would crow, smack his fist into his palm, and declare, "I knew it!" while taking advantage of rubbing it in, I was surprised when he didn't.

He said, "What's the other thing?"

"Mama said you can come visit again."

I'd no more said that when the bell rang. As

we walked back toward the school, I waited for him to react, to say he was happy, or act excited about it the way he would've before. He didn't respond, so I didn't either. I realized my invitation would put him in close proximity to Trent, and after what just happened, maybe he preferred not to be around him.

We were already at the double doors, and I said, "See you later?" but Daniel acted like he hadn't heard me.

Daniel was slipping away from me, somehow, and as he walked down the hall to his classroom, I kept glancing over my shoulder, wanting him to do some last-minute Daniel type of thing, like jumping up to tap his fingers at the very top of a classroom door. He disappeared without a backward glance. Our friendship was becoming frayed as an old rope, as weak as a rotten floorboard, and I spent the rest of the afternoon trying to compose a letter to him, only half-listening to Miss Young. I didn't like how I sounded so needy, so I eventually tore it up and threw it in the trash can after the final bell rang. I milled about with other students about to get on the buses when I noticed him making his way toward me. I hurried onto mine, and slumped down in the seat. Guilt hit me as I watched him frantically searching the windows, trying to see where I was. I hit my hand against the glass to get his attention. He made his hand like a phone receiver. I gave him a thumbs-up and then wanted to kick myself. I concluded I had no willpower whatsoever.

The smell of supper hit me soon as I got home. Mama wasn't in the kitchen and I eyed the covered dishes on the back of the stove with suspicion. I sniffed again. Youth Dew. Moments later she came into the kitchen dressed like she'd been before, and my heart plummeted.

I said, "Again? Geez!"

Mama said, "Oh, Sonny. It's just supper."

Like when she said, *he's just a man,* and we'd seen how that turned out. He arrived at six sharp, and Mama's, "We won't be long!" floated across the chilly night air. Mr. Fowler looked as if he was about to drop an arm around her waist, until he noticed I was still standing at the screen door making sure he'd see I had an eagle eye on them both. Ross had gone to work right after school, so that left only Trent and me to eat together.

He surprised me when he said, "Hey, let's eat in the living room and watch that new show, *Gunsmoke.*"

Although I was still mad about what he'd done to Daniel earlier that day, I didn't want to eat alone, and I softened a bit more when he apparently tried to make up for it by actually helping me clean up. Afterward, I sat waiting on Mama, my head down on the kitchen table. This time Mr. Fowler came in, and it was obvious they were in a serious conversation.

Mama said, "Soon."

The conversation stalled when they saw me sitting in the dark. I lifted my head and yawned.

Mama said, "For Pete's sake, Sonny, what're you doing sitting in the dark again? You ought to be in the bed."

Mr. Fowler sat down at the table, smelling like he'd been drinking.

He pulled his cigarettes out of his shirt pocket and said, "Go on to bed," and that made me twitch with irritability. I didn't want to be in the same room as him anyway.

I hugged Mama and said, "Good night," certain his eyes were on my back.

When I got in my room, I shut the door, and wished I could shut Mr. Fowler out of my head in the same manner. I grabbed Dolly off the bed and told her he was "a real sumbitch."

He showed up Saturday morning in a mood I'd never seen before, almost like he was . . . happy. I was sitting on the porch swing, bundled up against the cold, peeling apples for a pie, and listening to Mama sing in the kitchen. Ever since the other night, she'd been in a better frame of mind, as if some burden had been lifted. Maybe she'd worked out a way to pay him, and her happiness came from knowing we would no longer be so dependent.

He hopped out of his truck, and came up the steps whistling and when he spotted me, he said, "Where's your mama at?"

He plucked an apple slice from the bowl and ate it as I pointed with the knife and said, "In the kitchen."

He went right on in like he owned the place.

I had just picked up another apple when Mama stuck her head out the back door and in a quiet voice, she said, "Sonny, get your brothers. I need y'all to come on in here so I can tell you something."

It was the way she said it. I stared at her, noticing she had the same expression she'd had when we understood Daddy couldn't be saved. Resigned. I dropped the apple back into the bowl. My fingers curled into my palms and my stomach landed somewhere near my feet.

Mama said, "Sonny?"

I got up, and went down the back steps over to where Ross and Trent were working on a tractor. I simply pointed at Mama, who waved her hand in a beckoning way. Ross dropped the wrench he was holding with a *clunk!* He grumbled about not finishing as he headed for the house, while Trent hurried ahead, glad they'd been interrupted. I followed, looking back over my shoulder at Daddy's grave before

I went into the warm kitchen that smelled of coffee and cigarette smoke. I sat at the table, my hands folded in front of me.

Mr. Fowler said, "Might as well tell them now."

Mama began with what sounded like a fake cheeriness. "There's something we got to say. Frank and I"—and she glanced at him again—"have decided to get married."

Nobody said a word. Mr. Fowler looked at Mama. I was bewildered as I processed the news of what I was sure would never happen.

I found my voice first. "But, why?"

Mama cleared her throat and said, "There's lots of reasons, Sonny. You're too young to understand."

She said I was too young to understand, but I wasn't so young as to think it made any sense. It was like my teacher trying to tell me two plus two equaled three. I hoped Ross would say something, but he appeared dumbstruck.

Mr. Fowler made an absurd comment. "Just think of me as Daddy Frank."

Horrified, I said, "You ain't never gonna be my daddy!"

Mama said, "Sonny!"

I said, "Mama! You can't marry him! You don't love him, you love Daddy! You said so just the other day!"

Mama said, "But . . . he's not here, Sonny. He's gone. This is best for me, for us."

Trent said, "Neato."

I turned on him and said, "Oh, *you* would think so!"

Ross rubbed his hand over his head, back and forth and back and forth.

Distressed, I pleaded with her. "Mama, please don't."

Mr. Fowler looked put out. "Ain't this something."

I'd always believed, given my parents' relationship, you married somebody 'cause you loved them. Wasn't that the way it was supposed to work? Like it had with her and Daddy? I couldn't stop thinking about that, certain it was the one thing that ought to make this impossible between the two of them.

I insisted, "But, you don't love *him!*"

Mama said, "Sonny."

"You don't, Mama!"

Mr. Fowler said, "Well, of course she does."

Mama looked like something inside her hurt, her brows hinged together, and she nodded ever so slightly. Mama loved *him?* I didn't believe it. Couldn't believe it. In my mind was Daddy's shiny blond hair, his smile as rich and warm as the summer sun. Everything about Mr. Fowler stood out in contrast to him, from his black hair, dark brown eyes, his cold smile, his features always seeming to frown. Mama was only fooling herself into thinking she could love him. Or, she was trying to fool him.

Mr. Fowler said, "I done told your mama, she won't never have another worry. She'll be treated like a queen, ain't that right, darlin'?"

Mama actually blushed, while the look on his face made me sick, made me want to sob out loud. I noticed he said nothing about us and whether we were included in this blissful life they were about to start.

I faced Mama, persisting, "But, it ain't been that long!"

Mr. Fowler said, "Time makes no difference in situations like this."

Mama said what Aunt Ruth had said. "Trust me, Sonny. It's for the best."

This was like having confidence the devil would do right. Bile rose in the back of my throat, a vile bitter taste I fought to swallow. Mama hadn't *said* she loved him, and I held onto that.

Ross finally spoke, and he said, "It sure ain't what I expected."

Mr. Fowler said, "Women need them a husband. Men need them a wife. Simple as that."

I got up out of my chair, and Mama said, "Sonny, where are you going?"

It was like I didn't know my own mama any-more, like I'd lost her. She'd become somebody I didn't *want* to know. Without answering her, I left them in the kitchen and went to my room. I grabbed my burned up willow branch, and ran back outside, straight to the spot where Daddy fell. I concentrated hard, harder than I ever had. I felt silly standing there, embarrassed instead of in tune with the land below my feet. What was left of the Y stained my hands with a grayish ash. I sank down onto the freshly turned soil. My eyes filled with hot tears. I hated crying. Suddenly, I hated the blue sky too. And what nerve the sun had shining! Those birds shouldn't be singing, neither.

I whispered, "Daddy, how could you let this happen?"

A gust of wind came, the only answer I got.

Chapter 23

I'll never forget what Daniel said when I told him.

"Now you're really gonna be trapped. All of you."

I didn't like how he said it, his voice low and spooky sounding, like the way a scary movie comes on and you know something's about to happen, only you're not sure what. My dilemma momentarily diverted him from his own problems.

My voice high-pitched, I said, "What do you mean?"

I could hear him breathing rapidly on the other end, as if he was already thinking about some awful thing about to befall us.

He said, "He's *family* now."

I grew aggravated with Daniel in that moment for saying what I'd been thinking and for being right. He was no help.

I said, "I gotta go."

I hung up even though I heard him about to speak again. Mama came by carrying shirts to iron. I followed her, wanting to talk, hoping I might just say the right thing to make her think twice.

"Mama."

"Hm?"

"What would Daddy think?"

She headed for the kitchen where she'd set up the ironing board. It was cold outside, the grass coated like powdered sugar from frost. The silence stretched on. Maybe I shouldn't have said anything.

When I began to think she wasn't going to answer, she sighed and said, "We got no money to live on, Sonny."

"Not even with Ross's job?"

"It ain't enough."

"So, you're marrying him for money?"

"No."

"It sounds like it."

"There's no doubt he'll be a good provider."

I had to know. I had to ask her, even though she'd already said before she loved Daddy, this new decision undermined her words.

"Do you really love him?"

Mama focused on arranging a pair of pants on the board just so.

She said, "People get married for all different kinds of reasons. You'll understand when you get older."

I shoved my hands into the pockets of my dungarees. Mama licked her finger, quickly touched the iron, and it hissed. She kept talking, as if trying to persuade me to her side.

"We'll still be close by. I realize this is the only home you've ever known, but I think you'll like it over at Frank's. It's right nice."

I wondered when she'd been there. Was that where they'd gone one of the nights they'd gone out? It was odd thinking about her in that place. She wouldn't look right there, situated in those dark rooms that shut out the sunlight, different than our light, airy house that caught a sunbeam in every corner, depending on the time of day.

She continued, "It's gonna work out fine, wait and see."

I couldn't see how, remembering the ugly wallpaper, everything musty smelling and him there, every day, every night. Mama cooking in his kitchen. Us sitting at the huge dining room table. Come to think of it, I didn't even know what his kitchen looked like, but what I did know is it wouldn't be home. Could never be home.

Before I had time to even get used to the idea, and believe you me, that was all there was to do, try to get used to it, Mr. Fowler devised a way to make it all happen before Thanksgiving. We piled into his shiny vehicle on another cold and windy afternoon, when the sun dared to peek through a sky filled with chalky clouds while casting shadows across the plowed fields and bare branches rattled overheard, sounding like a string of bones. Mama wore a pale pink wool suit he'd surprised her with. It was a bizarre and intimate thing, him buying her clothes. He dressed in a suit, his hair near about as perfect as I'd ever seen it. Coal black, thick and shiny. Admittedly, Frank Fowler wasn't bad looking, and it was a shame him being such a jackwagon, as Ross had taken to calling him. He took her hand in his own, it got swallowed up the same way our own lives appeared to have done since he showed up.

We headed up to Kinston, to a justice of the peace, who asked a question or two, used his own wife as their witness, and then had them both sign a paper. And that was that. Mr. Fowler was now my stepdaddy, and I was so discombobulated by the entire thing, I couldn't speak. When he kissed her full on the mouth in front of all of us, I couldn't have been more shocked than if he'd slapped her. The justice of the peace congratulated them, and turned to do the same with me and my brothers, and I barely acknowledged the gesture. I shivered nonstop, like that cold wind that had been blowing for days had settled into my very bones. Ross pushed me toward the doors leading us out of City Hall. Outside the building, the American flag snapped sharply in the breeze and the clasps attached to the lines to raise and lower it clanged against the metal pole, giving off a slight echo that sounded like little church bells chiming.

Mama's face was pink as her suit, and Mr. Fowler was actually sweating, even though it was chilly. I kept picturing Mama and Daddy together. Ross, Trent, and I walked to Mr. Fowler's car, and got in. We sat piled together in the back seat, me staring straight ahead while Ross and Trent looked out their windows, all three of us absorbing what just happened. I think it was then I began to think about how there were moments in life that stood out more than others. Like when I knew I could divine water. Christmases. My first day of school. Daddy's passing. And today. Today was sure to be a day I'd never forget.

After we got back from Kinston, Mr. Fowler took us straight to our house. It was early evening, and the weak sun we'd had all day had finally given up. My brothers and I bailed out of the back seat, while he and Mama sat talking about moving to his house. I made my way to the back porch and into our kitchen so I wouldn't have to hear it. She came in after about five minutes, looking like she'd been standing over a hot stove cooking all day. Color high, hair a bit out of place and my stomach clenched. It was too early for bed, but that's where I was going.

I said "good night" in an abrupt manner and started out the door she'd just come in.

Quietly, she said, "Sonny."

I remained facing the door, my hand on the knob.

Mama said, "Please be patient with him."

I looked over my shoulder at her, trying to decide what she thought about today, about being married again. About being married to somebody like him. I couldn't hardly stand how he raked his eyes over her like she was one a them places where you could go and eat all you wanted.

She wanted me to accept him, and for her sake, I would try. "I will, Mama."

I went back to her and kissed her cheek. She grabbed at my hand and held it between the two of hers, urging my cooperation, while acknowledging a little as to what I was feeling.

She said, "It can't never be like it was with your daddy, I know that."

She released my hand and I went down the dogtrot for what seemed like the last time. The next day, a Sunday, we gathered up what we were going to take. Mr. Fowler came to help, and he moved so fast, carrying Mama's things out the door, it was like he believed she might change her mind. My brothers and I filled our station wagon with our own belongings. Looking at our small piles and then comparing it to the size of how I remembered the house, I was sure we'd be swallowed up, our presence like a smudge on the wall.

Mama and Mr. Fowler went on ahead. I went back to my old room one last time to make sure I'd got everything, and when I walked out, I stopped at the threshold, holding my dowsing branch. I took a moment to look around. I had Dolly clutched in my other arm, and it really felt as if we were betraying Daddy, and his memory.

I said, "We'll be back, Dolly."

She gave me that silent, lopsided look of hers.

I climbed into the back seat of our station wagon, and Trent turned around and said, "Why're you bringing that stupid stick? It's half burned up, and you can't do nothing with it."

Ross said, "What's it to you?"

Trent said, "I guarantee Daddy Frank will have something to say about it."

Ross cut his eye at Trent. "Daddy Frank. You sure are something else, Trent. Sure ain't taking you long to butter him up."

Trent shifted on the seat. "He said for us to call him that."

"You won't hear me do it."

I said, "Me neither."

Trent hated when we ganged up on him.

He mumbled, "You two ain't got the sense God give a turnip."

Ross drove slowly down Turtle Pond Road and I looked out from the crowded back seat, surrounded by piles of clothes. Passing by plowed fields, I let my imagination take over, and pictured us coming back just like this, going in the reverse.

A minute or so later, Ross pulled the car up Mr. Fowler's driveway and when the two-story white house came into view, he said, "Never did like the looks of this place."

I wanted to run back home. Mama stood on the big wraparound porch, dressed in a brand-new dress, a powder blue one. She waved and smiled. We stared at her as she came down the steps looking like she belonged in a fancy magazine. I didn't think she looked like herself. When she got closer, she even smelled different, something intensely sweet.

She said, "Ross, Trent, you each have a room. And Sonny, wait till you see yours."

Mama's nice clothes came with the look of someone focused on adjusting to a new situation the way a just-born calf would, wide-eyed and a little disoriented. We followed her into the house. Nothing had changed. The painting he'd told me not to touch, still there. The ugly wallpaper too, and it looked even more awful than I remembered. I turned around to go back out and help unload our car when Mr. Fowler appeared from out of the room where Daddy and I had gone to talk to him that very first time. He grabbed Mama around the waist and cinched her tight to him. I looked away. Seeing the two of them was like pairing a mourning dove to a turkey vulture. My sweet gentle Mama in the hands of a buzzard.

With a hint of embarrassment, she said, "Y'all come with me and I'll show you where your rooms are."

We went up the staircase, our feet clomping on the steps, sounding like we were marching. The walls were a narrow-planked wood that ran from one corner to the other, and on them were old black-and-white photographs of scary looking people with thin lips and hard staring eyes who seemed to observe us like trespassers.

Mr. Fowler came behind us and said, "This here's my family. Fowlers and Perdues. Mostly just aunts and uncles."

Mama said, "Your daddy Frank didn't have brothers or sisters."

She was going to call him that.

Mr. Fowler said, "Just as well. As a teen, I was wild as a buck Indian. Mama couldn't a handled much more'n me."

At the top of the stairs I saw five doors. Two on each side of the hallway, and one at the end. Mama pointed to the doors on the left.

"Ross, Trent, choose the one you want. And don't fight about it."

My brothers began looking over the two rooms, while Mama motioned at one of the doors on the right.

"Sonny, this one's yours."

She opened it, and it set off a loud creaking groan of protest. I peeked in and knew right away I hated it. The bed was set high off the floor, and I'd need a footstool to get up on it. The wallpaper was old and faded, a blue and yellow floral pattern that almost made me dizzy when I stared at it. It smelled like mothballs in there and I really, really wanted to be outside where I could gulp in fresh air. I would stifle in that room, I was sure. Mama noticed I'd gone pale, and sweaty.

She said, "Frank, can we open a window?"

He went across the room and yanked the yellowed lace curtains back. I saw a cloud of dust come off them, and the window only cracked a little before it stuck.

He said, "Ain't nobody been in here in a while. This was my own mama's room. I ain't allowed no one in it till just now."

I could tell. I had the horrible idea she might have died in it. I couldn't ask, but thought surely I was breathing the stale air that had been expelled from some old dying woman's lungs. I went over to the window and leaned down to the small opening and took several big gulps of air, and felt a little better.

Mr. Fowler said, "Thought you were a tough girl."

Mama said, "Oh, Sonny, look here. Isn't this a nice desk?"

Mr. Fowler said, "It was Mama's. Best she don't touch it."

Mama looked surprised. "Sonny would be careful."

He ran his hand over the wood top. "Tell her not to touch it."

Mama said, "She's right here, Frank, reckon she can hear for herself."

He said, "It's special made. I don't want it messed with."

Mama crossed her arms. "Fine."

Mr. Fowler said, "It's old, delicate. I can buy her one of her own."

Mama huffed.

Mr. Fowler said, "I will. Don't worry," misunderstanding her.

She let it go, and motioned around the room. "What do you think, Sonny?"

I gazed about. It was like being stuffed into a cramped little closet even though it was huge. "I like it fine, Mama."

Mr. Fowler said, "Shoot, this room's got to be twice the size of the one you had."

Mama said, "We'll get your things in here and it's gonna feel just like home before you know it."

I held back on that, and we finally went back down the stairs. I took a moment to look around, and found myself wandering to the spot in the hallway where I'd been with Daddy. Mr. Fowler caught me bent down, and looking at a picture of a fox crouched low, backed against a tree, and a pack of dogs snarling around it.

He said, "That there's a scene depicting a fox hunt in England."

I straightened up. I didn't know what to say 'cause I really didn't like it, but I wasn't about to tell him that. And then he asked me directly.

"Do you like it?"

I glanced at him, remembering how Daddy always said honesty was the best policy.

"Not really."

Mr. Fowler said, "You don't like me much either do you."

This was not a question. This was a statement. I was instantly on alert.

He said, "Maybe you just like little flits."

I said, "I don't even know what that is, so it don't matter none to me."

Mr. Fowler said, "It ought to matter. Looks like my first job as your new daddy is to teach you. Your friend? Folks don't take kindly to his sort around here. Them kind? They're no better than the Commies. And here you are, all moony-eyed over him. You can forget that. He ain't never gonna like you, and you might as well get used to it. Know why? 'Cause he likes boys. *Boys.* Not girls. I ever catch him over here, I'll fix him, but good. You hear me? My house is off-limits to the likes of him. He ain't got his shit together, and that's what I been wanting to say since Day One. You stay away from him, and you ain't got a thing to worry about. Understand?"

Through his entire little tirade, I didn't dare move, and minded my countenance. He looked satisfied, like he'd finally gotten something off his chest that had been eating away at him of a long time. Mama called him from some other part of this enormous house, her voice faint.

He pointed a finger at me. "You best keep that shit to yourself. Don't you go worrying your mama with your whining and carrying on. It's high time you learned who's boss."

After he was gone, I tried to sort out what he'd said about Daniel, searching back through my memory and recollecting instances where Mr. Fowler's words rang true. I considered how Daniel had acted around Trent, back to that most recent moment in the cafeteria. I stared at the wallpaper, at the fox cowering, at the dogs baring their teeth at it, and the blood pooling at its feet where it had been shot. I stared at its face, at the knowledge of its death which the artist had somehow captured and reflected back, as if I was an ethereal witness to the animal's end of life. The scene reminded me of Daniel, and how the world might come at him, relentless, unforgiving, and ruthless.

Chapter 24

Mr. Fowler was big talk.

He told Mama, "I want you to feel like this is your house. Make yourself at home."

He left one day, and Mama went through the place like a little tornado, dusting and straightening up. She put Ross and Trent to work outside, cleaning up the dead weeds from around the bushes near the foundation. She had me help pull back some of those heavy drapes to let the sun in. It wasn't much, but it looked and smelled better, until Mr. Fowler walked in, and got all pissy about it.

He said, "Why'd she move this here?" talking to himself again, like Mama wasn't there. What he was going on about was the couple of chairs she'd had my brothers help her move into the large hallway. He told them to put them back where they'd been. Mama stood with her hands folded in front of herself like a little school--girl being scolded. He walked around like a drill sergeant, looking things over, and then he stopped at a small side table where she'd arranged a couple pictures of us.

"Why're these here?" He grabbed the pictures and handed them to her. "Put'em in that room, there."

Mama protested, saying, "You said make ourselves at home."

He said, "Yeah, well."

He walked outside and looked at the wood rocking chair Daddy had given her and she'd set on the front porch. He picked it up and marched it around to the back side of the house, like it wasn't good enough to be seen. Mama remained quiet as he came back in and yanked the curtains closed, shutting off the light again, undoing all her work. She walked off, leaving him to mumble questions to himself about what was done and why. She went by me, tight faced, back ramrod straight. She made no move from that point on to change one single solitary thing in that house. She repacked boxes of pictures, and other small knickknacks she'd brought. She washed clothes, cleaned floors, but our possessions were nowhere in sight.

She said, "I feel like I'm walking around in a mausoleum."

On that, we could agree.

Just before Thanksgiving, she fixed Mr. Fowler's favorite meal. He'd handed her an old yellowed piece of paper with the recipe on it. Mama took it gladly and looked it over.

She said, "Oven-baked buttermilk chicken. Okay, I reckon that's what we'll have tonight."

He said, "I like to eat at six o'clock."

Mama said, "Yes, Frank, I know."

She worked in the kitchen all afternoon on the meal, and wonderful smells soon took over. Even though I didn't care about the big dining room and its gloomy interior, I wanted to see how it would feel to be sitting at that enormous table, which Mr. Fowler bragged could seat about twelve people and was made of solid oak.

We gathered round the table at six, and soon as we sat down, he said, "Mind your manners. This ain't no countrified kitchen you're sitting in here."

Mama went a little pink and said, "Pass bowls to the right and across."

Mr. Fowler put a couple pieces of chicken on his plate, and passed the platter to Ross. All was going along fine, and then Trent spoke up.

"Daddy Frank, this is one of my favorite meals too."

Liar. We ain't never had no buttermilk chicken. Mama had always fixed it like Granny Walters.

Mr. Fowler pointed his fork at him and said, "Button it. Unless you're spoken to, keep that piehole shut."

Trent's mouth clamped shut like a snapping turtle. Mr. Fowler kept looking at him until Trent's eyes fell to his plate and it was only then he got to passing bowls around again. Mama shook her head ever so slightly, and sat back in her chair.

Mr. Fowler said, "Vi? Darlin'? Ain't you gonna eat?"

Her eyes narrowed, and she didn't answer him.

Mr. Fowler said, "Children ought to be seen, not heard."

Mama joined our ranks, and said not a word.

Mr. Fowler got to looking a little twitchy. "I mean, I'm just saying, it's how I was raised and all."

Mama concentrated on a spot on her plate, rubbing it as if she was polishing silver.

"Here darlin', whyn't you get you some a this chicken. I declare, if it don't look just like what my own mama fixed. My, my, you've outdone yourself."

We looked to Mama. Mr. Fowler's kinder manner was more reminiscent of how he'd acted while at our house, and she finally took the bowl of peas I'd been trying to pass her all along.

She said, "Thank you, Sonny."

We started eating, although for me, it was more about pushing food about on my plate. I couldn't eat under such conditions. Then Trent evidently made another mistake. He put his elbows on the table, and quick as a spring-loaded mouse-trap, Mr. Fowler jabbed him in the arm with his fork.

Trent yelled, "Ow!" and Mr. Fowler jabbed at him again.

Mama said, "Frank! Stop!"

Mr. Fowler said, "Ain't these kids got no manners?"

Mama said, "We're at home, we're not guests somewhere. He's hungry, let him eat."

Mr. Fowler said, "I don't care if he eats, but no goddamn elbows on the table."

Mama said, "Trent, mind yourself."

Trent sat wide-eyed, stunned by Mr. Fowler sticking him. Slowly, we started eating again, but it was in a way like we weren't sure if we'd draw his eye by making some mistake we were unaware of. Mama had put a saucer of sliced bread on the table. Mr. Fowler folded a piece of bread over like a little pillow, slid food up and onto his fork, and then plunged it all into his mouth. His cheeks bulged, and he ate while smacking his lips the entire time. Mama kept looking over at him, like she was trying to figure out where he'd come from, or how we'd got here. She and I were of a similar mind-set in that regard, let me tell you. Somehow, the rest of supper passed without incident.

The ground rules had been laid. We tiptoed about in stocking feet. We talked in lower voices. We faded into the background. I saw this as a necessity. The only chance to get away from the dark, stuffy smelling house, and his ever vigilant oversight was at school, only there, I had to contend with the curious looks and whispers of my classmates.

"Heard he was Klan."

"My daddy said he killed somebody several years ago."

"I heard that too."

"Shoot, his mama? She was even crazier than he is."

I had no doubt some of what they said might be true. Daniel and I ate lunch together as always, but even then Mr. Fowler's presence messed things up. I found myself watching him closer than before, discerning his differences in the way a dog might sniff out a bone in the yard.

Of course, Daniel noticed right away. "Why're you looking at me like that?"

"Like what?"

He made a huffing sound as I answered his question with a question, which he hated. "You know what I mean."

"I'm not looking at you in any particular way."

"Yes you are."

"Geez. Fine. I won't look at you. At all. Ever again."

More moody than usual I sat ignoring him, and he ignored me through most of the lunch period and I was sure I kept my eyes everywhere except on him. Even when he talked to me.

The bell rang, and as we stood up to go back to

class, he said, "What's wrong with you anyway?"

I stared at the back of Junior Odom's head and neck. The buzz cut he wore showed several folds of skin, three rolls to be exact, and it was sort of fascinating how they disappeared, then reappeared every time he looked down, then up.

Without looking at Daniel, I said, "What do you mean, what's the matter with me?"

He made that aggravated noise again and said, "Never mind."

He walked off, and I got to feeling kind a bad. We didn't get much time together like before, and I shouldn't have been so ill toward him. I trailed behind him until he stopped abruptly and faced me. This time when I looked up at him, my insides went all soft and buttery, and my legs felt about the same way. Daniel had a way about him I found hard to ignore, how he leaned off to his left a little in a slouchy way that was appealing. I caught that scent of his too, and almost bent forward to sniff him. I caught myself and waited for him to speak, while trying to keep the soft spot I had for him vacant from my eyes.

He raised his chin in a knowing way and said, "Ever since you been over there, you've been acting different."

"What do you expect? I hate it there. I ain't used to it. He wants us to call him Daddy Frank."

He said, "That ain't it. It's something else."

I shook my head, denying it.

He gave me a disgusted look and said, "Yes, it is."

I wanted to reach out and grab him, hug him, but I kept my hands stayed at my sides.

"Just 'cause I looked at you? Don't be dumb."

"It was a different look."

I snorted.

He started walking again and I fell into step beside him. I only wanted for things to go back like they'd been before. It seemed like a long time ago at this point.

I said, "All I know is he's one crazy sumbitch, let me tell you."

Daniel actually smiled at that and my heart soared. We were almost at our classrooms. I could never tell him Mr. Fowler had forbid him coming. I grew brave with the idea of defying him and his ridiculous rule. My thoughts went in all directions, thinking of all the ways we could get by with it, and he'd never know.

Hurrying, so we wouldn't be late, I said, "You should see it."

"His place?"

"Yeah."

"What's it like?"

"Why don't you come over?"

"Am I allowed?"

"I told you Mama said you could come after the cotton was picked. There's all sorts of places we can go where we ain't got to be around him.

My room's huge, but he wouldn't dream of setting foot in there now."

"I don't know."

"Oh, come on. I dare you."

Even after Mr. Fowler's direct threat, my wish to be with Daniel outweighed my common sense. I knew this, but I couldn't help myself.

Daniel said, "Don't do that doggone dare thing."

Sensing he was giving in, I pushed. "Double dare!"

"Well . . ."

I pushed on. "Plan on Friday after Thanksgiving, at the pond, about one o'clock."

Daniel scratched his elbow, hesitated, then said, "Okay. What do you want to do?"

"We'll think of something."

Feeling victorious, I went into my classroom to tackle division of fractions.

Later that afternoon, after we got home from school, we found Mama and Mr. Fowler standing in the kitchen admiring her newfangled dishwasher. He was strutting around, his chest poked out as if he'd created the thing himself.

Just delivered, he was busy telling her, "Figured it would make a good, early Christmas present. Now you ain't got to stand at that sink washing dishes every night. Anything for my darlin'."

He spotted us standing in the doorway, and the smile he'd been wearing vanished. I had the impression his day had been going along fine till we showed up.

He looked at his watch and said, "Y'all are home already?"

Mama turned to us. "Look! Isn't it amazing? I ain't never heard of such. A machine that washes dishes! What will they think of next?"

Mr. Fowler played with a matchbook, opening and closing it.

He said, "Y'all need to get onto whatever it is you're supposed to be doing."

Ross didn't waste any time and left the room to go and get ready for work.

Mama, still mesmerized, said, "I declare, if this don't beat all."

Mr. Fowler glared at Trent, then me, and said, "Go on. Get on with your homework and your chores."

Trent tried to stall in his usual way. "How's that thing work, Daddy Frank?"

Mr. Fowler shifted his shoulders around like his neck hurt.

His reply was short. "You put dishes in, shut the door, turn it on. Now go do your homework."

Trent stomped out of the room while I waited on Mama to ask me how my day was, like she always used to do, but he said, "Go. Do what you're supposed to do."

Mama put a hand on his arm, and said, "Was there something you wanted, Sonny?"

"I wanted to talk to you for a minute, if Mr. Fowler doesn't mind."

He said, "Your mama's busy right now."

Mama said, "Maybe a little later, okay?"

I nodded, and turned to go.

Then, Mr. Fowler said, "Hold on."

I gave him a puzzled look. "Sir?"

"What's with the Mr. Fowler thing?"

I didn't answer.

"Seeing as how I'm putting food in your belly, and a roof over your head, it don't seem fitting, like I'm some stranger. Ain't you got used to me by now?"

"No, sir."

Mr. Fowler's head went back like I'd slapped him. "No?" He looked at Mama, incredulous, like he couldn't believe what I'd said. "You hear that?"

"Frank, honey, she's not ready."

"What's to be ready about? It's a simple thing."

He put his hands on his hips like we were going to have us a little showdown, yet the idea of attaching Daddy to him wasn't possible. I'd never do it, and I couldn't pretend I would.

He leaned forward and said, "What's the problem?"

"Nothing."

He said, "Good. Daddy Frank it is, then."

"No, sir."

"You defying me?"

"I'm saying you ain't my daddy."

Mr. Fowler looked to Mama again, like she needed to handle this. I didn't get why he was being so insistent about it. What difference did it make what I called him?

Mama twisted her fingers nervously and said, "Sonny, why don't you go on to do your homework like Daddy Frank said."

Silently I said, *thank you, Mama* as I hurried from the kitchen, the sound of my shoes declaring my ascent to the ears listening below. His loud voice carried up the staircase, and I was worried for Mama.

"What the hell, Vi? You let her get away with that? She's spoiled, is what she is, and ain't no kid under this roof gonna get away with being sassy."

"She's still upset over her father. It's not been all that long ago."

"Y'all have had plenty of time for that, and obviously we've moved on. We're married now, and that's the past. This is the present. Hell, he's been gone going on seven months. Now, I've been patient all along. I want us to have a nice Thanksgiving, everything pleasant. I ain't wanting to see a bunch a hangdog faces moping around my table."

Mama continued to try and soothe Mr. Fowler's irritation, talking to him like he was five years old. "Aw, honey, we'll make sure everything is perfect," but it was what she said next that had me wishing I'd gone on to my room. "You're so good to me, and the kids. We appreciate what you're doing, and I love you for it."

Hearing Mama tell him she loved him was even worse than her telling me they were getting married. I'd never heard her talk to nobody in that coddling way before. Did she sense something in him, like I had? Something gone bad, like meat that's gone off after it's been setting out too long. If she did, it made no difference considering what took place next. There was a scraping of chairs, and a skidding noise, like they were shifting furniture around.

Mama said, "Oh!" and then mumbled, "Frank, no. Not here!"

There was no answer from him, only more sounds, something like a struggle, a bump, and Mama hissing once again, "No!"

Then quiet. The creak of wood, and next, a sound like hands clapping, and Mr. Fowler grunting like a pig. *Uh, uh, uh!* I put my hands over my ears and hurried down the hall, avoiding the staring eyes of the gigantic deer head mounted on the wall. It looked just as stunned by what was going on in the kitchen as I was. Once, Junior Odom with his dirty mouth told Lil Roy about seeing two dogs doing what he'd called "fornicatin'" while making sure his description was heard practically across the playground. In my room, I stared at the faded wallpaper, and tried really hard not to think about what just took place.

After a while came slow, steady footsteps of someone climbing the stairs. I could tell it was Mama. She stopped at my door while I held my breath, waiting for the knock. I willed her to go away 'cause I didn't want to set eyes on her, not after what had just happened. I didn't think I could pretend. Thankfully she moved away and I had another pang, similar as to when I'd learned we were leaving our home. Mama and I had never had any awkward moments or cause to avoid one another, and Mr. Fowler was doing a real good job of changing that too.

At supper that night, despite the earlier happiness over her new dishwasher, she'd lost a bit of that glossy joy while Mr. Fowler ate like he'd worked up an appetite. He and Trent got into what sounded like a fake polite discussion about his gun collection, as if Mr. Fowler was wanting to pretend he'd not been short-tempered earlier.

He said, "I got'em locked up in a gun safe. I'll show'em to you one day."

Trent said, "What kinds?"

"Rifles, mostly. Couple a Remingtons, a Winchester, and a Savage 99."

Trent looked like he wanted to go look immediately, turning so his feet were pointing at the door like he might leave the table.

Mama said, "You need to go on and eat, Trent."

Mr. Fowler said, "Later. Maybe we'll shoot some this weekend."

"That would be swell!"

Finally, supper was over with and I carried our dirty dishes to the counter, and then watched Mama load them into the new dishwasher. Mr. Fowler leaned against the doorjamb smoking a cigarette, staring as she put plates in their special slots, unable to keep his eyes off her. It was embarrassing to the point I wanted to snap my fingers under his nose. It was only cause of the sound of a vehicle coming up the drive he finally quit ogling her.

Trent looked out the back door and said, "It's Ross."

Mama checked the kitchen clock on the wall and said, "He was only gone a couple hours," while Mr. Fowler yawned.

Ross came in, shook off his coat, and sat at the table. At first no one thought a thing.

Mama went about getting his plate of food out of the oven and as she set it down in front of him, she looked at him and said, "What's wrong?"

In a glum voice, he said, "I ain't going back."

"You mean they fired you?"

Mr. Fowler laughed and said, "Ha, he got canned!"

Mama said, "Frank," in the same tone she'd

use on us if we did something she disapproved of, while Ross gave him a dirty look.

Mama sat down beside him and said, "You've not been late, have you?"

He shook his head.

"You've not missed a day, and I'm sure you worked hard."

Ross said, "It don't matter."

"But, what happened?"

He raised his eyes, and stared at Mr. Fowler for a second before he lowered them again.

"I quit."

Mama sat back in surprise. "You quit?"

Mr. Fowler said, "A quitter. How 'bout that. We got us a quitter on our hands."

Ross looked at Mama and said, "People talk too much."

Mama got a confounded look on her face. "What do you mean?"

Ross looked uncomfortable, and he glanced at Mr. Fowler again, before he let his eyes drop back down to the tabletop.

Mr. Fowler caught the look and crossed the room in a second flat, and got in Ross's face. "Spit it out, kid. Who're they talking about?"

Mama said, "Frank. Calm down. It's all right."

Ross fidgeted and said, "About my mama marrying the likes of you."

Frank got even closer to Ross. "What did you say?"

Ross looked at the floor. Mr. Fowler leaned down and got even closer to Ross's face.

He spit his words out. "Tell me who, god-dammit."

Mama pulled on Mr. Fowler's shoulder. "Frank, stop it."

He straightened up and said, "Come on. We're gonna take care of this."

Mama was instantly afraid, and her voice shook. "Now, Frank, hold on a minute."

He ignored her. "Come on, boy, let's go."

Ross stood up, but Mama put her hand on his arm. "Ross. No."

Mr. Fowler yelled at him, "Come on!" and started down the hall. We hurried after him. He went to the gun safe, the one he'd just been talking about with Trent. I thought about what I'd heard at school. *He killed somebody several years ago.*

Mama said, "Frank! Ain't no need to go and start no trouble. People are gonna talk and we can't stop them!"

"Like hell we can't!"

Trent said, "Can I go too?"

Mama said, "No!" while Mr. Fowler said, "Both of you get in the truck."

Mama got to sort of half-crying, and begging him.

"Frank, please, please, Frank. Boys! I forbid it!"

Mr. Fowler turned to her and in a soft sort of voice like he would maybe use in those moments of love, he said, "Now, you hush, darlin', it's gonna be all right. Can't nobody talk about my wife, if I got any say in it. I'm just gonna give'em a little talking to."

Mama pleaded. "Frank, don't."

He only pulled her to him, and hugged her, his chin resting on the top of her head. That soft voice of his was as menacing as a gas leak with some unknowing person about to strike a match. Yet I saw with my own eyes, heard with my own ears, and concluded that if nothing else, Frank Fowler truly loved our mama.

Or, so I thought.

Chapter 25

Going to sleep was impossible, knowing Mr. Fowler was out there, likely doing someone some kind a hurt. Needing something to do, Mama baked cornbread. Then we started cleaning a whole mess a greens, pulling leaves off the huge stalk, and pushing them under the sink filled with cold water, as if we were trying to drown them. Mr. Fowler didn't have an outside work sink like we did at our old house. Here, in his kitchen, with its long row of pale yellow metal cabinets and fruity wallpaper, made me realize Thanksgiving was in two days, yet it didn't seem like the holiday at all.

She didn't talk much, and neither did I. When we did, it was about the food we were fixing. Should we stuff the bird or not. How much poultry seasoning to use. How much sage. Would this be enough collard greens, and should it be pecan pie, or pumpkin. She decided both, and casually mentioned she'd forgot to get some Karo syrup, her voice quivery and low. I didn't offer much to her comments. I still carried the embarrassment of overhearing what they'd done in here. I was upset at her for saying she loved him. It wasn't possible. I hadn't seen the same things between her and him I'd seen between her and Daddy. Lots of hugging. Lots of hand-holding. I reckoned Mr. Fowler showed his love to her in different ways, like going after someone bad-mouthing her.

She said, "You know, I overheard a few things myself when I went into Flatland the other day. Ain't no sense in him thinking he can stop it."

"You did?"

She nodded. "I had to buy stamps down to the post office. People ought to mind their own business. What do they know of our situation?"

I stripped leaves from a stem. Strip. Strip. Strip. Eventually, curiosity forced a question out.

"What'd they say?"

Mama shook her head. "It don't matter none." She changed the subject. "I hope he doesn't get the boys involved. It ain't the way to do things. It ain't proper like. He ought to know better."

This was the first small criticism I'd heard against Mr. Fowler out of Mama's mouth. She rested her palms on the edge of the sink, leaning forward to look out the window at the blackness blanketing what lay beyond the house, save for the little round light over the barn doors. It cast a small circular area of yellow on the ground right in front. She straightened up, and stuck her hands in the water again, the cold making them look chafed and rough. Our reflections in the window, me beside her, resembled a distorted photo, her brown and my blond hair, the muted color of clothing. I was almost as tall, but not quite. She shook her head, like she didn't want to think about what could be happening. Something scurried by in the shadows near the barn. Maybe a possum. Or a fox. My gaze went back to Mama's reflection.

She said, "I sure hope he ain't gone and done nothing crazy."

Mama's hoping was a little too late in that regard, since I considered the fact that Mr. Fowler was about as crazy as they come. She ripped at a collard leaf rather viciously.

She said, "Happiness is such a fickle little thing. It comes for one reason and goes just as quick for another."

I quit tearing up the greens for a second. "Ain't you happy, Mama?"

"My happiness ain't important. You kids, that's what's important."

"We could've done fine without him."

She stared straight ahead again, her hands gone still. "You know, your daddy was one to always talk about being prepared. It ain't until he's gone I realize we were about as prepared as a newborn babe left to fend for itself."

She sloshed her hands about in the sink, and held up the final leaf.

She stripped it, then waved the stem under my nose. "We'd have been down to nothing, just like this, if it weren't for Frank."

While Mama justified things, I remained quiet. She prepared the turkey next, and after we put it in the refrigerator, along with the pan of corn-bread dressing, and she'd set the collards in a big pot of cold salted water on the stove, we sat down to wait. I drank a Pepsi, while she smoked a bunch of cigarettes and drank cup after cup of coffee. I laid my head on my arm and wrestled with her reasoning.

Next thing I knew, she was nudging me awake, saying "They're back."

I was instantly alert. She went out the back door, and I followed. We watched Mr. Fowler's truck ease up the drive. It was almost midnight. He parked in front of the barn and we went out into a night as dark as I felt right then. Stars shimmered, clearer than usual, as if the cold snap had sharpened the air around us. I shivered, but it was more from dread. The driver's side door opened and Mama gasped as Mr. Fowler stepped into the faint glow of the barn light. A big stain adorned the front of his shirt.

He said, "Aw, darlin', don't you worry 'bout ole Frank. It sure as shit ain't mine."

He laughed in a weird sort of hacking way, the sound wet and croupy. Mama pressed her fingertips to her lips as she stared at him and my brothers. Mr. Fowler leaned against his truck, lifted a hand, and let it drop. He suddenly threw his head back, and laughed again, like someone told him a joke, which made him cough some more.

Mama said, "Frank! What's the matter with you?"

Ross and Trent's faces were pale white ovals.

They moved away from him, closer to us, and Ross said, "He's had a bit to drink."

Trent said, "Yeah, we had some too."

Ross whipped around and said, "Shut up, geez, Trent!"

Mama leaned in, sniffed near Ross, and wrinkled her nose.

She raised her voice and said, "Frank, what's wrong with you, what have you . . ."

Mr. Fowler cut her off.

He said, "Ain't a goddamn thing wrong now. A little correction has been made, is all."

"Frank . . ."

Mr. Fowler made an abrupt movement, standing straight and tall, no longer leaning on the truck. Mama fell silent. His face was partially hidden, and he wasn't smiling.

His eyes glittered as he put his finger up to his lips and said, "Shhh."

Mama stared, her arms folded.

Mr. Fowler said, "I'm going to bed."

Mama said, "Frank, what happened?"

He shoved his hands into his pockets, and sauntered over to stand at her side.

He said, "I made damn sure we'll be respected, that's what happened, Vi."

Ross looked like he wanted to punch him as Mr. Fowler stumbled across the yard, into the house, and disappeared inside.

Mama waited until he was gone and she turned to Ross. "What's he gone and done?"

Ross raised his chin. "You shouldn't ever have married him, Mama."

She put her hand to her throat, and stared at him, her face shifting from worry to anger.

She said, "And you ain't old enough to tell me what I should or shouldn't do."

"I reckon I was old enough to see what happened tonight, ain't I?"

She said, "It ain't on account of me not trying to stop it." Frustrated, she said, "Don't you forget yourself, Ross Creech. Don't you forget who it is you're talking to."

Ross gave her a pointed look and said, "I ain't forgetting a thing."

Mama said, "Neither am I. You ought to know if I could've stopped this, I would have."

She turned and went inside.

I wasn't sure he'd tell me, but I took a chance and said, "What happened?"

Ross shook his head and started walking to the house, and Trent followed.

"Why can't you tell me?"

My brothers ignored me. After they were gone, I crept over to the truck, peeked through the open window. There was a bloody white cloth laying on the front seat. I reached in, took it, and held it up. It had two holes in it, a place for eyes. I recognized what it was, and I threw it back on the seat and rubbed my hands down the front of my pant legs. Disturbed, I backed away and hurried inside. I could already hear Mr. Fowler's loud snoring. Feeling safe knowing he was passed out, I tapped on Ross's door. There was no sound from his room. I opened the door, and he was sitting on the side of the bed, his head in his hands.

I said, "I saw it. What was on his front seat. That hood thing."

Ross motioned at me. "Don't talk about it out there."

I went into the room and softly closed the door. I waited for him to confirm what I already knew.

He finally looked at me and said, "Klan."

Even the word. *That word.* I felt contaminated, and wiped my hands on my pants again. I realized then that sometimes people talked 'cause it was truth, not gossip or lies. Ross laid back on his bed, arms folded under his head. He stared at the ceiling.

He whispered, "He went clear off his rocker."

"What do you mean?"

He turned on his side and the look on his face was like he was seeing what happened all over again.

He said, "He took us down the road to some shack out in the middle of nowhere, a weird place. It was hidden in a patch of woods. There were a couple other cars there already. I saw three men standing around a fire, passing around a bottle. He told us to wait. He went over to them, and there was a lot a backslapping and all. He drank some, and then one a them men, he followed us over to Mr. Wells's house."

"What did they do?" I gasped, "Did they hurt him bad?"

Ross said, "Bad enough. He won't standing when we left."

"Did you and Trent do anything?"

"Hell no. He couldn't have made me, neither. He put that hood on and when he got out, he made us get out too. They banged on Mr. Wells's front door, and when he answered, they dragged him outside and beat him up. We weren't but about ten feet away. Then, he says to Mr. Wells, he says, 'You best keep your mouth shut, and anyone else working for you, they best do the same. Nobody, but nobody better say a goddamn thing about Frank Fowler, or his wife.' Mr. Wells, he couldn't even answer. I think all his teeth got knocked out. I wished I'd kept my own mouth shut."

"Ain't you gonna tell Mama?"

"What good would it do? She knows by the way he looked, all that blood. We're still here ain't we?"

"I heard at school he killed somebody."

"I can believe it, after tonight."

We both froze at a noise outside a Ross's door. He put a finger to his mouth. My heart beat loud as I imagined the door flying open and Mr. Fowler busting through to beat us up like he'd done Mr. Wells, just for talking. It opened with a slight creak, and I near about collapsed to the floor when I saw Trent.

In a loud whisper, he said, "What're y'all talking about?"

Ross sat up and muttered at him, "What do you think, dope head."

Trent's eyes were big, and even he looked scared. He came in, and shut the door.

He said, "I ain't ever seen nothing like it."

Ross shook his head. "Me neither."

I said, "I'm glad I didn't see it."

We sat for a few minutes, each of us having our own thoughts. Eventually, I left and went back to my room. I climbed up into the bed, but it was no surprise when dawn broke, I saw it. Now we knew what Mr. Fowler was capable of, Ross, Trent, and I crept around, expecting some irrational act out of him at any moment. He'd gone back to being his usual way around Mama, all soft-spoken and constantly hugging on her.

He told her time and again, "You're my every-thing, darlin'. I don't know what I'd do without you."

It was pretty disgusting if you asked me. Mama appeared to barely tolerate it, as if she was having difficulty with this new show of neediness and clinging.

Thanksgiving Day, Mr. Fowler loaded his plate with turkey, dressing, gravy, and everything else she'd cooked. He started eating without waiting for a blessing, and I wondered how somebody who'd done what he'd done could eat, much less not ask God to have mercy on his soul. Mama motioned for us to go on and fill our plates up too. Oftentimes the sharp edge of caution can be dulled by even a small amount of time passing, and I, without thinking, took a moment to bow my head for a few seconds, offering up a prayer.

I was almost to the Amen, when Mr. Fowler said, "What're you doing?"

I raised my head and encountered impenetra-ble, opaque eyes. He shoved his hair back off his forehead, and my eyes fastened on his hand. There was a fresh scratch, a vivid red streak I didn't remember. I looked at Mama, who was extra subdued. Was that a faint mark on her neck?

I returned his gaze and said, "I'm saying a blessing."

"Eat."

I nodded, but bowed my head again to say "Amen" when his hand smacked the table hard again, his favorite way to get our attention.

"I said eat!"

His sharp tone startled me and I dropped my fork.

Mama rose, and Mr. Fowler said, "Vi. Sit. If she'd done what I told her, she'd have a fork. She can do without."

Mama tried to placate him with a mild tone, and a hint of softness. "Frank, honey, she's got to have a fork to eat with. With mashed potatoes and gravy, and all."

She went into the kitchen and got me a clean one, then sat back down as if nothing had happened. Mr. Fowler carefully put his own fork down, and looked at her, then me, then her. Trent, forgetting how the slightest thing might start to snowball, was no help.

He said, "As usual, Sonny gets her way."

Mr. Fowler said, "Give it here."

By now, I didn't care if I ate or not. I handed him the fork and put my hands in my lap.

Mama's voice was disappointed when she said, "Oh, Frank. You said you wanted this to be nice. Let's try and have us a nice meal. I worked so hard on it."

Mr. Fowler ignored her, and said to me, "Eat. Like I done told you."

I picked up a piece of turkey, the easiest thing

to eat without a fork. I bit into it and started chewing, and chewing, and chewing. The meat seemed to swell, like I'd taken two, then three bites, and on and on. I tried to swallow it down and gagged.

Mr. Fowler watched me the entire time, and when I made that noise, he said, "Swallow that goddamn piece of meat, or else."

Mama said, "Frank!"

Mr. Fowler said, "She's got to learn."

"Learn what, for God's sake!"

Again, he acted like he hadn't heard her. He started that crazy talking to himself thing. "She ain't so sassy and full a herself now, is she? I'm gonna see to it, yessiree. Things are gonna be different here in *my* house."

Mama's mouth went into a straight line. She said nothing more. I could see her trembling.

He said, "Swallow, or else."

The bite of turkey continued to swell, and I gagged again. He jumped up, came around to where I sat, grabbed my jaws, and held them shut. I squeezed my eyes tight so I wouldn't have to look at him, look at that awful face above me.

"Swallow."

Mama's chair scraped the floor and hit the wall hard enough to cause the small decorative shelf with fancy plates setting on it to rattle. Mr. Fowler didn't loosen his grip.

She came around the table, and pulled on his

arm. "Frank. I said stop it. What are you doing?"

Ross, his voice a growl, said, "Let her go."

Mr. Fowler got to breathing real hard, like he was having trouble getting air in and out.

His voice had gone hoarse, and he puffed, "She's gonna do as I say."

I was about to be sick. Tears squirted out of the corners of my eyes, and ran down into my ears. The turkey wasn't going down, no matter what. It was a grotesque wad of meat. I gagged again and it fell out, and I had no idea where it went, and didn't care. The pressure on my jaws was gone suddenly as Mr. Fowler got to huffing even harder, like he was having trouble breathing. His face turned a funny shade, pale with a flush underneath, like a tomato having trouble ripening. Suddenly, it was Mr. Fowler in distress, not me.

Mama said, "Frank?"

He bent over, put his hands on his knees, and wheezed.

Mama said it again, more alarm in her tone. *"Frank? What's wrong?"*

A few seconds passed and his breathing grew clearer. He stayed bent over. Finally, his wheezing quieted. None of us moved, or hardly dared to breathe ourselves. There was the ticking of a clock on the mantel. Mama put a hand out, and touched Mr. Fowler's arm. Even Trent was speechless and looking sorry for once.

Mama said, "Frank, you all right?"

He straightened, wiped his forehead off, and the first thing out of his mouth was, "I knew Thanksgiving would be ruined."

Mama's concerned face smoothed out, and she went back to her place at the table, sat and put her head in her hands.

I slid my chair back as Mr. Fowler held onto the dining room table, and made his way back to his own chair. He didn't look so good. It was like something weak in him broke, something we'd not seen before had revealed itself. I couldn't feel a tinge sorry for him though.

When I got to the dining room door, I turned and said, "I hate . . . I hate it here."

I was sure Mr. Fowler knew what I really meant.

Chapter 26

Mama brought me a turkey sandwich and a glass of milk later on in the evening, but I didn't want it. She sat in the chair at the desk, and motioned for me to sit on the floor between her knees. She pulled a brush from her apron pocket. She used it, and her fingers to work over my scalp, and made it tingle. She talked while she brushed, and smoothed my hair, saying things meant to ease my mind, but it did just the opposite. What I wanted to hear her say was she'd made a mistake and that we didn't need to live like this, that we could make do somehow.

What she said was, "We got to have us a little settling in time, is all. We got to get used to one another, and soon, we'll be fine. I know he's a little more hot tempered than your daddy. It ain't like I hadn't noticed, but I see him trying. Don't you see it, Sonny?"

I said, "I guess."

What I saw was pure meanness, but Mama was trying so hard. For her, I too would keep trying.

She patted my hair, the weight of it laying warm against my back. "There. Better?"

"Yes, ma'am."

She gave me a wistful smile and said, "Good night, sleep tight."

"Night, Mama."

She drifted from my room, looking a bit like a child, the tall ceilings and doorway dwarfing her.

The day after Thanksgiving was sunny, and cold. I came downstairs slow, listening for voices. I hesitated outside of the kitchen, waiting to see if he was in there. It was quiet, only the sound of frying, and then the oven door opening. I sighed with relief and entered the kitchen, noticing how the sun coming up threw warm yellow beams at a slant across the tiles. Under other circumstances, I maybe could have liked the kitchen, out of all the rooms in this big, dark house. Mama smiled as I plopped into a chair at the kitchen table, while setting a big, hot, fluffy biscuit filled with crisp, salty ham in front of me.

She urged me to, "Eat, eat," as if feeding me would somehow make up for what happened, and what I was really missing.

It *was* like being hungry, I suppose, only in a different way 'cause there wasn't any kind of food that was going to make this particular emptiness in the middle of me disappear.

I looked at Mama and noticed her eyes were a bit red, and she looked sad when she said, "Just so you know. He said last night he would apologize."

I took the biscuit, and bit into it, waiting to see what else she would say.

She only lit up a cigarette and studied her nails. Well, I could hold onto the hope Mama's words from the night before would come true, and an apology might be a start.

"Where is everybody?" I asked.

"Ross went out looking for another job, thinking maybe Mr. Slater might hire him on for the Christmas season. They sell lots of hams, sweet potatoes, and pecans this time of year. People buying gifts and all. Frank and Trent are dove hunting." She gave me a peculiar smile and said, "Guilt."

As if on cue came the distant sound of a gun. I nibbled at the ham biscuit, my eyes on the time. Noon couldn't come soon enough.

Like Mama was reading my mind, she said, "What's Daniel been up to lately?"

I'd not talked much about him these days. She didn't even know about Sarah running away from home.

I mumbled, "Doing what he always does, I reckon. Sarah's done run off with some man, gone clear down to Georgia somewheres."

Mama shook her head. "Oh my. What's his mama doing about it?"

"He said his mama said, 'She made her bed, now she's got to lie in it.' "

"Sarah was always a bit too grown-up acting

for her age. I bet that makes him sad. Do you think he'd like to come visit?"

Cautious, I said, "What about Mr. Fowler?"

Mama sounded a bit put out when she said, "Sonny."

Puzzled at the sudden shift in her tone, I said, "What?"

"Can't you find it in you to call him Daddy Frank? It would go a long way in smoothing things over between you two. He's very sensitive about this."

I frowned at my biscuit, unable to believe Mr. Fowler could be sensitive about a thing.

Obstinate, I shook my head. "It doesn't feel right."

"Well, can't you at least call him Frank? Please, for me?"

I sighed and said, "I reckon."

She came over and hugged me.

She said, "Good."

She seemed to have forgot about Daniel.

"Mama?"

"Hm?"

"Can boys like boys? Like the way they would like a girl?"

Mama poked at the ham with a fork, and responded hesitantly. "I've heard of it, why?"

A little too quick, I said, "Some kids at school were talking about it."

Mama quit fiddling with the ham in the skillet and turned the burner off.

Casually, she said, "Oh? Is there someone they think is like that?" while giving me a steady look.

I played it safe and said, "I don't know. It was in the lunchroom, so I couldn't really hear it all."

Mama said, "People might would say those kinds of people ain't right in the head somehow. Maybe call them unstable. Folks can form their own opinion about such, I reckon, but if I know a person, and I get along with them, what does it matter?"

Mr. Fowler made sure it mattered.

She went on, "Ain't nobody's business, is my opinion."

I nodded. "Yeah."

Mama gave me a direct gaze.

"Yeah," she repeated after me, the way Daniel would.

She said, "I'm starting to decorate for Christmas. You want to help?"

I nodded, feeling like we'd talked about him without saying his name. For the next couple of hours, we brought boxes down from an upstairs closet. We wiped ornaments, and laid them out, ready for a tree. Mama swiped at her eyes time and again. By the time we finished, it was dinner-time, and I felt anxious about Daniel, afraid he was already at the pond, and might leave if I

374

didn't show up soon. I went in the kitchen and hurried to make a bologna sandwich.

On my way out the back door, I said, "Mama, I'm gonna go over to the pond for a little bit."

Distracted by the display of memories, she waved a hand. A last minute thought came and I ran back upstairs and got my old dowsing stick. It was time to try again 'cause I was needing a sign from Daddy, now more than ever before. Down the long driveway I ran, hoping I wouldn't encounter Trent or Mr. Fowler, wherever they were. I got lucky. I didn't see neither one, and I slowed to a walk as I entered the woods. Winding my way through the scrub and undergrowth, our old house appeared through the bare trees after I'd only gone a couple hundred feet. I came out on the other side and hurried to the pond. My heart gave a little gallop at the sight of Daniel pacing on the wood dock. He was wearing cuffed blue jeans, a flannel shirt, and a red wool hat pulled down to cover his ears. His hair stuck out from the bottom of it, looking like a thick brown fringe.

"Hey, Daniel!"

He pointed to his bike and said, "Come on, I got something to show you."

"What is it?"

"Here. Wear my hat."

Mystified, I pulled the hat on, still warm from his head, and breathed in the scent of his shampoo while I did so. I handed him my dowsing stick, and he stuck it in the saddlebag on the back, half of it poking out. He held the bike steady while I climbed on, awkward as usual.

"Where're we going?"

"It's a surprise. You'll see."

My rear end on the handlebars, I propped my feet on the hub of the front tire. I'd ridden the handlebars this way before, for short distances here and there. He pushed off, and we wobbled this way and that a bit at first, but once he got going, it smoothed out.

My job was to yell, "Pothole!" whenever a one came up, which on some of the roads was as frequent as seeing the carcass of possums that didn't make it.

And though it was chilly, I wouldn't have wanted to be anywhere else, my back within inches of his chest, his hands near my hips. I hoped wherever it was we were heading, it would take a while to get there. He peered over my left shoulder at the road ahead, and every now and then I would glance back at him, noticing how his hair glinted with sparks of gold.

I kept doing that until he finally said, "Quit it."

I grinned, and held on tight. It felt like I was flying. Down Turtle Pond Road he pedaled, his enthusiasm for this adventure evident in the small smile he'd allowed, even though he sounded annoyed at my attention. After a turn here and there, we ended up on a narrow dirt strip, the weeds on either side occasionally brushing our arms and legs. We were way out in the boonies, as Trent would have said. A few minutes later he took a delicate turn down another dirt path and that was when I guessed where we were going.

The tall silvery tank, which I'd only seen from a distance, showed a big red circle painted in the middle and the words *Lucky Strike* painted in black, the cigarettes Daddy smoked. I'd never considered the coincidence of this before, and my breath caught. Water tank. The brand of cigarette. The connection almost made me lose my grip on the handlebars. Daniel brought the bike to a stop, and planted his feet so I could slide off.

Looking around, I said, "This is great!"

"I've been coming here lately."

"You have?"

He stared up at the tower and said, "I like to sit up there. I can see your house. Plus, I can see all of Flatland, Trenton, and beyond. Come on, let's climb up."

I hesitated. "You sure? What if we get caught?"

"Ain't nobody coming out here."

I hesitated. "It's pretty high, ain't it?"

Daniel ignored my question and pointed at my dowsing stick. "You want me to bring this?"

I said, "I guess."

He stuck it in his back pocket, and started for

the narrow steps near one of the huge steel legs and said, "I'll go first and show you."

He grabbed onto the ladder, and after he'd climbed several rungs, he looked down to see if I was following. Nervous, I gripped the first rung. It was easy at first, but when we got halfway, I was clinging to the steel, and my legs were shaking.

I said, "Wait."

"It's worth it, I promise."

My voice was weak. "Okay."

"Think of it like climbing a tree."

"Ha. I don't do that much, in case you hadn't noticed."

"Just don't look up. And definitely don't look down."

We started again, and the higher we went, the more panicked I got.

I stopped again after a few seconds, and squeaked out, "Daniel."

I was shallow breathing, my damp hands slick and untrustworthy. I felt as if I was swaying. I hung on as stiff and unyielding as the steel I was squeezing so hard. I was certain I was leaving handprints. There was a slight breeze and even that scared me. Like it would blow me off, even though it was barely brushing across my face. Although it was cold, I was sweating under my clothes. The thought of continuing made me want to throw up. The thought of going down produced the same feeling.

Daniel's voice came from above. "Almost there. You're gonna be glad you did it. I was afraid the first time too. It gets easier."

I panted with fear, but knowing we were so close kept me moving.

I said, "Go!" my anxiety making me short-tempered.

I mumbled words of encouragement to myself.

"One step at a time. It's gonna be over with soon."

Seconds later, Daniel said, "We have to go across this. We can't go through the hatch."

"What?"

I gave a quick glance up, my arms wrapped tight around the ladder to see Daniel walking, *walking,* across a section that looked like a ladder laying on the ground, except we had to be at least a hundred or more feet in the air. After that, we'd be at the base, the part with a rounded, bulging end, where a circular platform went around it. The platform was the goal. I shut my eyes.

I whispered, "Dear Lord, dear Lord."

I finished the last part, then lay flat along the section he'd walked, my belly and legs against the steel, inching forward. My breath came in short gasps, like I wasn't getting enough air. I stopped.

Daniel's voice came from directly over me. "You ain't but about four feet from the last part. Come on."

"I can't do it."

"You can too."

"I don't want to."

"Come on!"

I licked my lips, which were dry as a clump of cotton and inched forward again. Inch. Inch. Inch. Like one of them little green caterpillars. I did it with my eyes shut.

Daniel said, "You're there. You ain't got but five more feet, and you're done."

Encouraged, I reached for the short ladder and crawled onto the platform where he was, only to lay flat again. I huffed some more and it was a minute or so before I could sit up.

Daniel said, "Gee whiz. You ain't ever said you were afraid of heights."

"You ain't ever asked."

He sat at the edge, his feet hanging over, arms resting on the safety rail. I shut my eyes to fight the dizziness. Slowly, I grew accustomed, and eventually I was able to ease my legs over the edge to sit beside him. I gripped the rail so tight it hurt.

He advised, "Look straight, off into the distance. Don't look down. Least not yet."

I did as he said and took in the scenery around me, and if I wasn't already feeling winded from fright, it would have taken my breath. Here I could see a view of the land as never before. I stared and stared. We studied the earth's browns, greens, and the creamy white of sandy areas, all of it cut into the square precision of fields, with clusters of trees breaking that perfection. I could see a slim sliver of blue off to our east, maybe the Atlantic Ocean, or maybe just the sky meeting earth.

I finally said, "Wow."

"It's great, ain't it?"

"It is. How long you been coming here?"

"Since Sarah left. I've come at night sometimes, when Brenda has company."

"At night? You must be nuts."

"Nah."

"But, it would be pitch black."

"I bring a flashlight. I've done it so much, I almost prefer it. I can see the lights of houses all around. I can see the light on in your bedroom window at his place."

I said, "You can?"

"Yeah."

"Are you spying on me?"

He started to give me a friendly bump.

I grabbed the rail and said, "Don't!"

He said, "Scaredy pants. How're you gonna use this if you're too afraid to move?"

He reached over and got the dowsing stick from where he'd laid it. I took it and put it beside me.

I said, "I need a minute."

"Yeah. I needed more than that my first time up here. How're things with *him?*"

If there was one way to get my mind off of the breathtaking height, it was to tell Daniel about Mr. Fowler. I told him about his rules, what he'd done to me at Thanksgiving, and what happened when Ross lost his job. I told him about finding the hood, and him being part of the Klan. About the scratch and Mama's neck. The more I talked, the worse it sounded. Daniel shook his head here and there. I finally had told all there was.

He said, "Geez. What're y'all gonna do?"

I lifted my shoulders. "Mama says it'll get better."

"That's hard to believe."

"She says I got to give him a chance. That we just need a settling in time."

"He's a real sumbitch, but who knew he'd be a crazy sumbitch."

"Yeah."

"Yeah."

Daniel stood up, and walked the narrow platform to the other side of the tower without seeming to care he was a hundred and fifty feet in the air. Without him beside me, I felt exposed, vulnerable.

After a few seconds, I called out, "Daniel?"

He came back and said, "If you move around, it helps. Wanna try?"

"It's too soon."

"You'll have to move eventually."

The thought brought back that queasy sensation, but I slowly got on my knees, and then my feet. I stood hunched over, clutching the rail while the idea of standing straight gave me a mental image of me toppling over it. I grew dizzy again. Maybe this hadn't been a good idea.

Daniel put out his hand, and I said, "No!"

"I was only going to help you. You're shaking like you're ninety years old!"

"It ain't funny!"

I sat back down quick. For comfort, I picked up my dowsing stick, gripping it in both hands, attempting to hide the tremor.

"If you could've seen yourself. All hunched over like an old woman."

"Ain't nobody up here but you, so who cares!"

My aggravation and nerves almost hid a different kind of tremor. I'd felt something. *Was it . . . ? Was that . . . ?*

Daniel said, "Sonny?"

"Sh!"

I don't know why I was telling him to be quiet. I shivered, but not from cold.

"You look funny."

"Wait, Daniel."

I let go of one end of my dowsing stick, and the sensation disappeared. I rose to my knees. Somehow got to my feet. My attention was no longer on where I was, or how high, or anything else except that distinctive awareness. I held it in both hands again, and felt a pull, as if it would turn me toward the tower. I faced the tank, staring down at the vibrating stick in my hands. Opposite of sensing water in the ground, here the flush of warm went along my arms first, then shot down into my legs, and the stick, instead of pointing toward the ground, flew up so fast even Daniel took a step back. It pointed at the tank.

"Sonny?" he said again, amazement in his voice.

It's back. I looked at Daniel and spoke that thought. "It's back. I got it back!"

Daniel said, "I ain't ever thought you'd lost it. You only needed the right place, the right time."

I held it properly again, wanting to be sure. The vibration started as soon as the ends touched my palms. I stared up at the huge letters spelling out Lucky Strike. If Daddy was finally sending me a sign, it couldn't have been any clearer.

Daniel said, "Ain't you glad you came now?"

I was breathing fast. I was more than glad. Suddenly, I wanted to try it again, at home, my real home.

I said, "I want to go try at my old house."

Daniel said, "Yeah, okay."

I would test it where it meant the most, on the land where I'd learned of it to begin with, near to the person who'd taught me. I waited for Daniel to lead the way. He drifted back to the rail and stared off into the distance again. When he finally started for the ladder, his expression sent a different sort of tremor along my spine. His eyes were lackluster, as dull as all of the browns of the dormant land below us. I realized he'd not talked of the things he usually did, his scenes, new movies, or any mention of being onstage at all. Given what I saw, I had the distinct impression Daniel no longer dreamed his big dreams, his eyes didn't shine with possibilities.

Loneliness was what I saw.

Chapter 27

When I think back on it now, the time at the water tower was a turning point, a moment when I'd realized my ability to divine water hadn't left me, and confirmed that Daniel had, in some way. When we'd started out, he'd seemed excited about showing me this special place, but once there, it was like it swallowed him up somehow, like he was looking into the distance and thinking of faraway places, maybe imagining he was anywhere but Jones County. Despite my fear, it was now a special, unique place for me too. I wanted to make it our spot, like the stage in the barn at the old house, or the pond.

On our way back, I said, "We ought to come back soon."

I was surprised when he said, "No."

"Why not?"

He didn't answer, and I took it to mean he regretted sharing his place, as if allowing me to come had taken something away from him. The ride back seemed faster, and soon we were zooming down Turtle Pond Road, then bumping down the tractor path. He stopped at the pond, and I got off the handlebar, grabbed the stick, held it proper, and walked alongside the water. It happened quick, and the wonder of it made me smile as the branch thrummed, and hummed, and sent the little signals I'd wanted so badly all those months ago. Daniel flopped down onto the dock. I pointed I was going to the field near the house, and he waved a hand in acknowledgment, remaining on his back, looking at the sky. I ran until I reached to Daddy's gravestone, certain my happiness would shoot through my feet, into the ground, telling him it had finally happened.

I placed my hand on his stone and said, "Watch this, Daddy."

I walked through the plowed field. My little damaged stick spoke without hesitation, sending messages of flowing water, pointing down with the consistency and accuracy of the sun rising and setting. I let the moment soak in, my doubts, at least about this, now gone. When Daniel finally came to see what I was up to, all I could do was grin.

He said, "It worked?"

"It did."

"I knew it would."

"It ain't happened for months."

He repeated what Aunt Ruth had said. "We've had enough rain now. Water tables during a drought are lower."

I should have figured he'd know the scientific

reason behind it. All that mattered to me was it had happened. I was contented.

Daniel said, "I got to go."

"When will you come back?"

"Ain't no chance of running into him over here, is there?"

I shook my head. "Not when it ain't planting season."

"This weekend, then?"

I was surprised, but nodded eagerly. "Yes."

And this was where I would say we entered a time when we settled back into a regular routine. Daniel's visits grew more frequent, with us spending hours at the old house every weekend. It was a lot like before, sometimes we'd be on the barn stage where Daniel got back into a bit of his acting, showing me a new scene from a movie called *Rebel Without a Cause*. Sometimes we'd end up inside the old house, using the key left under one of Mama's old flower pots by the back door. I wandered the rooms, touching this and that. We'd sit at the kitchen table, or we'd meander down the dogtrot to my old bedroom, where we'd lay on the bed, and I would be consumed by a heavy ache of homesickness weighing me down into the mattress such that I was sure I might not be able to get up. We grew comfortable, perhaps complacent, but if I thought my absences from Mr. Fowler's house went unnoticed, I was wrong.

• • •

A brand-new bicycle sat under the tree, a Schwinn Catalina, light blue, my favorite color. I wanted it, yet I didn't want it. He sat beside Mama on the couch, his hair all messy, like he'd had a rough night, stubble on his chin and cheeks, eyes bloodshot. They sipped hot coffee, and she'd brought in a tray of sausage biscuits. He wore a phony smile.

Mama said, "Oh my, Sonny, ain't it nice? You needed you a bike."

The shine of it seemed all wrong in this dull room. I got to thinking maybe a bike could be just what I needed. I could be quicker about where I was getting to. Freedom. That's what I realized came with this gift, and it was the only reason I accepted it by going over and putting my hand on the seat.

"Thank you," I said.

Mr. Fowler said, "No need to sit on somebody's handlebars no more."

Mama looked at me, then at Mr. Fowler. "What? Whose handlebars?"

Mr. Fowler grinned, a reaction that didn't fit with the tone of his voice or the look in his eyes. "She knows who."

My heart set to racing, like I was already pedaling hard uphill. He knew. Mr. Fowler took a deep puff on his cigarette, and let out a stream of smoke through his nose. His color was like he'd been working out in the hot sun. I was quiet while he gave a small nod of his head, as if to say, *yeah. I know all about that.* He looked like a pressure cooker about to blow.

He said, "Expensive gift is what that is. Hope it ain't a waste of money for being disrespected."

I was probably the only one who saw the intensity in that hot gaze, how his throat worked like something was trying to come out of him.

Mama said, "Frank, whatever are you going on about?"

He leaned over and patted her leg, more like pounded it, and gestured. "Hell, I'm only saying it cost me a pretty penny."

Mama moved her leg away and said, "Frank, dear, easy. You're gonna leave a bruise."

Mr. Fowler said, "Awww, sugar britches, don't you know how much I love you?"

Mama cleared her throat and said, "She appreciates it, don't you, Sonny?"

"Yes, ma'am. Thank you . . . Frank."

His gaze shot back to me, eyes narrowed. I'd conceded and finally said his name, for Mama's sake, and my own.

He relaxed and said, "Stuff's expensive these days. Took a good chunk out a my account, let me tell you what."

Mama's smile looked like somebody had pinned the corners of her mouth up.

Ross and Trent waited to open their gift, and

she sighed and said, "Ross, what did you get?"

Mr. Fowler's attention shifted, and it was as if the broiler I'd been under was shut off, at least for now. Ross had a large box near his feet, and he started to open it. We all leaned in as he lifted out a new record player, an RCA Victor, and a bunch of 45s to go with it. He went through them, calling out songs like "Sh-Boom," "Earth Angel," and "Shake, Rattle and Roll."

"Thank you," he said, a hint of surprise in his voice that Mr. Fowler had bought a gift he'd enjoy.

Mr. Fowler said, "Spent a half a week's groceries for it."

Mama said, "You shouldn't spend so much, Frank."

He said, "I didn't want a bunch a mopey faces."

Mama said, "The kids know better."

He said, "Hm."

Appearing exasperated, Mama turned to Trent and said, "Trent, your turn."

Trent's box was long, and I had all ideas what was inside it. He opened it and yep, just as I figured, out came a new shotgun. He was so excited his hands were shaking as he brought it up, and sighted on the chandelier overhead.

His voice cracked, like it had been doing lately, when he said, "Wow! A Remington!"

This was a gift Mr. Fowler seemed to take interest in.

He leaned forward and said, "It's a 12 gauge, Model 870 slide action. That's a good gun there."

"Gee whiz, thank you, Daddy Frank!"

Ross caught my eye, and rolled his. Trent knew what side his bread was buttered on. Funny that, cause after having asked us to call him Daddy Frank, every time Trent did, I'd noticed Mr. Fowler gave a little twitch to his shoulder like he didn't much like hearing it, as if it didn't suit him in some way.

He said, "Don't be shooting at the house."

Trent gave him a confused look.

Mama set things onto a more congenial path when she said, "Sakes alive, Frank, this is all too much!" and soon as she did, he became magnanimous, his back straightening up as he waved a hand.

"It ain't nothing, darlin'. Anything for my baby."

When Mr. Fowler wanted to play nice, he could be as smooth talking as a Sunday morning preacher. He hugged her, while over the top of her head his eyes trailed around the room, landing on each one of us like he was still trying to figure out how to make us vanish.

I said, "Mama, we got you something too."

Actually, Ross had been the one to get it with the money he'd saved up. Trent and I were part of it though, agreeing to do his share of chores for a month as a way to help pay.

Mama said, "Oh, you children shouldn't have done that!"

Mr. Fowler released her as Ross handed her one of the boxes under the tree. She tore the wrapping paper off, and instantly grew teary eyed. We'd got her a new winter coat. A pretty dark blue color with a soft inner lining she could zip and unzip as the weather warranted.

She held the coat up and said, "I love it! Look, Frank. Look what they've gone and done."

Mr. Fowler yawned and scratched his belly. He looked about as interested in Mama opening a gift from us as replacing a roll of toilet paper in the bathroom. She made over each of us, coming round to where we sat, squeezing us tight, and kissing the tops of our heads. Giving Mama a gift was the best feeling, especially to see her smiling and happy. She held it up again and sighed.

She said, "You kids outdid yourselves this year," and gave us that look, like she might come around and hug us again.

So wrapped up were we in our moment with Mama that when Mr. Fowler cleared his throat, and looked at his watch, it was like being thumped on the head.

Mama jumped, like he was reminding her of the time, and exclaimed, "If I'm gonna have Christmas dinner on the table at noon, I best get to it."

Mr. Fowler grabbed her arm and pulled her back down on the couch.

He said, "Hold on, darlin'."

He reached underneath the couch, pulled out a small thin box, and held it out.

She put a hand to her mouth, then to her chest, and said, "Frank. What have you gone and done?"

Like a kid on his first day of school meeting a pretty new teacher, he had an "aw shucks" look.

He said, "It ain't much."

She opened it, and once the paper was off, she held a red leather box, and inside it was a bracelet, diamonds galore, and even from where we sat, the sparkle of it could have lit the room had the sun hit on it just right.

Mama draped it over her fingers, staring at it, and said, "Frank! I never . . ."

"That's right, you ain't never had nothing like that, have you? That's what it means to be married to Frank Fowler. Look a that there, now. Ain't it something?"

Mama shook her head in confusion, staring at it like it wasn't real. She frowned, and seemed tongue-tied. He took it from her, turning it this way and that, admiring it. Ross and Trent had gone back to fiddling with their stuff, and missed the implications of Mama's reaction while Mr. Fowler preened like a peacock, proud, instead of considering the impracticality of such a gift. He stopped fawning over the bracelet long enough to notice his enthusiasm for it exceeded Mama's.

His head reared back. "What's the matter? Don't you like it? I paid . . ."

Mama interrupted him. "Frank, when would I wear this? I mean, it's beautiful, but . . ."

It got quiet. Oh. She shouldn't have said that. The entire time we'd been in the living room, supposedly having a nice Christmas morning, I'd viewed Mr. Fowler no different than a king overseeing his peasants. He snatched it from her hand.

"Fine."

He grabbed the box too.

Mama said, "Frank. I didn't mean . . ."

"No. It's fine. I shouldn't have bought it. I figured you'd appreciate it, is all."

"Well, of course I do, it's just . . ."

He snapped the lid shut and she stopped talking. She had a helpless look, as if she'd been going along a familiar path only to find herself now lost. Mr. Fowler stood up, his manner gone stiff and formal. Box in hand, he headed out of the living room.

Mama said, "Where're you going?"

He didn't answer. She got up to follow and by then Ross and Trent realized something had gone amiss. They stopped admiring their gifts and watched as Mr. Fowler exited the room with Mama trailing after him, one hand reaching out to touch his shoulder. He shrugged her off, a gesture of aggravation. We stayed put. Mama could handle him, and I was certain she'd persuade him to calm down, and that would be that. His gift didn't suit her, which proved he didn't really know her. She'd have loved something practical 'cause that was how she thought, even I knew that. He'd have done better to have given her a pretty dress for church, or if it had to be jewelry, a string of soft iridescent pearls that would lay against the creaminess of her neckline, something less expensive, and appropriate, although that would have seemed extravagant too.

Ross looked at Trent and me and with sarcasm, he said, "Merry Christmas."

I said, "Yeah. No kidding."

I almost didn't want the bike now. I honestly didn't want a thing from him. A loud noise came from the kitchen, a sound like something had been thrown. We jumped to our feet and next came raised voices. We rushed down the long hall, through the dining room, and into the kitchen. Mama was the only one in there, cleaning up a mess on the floor, her homemade cranberry sauce. She cried as she picked up pieces of a broken bowl. Strangely, *it* had been a gift from Daddy one year. Had Mr. Fowler known that? The red berries all over the floor looked like blood.

She refused to look up though, and all she said was, "The bowl slipped."

Ross put his hands on his hips and said, "Mama."

She shook her head, as if to dismiss any ideas it was anyone's fault but hers.

She said, "It got dropped, that's all."

"How?" he asked.

She repeated herself, and I suppose, technically, it wasn't a lie.

I knelt down beside her, and started helping get the berries up. It was quiet, nobody talking. Ross went outside, and I figured he might be going to find out where Mr. Fowler was, and maybe even ask him about it. Trent drifted back off to the living room, casting worried looks over his shoulder as he went.

When it was just us, I said, "Mama? You all right?"

She sniffled a bit and then said, "If I can just get us through this holiday."

Which said a lot more than she realized.

Chapter 28

It was after the New Year, and we were back in school, but all I could do was worry about Mama being at home alone with Mr. Fowler. Ever since Christmas Day he'd changed. Where he'd once catered to her, he'd started griping about everything she did. And where she'd once been able to quell his moods, if she even attempted to rationalize, he took it wrong.

"Are you telling me I'm stupid?"

"No, Frank, that's not what I'm saying, I'm only trying to tell you . . ."

"I'm your husband, not some imbecile. I don't need explanations."

"Frank, it's not a big deal."

"Says who? I'll decide what's what around here. Do you hear me? This is *my* house."

It went like that. Mama could not win. And all it took was that one mistake about the bracelet and it got him all twisted around, like he suddenly got turned inside out, revealing to Mama the Frank Fowler I'd seen all along. The atmosphere in the house went from murky to moldering. No matter how nice Mama talked to him, carrying on as if nothing happened, his responses were cryptic. He tried to pick fights, figuring out ways to nitpick. How she kept house. How she washed and ironed his clothes. She tried to bake him his favorite blackberry pie, using frozen berries she'd put up last year.

"My mama, she didn't fix this pie like this. It ain't nowhere as good as hers. She only used fresh berries. Why can't you do it right?"

Mama was gutsy enough to say, "You liked the way I cooked before, Frank," which earned her the sort of look that was the sole cause of my worry about her being alone. It was as if her comments about the bracelet had been a direct rejection of him.

I told Daniel at lunch, "He's done gone looney tunes."

Daniel made a disgusted noise and said, "No he hasn't."

We were standing at our spot by the fence on the playground, huddled up against the cold, and I pushed off it so I could face him. I was ready to give him what for when he clarified what he meant.

"He's always been that a way."

I relaxed and said, "S'truth. I don't know how he did it, but he fooled her. Now, all hell's busting loose."

I couldn't bring myself to concede to Daniel's original point about us being trapped.

The bell rang, and we headed for the school.

He said, "Hey, we meeting on Saturday, like usual?"

"Yep."

We parted ways in the hall, and if there was one thing I could be happy about, it was that Daniel and I had more or less regained our old footing with one another, even if I couldn't completely understand what was going on with him.

When Saturday came, Mama seemed out of sorts. She looked pale, sickly, with the shine of sweat on her forehead, while the house, if anything was cool and damp.

I studied how she looked and said, "Mama, you feeling sick?"

"I'm a bit off this morning. I probably just need to eat something."

I said, "I'll fix toast. Can you eat that, you think?"

Mr. Fowler came in at that moment, smelling to high heaven of aftershave, and the scent of it made Mama go green. She covered the lower half of her face with her hand. He had on a pair of clean pants, creased sharply, and I pictured Mama ironing and ironing them creases until they would just about cut your finger. That's how he liked them. Same with his shirtsleeves. He looked from the stove to Mama, and back to the stove.

He said, "I told you yesterday I was going

down to Swansboro to look at that new tractor this morning. Ain't nothing cooked for breakfast? I mean, can't I get a simple egg sandwich?"

Mama went to stand up, and I got between him and her and said, "She ain't feeling up to it. Mama, sit back down, I'll do it."

All he said was, "Yeah? That's too bad. Get to it, kid. I got to get going."

I hurried to fry the egg, and toast the bread. I laid out ten slices, thinking of Ross and Trent while I was at it, knowing they'd be up soon. I put it all on a cookie sheet, dotted all but two slices with butter. Mr. Fowler watched every single thing I did, and knowing that made my fingers to feel stiff and clumsy, what with his eyes boring into my back. The one time I glanced at him, he made a point of looking at his wristwatch. I went faster, scooping bacon grease into the skillet and turning the burner on high. I cracked two eggs into it, and slid the bread into the oven. I had it all done in three minutes, if that. When I handed him the sandwich wrapped in wax paper, he leaned across the table. Mama was sitting in the chair, looking like a broken doll. He put the food under her nose and she averted her head quick.

He said, "That's all I asked for."

Mama's voice was weak, and she said, "Frank, I'm not feeling well."

He mocked her, "Fraaaank, I'm not feeling well."

My voice low, I said, "Leave her alone."

How obscure them eyes of his could get, black as night, and cold as the winter wind outside. I braced, waiting for him to yell at me, only his focus was on Mama. Like he couldn't stand she wasn't waiting on him.

He said, "I want my supper on the table when I get back."

She nodded and he went out making sure he slammed the screen door, acting like a spoiled child. Mama's nerves were as ragged as a torn, frayed sheet. I let my breath go and sank into the chair opposite her. A single fat tear rolled down her cheek.

I said, "Mama, don't worry. I'll cook supper."

"It ain't about supper."

"What is it?"

She reached across the table and grabbed at my hand. "Oh, Sonny. I can't hardly believe it."

She sounded alarmed, almost panicked.

My own voice rose to match hers. "What Mama, what is it?"

She let go of my hand and said, "I need to eat a piece of toast."

I jumped up to get one of the slices I'd left unbuttered. I put it on a saucer and brought it to her.

"You want some coffee?"

She shuddered. "No."

I noticed she also wasn't smoking her usual

morning cigarette either, the one that always, always accompanied her first cup.

She nibbled at the toast, set it down, and without any further preamble, she said, "I'm pregnant."

"Mama!"

Those were two words I'd not expected to hear. Pregnant! I didn't know how to react. I couldn't hardly believe I'd heard her right. She was almost full-out crying now, and sort of clenching and unclenching her hands.

I said, "Maybe you ought to call Aunt Ruth, Mama. She'd know what to do."

Mama acted like it was the last thing on her mind. "Ain't nothing to do, Sonny. I'm gonna have a baby in about seven months. Lordy, I can't believe this happened after all these years. I figured I was getting too old for this. I'll soon be thirty-nine, and . . ."

Ross and Trent wandered into the kitchen, hair wet, and dressed ready to work, a habit they'd formed after the first morning here. They'd learned not to come to the breakfast table in their pajamas, hair stuck up all over the place, like they used to do at home 'cause Mr. Fowler had sent them back upstairs, yelling at them that nobody was allowed at *his* table looking like they'd just rolled out of bed.

They immediately noticed Mama's tear-streaked face.

Trent said, "What's the matter?"

Mama couldn't seem to get the words out again, but Ross read it a different way. He was instantly mad, like he already figured it had something to do with Mr. Fowler. He looked like Daddy in that moment, same squared jaw, almost the same posture too.

He said, "Mama, it ain't right, him acting like he is over a damn bracelet. How's he gonna be when it's something more serious? It worries me."

Trent sat in one of the kitchen chairs and grabbed a piece of toast. "He ain't gonna do nothing. He's all bark and no bite."

Ross said, "Oh yeah, Mr. Know-It-All, and what about Mr. Wells? Huh? What about what he did to him?"

Trent pointed at Mama. "He ain't gonna mess with Mama like that."

Ross said, "How do you know what he'll do or not do, he's liable to . . ."

Mama put her head into her hands. "Boys. Stop. I ain't up to hearing no arguing."

She lifted her head from her hands, and sighed.

I said, "You want this other piece of toast?"

She shook her head. "Boys, I'm expecting."

Ross sighed deep, and Trent said, "Expecting what?"

Under any other circumstances I'd have laughed.

Ross shoved him and said, "A baby, you yo-yo."

Trent gaped at Mama, his mouth open. Both boys turned a shade of red usually reserved for when some girl at school paid attention to them.

Mama spoke carefully, like she was testing the words out for herself. "A baby." She pushed away from the table and said, "I'm going to go lie down."

I said, "Don't worry about nothing. I'll fix supper tonight. You rest."

She lifted a hand in acknowledgment, then let it drop. She didn't look strong enough to carry no baby.

Ross said, "Son of a bitch," and though it sounded like an exclamation, maybe he was calling Mr. Fowler that name too.

Trent said, "Damnation."

I thought of something and rushed after her. She was already at the top of the stairs.

I said, "Mama, does he know?"

She shook her head.

I said, "Okay," and when I heard the door to their room close, I stood still, unable to wipe out the ugly memory of what I'd heard happening in there. Him after her like a dog in heat. Him pawing at her with those big meaty hands of his, and how she'd winced a time or two when he grabbed her in that boisterous, energetic way of his. I drifted back into the kitchen where Ross and Trent had cleaned out the pan of toast and were now eating bowls of cereal.

I grabbed a couple of bananas, and Trent said, "You gonna meet what's his face?"

Aggravated, I said, "Yes, but I'll be back so Mama ain't by herself."

I went out, and jumped on my bike, rounding the big loop of a drive until I was on the road, where I pedaled furiously. Soon I was flying down Turtle Pond Road, and bad as I hated to admit liking anything to do with Mr. Fowler, the bike sure did get me over to our place quicker. Daniel was waiting for me by the barn. I jumped off the bike and tossed him a banana.

He said, "I wondered if you were coming."

I looked up at that sky with not a cloud in it, appreciating that deep blue it could get in the wintertime. I sighed and looked at Daniel.

"Something happened," I said.

He gave me a nervous look. "What?"

"Mama's pregnant."

He did the same thing we'd done, repeated the fact as if by saying it out loud, it might clear up the confusion he had. "Pregnant?"

"Yeah. She's not feeling good. Why don't you come to his place?"

"No."

"He ain't there, Daniel. He's gone to Swansboro. And Ross and Trent are gonna be in the fields today, and I don't want Mama to be alone, in case she needs something."

"I don't know."

"Just for a little while. He won't be back till suppertime. You can leave right after lunch. He won't ever know you been there."

He paused, then with a hint of doubt, he mumbled, "All right."

We hopped on our bikes, and it was fun riding side by side down the road, although I wouldn't have minded being up on his handlebars if only to be closer to him. I found myself looking back over my shoulder now and then on that short ride back to Mr. Fowler's house. He almost looked like the old Daniel, his hair whipping in the wind, his cheeks pink from the cold, and eyes as soft and warm as honey. Daniel was something else in my book, and I got to wishing he wasn't, wishing it had been like it was when we were ten.

Up the drive we went and around to the back side of the house. I showed him where he could stow his bike so it was out of the way. We entered the kitchen, and found Mama back at the table again.

At the sight of Daniel, she smiled big and said, "Daniel, how nice to see you!"

"You too, Mrs. Cree—, I mean Mrs. Fowler."

Mama said, "I'm not used to my new name yet neither."

She asked how he was getting along, and then she took on a bad spell again.

She said, "Whew. I best go back upstairs and lie down. Did Sonny tell you the news?"

Daniel's feet did a little shuffle and he mumbled, "Yes, ma'am. Congratulations."

Mama said, "Well, it's really too soon to be sharing the news outside of our little circle here."

"Yes, ma'am."

Mama put her hand on his cheek and said, "Now, honey, you come back to visit soon. I'll be feeling better, shortly, I'm sure."

She gave me a little smile and turned to leave. She was still in her nightgown and robe and I saw a big bruise on her calf, and wondered how it got there. Daniel noticed too, and looked at me. I shook my head, and shrugged. Maybe she'd just bumped her leg.

For the next little bit, I showed Daniel the house. He agreed with me about the wallpaper, saying it was "downright disgusting." He stared up at the tall ceilings, and at the artwork, and at all the mounted animals.

"Sumbitch has money, but Brenda's got a better-looking sofa than that," he declared, while pointing at the hideous orange and brown patterned monstrosity sitting in the study.

I snickered and said, "Darn thing's ugly as all get out," and then I got nervous about Daniel in enemy territory.

I said, "Come on, let's go outside."

We crossed the yard, heading for the big barn. The door had been pulled back and I could see Ross and Trent. Ross was filling up a gas can, and Trent was oiling one of the implements, and it got awkward 'cause of what had happened between Trent and Daniel in the cafeteria.

My plan was to simply ignore Trent. "Come on, Daniel, I want to show you something."

To my surprise, Trent spoke to him. "Hey, Daniel, you seen any a them 3-D movies yet?"

Daniel sort of stuttered, and feeling protective, I said, "What do you want, Trent?"

Trent got huffy and said, "Nothing! I just asked him a question. I mean, I know he likes movies, and acting and all."

"And since when did you decide you're interested in anything Daniel does?"

"Well, just forget I asked, then!"

Daniel was a bigger person than me.

He said, "It's okay. Yeah, I've seen one. It was really neat, like you were actually right there, in the scene."

Trent nodded and said, "That's what I heard. I want to go see one, myself, one a these days."

Daniel said, "If you do, go see *Inferno*."

Ross said, "Oh yeah, that's the one I heard about."

Considering how the day got started, this was

an unexpected turn and a good one. Trent was likely feeling guilty.

And after a bit of an awkward silence, I said, "Well, come on, Daniel, there's something over here I found."

At the back of the barn was a set of old velvet curtains that had probably hung in one of the living rooms. They had some moth holes, but I'd thought of taking them over to the barn at our house, and using them for our stage. Considering where they'd been thrown, I had a feeling they wouldn't ever be missed. Daniel and I were in the process of stretching them out to see how long they were—twelve-foot ceilings made for some really long ones—when I heard several vehicles pulling up into the drive and then doors slamming. One, two, three, four. The sound of footsteps coming in the direction of the barn made me catch my breath, and hold it. Daniel reminded me of a baby robin out of its nest too early, how they go absolutely still even if you walked right up to one, picked it up, and put it in the palm of your hand. They would remain frozen in place, as if not moving could somehow render them invisible.

I whispered to Ross, "We got to hide Daniel!"

Ross gave me a confused look and said, "Why?"

I was almost in tears, my voice hitching a little. "He told me to not ever bring him here.

I thought it would be okay 'cause he wasn't supposed to come back till tonight!"

Ross looked like he wanted to smack me for being so stupid.

He said, "Damn, Sonny. That's gonna really piss him off. Geez."

Daniel upon hearing that ran for the back of the barn. I followed, looking over my shoulder as four men filed in, one of them Mr. Fowler, and the other three wearing those scary hoods. An ice cold rush came over me. Suddenly, light from the sun was gone when one pulled the big barn door closed. They had shotguns, resting up on their shoulders, and aside from the sound of the door sliding to meet the wall, they were quiet, moving and doing without saying a word, like it was planned. Daniel stood with his back against the barn wall, tucked into a corner, hands clenched together, and I could hear him breathing hard. I crammed in beside him.

He whispered, alarm strangling his words so they came out high-pitched, "Why are they here?"

I shook my head, just as confused, and scared. "I don't know!"

Mr. Fowler called out, "Where are you? Ain't no sense hiding. Come on, you two, come on out and face the music. Go on and get'em, Stem."

Ross said, "What're you wanting?"

Mr. Fowler said, "You'll see."

I was terrified, and couldn't believe I'd been so stupid. This was happening 'cause of me. I'd only been thinking about what I wanted, going about without concern for getting caught. The tall thin hooded figure didn't take long to spot us, crouched in the corner at the back of the barn. He looked like something out of a horror movie.

He spoke, a strong twang to his voice. "Aw, hell, Frank. It ain't but a couple kids."

"Don't matter none. The girl knows she's done disobeyed her daddy Frank."

When the tall man called Stem went to grab Daniel, he went wild, biting, kicking, and yelling.

I hollered, "You leave him alone!" pulling on the man's arm and trying to grab at the hood to pull it off.

Ross yelled the same thing. "Leave them alone!" and when he started to come help, a fat man jabbed him with the shotgun.

"Stem" shoved me aside, and Mr. Fowler told another man to help him, and between the two of them, they hauled us to the front of the barn, both of us bucking and kicking the entire way. The man who hit Ross and who was as fat as the one was skinny, had my brothers lined up against the side wall, holding the gun on them. It was like some true-to-life movie script of Daniel's run amok.

Mr. Fowler said, "See. I been watching the both

of you, all along. Traipsing around over at the old place. I was gonna do something about it then, but I said to myself, nah, let it go and see what happens. And look what happened. I can't even say I'm gonna be gone for a day that you don't contravene my number one rule."

I struggled to speak. "Please, please, it was a mistake. My mistake."

He reared his head back and said, "What did I tell you?"

I gritted my teeth, and looked at Daniel. His head was down, hair covering his face. He was shaking. My heart clenched, seemed like it would stop.

I said, "You said to stay away from him, and I wouldn't have anything to worry about."

He chuckled. "Girl, least you remembered what I said, even if you didn't *do* as I said. All right, boys, let's get this show on the road."

He spoke to the hooded fat man holding the shotgun on Ross and Trent. My brothers were as stunned as I was, both of them unable to move.

Mr. Fowler said, "Big Boy, make sure them boys watch so they see what happens when someone like him"—and he gestured at Daniel—"goes and gets themselves confused. We're gonna make it so the confusion is gone. Hell, if anything, we'll be doing him a favor, and later on down the road, when he's married, got kids and all, he'll be thanking us. Stem, bring his little ass over here, and Rufus, you control that girl."

Mr. Fowler walked to the stalls in the rear. The man called Big Boy drew closer to Trent and Ross, almost touching them with the gun, and nudged them to follow Mr. Fowler, while Stem grabbed Daniel by the arm and yanked him along to the back too. Daniel had quit fighting. He stared over his shoulder, his gaze locked on mine. Rufus kept a tight grip on my arm, preventing me from going after them, but upon seeing Daniel's expression, I couldn't even stand on my own two feet.

I sank down to the barn floor, repeating, "Don't hurt him. Don't hurt him!"

I was certain we'd entered hell.

Chapter 29

Though I was watched over by the man called Rufus, I wouldn't have gone anywhere. I wouldn't have left Daniel. Rufus wasn't really paying attention to me, anyway. He faced the back of the barn, licked his lips over and over, and rubbed on himself. I shook and my heart felt as if it split right in two. Soon, another emotion I could only identify as rage, an anger unlike anything I'd ever experienced, with the sort of thoughts I'd never had, took over. If I'd have had a gun, I'd have shot them all dead. I knelt in the dirt, folded over, my chest against my knees, my posture like I was praying, and I was. Hard as I could. I prayed for Mama to come. I prayed hard as I've ever prayed, harder even than for Daddy to come back. I was petrified they would kill him. That *this* would kill him.

Time left me. There was no talking, only scuffling sounds, a thump, and more scuffling. A buzzing noise, like a shaver.

That went on forever, and when it stopped, I heard Mr. Fowler say, "Hold him steady."

A sticky, scraping noise like tape being

unrolled. A second of quiet. A muffled crying overridden by the disgusting grunts I'd heard before. I squeezed my eyes tight, pressed my hands over my ears hard as I could. I began to hum. Louder, louder. Rufus kicked me in my backside, hard enough to knock me over.

"Shut the hell up, kid."

I heard the man called Big Boy say, "Boys, uh, uh, don't you turn away. You keep watching."

I hummed even louder, and hoped Rufus would kick me again. And again. I deserved it. I wanted to hurt like Daniel was being hurt. A few seconds later, I was aware it was over. I took my hands from my ears. I unfolded myself, and dared to look down the length of the barn. Daniel came forward, slow, and hesitant. He stared straight ahead, neither left nor right, eyes fixed on the door behind me. He had no expression on his face. The tape was left on his mouth. Symbolic. He passed me as if I wasn't there, only two feet away from him. His head was shaved erratically, some wispy strands left, but mostly, he was bald. There was blood on his scalp. Mr. Fowler stood just outside the stall, fastening his belt.

He called out a warning, "You best not forget what happened here today, boy."

I whispered his name, "Daniel."

He slid the barn door open. Sunlight flooded inside. He walked outside with purpose. After being in the dim interior, I had to squint against the brightness. The shadowed shape of him in the doorway lasted seconds and then he was gone. The sunbeam revealed flecks of dust that swirled. A fresh breeze blew in, dried the tears on my cheeks and things took on a dreamlike appearance. I stood up, wobbly legged as a newborn baby deer.

Mr. Fowler pointed at Trent and Ross. "You two. Get over there by your sister."

Couldn't none of us make eye contact. I'd gone rigid with horror, repulsed by such awfulness. Trent and Ross came and stood by me. We were lined up like tin soldiers. I refused to look anywhere except at the ground. Mr. Fowler approached us, and I could smell him. For the first time since I'd met him, he stunk. He smelled foul, like sweat dried several times over. I put my hand up to my mouth to stop myself from gagging.

He spoke in a whisper, and I had the impression he'd gone crazy. "Any one of you even so much as breathes a word of this, you'll get the same thing. We'll get'em, won't we, boys? What say we go again?"

He chucked Trent under the jaw, and Trent's face folded, collapsing in on itself like a crushed paper cup. Mr. Fowler loved weakness, it was obvious in the way he spoke, milking the moment for all he could.

"Aw. Wah-wah. He's crying."

He made a dismissive sound, and then he was in front of me, so close the toe of his boots almost touched mine.

"I ain't foolin'. Don't you breathe a goddamn word to your mama, or there'll be hell to pay. Y'all hear me? And I want a goddamn answer. Let me hear it. You first, since you're the one who caused this."

He prodded my shoulder and what I had going on in my head was sure to have reflected back to him as I raised my eyes to his.

I piled branches high around Mr. Fowler. His ankles were tied and he begged me for mercy. I laughed as I squirted gas on the wood, flicked a match nonchalantly to it. I watched without a care as he burned, while screaming bloody murder. Daniel forgave me then.

Ross said, "Sonny."

I ground out my answer, while I killed Mr. Fowler with my eyes. "I heard you."

He said, "See? That won't so hard now was it? Good. Good. Now, all of you, get the hell out of my barn. You two, get on to your work. And don't let me catch you lollygagging about. You." His finger was under my nose. "Inside the house. Don't you come out till I tell you."

And that was how it ended. With us walking out of the barn, and Ross and Trent sent to work. As I went toward the house, barely able to put one foot before the other, I was sure Mr.

Fowler watched me. I looked out of the corner of my eye to where Daniel had put his bike. It was gone, and with that came a tremendous sense of loss. Somehow I ended up in my room and watched from the window as Mr. Fowler and his "friends" backslapped one another. They'd removed their hoods, but they were too far away to see much other than their hair color. All brown. They finally climbed into their trucks, and went down the long driveway.

I sat on the edge of the chair at the forbidden desk, and waited, for what, I wasn't sure. It was so quiet in the house, I could hear the occasional car passing by on the road. I listened for Mama's movements within her room. Wasn't it possible for somebody to sense such horribleness, after what took place in the barn? I imagined I could signal her in the same way I'd hope to contact Daddy, as if the sheer force of my need for her would hit her, pummel her into awareness. After a few minutes, I got up, and went across the hall to her door. I put my ear to it. Nothing. There was no sound from her room, whatsoever. My urge to tell her was strong, but so was my fear.

I went back downstairs and outside, not caring what he'd said. I heard the tractor running in the distance. As I ran toward the sound, I forced away the images of what happened earlier every time they tried to come. I wasn't going to stay, is what I'd decided. I was going back to our old house. I didn't know how that would work, I only knew I couldn't stand being near *him.*

I made it to the edge of the field. Ross idled the tractor down, looking like he was afraid for me. He kept looking over his shoulder. I climbed up and he put his hand out, and grabbed hold of mine tight. He squeezed it hard, but I didn't care. I needed that steadiness right then, needed his strength. I didn't let go once I was beside him, standing on a metal piece by his boot, leaning into him. He put his arm around my waist.

I sobbed, "I ain't staying there no more, Ross. I can't. He hurt Daniel. He ain't right. I want to go home."

His gaze went toward the woods, in the direction of our real home. I'd never seen him look the way he looked right then, almost old, his features compressed. Every bit of his color was gone as if he'd been bleached white from the inside out.

He said, "I reckon I ain't either. Matter of fact, I ain't doing none of his work. Let's get Trent."

He left the tractor where it was, and we walked alongside the row of scrub growing in between the fields. When we came to where Trent was supposed to be tilling, he was on the tractor, but it wasn't moving. He was just sitting there, in the middle of the field, motionless. Ross motioned with both his arms.

Trent got off and we met him halfway, and Ross said, "Come on."

Trent didn't speak. He was like I'd been, just moving, doing without thinking. The three of us went into the woods without having to say a word. We walked in silence, and when we came to the pond, I grew teary eyed as I stared at the dock. At the edge of our old backyard was the post that would be covered with honeysuckle in a few months, and there was our toolshed, and our barn, and our house with the sugar maples, and the oak tree. I had a deep need to touch the things that had meant love, constancy, and safety.

We went up the back steps and into the kitchen. I got glasses out and we got water from the sink. We sat down and I noticed how the kitchen carried the odor of all the meals Mama had ever cooked here. I heard the echo of our laughter, back when Daddy was alive, the memory strong with the five of us sitting around the table, eating, and talking, and sharing our day. It made my chest ache for the want of it.

I said, "We got to tell Mama."

Ross said, "Not yet. We can't go and set him off. I think he's capable of just about anything, what he said he'd do, and more."

I said, "But, what if he does something to her. Does he know yet, about . . . you know, the baby?"

Ross and Trent looked at me. None of us knew if he did or not.

Ross said, "We'll stay here tonight, in the living room. Lock the doors. I'll get Daddy's shotgun. It's still in their bedroom. He wouldn't let her bring none a his things."

It made me feel better as Ross took charge. I went to the part of the house where Mama kept some blankets. The house was almost as cold as the outside, but it would be all right if we piled blankets on, and I would rather be cold here than warm over there. I took several back to the living room and we spread out on the chairs and the couch. Ross made sure the gun had shells and sat in a chair facing the door, keeping an eye out. After that, there wasn't anything left to do but sit, watching and waiting. No one talked. We were exhausted, and worried, yet somehow, at some point, we must have fallen asleep, slept through the rest of the day, and into the night.

Dawn came, that time of the morning when the sun isn't up fully, and clouds in the sky hold onto the pinks and oranges for only seconds when the footsteps outside woke me up. Ross was already up. He lifted the shotgun and went into the kitchen. Trent and I followed and through the curtains was the shape of Mama at the back door.

I hurried to open it, only Ross said, "Wait!"

"It's Mama, Ross!"

"I know that, but just hang on a minute. I want to see if he's with her."

He went to the window over the kitchen sink and looked out. I could see Mama searching for the key under the flower pot, but we hadn't put it back.

He said, "Go ahead, it's just her."

I wrenched the door open, and she rushed in, crying, and so upset she couldn't speak. Her lips were blue, even though she was wearing the new coat, and her hair was messy. She'd obviously rushed from the house, still in her nightgown and slippers. They looked pretty bad, dirt stained, like she'd run through the woods, and straight across the fields. She was shivering, her arms wrapped around her waist. She looked at us like she didn't know who we were.

I said, "Mama, we . . ."

Ross interrupted and said, "Mama, sit."

"No! What in hell are you all doing here? Frank is furious! We were at breakfast this morning, and we waited and waited."

We hadn't prepared a story for this. We looked at each other, unsure of what would sound right.

Mama noticed the exchange and said, "What's the matter?"

We shuffled, and shifted, and no one spoke, remembering all too well. The short passage of time wasn't enough to dull our memories. She put her hands to her stomach, and bit her lower lip. She looked to be in pain.

I said, "Mama, you okay?"

Her face was splotched, an uneven and unhealthy look. "I'm fine! I only want to know why my children ran off without a word to me. Without telling anyone where they were going. Frank liked to have had himself a fit. He was coming over here himself, but I said I'd handle it. Tell me what made you do this!"

Trent spoke up. "It ain't nothing, Mama. We just miss it here, is all."

Ross and I looked at Trent like *where did that come from?* He raised his shoulders as if to say *it was the only thing I could think of.*

At that, Mama got emotional again, and she said, "I miss it too. God, how I miss this place. Don't you know?"

We didn't, but I said, "We know, Mama."

Her voice hitched a couple of times when she said, "Come on. Let's go back, okay? I don't want to upset him any more than he already is. He's doing the best he can. He doesn't even know about . . ."

She stopped. She gestured at herself weakly, like she still couldn't quite get her head around the idea either.

Ross said, "It was just a spur of the moment thing. We shouldn't have done it."

The sound of his truck coming down the drive

struck us all silent again. I couldn't hardly stand the thought of seeing him, knowing what he'd done. I dropped my head, clenched my trembling hands.

Ross looked out the window and said, "Damn."

Mama said, "Listen to me. It ain't like I don't see how he is. I thought I was doing right, seeing a way to keep this place here. He . . . changed. And now . . ."

Before she could finish, he began hammering on the kitchen door and hollering, "Vi! Vi! Open this goddamn door!"

Mama opened it, and spoke as if she wasn't nearly as upset as she'd been seconds before. "Have mercy, Frank, calm down."

He came barreling in, wild-eyed and agitated. Ross, Trent, and I stood clumped together like sheep while Mama put her hands on her hips, showing some of her old gumption.

Mr. Fowler pointed at us, while speaking to her. "I don't know why you're telling me to calm down! Things would be going along fine if these young'uns minded me. I ain't got to do a goddamn thing for them, if'n I don't want, but out of the kindness of my heart, I try to do right. And lookit how they show their respect."

Mama said, "I've told you before, it's going to take time."

"I been around them long enough now to have earned it, don't you think?"

He was flailing his hands around, and I could see an edginess to him I'd not seen before. He was uneasy about yesterday. About what we'd said or not said. He was worried we'd tell her.

Mama said, "Frank, the way you're behaving, you're not helping."

He rushed at her and she ducked, an involuntary move like the way a dog does when it's been hit.

I said, "Don't!"

Mr. Fowler spun around and said, "What? You think I'm gonna hurt your mama?"

Mama suddenly blurted out, "I'm pregnant, Frank."

He turned and stared at her like she'd said something so bizarre, he was having trouble cogitating the meaning of the words.

Mama said, "That's why the kids are here . . . they were upset about it."

He repeated it. "You're pregnant?"

Mama nodded, and Mr. Fowler looked down at her stomach. He went to her, and carefully placed a hand over her belly. He bent down and put his head against her, and closed his eyes. I could only see him as he was in the barn, while Mama saw him in this moment of rare tenderness, and I was certain she still didn't know what he was capable of, how evil he was.

He murmured, "We'll have us a son. Me and you, Vi. A son."

Mama said, "Could be a little girl."

"No. Fowlers have boys."

Mama said nothing more, letting him think whatever he would.

He straightened up and said, "Let's get you home."

He put his arm around her shoulders, and held her arm with the other, helping her along as if she was unable to walk for herself.

She said, "I'm fine, Frank. Just a little queasy."

"It don't matter, you ain't gonna lift a finger from here on out, I'll see to it."

He eased her down the back steps, and she stopped at the bottom. Ross, Trent, and I stood at the back door, watching, wanting to be with her, yet not wanting to leave the sanctuary of this house.

Mama begged with her eyes and said, "Come on."

It was only 'cause of her sallow skin tone, and apparent frailty, I knew I'd go, even if my brothers didn't. Ross motioned at Trent. For now, we were backing down.

Mr. Fowler's face was like granite, his voice tight and hard when he said, "Lock that door, and give me that key."

Ross hesitated, and then did as Mr. Fowler said. We understood it was his way of ensuring we had nowhere to go.

Chapter 30

Mr. Fowler got to stewing over how things went that morning back at our old home. It resulted in an argument at the breakfast table before we left for school a couple days later. He talked about me and my brothers as if we weren't there.

"I don't get why you told them first."

"It just happened that way."

"How?"

"Frank."

"I want to know how it is you told them before you told me."

"What difference does it make?"

"I ought to have known first. I'm his daddy."

"Ain't a thing I can do about it now, is there?"

I felt sorry for that baby already. At least it would have a wonderful Mama. I got up from the table, and carried my plate to the sink. Mama sounded exhausted, always having to carefully choose her words, so when her frustrated reply was followed by a marked silence, the hairs went up on the back of my neck. I looked over my shoulder. Mr. Fowler was giving Mama *that* look, and I felt compelled to distract him.

I said, "Daniel said he talked to Sarah the other day."

This was a lie 'cause even though I'd snuck in several phone calls, I hadn't talked to Daniel at all.

I'd done it enough that Eunice would hear my voice and say, "Stand by, placing call to 4289."

Still, it got the reaction I wanted. Ross and Trent looked at me like I'd lost my mind and Mr. Fowler shifted his attention to me.

I kept talking normal, like there wasn't a thing wrong about bringing him up. "Yeah. She's still in Georgia, so he said."

Mr. Fowler narrowed his eyes and said, "What're you up to?"

Mama sighed with exasperation. "Frank, she's only talking."

"If she knows what's good for her, she better mind what she says."

Mama got up and said, "Can't we eat one meal without an argument?"

Mr. Fowler stood at the same time, and kicked his chair back with his foot and it hit the wall behind him.

He said, "We could if these damn kids of yours could learn how to talk to me right."

Mama spoke with control, but her voice shook. I wasn't sure if it was anger, or fear. "They ain't the ones causing the problem, Frank."

"You saying I'm the problem?"

"You're always on them. They can't do anything right, according to you."

"They could if they'd listen. Maybe their manners ain't up to my standards."

"Can't nobody meet them, Frank. Not even me. You're always nitpicking."

"Nitpicking."

"I don't want to argue."

"This is your fault. I say what's what."

Mama waved a hand like she was done with it. "Okay, Frank, you're the boss of everyone."

He looked like he was about to explode. His neck bulged, and I could actually hear his teeth grinding. He turned that off color again. Not one of us saw it coming. His open hand smacked her across the face so hard she stumbled backward, and the only reason she didn't fall was Ross catching her.

I screamed, "Mama!"

Mr. Fowler instantly realized he'd gone too far. All the tiny little signs of his overreacting flared bright and hot as a noon-day sun in August. His mouth turned down like a baby about to cry. He rubbed his hands like he was washing them, like they were dirty.

"Vi, darlin', I'm sorry. Don't be mad. You know I can't take it when you get mad at me. I don't know what come over me. Darlin', it's just . . . I love you so much."

Ross gripped Mama, who was gasping for

breath while the side of her face displayed a perfect handprint. Ross gave Mr. Fowler a deadly look, one that said if he didn't have a hold of Mama, he'd beat the crap out of him.

Trent yelled, "You ought not hit our mama!"

Mr. Fowler, still agitated, yelled back, "Boy! Don't you be back-sassing me!"

Mama put her hand over her cheek and closed her eyes.

She said, "I need to go lie down. Now."

Mr. Fowler moved forward, saying, "Darlin', let me help you."

Mama put a hand out and said, "Don't touch me."

Mr. Fowler spoke anxiously, and I could see he was very disturbed by this. "But, darlin' . . ."

Mama shook her head. "No."

He backed down, but trailed after her as she left the kitchen with Ross helping her.

When it was just Trent and me, he said, "Whoa."

I said, "He scares me. He's done that before, I bet."

"I think so too."

Ross came back into the kitchen a few seconds later.

I said, "Where's he?"

He said, "I have no idea. After I came out of Mama's room, I didn't see him."

We were going to miss the bus, if we didn't

hurry. We grabbed our books and went out the back door, half-running down the drive as the squash-colored bus showed up. When I got on and got a seat, I looked back at the house. Mama stared from her bedroom window and then she turned away quick, like somebody came in the room. Ross got a seat behind me, and Trent slid in with me.

I said, "I hope she'll be all right."

Ross said, "Mama can handle him."

I shook my head. "I don't know. It ain't possible to reason with somebody who's gone off their rocker."

I worried about her all day, anxious to get home and look for the signs he'd made her pay some more for what she'd said. While at school, I was also on the lookout for Daniel too. He'd not been in some time, and he was running the risk of being turned in to social services or his mama fined for nonattendance. We'd seen that happen with Buddy Crandon, who finally dropped out altogether when he turned sixteen.

I tried to listen to what Miss Young said, while the hands on the clock above the blackboard got more of my attention than anything. The last bell rang finally, but instead of hurrying out, all of the sudden I dreaded going back to that house. I walked to the bus slowly, and ended up having to sit in the short seat, right behind the bus driver, which I hated. Ross and Trent were already on, sitting together. Junior and Lil Roy got on, making stupid faces at me before working their way to the back. The bus jolted into gear, and I spent the entire ride staring at my hands.

After we were dropped off, we looked for Mr. Fowler's truck, or some sign of work being done in the fields. It was quiet as a Sunday afternoon. We went inside and I half-expected him to pop out of some room like a ghost. Usually we'd smell whatever Mama was fixing for supper, but the only scent I caught was the usual stuffiness. With Ross leading the way, we went up the stairs and stood outside of their bedroom door. Ross knocked, but there was no reply, no "Come in," not a thing.

I said, "Wonder where they're at?"

Ross sighed and said, "I don't know, but I got to go to work."

Trent said, "I'm gonna go to my room."

I went to mine too, but I couldn't concentrate on homework. I grabbed Dolly off my bed, and hugged on her some, but she offered about as much comfort as hugging on a loaf of bread. I stood by my window, and considered getting my bike and riding to Daniel's house. I wanted to talk to him, tell him I was sorry. I wasn't sure he wanted to stay friends with me. He'd never trust me again, of that I was certain. And, selfishly, I wanted to talk to somebody about what was happening, and I'd always been able to talk to him.

Worried and restless, I ventured across the hall to Mama's bedroom door. I tapped on it, knowing good and well she wasn't in there, yet caution made me act accordingly. I pushed the door open and the pink rose wallpaper mixed with the scent of Mama's powder drew me in. This room was filled with old, but nice furniture. I went to Mama's side of the bed and picked up her brush setting on the nightstand. I sniffed the bristles, smelling her lemony shampoo. I went to his side, and feeling incredibly brave, I opened the drawer of the nightstand. There was a handgun. I was used to guns, but the sight of this one gave me a chill. There was a watch, and an old wallet. The wallet was curious, and I picked it up. Before I opened it, I went to the window and looked out. They were still gone.

I unfolded it, and saw an old driver's license of a younger Mr. Fowler. A military ID of some sort. Some foreign money, and that was it. I put it back and as I went to shut the drawer, it went crooked. I pushed hard, and it jammed. Panicking, I yanked it back out. As I went to set it back on the wooden track, I spotted what looked like a newspaper article taped to the side. This was a time when I wished I had finger-nails. I picked at the edges, starting to sweat.

Finally, one side came loose so I could partially unfold it. It was a picture of a woman, an obituary for a Delores Fowler. I wanted to read the whole thing, only I was afraid they'd come back any minute. I retaped the side, and fixed the drawer, then hurried from the room, curious about who she was.

I hurried down the stairs and outside to find Trent sitting on the rail of the back porch, pitching rocks into a bucket. The noise was nerve-wracking.

I said, "He knew someone named Delores Fowler."

Trent said, "How do you know?"

"I found an obituary. In their room."

Trent raised an eyebrow. "What were you doing in there? Snooping?"

"Maybe."

"Geez, Sonny. That's either brave or dumb. I ain't sure which."

He pinged and ponged rocks while I went to pacing and chewing my nails. Leaving him to his rock throwing, I went around to the front of the house, and sat on the front porch steps, watching the road. Off to the left, the top of the Lucky Strike tower poked above the pines. It gave me chills thinking about Daniel sitting way up there. Alone. Thinking how he might be thinking. As the sun set, losing its final grip on the edge of earth, the countryside looked as if it was on fire, and it was easy to see spring was around the corner as shadows of the barn and sheds changed and lengthened. A few minutes later, Mr. Fowler's car eased along the drive. Mama stared from the passenger side window, and that one side of her face looked horrible. She wasn't smiling, even though Mr. Fowler was. I rose from the steps, and followed the car as it went around to the back. As he hurried around the front to help her out, she waved at me to come over.

Her voice was tight, and careful when she asked, "Sonny, how was school?"

"It was a long day."

She smiled, then winced.

She said, "Yes."

Now Mr. Fowler strutted to the trunk of the car and opened it. I couldn't understand how he kept that pride when he'd left such marks on my mama.

He said, "Help me get this stuff."

No please, just do. Inside were all sorts of baby things. All of it blue. If a girl came out instead, what would he do?

He said, "Don't you drop none of it."

"No, sir."

"Put it in that extra room. That'll be the nursery."

"Yes, sir."

He watched me lift out several bags, and

then he went back to Mama. She was leaning against the side of the car.

He said, "Come on, darlin'."

Mama said, "Leave me be, Frank."

That told me a lot about the kind of day they'd had.

The rest of that week at school, there was still no sign of Daniel, and I finally broke down and asked Miss Young about him. Teachers talked. She might know something. My hands grew sweaty as I approached her when the lunch bell rang.

I said, "Miss Young? My friend, Daniel Lassiter, he was in Mrs. Driver's class, and I haven't seen him in a while. Has he been sick?"

She hesitated, and then she said, "No, Daniel probably won't be back this year."

I was so stunned, I only nodded and walked away.

She called me back, and when I stood beside her again, she said, "It's for the best, don't you think?"

I didn't know what she meant until she said in a low voice, "Don't misunderstand. Daniel's very nice, but he's a troubled boy."

"Why, did he do something bad?"

Miss Young said, "No, but look you're such a pretty girl, you can make new friends, the kind you should have. Now, go on to lunch, and don't worry about him, okay?"

March came, and went, and with it, my thirteenth birthday passed and so did his. They were only a week apart and we'd always done something together. Mama managed to bake a cake for me, but other than that, the day came and went like any other day.

I kept trying to call, time and again, to wish him a happy birthday, until finally, Operator Eunice said, "Honey, call him all you want, but take it from me. If he ain't called you back by now, he ain't gonna."

Embarrassed, I hung up, and sat with my hands clenched in my lap, unaware I was scowling. Mr. Fowler went by carrying a glass of ginger ale for Mama. She wasn't holding up so well, each day more sickly and weak.

He said, "What's the matter with you?"

I said, "Nothing."

"You best not be using that phone for what I think. I can find out, you know. Do I need to find out?"

He had a way of making threats that loosened everything up inside me, like if I tried to walk, my legs wouldn't work.

I said, "No, sir," and prayed he wouldn't.

I was spared when Mama called from the bedroom, but he shot me a warning look before he went to her.

One unseasonably balmy Saturday morning in early April, Ross said, "You know, I've been saving just about every dime I've made. What if I go to Slater's and we plant a few acres on our farm? In honor of Daddy."

I nodded vigorously, and even Trent agreed, as much as he hated field work. I thought about Mama, and it almost made me guilty to think of leaving her every afternoon after school. When I mentioned this to Ross, I was shocked at his reply.

He said, "It's her fault. She shouldn't have married him."

Ross was spitfire mad at Mama, and this said how much.

I said, "Maybe if we tell what he did to Daniel, she'd want to leave."

Trent said, "Yeah."

Ross said, "You go and do that, all hell's gonna break loose. He made it clear what he'd do, him and his so-called friends."

I said, "What if he gets mad at us working over there."

Ross said, "We'll deal with it."

When we went to work in our old fields, I couldn't speak for my brothers, but I felt like a different person, the weight of worry temporarily gone. I was happier there. The familiar land lay before us, and it became a ritual for me to bring my old dowsing branch, and to take a turn or two up and down the rows. Without fail, the message was clear, and I celebrated those little tiny victories each time it signaled water. Even Trent no longer poked fun. I came to cherish those early spring afternoons away from Mr. Fowler's while I was still very much aware of Mama's ever increasing weakness, and ever growing belly.

Chapter 31

A thump came from their bedroom, along with raised voices. I hurried out of my own room knowing Ross was already gone to our farm, and maybe Trent too. I heard it again, and crept toward their door. I hesitated and then put my ear to it.

Mama said, "Frank, please, stop now. I'm not up to it."

He said, "You ain't never up to it lately."

Mama said, "Would you be, considering?"

I could picture her pointing to the small swelling one might consider more of a holiday weight gain than a baby just yet.

Mr. Fowler mumbled something, and I heard Mama repeat, "No," like she was gritting her teeth.

I jerked when I heard sharp slaps. It got quiet until that horrible noise he made told me the thing between a husband and wife was happening again. I backed away from the door, considered what made him so damn mean as I rushed downstairs, my face hot as a firecracker. I grabbed two slices of bread, some bologna, and made a quick sandwich. I stood at the counter eating it, but not tasting anything. I moved to the screen door, and breathed deep, noticing how spring made everything smell different. The sweet scent of pollen and flowers poking up through the ground usually would've made me happy 'cause it was my favorite time of year, except we were *here*. I finished eating and brushed my hands off. I wanted to check on her, but didn't care to hear what was going on behind those closed doors.

I went outside, down the back steps, and made it across the yard to the edge of the woods, when out of nowhere, Mama's voice higher pitched than I'd ever heard before, shouted, "Sonny!"

She stood in the kitchen doorway, clutching her stomach. Even from that distance, the red streak on the front of her gown stood out as bold as a splash of red paint would on this white house. Shocked, I ran toward her as she sagged against the doorframe, her legs giving way until she sort of slid down it. He was behind her, a big looming figure shadowed by the interior of the house, like a phantom hovering, or the devil, about to snatch her back into that hell he'd created.

He bent down, and I yelled at him, "You leave her alone!"

He yanked her to her feet, gripping her upper arms as he stared down at her nightgown.

Despite the hold he had on her, she tried to double over, as if the act of standing straight were too painful to bear.

I ran up the steps, crying, "Mama! Mama!"

Mr. Fowler was saying, "Goddammit, Vi!"

She struggled to get away from him, reaching for me. The sweat glistened on her brow, and the sickly gray of her face was alarming. He let her go as I grabbed her hands and pulled her away from him. She gasped, holding her stomach like she was cradling it.

She panted, "The baby. The baby."

Mr. Fowler's hands were bloody, and he looked at them like they weren't his, like they belonged to someone else.

I said, "Get the doctor!"

He wiped them down the front of his pants, and he looked furious about what was happening. He lowered his voice, and spoke so quiet, it was almost a whisper.

He said, "She better not lose that baby. She just better not." He took a step closer, pointed at Mama like she could magically stop what was happening, and then his voice turned eerie as he said, "Ain't a thing wrong. It's just a little blood."

I stared at him like he was insane.

I said, "I'm gonna get Ross."

Mr. Fowler said, "Hell no you ain't."

Mama's body spasmed like it had a mind of its own. She leaned to the side, away from me, panting with pain. Tears coursed down my own cheeks as she doubled over. Mr. Fowler grabbed under her arms and hauled her up. She cried out as a rush of blood poured down her legs and I was sure she was gonna die.

I cried out, "She's losing the baby!"

Mr. Fowler looked over at me and said, "Shut up! She ain't doing no such thing!" He held Mama upright and said, "Now, Vi, you got to stop this. Don't you let it happen!"

Mama could only cry. He would blame her for this, he might even kill her for it. I looked toward the woods, frantic, wishing Ross or Trent would appear. I was afraid to leave her alone with him, but she needed help, and quick. Her face went from gray to white. He let her go like she disgusted him, and she collapsed to her knees on the porch, rolled over, and balled up onto her side. Mr. Fowler took off down the back steps, cussing a blue streak. He jumped in his truck, tore down the driveway, the back end fishtailing, and causing gravel to shoot out from under the tires. I heard them screech when he hit asphalt. Mama gazed up at me, eyes dulled by the pain.

She said, "Oh, Sonny. I prayed and prayed . . ."

"It's okay, Mama, he's gone to get the doctor."

Her eyelids sort of fluttered, then closed, and in that instant, it was like I'd jumped into the pond in the middle of winter. I bent down and put my ear to her mouth. A single puff of air. Then another. I stroked her arm, thankful she was still with me, if barely. I waited for Mr. Fowler to come back, to bring some help. Minutes went by. A half hour. Finally, I jumped up and ran into the house and dialed zero.

Eunice sighed and said, "Four, two, eight, nine?"

"No! No! Doctor Meade, quick!"

For once she didn't prattle on about the weather, or give me advice about calling boys. I heard her sharp intake of breath.

"Hold the line."

The clicks in my ear were loud, going on forever until Doctor Meade came on. I told him what was happening, and I was sure Eunice was listening in too, but I didn't care.

I said, "Hurry! It's bad!"

He said, "I'm on my way."

I hung up the phone and went back to Mama, rubbing on her back, doing anything I could to let her know I was there. A few minutes later, Ross and Trent found me, holding her hand, and sort of humming an off-tune song. I kept fanning her face to keep the flies away. She'd not woke up, and neither one of them seemed to understand what they saw. Blood pooled in a large sticky puddle by the back door, the smell of it a steely, metallic odor.

Stunned, Ross said, "The baby?"

Trent said, "What happened?"

I was speechless, unable to tell them how horrible it had been, how Mr. Fowler acted, and how I'd hoped he was going to the doctor, only he'd yet to come back. It was like he'd simply run off.

Ross said, "Should we move her?"

I gave a shaky answer. "I-I g-guess."

The sun would soon hit that side of the house and I didn't want her in it. Ross lifted her shoulders, while Trent and I got her under the legs. Where the blood hadn't dried, her skin felt slick and sticky. We stumbled through the doorway, clumsy but careful.

I said, "Let me get some towels, then we can put her on the couch."

They laid her on the floor, and she moaned. We watched intently to see if she was waking up.

I knelt beside her and touched her arm, "Mama?"

She didn't open her eyes, but she gripped my fingers.

I told Trent, "Get them old towels underneath the sink in the kitchen."

For once, Trent didn't say, "Don't tell me what to do."

As he hurried off, Ross still wore the look of disbelief, and he said, "When did all this start?"

I put my finger to my lips and mouthed, *wait.*

Trent hurried back with an armful of old bath

towels Mama saved for rags. I went into the study with the hideous couch and laid them out. We got Mama situated, left the room, and only then did I finish what I wanted to say. It came out in a rush, my words, one after the other, like little tumbleweeds blown in the wind.

"I was coming to help y'all when she called out from the back door. She was bleeding. He wouldn't let her alone, kept saying she'd better not lose the baby. I wanted him to get a doctor, that's what I thought he was doing. I haven't seen him since he left. I called Doc Meade myself, and he's on his way."

Ross's hand shook as he scrubbed his hair. "We're gonna do something. We're gonna get out of here, somehow, someway. I'd rather take the chance at our own place. I'll work day and night. Even if it means we eat nothing but beans, I'd rather do that than to stay around him any longer."

Trent and I agreed. Doc Meade arrived about fifteen minutes later. When he came rushing in, he smelled of healing, of making hurts go away, bringing a sharp scent of alcohol and something else clinical I couldn't place. Doc Meade took one look at Mama's waxy appearance, and sent us back out of the room.

"I'll let you know when I'm done."

We went into the kitchen and sat down at the table. I chewed on my nails while Ross began an incessant polishing of his head, and Trent went from the back door to the window. It didn't take long for Doc Meade to poke his head in.

He said, "She really needs to go to Duplin General over in Kenansville. They got a new hospital, just opened up. Where's your step-daddy?"

We looked at one another, and then Ross said, "We thought he was coming to get you."

Doc Meade grunted, rubbed his chin, and said, "Maybe I passed him on the road."

I said, "What about the baby?"

Doc Meade shook his head. "She ought to have come to see me before now. I could've give her something to help. Her age and all. I guess it wasn't meant to be, but the Lord knows about such as this. He's spared her, but not the baby. I sure am sorry. I need more old towels, if you have them?"

I rushed off to get him what he needed. I didn't know what to make of this news, not only hearing him say Mama needed the hospital, but that the baby was gone too. Before we even knew what it was or nothing.

When I came back into the kitchen, Ross was saying, "Damnation. It ain't right. If it wasn't for him . . ." and he stopped, then he went on. "Sorry, but, I'm thinking he won't like her going to a hospital."

Doc Meade studied the floor and said, "That

don't surprise me none. I'll see what I can do for her."

He took the towels from me and when he came out minutes later, he was carrying a bundle. I could only imagine what was wrapped up in it. My tiny, barely there baby brother or sister. Innocent, blameless, *murdered*. I couldn't think any other way. It rankled and gnawed at me. I felt like it would leave a hole in my middle.

He said, "I've given her a shot to help stop the bleeding, and penicillin. She can take these for pain." He rattled a big bottle, and set it on the table. "She doesn't need to be up and about too soon. She needs to stay off her feet. Make sure she eats. Tell your stepdaddy what I said."

We only nodded, like what he said would be so simple. We knew better than that.

I said, "How long?"

"Least a week. And then, when she does get up and move around, it still doesn't need to be doing anything too strenuous."

I pictured Mama waiting on Mr. Fowler the way she did, coddling him, and cooking and cleaning, and all the things he'd got used to.

Doc Meade went out the back door, and his final words were, "Call me for anything, anytime, 'specially if the bleeding gets worse."

Mr. Fowler, he didn't come back for two days and when he did, his clothes were torn and dirty, and he reeked of liquor and vomit. By then Mama was in the bed where she could lay on soft, clean sheets. I held cool cloths to her forehead, plied her with chicken broth I'd made myself, enticed her with soft scrambled eggs and buttery toast. I brought her cups of hot tea loaded with sweet honey. I read to her from the paper and magazines. I told her it was going to be fine as she stared at me, them hollow eyes of hers empty as a dried-up well. I talked about what a fine day it was, and didn't the food taste good, and did she want a pain pill. She couldn't seem to heal, and I kept hoping some color would return to her cheeks. It scared me bad her being so sick, but when he finally showed up in the bedroom doorway, I witnessed something in my Mama I'd never seen before. Pure, raw fear.

Chapter 32

Being around death, you can't never get used to that feeling it gives you, just plain powerless in the face of it. The little brother or sister lost ignited an uncommon sadness, even though I couldn't hardly bear the thought he or she would've been part of Mr. Fowler. Although Mama was frail, I believe we could have moved on, except Mr. Fowler got to behaving like she'd done it on purpose. A pall fell over the house and stayed put, and even if we'd been allowed to open the curtains to allow the sun in, it wouldn't have helped. This was a different sort of gloom, one you sensed more than saw.

He said, "You didn't want him, did you."

As with me, this was not a question.

"You didn't want him, so you done something to yourself."

Mama was still weak, and she could only repeat herself, as before. "No, Frank. That's not true. Doc Meade said there was probably something wrong."

"With you, maybe. Not with my boy."

"Frank."

"What. You don't think I don't know about these things? I know aplenty. Oh yeah. How women shove things up in there, and poke around. Messing with God's business. Did you do that, Vi?"

"Frank!"

He'd taken to staring at her, until she dropped her eyes, shook her head, maybe trying to think of the right thing to say to fix this crazy notion of his. His mouth stayed turned down, and a new tightness consumed him that made his movements jerky. Who'd have ever thought a man like Mr. Fowler would've wanted a baby so bad? It was the most unlikely thing I would've ever associated to him, yet I began to think maybe it wasn't about a baby at all. It was about the idea of it, a way for him to keep Mama here, and now he'd lost that advantage. As for us, when he'd look our way, it plumb scared me how his pupils would go large, making his eyes bottomless and cold. There was a threat hidden away in there.

I spent a lot of time thinking, and periodically my mind went to Delores Fowler, wondering about her, while watching Mama's zest for life get eaten up by him bit by bit. It was inside our old home, after we'd worked in our fields, that we decided we'd tell Mama what happened to Daniel. Ross had jimmied a window open, climbed through, and unlocked the door, and it was there we'd gathered late one afternoon and talked. I was sure this would save us, only finding the right moment was more difficult than we'd anticipated. We were afraid, not only 'cause of Mr. Fowler's threats, but also 'cause Mama had a particularly bad spell when the anniversary of Daddy's death came. We didn't know how much more she could take.

Then it was May, and then June, and we were once again free of school. By the time it was July, it was hot as a furnace outside, and cicadas sang nonstop. Mr. Fowler put big fans in the windows to draw out the hot air, but the house stayed dank and stale. Mama came out of her bedroom one day and I was struck once again by how thin, gray, and sickly she still looked, as if the house itself, and Mr. Fowler drew the essence of life straight out of her. She moved in a manner she'd never had before, hesitant and unsure.

She was trembling as she walked, but she smiled a little at me and said, "Hey, Sonny."

I said, "Hey, Mama. You want I should get you something. You hungry?"

She said, "No."

She looked so strained, so odd that, with alarm, I said, "What is it?"

She grabbed my hand and said, "Oh, Sonny! I wished to God I'd never married him. He's got something wrong with him. Really wrong."

She looked over her shoulder as if to make sure we were alone, and then she gripped me hard, the tips of her fingers digging into my shoulder bones. She plumb scared me the way she looked, sort of crazy eyed, her hair hanging in limp strands against her washed-out face.

She said, "He makes me . . . I can't tell you . . . dear Lord, how I wished I could undo this mess!"

This was it. The opportunity. Even though Ross and Trent weren't here, I couldn't delay it any longer. I licked my lips. I would tell her, I would convince her we had to leave, that it was only going to get worse.

"Mama, he did something else really bad."

She sucked in her breath, her eyes big and wide. Her voice dropped to an almost whisper.

"Has he done something to you kids?"

"Not to us. Him, and some other men, they got Daniel. They hurt him, Mama. They wore hoods, and they did it in the barn. Mr. Fowler, he made Ross and Trent watch. I could only hear it, but I know what he did. That thing he does to you."

Mama reared back in the same manner as when Mr. Fowler slapped her.

She pressed her fingers to her mouth, and her eyes watered. "Don't tell me that."

I was relentless. "He said he'd hurt us if we told. Mama, we can't stay here with him!"

"It ain't that easy."

"What do you mean, it ain't easy! We just leave . . . !"

"Listen to me. We can't do that. You don't

know all there is to know. What he's capable of."

"What about Aunt Ruth? Can't we sneak away, go to her and . . . ?"

Mama didn't answer me. She went down the stairs, and I trailed behind her, worried sick this would get out of hand now she knew. I was afraid she'd confront him and no telling what he'd do then. We went into the kitchen and she grabbed a cigarette from the pack on the table. I realized I hadn't seen her smoke in weeks, not since she'd lost the baby.

When she struck the match and brought the flame up, her hand shook so bad, I started to do it for her, but she somehow got it lit.

She blew the smoke out and nodded. "We could go to Ruth's."

That gave me hope and now I wanted to rush things along. I wanted it to all be over with. I didn't want to wait any longer than I had to.

She said, "Is Daniel okay?"

"I don't know. I ain't seen him since it happened."

Mr. Fowler came in, screen door slamming behind him, and making Mama jump. She fell silent, and her shoulders rounded, visibly shrinking from his presence.

He squinted at her and said, "What're you talking about?"

Mama brushed a hand through her hair. "Nothing. We weren't talking about nothing."

Mr. Fowler said, "You look guilty."

"No I don't . . ."

"Yeah. You look guilty. You got the look of somebody up to no good."

"Don't be silly."

"Silly? Maybe what you really mean is stupid."

He grabbed her arm, and Mama said, "Frank, careful, you're hurting me."

I said, "Don't hurt my mama."

His gaze shifted to me, and it was like I'd fell into a cold black pit.

He turned back to Mama and said, "Come on, you come with me."

He grabbed at her, but she moved quicker than I would have thought she could, so his hand swiped through an empty space.

He clenched his mouth. "What're you up to?"

Acting like she didn't hear him, she said, "Sonny, you want to go with me and see about them blackberries?" She turned to him and sighed. "If you must know, I was thinking about baking you them blackberry pies you love so good. That's what we were talking about. It was going to be a surprise."

Mr. Fowler said, "Well now, that would be something else, you actually lifting a goddamn finger around here. What is it about women? The moment you marry'em, they ain't worth a dime. Forget about that pie for now."

He went after her, stalking her, his mouth

curled in a leery smile while the rest of his features were dull, like he was bored.

Mama's voice held a warning. "Don't."

He whistled a little airy tune, advancing on her as she stepped backward.

I had to do something, so like before, I blurted out a name, "Who was Delores Fowler?"

Like when I'd mentioned Daniel, it worked.

He spun on his heels, facing me. "Who told you about her?"

"Everybody knows. It was in the paper, remember?"

Mr. Fowler snort laughed while Mama looked puzzled. "You think you're smart, eh, kid?"

He looked too confident.

He said, "It won't in no local paper here, that's for sure. That was in Parris Island, where I was stationed."

How I wished I'd not said a word. How I wished I'd taken a chance to read the whole thing.

He gestured at Mama. "What you got here is a little snoop. I can't abide by that, no sirree."

He folded his arms across his chest. "Delores was my first wife. Man who looks like me, you think I ain't never had any other woman?"

I said, "She's dead, Mama."

Mr. Fowler's arm shot out. He grabbed me so quick I squeaked like a mouse caught in a trap.

Mama said, "Let her go, Frank!"

He held on tighter like he wanted to tear my arm out of the socket. He went for the back door, and all I could think was *the barn.* I grabbed hold of the doorframe and held on, only he jerked hard, and one of my shortest, stubbiest nails came loose.

I screamed, and Mama yelled, "You crazy son-of-a-bitch, let her go!"

I think calling him crazy was what stopped him cold.

He let me go, and turned to her and said, "What did you call me?"

Mama raised her chin a little. "You heard me."

Quick as a flash of lightning, his fist connected to her cheek, and she dropped where she stood. He couldn't let it go with that. No. He had to kick her too, right in the stomach, as if he was still furious about her losing that baby. I ran at him, and he shoved me, and sent me flying backward, hitting the floor. I lay stunned.

Helpless against his strength, I rolled over, hid my face, crying, "Mama, Mama!"

I heard her faint whisper, "Sonny, it's okay, shhh."

I kept my face hidden until it got so quiet, I feared he'd done to Mama what I suspected he'd done to Delores Fowler. I lifted my head. I was alone. Where were they? I slunk into the hallway, and looked up the staircase. Kids at school had whispered it, hadn't they? *Heard he killed someone*. I crept step by step. I wanted to call out to her, let her know I was there, but I was too scared of making things worse. Again. I posted myself like a sentry in the hall, waiting, and like with Daniel, I hummed. There would be no going back from that afternoon.

Ross glared at Mama's face, again the color of eggplant.

He said, "I'm gonna kill him."

She put a hand on his arm, and shook her head. That wasn't good enough for Ross. He decided to handle it another way, and took a chance when Mr. Fowler was overseeing work in a distant field, and when Mama was lying down on the couch, holding ice to her bruised face. He called the sheriff. The sheriff, when he came, rolled along the drive real slow, and that was odd, considering what Ross had told him. My brothers and I waited on the back porch, all of us nervous as a dog that's been left on a chain too long. The sheriff put the car in park and sat smoking with the engine idling. After a while, he flicked the butt out the window and opened the door. I got the shakes, like Mama, when I saw who got out. Big Boy looked just as ornery as that day in the barn. Ross, having spilled his guts over the phone about an assault, looked like he might get sick.

Trent mumbled, "Shit."

Big Boy came forward and we learned his real name.

"Sheriff Ralph Biggs, what can I do for you, son?"

Ross said, "Nothing."

Sheriff Big Boy smirked. "Hate I had to waste my fried fish dinner coming all the way out here for nothing. What's this about an assault?"

"I made a mistake."

"I thought you said your mama got beat up by your stepdaddy."

"I found out she fell. Everything's fine."

"I see. So, without talking to her first, you called me, and then you went and talked to her?"

"Yes, sir. That was dumb."

"Sure enough it was."

Big Boy spit on the ground.

He said, "I want to hear you say it, and maybe that way you don't forget. I want to hear you say, 'I am dumb. Dumb as a rock.'"

Ross had lost all the color in his face, and it made him look sickly as Mama. Trent was clenching and unclenching his fists, like he was looking for an opportunity to punch the man.

Ross repeated what Big Boy told him to say. "I'm dumb. Dumb as a rock."

Sheriff Big Boy moved closer, smelling of old frying grease and another underlying rank odor. I wanted to pinch my nose against it, only I was afraid to move.

460

He said, "Again."

Ross repeated it.

Sheriff Big Boy looked over at Trent. "Ain't you right pretty, yourself. Didn't notice that when we were having our little bit of fun, but I see it now. Hm."

Her soft voice came from behind us through the screen door, her words muffled sounding 'cause Mr. Fowler had loosened a couple of her teeth. "Sonny, what's the sheriff doing here?"

She held the towel she'd used to wrap ice in, her black eye and cheek standing out in contrast to the white of her skin. She looked like she was dead. I looked at Ross, and then the sheriff. Even he had trouble looking at Mama's face.

I said, "It ain't nothing, Mama. Sheriff was just about to go. He was only telling us to be careful. There's a rabid fox in the area."

Sheriff Big Boy said, "That's right, ma'am. No cause for alarm. I'll just be on my way. Give my best to your husband. He and I go way back."

Sheriff Big Boy strolled to his car, and as he went to get in, he said, "Don't forget what I told you."

Nobody said a word. Nobody moved until the car was out of sight.

Chapter 33

There was a pattern when it came to Mr. Fowler's tirades. After he'd beat Mama black and blue, he'd mellow out for days on end. It was as if he'd expelled a badness in him, and we were safe until it boiled over once again. A couple days after Sheriff Big Boy showed up, Mama approached me early in the morning with the idea of baking them blackberry pies Mr. Fowler favored, as if she thought it was a way to soothe his temper.

She said, "Let's go to the patch off Turtle Pond Road. It'll be like old times, won't it?"

I agreed. "Yes, ma'am."

We got a couple of buckets from the root cellar, and took the path through the woods. In another time and place, I could have held onto this moment as a happy one, but with her looking like she was, I could only worry if she felt well enough to pick.

I said, "We don't have to get a lot. Just enough for a pie."

She said, "I want to bake two. If I'm gonna bake, I might as well make sure it's worth it. Besides, Frank will eat one almost by himself."

I'd seen him do that, so Mama was right.

I said, "Well, there ought to be plenty. We'll be able to pick 'em fast."

She smiled, which made her flinch in pain.

She lifted her face to the sun and said, "I'm fine, don't worry. I declare, if it don't feel good to be outside again."

I nodded and smiled when she pointed out a butterfly, or some wildflower growing along the way. If Mama could put what he'd done behind her, then I had to try too. When we got to the blackberry patch, the briars were loaded, and in various stages of ripening. It was right pretty, the red and blackish-purple berries set against the bright green leaves. We were right out in the sun, and though it was hot, once we started picking, I didn't even notice. We were quiet, and the only sound was the occasional clink of a bucket as we set them down, and a few crows ca-cawing overhead.

After a while, Mama said, "I'm going over there, Sonny."

"Okay."

She went across the road to where Daniel and I had stood eating them, while I kept picking where I was 'cause there were so many. I was eating them too, and despite the fact we were doing this for him, I couldn't help but appreciate it was a nice day, and Mama and I were doing something together like old times. I would occasionally glance her way and a time or two, she wasn't picking at all, but simply staring into her bucket. That was okay, her resting and all. I still thought of her as strong, no doubt about it. After all she'd been through, and here she was picking blackberries in the hot sun.

She eventually came back over to me and said, "I think we have enough, don't you think?"

My own bucket was over half-full.

She said, "I have the same as you. We'll have enough for a few jars of jam too. Let's go."

I nodded. "Okay."

Back at the house, Mama said, "You measure out the flour, get the lard and all together, while I'll wash these up real quick."

I nodded and set about getting what we needed. I put cubes of ice in water like Mama had showed me, and set it on the table for when she was ready to assemble the crusts. All the while she hummed and washed, washed and hummed. My mouth watered at the memory of how a warm blackberry pie tasted. It was the only thing Mr. Fowler and I might have in common, our love for them. I went into the pantry and measured out flour, and set that on the table and when I went back into the pantry, I was in such a hurry I dropped the bag, and flour went everywhere.

"Oh! Darn it!"

Mama said, "What is it?"

"I made a mess."

Mama poked her head in and said, "Well, get the broom, and then you'll have to get the rest up with a mop. Get it good and clean. You know how he is."

"Yes, ma'am."

I spent a while getting it up 'cause every time I thought I was done, I found something with flour on it. I wiped and swiped at everything and by the time I came out of the pantry, she was just about done, already busy scoring the tops of the pies. She put star shapes on one, and cross marks like Xs on the other.

She stood back to survey her work and said, "I did it like that since I put more sugar in that one there. That's how Frank likes it."

I said, "I like mine with less, like Daddy."

She smiled and said, "Ross and Trent too."

I spent the rest of the day helping her cook Mr. Fowler's favorite things. Mama was trying to stay on his good side, so she fixed that buttermilk chicken he liked, mashed potatoes, corn, and okra.

When he came in from work, all he had to say was, "Well, I'm glad to see you finally got out of the bed to cook for a change."

Mama didn't say a word, like she'd developed a callous when it came to his way of talking to her. I wasn't sure she even heard him. She put the food on his plate and set it in front of him.

She said, "Boys, Sonny, y'all go on and get your plates. Don't let this food get cold."

Mr. Fowler said, "Like your mama."

It was hard to enjoy eating when he seemed to want to make it unpleasant, but like Mama asked, we did our best to not waste it. Mr. Fowler had no problem emptying his own plate.

When he was done, she said, "I made blackberry pie."

He said, "Well? What're you waiting for?"

She went into the kitchen and brought out several slices, giving him his first. He attacked it like it might get away. We began to eat the pie, and I decided it might be the best she'd ever made. Ross and Trent agreed, eating theirs like Mr. Fowler, barely breathing between bites.

He finished and said, "I don't know. Lemme have another. It might be close to my own mama's, but I ain't sure yet."

Mama got him another slice.

He ate it, and like he was playing with her, he said, "Um, not yet. Lemme have another one, just to be sure."

Mama smiled graciously, and went and got it.

He ate that one too, and when he was done, he finally sat back, wiped his mouth, and said, "Nope. Not as good."

Mama said, "I followed my own recipe this time. I couldn't find your mother's."

Mr. Fowler tossed his napkin on the table, and stood up, holding his stomach like it was bothering him and I reckoned so, considering.

He said, "Whew. I probably shouldn't have eaten that last piece."

Mama said, "Go sit down and I'll bring you some seltzer after I get this cleaned up."

Mr. Fowler burped loud and gave her no argument. I could hear him in the study as he settled into a favorite chair with a groan. I helped Mama, and maybe it was her general feeling of weakness or soreness, but it took us a long time to get the kitchen clean. She placed towels over the leftover pies. The one I liked with less sugar was only half-gone, but holy cow, Mr. Fowler had just about eat all of one by himself. No wonder he was miserable.

Ross and Trent disappeared to their rooms, avoiding any further contact with him. I looked at Mama as she rinsed and rinsed a glass until I figured she'd used a gallon of water on it.

Mr. Fowler called out, "Vi! You getting me that seltzer?"

Mama said, "In a minute, I'm almost done!"

I wiped the dishes dry and thought about Daniel, wondering what he was doing at this very moment, if he even missed me, or was he spending his days and nights at the water tower planning his escape from Jones County. Maybe he'd take a chance on Sarah and that man down in Georgia. At this point, it would be better than here. Maybe if I got brave enough, I'd ride out to the water tower and find out for myself. I could apologize properly, and give him a way to try and forgive me. I finished wiping the last plate and put it up and looked to see Mama sorting out the utensil drawer.

I said, "Mama, don't you reckon Mr. Fowler wants that seltzer you mentioned?"

She cocked her head, listening, and said, "He ain't yelling no more for it. He's probably asleep after eating like he did. I been wanting to do this, and now I'm into it, I'll just finish this up and go check on him."

She sorted, and sorted. She talked while she did so, reminiscing about Daddy. It had been a long time since she'd mentioned him. It was probably too painful for her, and she'd buried her feelings. Tonight, they'd resurfaced and what was odd was she'd always acted like she had to look over her shoulder when talking about certain things and now, she talked openly, and freely, like she didn't care. After sorting the utensil drawer, she sat down to smoke a cigarette. A couple hours had passed since we ate and I was surprised Mr. Fowler hadn't demanded she wait on him. I paused to listen when an unexpected noise came from the study, an odd spongy sound I couldn't figure out.

I said, "What's that?"

Mama frowned and said, "I don't know."

She left the kitchen, and seconds later, called out, "Sonny, get Ross."

I went into the hallway and said, "Is everything okay?"

Her voice was sharp. "Just do as I say!"

I took the stairs two at a time and banged on Ross's door, then stuck my head in. He'd been practicing camel hops with a towel tied to his closet door handle, and looked a bit aggravated at the interruption.

"What?"

"Hurry. I think something's wrong with Mr. Fowler."

He rushed out of the room, with me on his heels. Mama was still by Mr. Fowler, shaking his arm, and calling his name. He continued making that strange sucking noise, his tongue protruding like he was trying to throw up. I developed an odd sensation of wanting to breathe for him.

Ross knelt beside Mama and said, "He's having some sort of an attack."

She said, "Jesus, Lord, God, yes he is." She put a hand on his chest and said, "Frank?"

Mr. Fowler's eyes widened, and to our horror, he went rigid as a board and his own face turned that horrid color it had before and then, if it was possible, it went even darker, almost like Mama's eggplant-colored bruising.

She drew back and whispered, "He ain't gonna make it."

It was horrible to see, and despite how I felt about him, I had a moment of compassion and said, "Help him!"

As soon as the words came out of me, Mr. Fowler seized up once more and his chest collapsed as the air went out of him. It didn't rise again. He stared straight up while Mama, her hand on her mouth, stared down at him. Mr. Fowler was beyond helping.

Mama said, "I will be damned."

There was talk it had been his way of living. Mr. Fowler had a reputation for being high-strung, while some said it was his heavy smoking and drinking.

At his funeral, Doc Meade told Mama, "He's had health problems for some time now. I figured after he got married, he'd eat better, drink less. Course, y'all weren't married long enough to do him any good." Doc Meade looked close at Mama, leaned in, and said, "I reckon he hadn't done you much good neither."

Mama shook her head, her expression partially obscured by the black veil.

She said, "Frank had his ways, that's for sure."

He said, "Lots to think about, what with two properties."

Mama said, "I'll call my sister Ruth, see if she ain't interested in a new career."

That made me so happy, I quivered with excitement.

Acquaintances, and I think maybe even a few strangers came from all over Jones County to see him laid out in his coffin. I had the distinct impression many were glad about his death, although what business he'd had or done with them, well, I could've cared less. Three that didn't attend were Stem, Rufus, and Big Boy. Maybe they didn't dare. I'd never considered before that death could make a person feel happy. Maybe it's a sin to say or think it, but if I'm being truthful, I was glad he was gone, out of our lives.

Yes, his death had made me happy.

Chapter 34

Quick as Mr. Fowler had moved us in, we left the big, ugly house even faster. There were no good memories there. Not a one I could count. We got our things, packed the truck and the station wagon with as much as we could carry, and still have room to sit. There were no tears. My feelings, though I tried to keep them tamped down out of simple respect for death, were in direct contrast to when we'd moved to his place. Giddy comes to mind. Soon we'd settled back at the old house as if we'd never left. Despite my relief and happiness, for some reason, Mama couldn't completely let go of Mr. Fowler. Every now and then she'd bring up something he'd done in the early days, when he'd been a nicer person—at least to her. It could have been her way of getting past the awfulness, a way to paint a prettier picture, or to justify why she'd even considered getting mixed up with someone like him. I didn't mind her talking about him now. He was gone, and it was just words.

We worked the small bit of cotton on our own land, and one day, while on that side of Turtle

Pond Road closest to his property, we noticed his cotton needed tending pretty bad. The workers he'd hired had drifted off to who knew where. Ross wasn't necessarily inclined to labor on his land, but he couldn't see a crop going to waste either. When he brought it up to Mama, it was understood it was more than even the four of us could do.

Mama said, "We'll get enough in to get by on. It'll be fine."

I didn't care none too much being over there and if I never set foot on any part of that man's property again, I'd have been all right, but there we were, working his fields, his presence seeming to hover over us. I did the spot where Daniel and I had run underneath the irrigation's sprinkler system. It seemed like it had been ten years ago instead of only last summer. I felt embarrassed when I recollected how I'd kissed him, and his reaction. We'd been completely unaware of the event about to happen that would change us, who we were, forever. The echo of Daniel's voice came as the sun beat down on me. It renewed my sadness over him, being in that place, and so I left, and didn't look back.

It was late August when Aunt Ruth finally came, and Mama, who hadn't looked herself in ages, was transformed. Aunt Ruth's presence filled an empty spot left by Daddy, albeit in a different way. Ross and Trent looked as happy as I felt. When we sat down to eat supper the first night she was there, Mama shared some news.

She said, "County sent me this deed. What you reckon we ought to do?"

She and Aunt Ruth sipped on glasses of sweet tea, a curl of smoke circling Mama's head, like a halo. The deed was for Mr. Fowler's property.

Ross said, "It ain't no reason to ever want to set foot there again."

Trent said, "Nope."

I was suddenly consumed by the notion Mama might be thinking about cutting down the woods, like he'd wanted to do, and combining properties.

I said, "I hate that place."

Mama said, "I can't blame you kids. I've been thinking on this idea a while. What if we donate it to your daddy's college, let them use it in whatever way they want. That would give us a little peace of mind, using it in his memory."

Aunt Ruth said, "Perfect."

We agreed, and over the next few days Mama stayed on the phone, talking to people at the college, and then to the Register of Deeds for Jones County. The college was more than happy to accept such a generous gift and Mama's only request was for it to carry Daddy's name. During one of the phone calls I heard her repeat what it would eventually become, The Lloyd Simpson Creech Cooperative Extension. Mama's decision would turn the property and all the bad memories into something good, so that whenever we rode by, we'd no longer think of it like before. Eventually signs would be put up pointing to the different work studies being done there, from horticulture to specialty crops to pest management. Knowing it would soon be filled with people doing the sort of work Daddy had been interested in was like plowing weeds under.

It was right before school was going to start, when I went to Daddy's grave, sat, and leaned my back against the sun-warmed stone. There was something at the back of my mind bothering me, something I could only share with him.

Daddy, I sure do miss you. I wish you were here, but you already know that. I reckon you know by now about Mr. Fowler, and there's something I can't stop thinking about. That day Mama and I picked blackberries, and she made them blackberry pies, she marked them different. She mentioned the sugar, and it wasn't nothing really since she's scored pies different before. Only, when I went into the kitchen the next morning, I couldn't find the leftovers. The pie plates had been washed and were in the sink drain. I looked outside in the burn barrel, and there wasn't anything there. It was like we'd never made them. And then, there's where she'd been picking that day, the spot where Daniel showed me them pokeberries. I don't know. Maybe it doesn't mean anything. Mama is better now, Daddy, and I guess that's all that matters. Well, I got to go in. I love you. See you later.

I watched Mama close, always looking for a sign, some word she might say or a look of guilt if I casually brought up how quick Mr. Fowler had died. Aunt Ruth wasn't compassionate at all.

She'd said, "Good riddance."

As to Mama, she was slowly returning to her old self, gaining weight from Aunt Ruth's cooking, a pink flush coloring her cheeks once again. The idea she'd do something like that seemed so far-fetched, until I thought of how he'd been, knowing he could've killed her, and then it wasn't.

I started to the same junior high school Trent was attending for his last year, and it intimidated me, this concept of having a locker and changing classes for each course. When I went from one room to another, I looked for Daniel, having to remind myself his hair would be short, although it had to have grown out some by now. The first few days, I got so wound up with wanting to see him, my stomach hurt. It wasn't until the second week, when I no longer scrutinized the masses of students moving through the hallways that I spotted him coming toward me. I came to a dead standstill, disrupting the flow of bodies, like a car blocking a lane. It had been months since I'd seen him. He still carried the tan of summer, and his hair was cut like Ross's now, like every other boy I knew, a purposeful crew cut.

Excited, yet nervous, I called out, "Daniel!"

He stared right through me as he went by with two other girls I didn't know. They hung on to him, laughing, flirting, and why not. Daniel was the best-looking boy in the entire school.

I heard one girl say, "Isn't that the water witch?"

For all the sorrow and anguish of the past year, nothing hurt as bad as what I heard him say in passing.

"Her? I don't know who she is."

"Well, she knows you."

"I don't know how."

He did look at me then, eyes empty of any recognition. A rush of heat, a knot of pain blossomed in my chest. I moved on, feeling awkward while fighting the prick of tears behind my eyelids. The pain in my heart was as intense as when Daddy died. I knew then, that was my last attempt to fix what I'd done. It was getting to the point of embarrassing myself. If Daniel wanted to associate himself to me in any way, it would have happened by now. I had to accept what he wanted. He'd found a way to go on, and I would have to as well.

Becky Hill was in my class and I began to eat lunch with her. She introduced me to Doreen Walker and another girl, Crissy McLamb, who said she'd had a crush on Trent since first grade. It became normal, somehow, to be with them, and when I found out Crissy was only about five miles down the road from us, in the opposite direction of where we usually went into town, we agreed to visit one another. Her daddy farmed too, but she didn't like working the cotton like I did.

One day during lunch, she said, "Is it true, you can find water? With a stick?"

I looked at her carefully, assessing if I ought to talk about this with her. I didn't know if I could trust her yet. She bit into an apple, and crunched on it enthusiastically, leaning forward with an openness, appearing eager to hear about it. I decided I ought not be ashamed. Daddy never had been.

I nodded and said, "I don't talk about it much."

She said, "I wish I could do something like that. The reason I asked is my daddy, I think he's gonna call your mama. He wants you to come find water on our farm for next year. After that drought, he told Mama he ain't inclined to go through it again. Your daddy told him once you were just as good."

Hearing Daddy had talked about me like that was a comfort and it was good to have new friends, but even as I tried to forget Daniel, my mind refused. He'd been by my side for so long, not having him around disturbed me to the point Mama threatened the castor oil again. That, or she thought it might be something else.

She said, "Remember what we discussed. Your monthlies might be about to start—if they haven't already."

The question hung in the air, and it was like her eyes bored into my head, trying to see what had me in such a mood.

"No, ma'am."

She finally said, "Is this about Daniel?"

I broke down. Holding it in had been like trying to drag a hundred-pound sack of cotton around.

I sobbed, "He doesn't want to be my friend anymore."

Mama rubbed my shoulder. "Time will take care of this. I promise."

She didn't understand. Time wasn't doing a thing except making it worse. My self-respect went missing once more as I again rode my bike to his house just to see if I could see him. I rode to the water tower at least twice. I stared up at the Lucky Strike sign, and wished with all my might Daniel would appear at the railing and at least wave to me. My sense of loss was so real, so difficult, that when I went to Daddy's grave, I couldn't bring myself to talk to him like I usually did. Silent, I pictured my grief coming out of all sides of me, through my feet even, penetrating deep into the ground like the water that flowed there.

The days at school passed one after the other, all of them sort of blurring together. One evening there was an early chill in the air, and I realized it wouldn't be long before we'd be ready to pick again. I was looking out over the fields, the white of the cotton against a sky growing dark earlier and earlier. I had my arms wrapped around my waist, and shook ever so slightly. I was about to go in when I saw a small yellow flash in the distance. I was always on the lookout for shooting stars, and instantly made a wish even though I'd lost sight of it. The small flicker came again, only it appeared precise and without the thin trailing tale a meteorite would have.

And, again.

Blink. Blink. Blink.

My hands grew sweaty, despite the chill. I ran inside, rushing by Aunt Ruth who stood at the sink.

Mama was sitting at the table and said, "What in the world?"

I dug around in the hall closet. "Where's that big flashlight of Daddy's, the one he used when he was working at night?"

She said, "What do you need that for?"

"I just do!"

"It was out in the barn, remember? Sonny, what . . . ?"

Bang! went the screen door. I ran, stumbling around in the dark in the first stall until my hands felt the square box with the big bulb. Praying the battery wasn't dead, I pushed the button on top. It came on, flooding the barn with light. I turned it off, and tried to ignore the strange lights floating in front of my eyes. I ran back into the yard, my legs tingly, and my arms too, almost like when I would divine water. I pointed the light toward the Lucky Strike tower. I turned it on, off, on, off, on, off. I waited, and five seconds later came an answer. Blink. Blink. Blink.

Daniel. It was Daniel.

I remembered him saying he took a flashlight up there sometimes when he went at night. I turned my light off and on again three times more.

He did too.

I grew warm all over. I didn't know what it might mean. I didn't know if it would change anything between us. I smiled at the heavens, and hugged the light, sitting down on the damp ground to face the tower. Grateful tears trickled down to my neck. All that mattered was Daniel had sent me a sign by way of a tiny, twinkling light, an offer of forgiveness, and for me, that little light was big as the night sky above us.

Author's Note

Not far from where I live today, there used to be a sign along a stretch of I-95 South near Smithfield that declared, "You Are in the Heart of Klan Country! Welcome to North Carolina! Join the United Klans of America, Inc.!" And below that main billboard sign, a smaller one that said, "Help fight integration and communism!" There are varying dates for when it's said to have existed, from 1970 to as late as 1982. As I set out to write *The Forgiving Kind*, I thought about how I'd never tackled the difficult topic of bigotry in the stories I've written thus far. Writing about this narrow-mindedness and prejudice which used to saturate my lovely home state's early history, and yes, still exists to some degree today, is not easy. Progress is being made in North Carolina. It's much different than it was in the 1950s, but there is always room for improvement, because for all of the idyllic living, the Southern hospitality, the genteel way of life, intolerance and narrow-mindedness can still be found. It is not completely gone. Bigotry is a huge topic and not one I feel I can address adequately in this space, and shouldn't.

What I do want to talk about is my antagonist, Frank Fowler, and Daniel Lassiter, the lovable, affable, and utterly confused twelve-year-old best friend of my main character, Sonny Creech. Frank Fowler's backstory, while not too in-depth, gives hints here and there of his upbringing in a well-to-do family. We learn of the abrupt, mysterious demise of his father, and his feeling of uselessness when it came to his mother's needing him on their own farm, so he goes off to war to "kill him some Nazis." As I wrote, I kept circling back around to the question: Why is Frank Fowler like he is? What are his motivations, his reasons for being so hateful and cruel to Daniel? Why did he do what he did? I toyed with the idea that maybe he was having his own identity crisis, but then it struck me sometimes there doesn't have to be a definitive reason. What I believe is sometimes people are the way they are simply because they're born that way and perhaps a characteristic evil is then influenced by societal norms for the given time period in which they're living. The nature of what was taking place with regard to Daniel's confusion was against the law back then. Even within our own government, individuals were called "lavender lads," and removed from job positions. *Purged* is the word I want to use.

Frank Fowler, as a character, is a person who

is inherently evil. It's in his nature. I knew what was going to happen between him and Daniel. Writing scenes like these is never easy and there are risks as a writer when taking on such a challenging subject. There is worry and concern it will be misunderstood, or not written about with enough knowledge or sensitivity and regard for those who've been on the receiving end of such hate. I tried to do my best. I tried to put myself into the shoes of a bewildered, twelve-year-old boy who understands he is different, yet is having difficulty grasping this uniqueness. I hope I did him justice. I hope I captured the complexities and difficulties a child going through this, during this timeframe, would have experienced. Most of all, I want the reader to know that I tried to write about this sensitive issue with compassion and empathy. What I came away with was the knowledge I cared deeply about Daniel, and his emotional well-being, and I hope I've conveyed this through my writing.

Discussion Questions

1. What did you like best about this book?

2. What did you like least?

3. How believable were the characters, and did they remind you of anyone you know?

4. The story takes place in 1955. Do you think the author did a good job at depicting this time period and setting for the story?

5. Issues of racism, bigotry, and intolerance are introduced, highlighting the era Sonny and her family lived in. Do you like stories that address these issues, or not?

6. How did you find the pacing of the story, do you think it was too fast, too slow, or just right?

7. The Creech siblings, for the most part, have normal, typical relationships with one another. What did you find special or

different about the bond between Ross and Sonny, and Trent and Sonny?

8. Sonny's best friend, Daniel, struggles to understand what sets him apart from the rest of his peers. When did you first have an understanding of what was going on with Daniel?

9. Do you believe the author had a purpose in writing this story, and if so, what do you think was the message intended?

10. The title of the book is *The Forgiving Kind*. Did it suit the story told? Is there a different title you would have chosen?

Center Point Large Print
600 Brooks Road / PO Box 1
Thorndike, ME 04986-0001 USA

(207) 568-3717

US & Canada:
1 800 929-9108
www.centerpointlargeprint.com